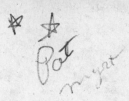

HOLLY'S HEART
Collection Two

BEVERLY LEWIS

HOLLY'S HEART

Collection Two

BETHANYHOUSE
Minneapolis, Minnesota

Published by Bethany House Publishers
11400 Hampshire Avenue South
Bloomington, Minnesota 55438

Bethany House Publishers is a division of
Baker Publishing Group, Grand Rapids, Michigan.

Printed in the United States of America

Library of Congress Cataloging-in-Publication Data is available for this title.

ISBN 978-0-7642-0459-3

About the Author

BEVERLY LEWIS, born in the heart of Pennsylvania Dutch country, fondly recalls her growing-up years. A keen interest in her mother's Plain family heritage has inspired Beverly to set many of her popular stories in Amish country, beginning with her inaugural novel, *The Shunning*.

A former schoolteacher and accomplished pianist, Beverly has written over eighty books for adults and children. Five of her blockbuster novels have received the Gold Book Award for sales over 500,000 copies, and *The Brethren* won a 2007 Christy Award.

Beverly and her husband, David, make their home in Colorado, where they enjoy hiking, biking, reading, writing, making music, and spending time with their three grandchildren.

Books by Beverly Lewis

GIRLS ONLY (GO!)*
Youth Fiction

Girls Only! Volume One
Girls Only! Volume Two

SUMMERHILL SECRETS†
Youth Fiction

SummerHill Secrets Volume One
SummerHill Secrets Volume Two

HOLLY'S HEART
Youth Fiction

Holly's Heart Collection One†
Holly's Heart Collection Two†
*Holly's Heart Collection Three**

www.BeverlyLewis.com

*4 books in each volume   †5 books in each volume

HOLLY'S HEART

Second-Best Friend

To

Kirsten Brown,

who loves cats so much

she wanted to take Melissa-Kitty

home from Swiggum's farm.

And . . .

to the memory of Kitty Tom,

a cool Kansas cat who lived

his life spoiled rotten.

Chapter 1

"I'm sorry, Goofey, but you have to stay in my room tonight," I said, bending down to stroke my cat's motley fur. "Our stepdad's off his allergy pills for the weekend."

Goofey looked up at me. A brown patch of fur colored the gray around one eye. "Me-e-o-ow." It was as if he were apologizing for making my stepdad so miserable.

"It'll be okay, baby," I whispered. Not having the heart to tell him Mom's plan, I softly closed the door. Spending the entire weekend—every weekend—from now till who knows when locked away in a room was not something you discuss with your beloved thirteen-year-old tabby. But it was Mom's only solution to Uncle Jack's reaction to his allergy pills. For now.

Hurrying downstairs, I thought about Uncle Jack—no blood relation—who was once married to my dad's sister, now in heaven. The only allergy medicine that worked for him was making him drowsy. And for an upbeat, fun-loving guy, that was bad news. Tonight, though, things would be back to normal.

"Party time!" Uncle Jack called, tossing a round pillow at me as I entered the downstairs family room.

"Hooray!" cheered eight-year-old Stephie.

"Let's watch a Meredith home video," Carrie, my nine-year-old sister, suggested, pulling out one of our family before Daddy divorced Mom.

"Forget that," I said, playfully tugging it away from her.

"Let's rent *Deep Space Invasion,*" suggested Mark, my nine-year-old cousin-turned-stepbrother.

Phil, ten, tossed a baseball cap into the air. "Cool! Let's gross everyone out."

"Yeah, and when we get scared, we'll crawl into bed with Mommy and Uncle Jack," Carrie said. She scooted across the floor on her stomach, making room for me in front of the TV.

"Think again," fifteen-year-old Stan said, sprawling on the floor next to me. It was still weird having four cousins turn into three stepbrothers and one stepsister overnight. "How 'bout a John Wayne movie?" Stan suggested.

"Not tonight, pilgrims," Mom said, snuggling up to Uncle Jack. I sneaked a glance at them as they kissed. Still enjoying the honeymoon stage, no doubt.

"So . . . what are we watching?" I asked.

A comical grin sparked mischief in Uncle Jack's eyes. "You'll love this one," he said, popping a DVD into the player.

Everyone cheered when the title came on the screen. But *102 Dalmatians* wasn't exactly the kind of movie I was hoping for. Especially with Goofey stuck upstairs in my room instead of here purring next to me.

Halfway through the movie we had intermission. Carrie and Stephie raced upstairs to their bedroom while Mom and Stan went to the kitchen to make ice-cream floats.

Thanks to the movie, I missed Goofey more than ever. I trudged upstairs to my room. When I got there, the door was open!

I scurried around my room, searching the closet and under my four-poster bed. "Here, kitty, kitty," I called frantically. Man, would I be in big trouble if Mom found out Goofey was on the loose in the house.

And poor Uncle Jack! He'd been off his medicine since this morning, hoping for a stupor-free weekend.

Dashing downstairs, I looked everywhere. The living room, under the dining room table, in the kitchen. Worried, I ran to the lower level. That's when I saw disaster waiting to happen.

Loaded down with a tray of root beer floats, Mom couldn't see that Goofey was right on her heels! As she made her turn to the round coffee table, my cat leaped onto the sectional.

I crouched behind the sofa as Mom placed the tray of sodas on the wood surface. Quickly, I tried to grab Goofey before Mom or Uncle Jack noticed him. But he leaped away, out of my grasp.

Oblivious to Goofey, Uncle Jack munched on popcorn. Then, reaching for an icy glass of root beer, he took his first drink. Meanwhile, Goofey—whose slightly torn ear flopped, reminiscent of his tomcat fight days—padded straight across the top of the sectional.

Then it happened! Goofey did the unthinkable. He curled himself around Uncle Jack's neck.

My stepdad jumped up. "What on—ah-ah-aw-*choo!*" He sneezed once, then twice, then three times! Before I could grab Goofey, he leaped from Uncle Jack's shoulders and darted out of the family room and through the furnace room door.

Mom spun around. "Goofey!" she yelled, casting accusing eyes at me. "Where is he, Holly?"

"Honest, Mom, I didn't let him out," I said.

I fled to the furnace room to look for Goofey. There I found him crouched on top of a heat duct.

"Please, Goofey," I pleaded, "come down here. You've caused enough trouble already."

He refused to budge. His whiskers twitched as if to say, "I'm not bothering anyone up here, am I?"

Stan came in just then and saw my predicament. "Here, I'll get him for you." He pulled out a stepladder and climbed up, but when he reached for Goofey, the cat slithered away. "Your cat's wreaking havoc with our family night, little sister," he said—John Wayne style, of course.

"You can say that again," Mom said, peering through the doorway with Carrie at her side.

"Your cat's wreaking havoc with—" Stan began again, but stopped when Mom looked at him cross-eyed.

"Carrie," I said. "Bring Goofey's dish down here with some of his favorite food in it."

"Okay!" She bounded away, giggling.

Mom sent me a stern look, then left to see how Uncle Jack was doing. Meanwhile, Stephie, followed by Mark and Phil, squeezed into the furnace room to watch the excitement.

"I know what'll get him to come down," Phil said. He rolled his eyes and howled like a hound dog. "Ah-whooo! Rowf! Rowf! Rowf!"

"Oh, *that's* really gonna help," Carrie said as she brought in a dish of tuna-flavored cat food.

Stan took the dish from Carrie and held it up. Sniffing his favorite meal, Goofey inched out, away from the wall, step by kitty step. Slowly, Stan slid the dish down the heat duct as I steadied the ladder.

Stan grunted as he leaned forward. Mark made alien faces, Phil whined softly like a puppy, and Stephie made weird kissy sounds with her lips.

Closer . . . closer . . . Goofey crept toward the dish.

In a flash, Stan grabbed my cat with his free hand. Frightened, Goofey spit and hissed. I snatched up the cat dish just as Stan lost his balance, toppling into a pile of laundry.

And Goofey? He ran for his life!

I chased him upstairs and into my room. And Mom was close behind. She closed the bedroom door firmly behind her.

I was expecting a full-blown lecture, and she didn't disappoint me. "Holly-Heart," she started in, "this is serious business." She stood across the room as I sat huddled with Goofey on my window seat. Her soft blue eyes squinted slightly. "I think it's time you found another home for your cat."

I looked up at her, shocked. "But he's part of our family!"

Mom wasn't listening. "The pills make Jack listless. He's not himself, and I'm really tired of it."

I took a deep breath, thinking of Goofey. And of myself. The purring on my legs rose to a gentle rumble as he relaxed into my lap. I kissed the top of his head.

Mom sat opposite me on the window seat. "Listen, honey, I don't want to make things difficult," she said. "I know how much this cat means to you."

This cat? What a way to refer to the precious bundle of fur who'd seen me through Daddy's leaving and the divorce. Who'd been with me ever since I'd learned to walk . . . and so much more.

"I'm sorry, Holly-Heart." She touched his drowsy head. "My decision has nothing to do with how I feel about Goofey."

"Please, Mom!" I begged. "I'll do anything to keep him here. I'll even make a place in my closet for him when I'm at school. He could eat and drink and sleep in my room, even on weekdays. I promise he'll never go out unless I carry him."

Mom made a sad little sighing sound. My speech had tugged on her heart strings. Perfect!

She stood up to leave. But I could see by her face that I had lost the argument. "Please don't do this, Holly," she said. "I think it's best that Goofey leave. I'm sure you can find a home for him by the end of the weekend."

"But, Mom—"

"I'm sorry," she said and headed down the stairs.

I held my beloved cat close. "It's obvious no one loves you the way I do," I whispered in his tattered ear. "We have to find you a home. One where we can still spend lots of time together."

Pushing my shoe rack aside in my closet, I arranged a soft bed of blankets. "You'll be safe and warm here," I told him.

"Show time," Stan called to me from downstairs.

"Coming," I answered. I didn't feel like watching a silly DVD about pets. But I clumped down the steps anyway, thinking only of Goofey's future.

Chapter 2

Saturday morning after breakfast, I pulled on my ski jacket, mittens, and scarf.

"Where are you going?" Mom called to me from the kitchen.

"To find a home for an outcast," I announced, running upstairs to get Goofey. I wrapped him in an afghan, and as we came down the steps, I held him up, giving him one last look at his home. "Say bye-bye to the lamp. Remember, you knocked it over the first Christmas you lived here?"

I glanced toward the kitchen. Could Mom hear my going-away speech?

Going-away parties, after all, were never much fun. Especially if the person . . . er, pet was a close friend like Goofey. He'd shared my window seat, curling up next to me as I wrote in my journal each day. He'd been my companion all through the crazy days of grade school. Not to mention the trials of last year—seventh grade. And Goofey had snuggled near me through every prayer I'd ever prayed, except for the ones prayed in California, where Daddy and his new wife lived.

Staring down at his furry face, I whispered, "How can I say

good-bye to you?" A lump sprang up in my throat as I lowered my face to cuddle him.

Just then the front door swung wide. Stephie, Mark, and Phil burst in, followed by Uncle Jack. "It's gonna be a big one," said Uncle Jack, grabbing my shoulders and guiding me to the living room window, Goofey and all. "Look up there. Storm clouds are dying to dump." He pointed to the snow clouds hanging over the mountains. Uncle Jack looked down at the bundle in my arms. "Whatcha got in there?"

Faster than lightning, Goofey hissed and swatted his paw at Uncle Jack's nose. I pulled the cat away.

"Sorry," I said, amazed at the sudden increase in Goofey's intellect. My cat had recognized his own mortal enemy! Not bad for a lazy feline.

Uncle Jack sneezed three times, which brought Mom running. "Holly!" she said as she came into the living room. "I thought you'd already left."

"I'm leaving now." I spun out the front door.

A quick jog down the street brought me to the city bus stop. In a ski village like Dressel Hills, the transportation system was free. Hop on, hop off, anytime—day or night. I pushed my fat friend into the afghan, hiding him. It would be easy to conceal him. Old and pampered, Goofey had slept through longer things than bus rides to my best friend's house.

Soon we were on Andie's street. I pulled the cord and waited for the bus to come to a complete stop before standing up.

Outside, I hurried to the Martinez residence. The wind was picking up, and I kept Goofey covered. "You remember Andie Martinez, don't you, little guy?" I said to the puff of gray nestled in my arms. "She's my best friend ever. If everything goes as planned, she'll be taking very good care of you from now on." I pushed the doorbell with the thumb of my mitten.

Andie's mother opened the door, eyeing my afghan-wrapped bundle. "Quick, come inside, it's whipping up a storm." She hurried through the living room and called up the steps for Andie.

"Be down in a sec," Andie hollered down.

I waited silently, even though Andie's mother cast curious glances at the quiet lump in my arms.

"My toy . . . mine!" a husky shout came from the kitchen. One of Andie's twin brothers, no doubt. The three-year-olds weren't identical in looks, but their vocal chords definitely had matching decibel levels.

Mrs. Martinez excused herself to investigate the battle, leaving me alone with my precious Goofey. It was sweet having these last few minutes together. Just the two of us. For all too soon, Andie and her family would be the proud new owners of a weird-looking cat named Goofey Meredith.

Meredith's my last name. But Mom traded it to marry Jack Patterson at Thanksgiving, two and a half months ago.

I figured as long as the honeymoon lasted, Goofey was safe. A kind-hearted man like Jack Patterson could take allergy pills off and on, no problem, no complaints. But I'd guessed wrong. Mom was completely bummed out by the medication's side effects. And who could blame her? Uncle Jack was flat-out droopy.

"Hey, Holly." Andie appeared wearing dark blue jeans and a black sweater. Her dark curly hair framed her chubby cheeks. She eyed the afghan suspiciously. "What's that?"

"We have to talk," I whispered.

She came over and peeked under the afghan. "Oh, it's Goofey," she said. "What's he doing here?"

"It's a long story," I said. "But here's the deal. Goofey's up for adoption, and I'm giving you first chance to—"

"Wait a minute," she interrupted. "I don't want your cat." A look of horror spread across her face. "He's the ugliest thing I've ever seen."

"His looks never bothered you before," I snapped. "All those times at my house—shoot, you even slept with him."

"That's different than claiming him. *You* keep him."

"Can't."

"Why not?"

16

"Uncle Jack's allergic, and Mom's sick of the pills."

She tried to keep from laughing, but a giggle escaped. "That was so funny at their wedding when your uncle sneezed all over the place. Remember?"

How can I forget?

"Look, I didn't come here to discuss that," I said. "I'm here because I thought you might consider helping me out."

She motioned me up the stairs. Once in her room, she closed the door. Clothes were strewn everywhere. The pink floral comforter had slid halfway off her bed.

"Honestly, Holly," she said, "I'd consider taking your cat for you if I could. It's just that I'm in the middle of real important stuff right now."

I studied her. What was she trying to say?

"I don't know how to tell you this," Andie sat on the floor cross-legged, leaning her back against the bed. Goofey jumped out of the afghan.

"Tell me what?" I asked.

"Well, it's just that . . ." She stopped.

I sat down. "You can tell me anything, Andie," I reassured her. "We've been best friends forever. What is it?"

"Your fourteenth birthday," she said, twisting a dark curl around her finger. "I can't come to your party. It's not that I don't want to. It's just that we're going to Denver Friday evening, and we won't be back in time."

I glared at her. "Why are you telling me this now? The party's a week from today."

"We—my family and I—have been waiting for some paper work," she admitted.

I fumed. "What paper work . . . and what's going on in Denver?"

"Christiana's coming."

"Who?" The way Andie sounded, Christiana might have been the Queen of England or something.

"My pen pal from Austria. Christiana's coming to stay with us for five weeks. It's a private exchange program her parents set up with us." Andie was silent, like she was waiting for me to respond.

I jumped on it. "Why didn't you tell me this?"

"We didn't know if it was going to work out or not."

I felt totally left out. "When were you going to tell me?"

She shrugged. "Soon enough."

"So you're saying you can't adopt Goofey because of some overseas pen pal? And you're skipping my birthday to pick her up?" I stared at Andie.

"It's just one of those things," she said apologetically. "I'm sure you'll find someone to take your cat. I hope so, Holly, for your sake."

"C'mon, Goofey," I said, rewrapping him in Mom's afghan. "We have to go."

"Sorry. I really am." Andie's face drooped, and she played with her leather watchband.

I headed into the blustery February afternoon without even saying good-bye.

Chapter 3

By the time the city bus arrived, I felt like a human icicle. Sliding into the first available seat, I cuddled Goofey close. Feelings of frustration swept over me. I couldn't decide which was worse, losing my precious cat, or not having Andie at my birthday party this year.

Without Andie, there was no need for a party. Who wants to celebrate turning fabulous fourteen without your best friend?

I stared out the window. Snowflakes were beginning to fall. Uncle Jack was right; it looked like we were going to get dumped on.

Downtown, the bus stopped to take on more passengers. Paula and Kayla Miller got on, loaded down with shopping bags, probably filled with designer clothes. They wore their brown hair down, matching as always.

"Hey," I said when they saw me.

They sat in the seat behind me. Paula stared at the afghan in my arms. "Did I hear a cat crying?" she asked, flashing her sickening-sweet smile.

Glancing around, I slowly revealed my cat. "This is my homeless pet, Goofey."

Paula's eyes blinked, a week's worth of mascara weighing them down. "He doesn't look homeless to me."

Kayla spoke up. "We heard about Mr. Patterson's allergies. Our father told us."

Paula and Kayla's dad worked with my stepdad in a consulting firm. I wasn't surprised that they'd heard about the problems with Goofey.

"What a shame," Paula cooed over my shoulder, nearly in Goofey's face. "He's so sweet." Then she got up and slid into the seat beside me. "Mind if I pet him?"

"Okay," I lied through my teeth. I didn't want her talking to me, let alone cuddling my cat! This girl had caused me enough trouble to last a lifetime.

I cringed silently as Paula took Goofey from me.

"I've always wanted a cat," she confessed.

And that's not all, I thought. She wanted to take away my guy friend, Jared Wilkins, too!

Kayla hung over the back of my seat. "He really is cute, in an odd sort of way."

I couldn't bear all this ogling, so I changed the subject. "Where are you two headed?"

"Home," they said in unison.

"We ran into Miss Wannamaker at Plain and Fancy Things," said Kayla. "She's so sweet. We just love her."

Miss W was popular with lots of kids. Whether she taught grammar or creative writing, she made words come alive.

"I think Miss W's in love," Paula continued. "We saw her pricing wedding dresses."

This news was really something for a woman in her fifties who'd never married.

"I think she'd make a fabulous wife," I said. But I was more preoccupied with the twins than with Miss W. I'd made it a point to avoid them ever since they'd moved from Pennsylvania last year. They were so perfect looking and rich it made me sick. They chattered constantly about shopping trips to the mall. Especially

Paula. She had a habit of showing off her expensive clothes. But worst of all, she'd been after Jared for months. She still glazed over whenever he was in close range. And even though he had assured me she wasn't his type, I didn't trust her.

"Is this your street?" Paula asked.

"Uh, yes, it is," I stuttered, turning toward Goofey. Still wrapped in Mom's afghan, he was snuggled against Paula's white fur jacket. I stood up and the bus jolted to a stop. I lurched forward, reaching out to stop my fall.

I felt Paula yank the back of my ski jacket, steadying me. I regained my balance but didn't bother to thank her.

"Downhill Court," announced the driver.

"Coming," I called, reaching for Goofey.

"May I keep him?" Paula pleaded. "Just for a couple of days? I promise to take good care of him."

"You can visit him whenever you want to," Kayla added.

"Please say yes," Paula begged, her violet eyelids blinking at me pitifully.

The driver waited. Passengers jostled grocery bags, young children, and packages. Their faces spelled impatience.

"Okay . . . uh, I guess," I said.

Before the bus doors swooshed shut behind me, I heard Paula say, "I'll call you, Holly."

Oh, fabulous.

Talking on the phone with Paula Miller or her look-alike twin was the last thing I wanted to do. I watched sadly as the bus made its turn onto Aspen Street, carrying with it my little Goofey—in the arms of the enemy.

♥ ♥ ♥

After supper I made a big deal in my journal about losing Goofey.

Saturday, February 5: My poor little Goofey is being cared for, right this minute, by strangers. It wouldn't be so bad, but

I refuse to set foot in Paula and Kayla Miller's house. And
that's where my Goofey is, at least for now. Hopefully I'll per-
suade Andie to change her mind.

    Christiana Somebody from Austria is coming to stay with
Andie and her family next week. I wonder how it'll work out.

    Not every girl is lucky enough to have a Valentine birth-
day. Daddy always said it meant I was extra special. That's
why Mom nicknamed me Holly-Heart. Without Andie,
though, the party's a flop.

I closed my journal and sighed. Goofey was gone, and I missed
him. Who knows how he was doing, poor, homesick thing. Of
course, I could find out in a flash, but it would mean calling Paula
Miller. No way.

Curling up on my bed, I stared at my lavender and white
bedroom—private domain regained. It felt good having my room
all to myself again, without the super snoopers, Carrie and Stephie.
The two of them were roommates now, down the hall.

My sister had reclaimed her old room, the one she'd had before
Uncle Jack married Mom. It was great to have Phil and Mark off
the second floor and in the new addition at the back of the house.
Stan, the oldest of our tribe, took the other bedroom in the addition,
vacating the family room. It was a good thing, too. I was tired of
having to miss good TV shows just so Stan could pull his bed out
of the sofa and lounge around watching John Wayne videos—his
current obsession.

Br-ring! I dashed to the hall, reaching for the phone on the
second ring. Too late. Picking it up, I recognized Andie's voice on
the line. No doubt she'd called to talk to Stan. They actually liked
each other. Mind-boggling.

"Did Holly find a home for Goofey yet?" she asked Stan as I
listened.

Dying to hear what he would say, I continued to eavesdrop.
"Haven't seen much of Holly today," Stan said. "And . . . who's
Goofey?"

Andie laughed.

I wasn't surprised at Stan's remark. He'd never liked Goofey. But it didn't matter. He and I just so happened to be getting along better than ever. I decided to let it go. This time.

Afraid they might hear me breathing, I hung up the phone.

Mom came upstairs just then, dressed in a blue wool sweater, her blond hair pulled back in a gold barrette. "Holly, let's talk." She motioned to my room.

Settling on my bed, she said, "It's almost party time for my birthday girl."

I smoothed the quilt. "Yeah, it's countdown to nothing much."

"What about the make-over party we planned? Sounds like fun, doesn't it?"

"Who cares," I grumbled.

"But Jack and I—"

"Please don't make plans behind my back," I snapped. "Honestly, I feel like calling the whole birthday thing off."

"Holly-Heart," she protested, "what's happened?"

I got up and wandered across the room. Without looking at her, I blurted, "Andie won't be coming."

"Well, why not?"

"She has plans. With Christiana of Austria." I grabbed Bearie-O, Andie's teddy bear, off the shelf. Hugging him, I told Mom about Andie's pen pal and the exchange they'd planned.

"Does this mean Andie will go to Austria next summer?"

I hadn't thought of that. Andie was probably holding out that tidbit of information for a later date. Unpredictable Andie, always full of surprises! Not always happy ones, either.

"It's not easy having a best friend who can't even tell you the important stuff ahead of time." I squeezed the stuffed bear extra hard.

Mom came over and sat near me on the window seat. "This has you very upset, Holly. If you'd like, we could arrange to have

23

the party on Monday, your actual birthday." She sighed. "Could Andie come then?"

"She'll be up to her eyeballs introducing Christiana to Dressel Hills by that time," I responded. "I can see it now—"

Mom interrupted. "Holly-Heart, I don't like the sound of this. I think you're jealous."

"Isn't that a shame," I said sarcastically. "And I haven't even met Andie's friend yet."

Mom stood up. "Be careful you don't let these feelings come between you and Andie. It would be a sad thing for a lifelong friendship to be marred by your bad attitude."

Mom's lecture bored me. I knew all that stuff. What I didn't know was how I could possibly fit in with Andie when Christiana arrived.

As far as I was concerned, second best might as well be zero!

Chapter 4

Sunday morning I slept in longer than I should have. Through a sleepy haze, I rubbed my eyes. Bearie-O, the droopy-eyed teddy bear Andie had traded for mine in first grade, stared down at me from the shelf near my window seat. Since Goofey was gone, I'd have to revert back to my childhood and sleep with Bearie-O. It was an option, at least.

Getting up, I hurried for the shower. On the way, I noticed Mom's bedroom door open. For a moment I stood, listening. It was unmistakable. Classical music wafted down the hall, interspersed with the clinking of fine silver against china. Could it be?

I strained to listen, inching my way down the hallway. Mixed with the music was soft laughter. Uncle Jack was serving Mom breakfast in bed!

How romantic, I thought, making my way to the bathroom. *Someday . . .*

I allowed my mind to wander as I lathered up in the shower. Jared Wilkins, the first real crush of my life, instantly came to mind. Though hundreds of miles distanced us, I thought of someone else, too—Sean Hamilton. Sean lived in Southern California, just down the beach from Daddy.

Sometimes I regretted not meeting him on Christmas Eve for a walk on the seashore. Now I would never know if he hoped we might someday be more than friends.

My dad was probably right. *"Develop lots of friendships with guys,"* he'd said when I visited at Christmas. *"There's plenty of time for romance later."*

Andie didn't agree when I told her about my talk with Daddy at Christmas. "What's wrong with a little mushy stuff?" she'd said, laughing. Andie's parents didn't seem to be as strict as mine.

I grabbed a towel and hopped out of the shower. My thoughts went back to Sean and the moonlit walk I'd missed. Daydreaming about the possibilities, I didn't hear the knock on my door.

"Holly, I have to go. Hurry up!" It was Carrie.

"Okay, okay." I reached for my robe. Little sisters!

♥ ♥ ♥

As was our custom since Uncle Jack married Mom, we attended the early service at church on Sundays. Today I asked permission to sit with Andie. Usually, all eight of us filled up one long pew. Mom liked it that way: family togetherness in worship. But I needed space.

Sitting next to Andie and her entire family, I sensed something was wrong. I could feel the tension. And she seemed preoccupied, probably with her pen pal's arrival.

"A cat like Goofey would make a fabulous contribution to Christiana's stay in America," I whispered in her ear, then reached for the hymnal.

She fluffed her short, springy curls. "I know you love your pet, Holly," she said, "but why don't you let Paula adopt him?"

Paula? How does she know?

"Would you want someone you love spending day in and day out at the Miller residence?" I whispered.

She shrugged halfheartedly, like she wasn't really listening.

I couldn't talk about how I disliked the Miller twins—not in church, of all places. So I sat there fuming about everything imaginable. Goofey staying at Paula's . . . and Miss Christiana So-and-So living at Andie's!

Jared waited for me in the church aisle after the benediction. His dark hair was neatly combed, and his eyes lit up when he saw me. "Hey, Holly. You look great today."

I blushed. "Thanks." He looked fine himself, wearing a blue cotton shirt and khakis.

"Coming to youth service Thursday?" he asked.

"Wouldn't miss it." I couldn't help grinning. Jared was so easy to be around. Then an idea struck me. "Uh, Jared," I said hesitantly, "how would you like to adopt my cat?"

Jared scratched his head and stuffed his hands into his pockets. "I have a problem . . . with cats," he admitted.

"What's that supposed to mean?" I felt rejected. "Cats are fabulous," I told him. "I'd have a dozen of them if I could."

He smiled that adorable smile, but it didn't do a thing for me. Not today. "I'm a dog person," he said proudly.

His comment ticked me off. "Can't you at least keep Goofey for a little while?" I pleaded. "It'll buy me some time."

"Holly," he said, as an exasperated frown appeared. "It wouldn't be fair to your cat—hanging out with someone like me."

"But you're my friend," I argued. "I should be able to count on you no matter what."

"Hey, friends can't bail each other out *all* the time," he said. "You should know that."

"He's right." Paula Miller sidled up to us. "Only God can do that. He's the only one who can be there for us all the time."

I glared at her. *Who asked you?* I thought, watching her like a hawk, especially since she seemed to be showing off her new dress. Probably for Jared's benefit. He straightened his collar while Paula flashed another Colgate smile.

Grudgingly, I asked Paula how my cat was doing. Even though I disliked her, I loved Goofey.

"Oh, Goofey's just fine." Paula grinned wider than ever. "He's absolutely wonderful."

"That's nice," I whispered. But I wasn't so sure. If Goofey had any good taste, he'd hate being around Paula.

Just then, out of the corner of my eye, I noticed Andie and her family leaving by the side door. "I'll see you tomorrow," I said abruptly to Jared and Paula, hurrying to catch up with Andie.

I spotted her in the parking lot, heading toward her car. "Andie, wait!"

She stopped and turned around. "This better not be about that cat of yours."

"It's about my birthday party. Can you come if I change the day?"

Her dark curls blew against her face. "To when?"

"Valentine's Day, a week from tomorrow." I realized I was holding my breath, waiting for her response.

"I'll have to let you know," she said. Then she hurried to catch up with her family.

♥ ♥ ♥

I called Paula on Sunday night and then again on Monday after school. I simply had to know how Goofey was. I missed him terribly.

"Oh, hello, Holly," Paula cooed when she answered the phone.

Carrying the portable phone, I paced nervously around my bedroom. "How's Goofey eating?"

"Very well, and Kayla thinks he's beginning to bond with me. I've been giving him lots of attention, including a bath every day. He loves the rose-scented bubbles."

I couldn't believe my ears. "You're kidding! He likes bubble baths?"

"Oh yes," she said. "And I'm making him some little pajamas to wear at night."

I gasped. "Pajamas?"

"They're darling. You should come over and see them."

"Um, sometime." I switched the phone to my other ear. "But

you don't have to sew him pajamas, Paula. I only wanted you to keep him until I could—"

"Oh no, no!" she exclaimed. "Please don't take Goofey away."

Oh, puh-leeze. This is too much!

"I couldn't stand the thought of losing him," she insisted.

"Hey, I know the feeling," I said. "I'll be right over."

It was time to put a stop to this bonding Paula Miller had going on with my cat. Rushing downstairs, I swung open the coat closet in the front hall. My pink-and-purple ski jacket was handy, so I flung it on.

"Where are you going?" Carrie said, looking up from her book. She was snuggled up on the sofa in the living room.

"None of your business."

"We might be gone when you get back. Uncle Jack's taking us to get fitted for our own skis," Carrie said.

"He is?"

"Yep, we're going skiing soon. He wants each of us to have our own equipment." Carrie slouched against the sofa. "Isn't it great having a rich uncle in the family?" Then she burst into giggles.

"You're a nut case," I said, looking around for Mom and Uncle Jack. "They'll hear you."

"It's no secret. Do you know how much money we have?" She stared at me. "Well, *do* you?"

"What are you talking about?"

Carrie motioned to me with her pointer finger. "How do you think we paid for the addition on the house?"

"Uncle Jack did, of course. Who else?" I sat on the arm of the sofa.

"Last night I heard him telling Mom about the money he got when Aunt Marla died. You won't believe it," she said, her eyes sparkling.

"People get insurance money when their spouses die. It's no big deal."

"Three quarters of a million dollars is a big deal." Carrie shoved her finger into her book, marking the page. "How much is that?"

"Figure it out." I leaped up and dashed out the door. *Whoa, she wasn't kidding. We are rich, all right!*

Carrie's news cast a spell over everything in my path. Running down the street toward Paula Miller's house, I felt strange. No wonder Uncle Jack had tripled my allowance. It was nice of him, but really, kids my age didn't need that much money. I was putting most of it in the church offering. In fact, last Sunday before the service I'd stopped by the church bulletin board in the foyer and studied a display of missionaries and their families. I wanted to support one of them, but I wasn't sure whom. Then another picture had caught my eye—of a thin, naked child, crying from hunger. I resolved right there to use my allowance to help starving children, too.

Just ahead, the Miller twins' house came into view. Set on the side of a hill, the house was in one of the lah-dee-dah-est areas of Dressel Hills.

I groaned as I made my way up the steep driveway, praying. *Dear Lord, if Carrie's right about the money, please don't let me become like Paula Miller—constantly buying new clothes and living for the next shopping spree. I want to help people with my money, not hoard it to myself.*

When I rang the doorbell, it played some long excerpt from Mozart or Beethoven, I wasn't sure which. Anyway, I was surprised when Paula answered the door. Minus Goofey.

Chapter 5

"Won't you please come in?" Paula said, opening the door wide. She showed me into the large foyer, where a wide tapestry of an English garden graced the wall. Fresh roses, yellow as buttercups, brightened a cherrywood table nearby.

"Where's Goofey?" I asked, gazing overhead at a twinkling glass chandelier.

"Upstairs," she said.

I sneaked a peek at the living room as we headed for the curved staircase. Lily-white chairs and sofas were dotted with satiny pillows of black and red. A slate-black coffee table held a tall, white vase bulging with more flowers, this time in dramatic shades of red. At the top of the curved staircase, Paula's massive room awaited.

"Kayla's resting, so let's keep our voices low," Paula suggested.

What century was she born in? I wondered, amazed at the golden Cinderella-like mirror hanging over her dresser. The bedspread of pastel blues and greens perfectly coordinated with the throw pillows on two powder-blue easy chairs.

"Would you care for a soda?" Paula offered.

I nodded. "Sure, thanks."

Paula opened a miniature refrigerator near her closet and pulled out a Coke. "I hope it's cold enough."

I took the soda and thanked her. A *refrigerator* in her *room*? What else did this girl have—diamonds and pearls in her jewelry box, maybe?

Paula directed me to one of her soft chairs. "Wait here while I get Goofey up from his nap," she said.

Goofey had been spoiled rotten at my house, but this . . . ! I took a sip of my soda, surveying the picture-perfect view. Getting up, I went to the window and leaned my knee on the padded window seat, in awe of the mountains. Looking down, I caught my breath. What—a window seat? Paula had a window seat just like mine!

I don't know why her having a window seat bothered me, but it did. For some reason I didn't want to have a single thing in common with this girl.

"Here we are," Paula said cheerfully, returning with Goofey in her arms. "Isn't he simply adorable?" she cooed. Cooing was one of her trademarks. Hers and Kayla's.

"Simply," I echoed. "Now, what's this about bubble baths?"

"Oh, that," she waved her hand as though it was an ordinary thing for a cat to take bubble baths. "Would you like to witness it for yourself?"

"Now?" It was hard to believe that's all Paula could dream up for after-school entertainment. What about friends? Didn't she have anyone besides her twin sister to hang out with?

"Goofey really loves his baths," she continued. "I'll draw his water now if you'd like."

"Actually, I'd rather just play with him if you don't mind." I really wanted to take him back home where he belonged. But Mom would never hear of it. If only I could talk some sense into Andie. Or Jared.

Paula put Goofey down. He stood close to her for a moment, then wandered over to nuzzle my leg. Stooping down, I picked him up. He smelled like roses. Probably the bubble bath variety.

"I've missed you," I whispered. Purring contentedly, Goofey rubbed his head against my chin.

"If it would make you feel any better," Paula said, "I'd be delighted to purchase him from you."

"Buy my Goofey?" I was still shocked that the facts hadn't sunk into her brain. "Goofey's not for sale. He's only here for a few days, like we agreed."

"I really wish—"

"Well, I have to be going," I interrupted. "I've got important stuff to take care of."

"You can't stay?" She sounded disappointed.

"Sorry," I said. Then I gave Goofey a kiss on his pink nose and left the room. "He's yours till Wednesday."

"Wednesday?" she asked. "What happens then?"

"I'll find a permanent home by then," I said.

Paula followed me down the long staircase. "Thank you, Holly, for allowing me this time with your darling cat."

This girl is about as flaky as a Barbie doll, I thought as she opened the front door.

"Remember, Holly, you're welcome to visit Goofey any time," she said as I stepped out into the cold.

I turned to face her and noticed with a shock that her eyes looked misty, like she was about to cry. "Thanks," I said uncomfortably, eager to get away before she started bawling on my shoulder. "I'll come get Goofey in two days."

"Rest assured, I'll take good care of him for you," she said as I headed down the flagstone steps toward the tree-lined street.

A twinge of guilt haunted me on my walk home. It was rude the way I'd treated Paula. I'd called her rotten things like *pathetic* and *pitiful* behind her back. But her only real problem was she was different. *Very* different.

When I finally arrived home, the gray van was gone, which meant only one thing: Carrie was right about Uncle Jack spending big bucks on the family. I loved to ski, but somehow I couldn't picture Mom on the slopes. Guess Uncle Jack was opening new horizons for her.

Instead of going into the house, I hopped on the city bus. With any luck I'd link up with my family at the sporting goods store.

On the bus I spotted Mrs. Martinez seated near the front.

"Hello there, Holly!" she called.

I hurried to take a seat beside her. "Andie told me about the guest you have coming next weekend."

She smiled. "We're excited about having Christiana in our home. From her letters, she seems like a lovely young lady."

And I'm not? The resentful thought jagged across my mind. I forced it out of my head. "Sounds like fun," I lied.

"Andie has been wanting to do something like this for quite some time now."

Funny, she hadn't told *me* about it.

"She hopes to learn from Christiana while she's here, and if things work out, Andie may spend some time in Austria next year."

So Mom guessed right. Why was I not surprised?

"Well, tell Andie hi for me." I stood up when I saw the doughnut shop next to the sporting goods store. "Here's where I get off."

"Nice seeing you, Holly," she said.

"You too, Mrs. Martinez." I hurried off the bus and headed into the sporting goods store. Sure enough, my family was there. All of them.

Carrie and Stephie were modeling matching ski outfits, completely ignoring the price tags. Mom was trying on ski boots, and the boys were off in another corner of the store, checking out the most expensive skis.

This bothered me. A lot. There were tons of starving children in the world, and here we were spending zillions on ski gear.

"Holly, I'm glad you found us," Mom said, looking up as she buckled the shiny ski boots. "What do you think?" She held her foot up.

"I can't believe you're actually going to hit the slopes." I was laughing. But not at the pricey boots she wore.

Uncle Jack sat next to her, wrapping his arm around her. "She'll have plenty of time now for sports and leisure activities," he said with a twinkle in his eye.

"Mom's quitting work, right?" I said gleefully. All this money in the family had its advantages, after all.

"Yep, and she's going to join a health club to get back in shape," Carrie announced.

"She's not that much out of shape," I defended Mom.

"Thanks, Holly-Heart," Mom said, touching my hand.

Uncle Jack led me to the shelf displaying boots my size. I picked up the cheapest pair.

"Those might make it down the hill twice." Uncle Jack chuckled. He picked up another pair. "Now, here's something that'll last a good long time."

Eyeing the price tag, I said, "But they cost so much!"

Uncle Jack sat me down near Mom and helped me slip on the boots. "It's better to pay a few more dollars and have them last for several seasons," he explained. "Besides, your feet have stopped growing. Who knows how long you'll be stuck wearing these."

I could see his point. Still, I couldn't get that picture of the starving child out of my mind.

Chapter 6

Wednesday in science class, Andie was so engrossed in taking notes she scarcely noticed me. After class, she stayed to talk to Mr. Ross, our teacher. A major switcheroo.

I waited as long as I could at her locker. Finally giving up, I headed off for English. Miss Wannamaker looked thinner, like she was losing weight. I was curious about that. Was she trying to impress Mr. Ross?

Jared slid into the desk across the aisle. "Hey, Holly-Heart. Got your homework done?" He flashed that wonderful warm smile.

"It's right here." I patted my school bag.

"I hear we're having a visitor from Austria."

"Yep. That's all Andie's talking about." I searched for my English book in my bag. Miss W was getting ready to begin class. "See you at lunch, okay?"

"Perfect," he said, using my word. When he winked at me, my heart did its usual wild flip-flop.

♥ ♥ ♥

At noon, Paula slipped into the hot-lunch line behind me. "You should see Goofey in his new pajamas," she purred. "He looks so adorable."

"You made them already?"

"They weren't difficult," she said, tossing her hair back over her shoulder. "I followed the pattern for a doggie sweater."

"You what?"

"I crochet," she explained. "It's lots of fun."

I could just see it now—my Goofey in pink poodle pajamas. It was enough to give me a hissy fit. "Poor thing," I muttered under my breath.

"He seems to like them," she said, following me to the table where Andie sat saving places for both Jared and me.

"Mind if I join you?" Paula asked, holding her tray till I answered.

I studied Andie, still writing notes. "Hey, relax, it's lunchtime," I teased, motioning for Paula to sit on the other side of me.

Andie kept her nose stuck in a book.

"Whatcha studying?" I asked, peering over at Andie and her mammoth book.

"Stuff about Austria," she said without looking up.

"Oh, I know. You want to communicate with your new friend, right?"

"She speaks English fluently. Started studying it in fifth grade."

Paula leaned forward, talking around me. "What does she know about Colorado?"

"I've already described Dressel Hills to her, if that's what you mean." Andie looked up momentarily.

"And what about when you go over there?" I asked. "What then?"

Andie closed her book. "Well, if things work out, I should have enough money saved by a year from now." She had a faraway look in her brown eyes. "I want to travel the world. See the sights, meet different people."

"It's a good goal for you," I said, not realizing it sounded like a put-down till it was out of my mouth.

Andie ignored the comment, or maybe her head was in a cloud somewhere in the Alps. "Mr. Ross is giving me extra-credit work to help pull up my science grade. My parents said if I work extra hard this semester they'll help me with my plane fare—to visit Christiana."

"Wow, sounds like you're serious about this," I said.

Andie leaned on the table, looking at Paula on the other side of me. "So . . . how do you like Holly's cat so far?"

Paula was munching on a hot dog. "Uhmm," she mumbled, wiping her lips.

It was the first unintelligible remark Paula had made since she moved here last April.

"Her mouth's full," I explained.

We both waited for her to swallow. At last she said she'd been praying about Goofey's well-being. That the right person would end up with him.

Man, this is getting nutty, I thought. *Paula's talking to God about my cat.*

"You sound like Holly," Andie said, chuckling. "She prays about things like that. And you know what's amazing? God answers her prayers."

I spooned up some chili for my hot dog. "But sometimes the answer is 'not yet' or just plain 'no.' "

"Which reminds me," Andie said. "About next week and your birth—"

I made a cut-throat gesture for her to stop talking. Paula had *not* been invited to my party. This could be embarrassing.

Andie glanced down awkwardly, playing with her napkin. Then she said, "I've gotta run. Stan has a book he bought in Germany last summer. I'm supposed to meet him at his locker. See ya."

I knew by the look on her face she wasn't coming to my party no matter when I was having it. I just hoped Paula hadn't heard. She was the last person I wanted hanging around.

Now . . . what to do about Goofey? There was no changing Andie's mind. That was obvious. She seemed determined not to have anything to do with my cat. On the other hand, here was Paula, a girl who loved him almost as much as I did.

I needed some time to think. What I really needed was a backup plan. So I mentioned my preliminary idea to Paula, who was finishing her lunch. "Do you think you could keep Goofey for a few more days?"

Her face broke into a grin. "Do you mean it?"

You would've thought she'd just won a shopping spree.

"Only a few more days," I said, "till I can work something out."

She sighed. "Oh my! How can I ever thank you, Holly?"

"I'll think of a way," I said a bit too sarcastically.

Jared showed up just then, and Paula excused herself promptly. Strange. If I hadn't known better, I would have thought Paula was trying to avoid Jared. How weird was that?

"Heard you have a cat for sale," Jared said, sitting beside me.

I bristled at his remark. "I would never part with Goofey for money," I declared. "I couldn't possibly put a price tag on him."

"You're one loyal and dedicated owner." He smeared mustard, ketchup, and mayonnaise all over his hot dog. "Paula seems to love him, too," he said. "Why don't you let her keep him?"

"Never in a zillion years," I said.

Jared shot me a surprised look. I didn't want to explain why I disliked Paula, so I made a point of looking at my watch.

"Going somewhere?" he asked.

"I need to pick up some library books before my next class. Wanna come?"

He held up his hot dog. "I'll catch up with you later."

"Okay. See ya." I rushed off to the library, hoping to find a book on Austria. Then just maybe I could get Andie's attention. Finally!

Chapter 7

Paula called after school. "Something's wrong with Goofey," she said, her voice quivering.

I gripped the phone. "What do you mean?"

"He's acting very strange," she answered. "He won't eat, and he's throwing up. I called the vet."

"What did the vet say?" I tugged on my hair nervously.

"He said to bring him into the animal clinic right away."

"Thanks for telling me, Paula. I'll get Mom to drive me. I'll meet you there." I hung up the phone, trembling as I dashed down the steps to the main level.

What had Paula done to my precious kitty?

"Mom!" I called.

No answer.

"Where is she?" I said through clenched teeth, disgusted at her lack of immediate response. "Mom!" I called again. Louder this time.

Carrie and Stephie came running upstairs. "Mom's gone," Stephie said.

"Yeah, she left a while ago," Carrie informed me.

"Just great," I muttered, wishing the city bus route went as far as the vet's. What could I do?

The TV blared in the family room downstairs. Maybe Mark knew something. I dashed down another flight of stairs. Carrie and Stephie followed. "When's your dad coming home?" I asked Mark.

"How should I know?" he blurted, making one of his disgusting alien faces at me. Stephie giggled.

"Doesn't anybody know anything around here?" I shrieked, growing more irritated by the second. "Goofey's in trouble, and I have to see him before—"

"Before what?" Carrie asked, her eyes ready to pop.

"He's sick, really sick, and I have to get to the vet's. Goofey will be scared if I'm not there," I said, tears blurring my vision.

"Is . . . is he gonna die?" Stephie cried.

A hideous thought. One I couldn't bear to face. "I hope not," I answered.

Running upstairs to the kitchen, I reached for the portable phone. Maybe Andie's mom could drive me across town.

Andie answered on the first ring.

"Is your mom home?" I asked.

"She's out buying groceries for next weekend when Christiana comes," she said.

"Oh, I just thought maybe she could drive me somewhere. Goofey's real sick . . . at the vet's. I need to get there somehow."

"What about your mom? Can't she drive you?"

"Mom's gone. I wish I could drive!" It looked hopeless for transportation. And Goofey needed me. No one else could give him the kind of love and attention he needed now.

"Sorry, Holly. Wish I could help," she said.

"I'll work something out." I said good-bye and hung up.

In desperation I grabbed the phone book and called a cab. It would probably eat up every dime of my mission project, but it was well worth it to be with Goofey.

I dashed back to the family room, informing Mark and the girls where I was headed.

"Mommy won't be happy about this," Carrie said. "You're supposed to be in charge of us while she's gone."

"Don't worry," Mark said, "I'll make sure nothing bad happens."

I eyed him. "That's what I'm afraid of."

"We'll sit right here and watch Mark make alien faces till Mommy comes home," Stephie said. "We promise."

Mark started his gross facial repertoire.

"You're hopeless," I said, turning toward the stairs.

The cab pulled into the driveway just as I stepped onto the porch. I hurried to get in.

Rush-hour traffic was appalling in a ski resort in winter. We weaved in and out of traffic on Aspen Street. Afternoon skiers were coming off the slopes in droves. The latest snowfall provided the perfect conditions—packed powder.

"Can you go a different way?" I pleaded with the driver.

"We're almost out of the worst," he said. "What's your hurry?"

I told him about Goofey.

"Maybe he caught a simple flu bug," the cabbie offered.

"Flu can be deadly for a cat as old as Goofey," I said, praying silently.

When we arrived at the vet's, I paid the cab fare and made my way up the snowy steps to the animal clinic. Inside, Paula sat on the edge of her chair.

"Where's Goofey?" I asked.

"The vet took him in there." She pointed to a door across from us. I noticed her eyes glistening.

I didn't wait to hear more. Making a beeline for the door, I darted inside, looking for my cat.

"May I help you, dear?" It was the vet's assistant, peering over the top of her granny glasses. She was filling out some papers. I saw "Goofey Meredith" written at the top of one of them.

"I'm Holly Meredith," I replied. "Goofey belongs to me."

Slowly, she removed her glasses. "Please sit down." She motioned to a vacant chair.

A giant lump crowded my throat. I could almost predict what she would say. Goofey is dying. It will be a slow, painful death, unless . . . No! No way would I let them put my darling Goofey to sleep.

I studied the woman momentarily, then blurted, "What's wrong with my cat?"

The woman smiled sweetly. "We're doing everything possible for him," she said. "He has a severe intestinal problem, caused by ingesting large amounts of soap. Actually, bubble bath."

I took a deep breath. Paula was responsible for poisoning my cat! Wanting to scream, I managed to force polite words out of my mouth. "May I see Goofey now?"

"Certainly." The assistant led me into another room. She explained that the technician was giving Goofey liquid charcoal to absorb the soap in his stomach. I watched, willing the tears back, trying to focus my eyes on Goofey.

"We'll have to keep your cat for several days," the technician said.

"What for?" I asked.

"We'll put a tube down his stomach for starters, and after a while he should be as good as new. But you'll have to help us," he said, smiling.

"I'll do anything," I said, inching closer to the gray form lying deathly still on the table.

"You'll have to monitor his eating and drinking habits for a week after we release him. I'll give you a prescription for Goofey—fifty milligrams of Amoxicillin, twice a day. In addition to that, he'll need an anti-inflammatory to make sure the liquid charcoal doesn't irritate his stomach." He stood up and walked me to the door. "I'll make a list of things for you to follow."

"Thank you very much for saving Goofey's life," I said, following him to the waiting area.

"Well, you can be sure we'll give him the best of care," he said. "But when he's released, it would be a good idea if Goofey returns to his home." He glanced at Paula just then. "He'll get well much more quickly if he's surrounded by those he's accustomed to."

Another lump swelled in my throat. This was turning into a nightmare.

After the vet left, I glared at Paula. "Thanks for trying to kill my cat," I whispered.

Paula wiped a tear. "I never thought . . . it's just so awful . . . I'm truly sorry, Holly. I really am."

I couldn't stand her blubbering. I turned to the receptionist's desk. "May I use your phone, please?" I asked.

The phone rang twice before Uncle Jack answered. "I'll be right there," he said after I told him my dilemma.

Thanking the receptionist for the use of her phone, I turned around. Paula was gone. *She's out of here for good,* I thought, seething silently as I waited for Uncle Jack.

Then I heard a familiar cooing sound coming from the open door. I stood up. Yep, it was Paula's voice all right. Who could mistake it?

Moving closer, I peeked around the doorway and saw Paula standing near my cat, stroking him. Furious, I headed down the hall toward her. "Don't touch my cat!" I said.

Paula jumped. "But I had to say good-bye to Goofey," she sputtered, eyes a-flutter.

"Well, you said it, now disappear."

She looked at me sorrowfully. "Oh, Holly, please forgive me. I wouldn't hurt Goofey for anything."

"Well, you did, and it can't be changed." The angry words surprised me as they tumbled out.

Paula rushed past me, sobbing.

I said my good-byes to Goofey in private. His fur smelled of roses, the scent that Paula had been smothering him with every day. He didn't move, or purr, or anything. His eyes were glazed over, unseeing.

"Please get well," I whispered, touching his tattered ear. "I can't live without you."

Chapter 8

Settling into the bucket seat of Uncle Jack's van, I thanked him for picking me up.

He apologized all over the place about what had happened. "I'm sorry it had to be my allergies that sent Goofey away."

I wouldn't let him take the blame. "It's not your fault. You couldn't help it."

He offered to pay for the entire bill. "Don't worry another second about this, Holly," he said. "That's what stepdads are for, right?" He grinned at me.

"Thanks," I said, still unsettled about what to do when Goofey was well enough to come home. If only Andie would agree to keep him, the problem would be solved.

♥ ♥ ♥

After supper, Mom and Uncle Jack went to Bible study. I spent the evening doing pre-algebra with Stan. He assisted me, with occasional comments from "John Wayne."

When the phone rang, I hoped it was Andie, not Paula.

I got my wish.

"Hey," Andie said. "What're you doing Friday night?"

"Nothing much," I replied.

"C'mon, Holly, you sound morbid," she scolded. "You'll have a very cool make-over party."

"Don't rub it in." I felt a sickening lump in the pit of my stomach. She was ruining everything by not coming.

"Relax," Andie said in her quirkiest voice. "I'm still invited, right?"

I almost dropped the phone. "What are you saying?"

"Christiana's arriving earlier than we thought. We're picking her up on Friday morning."

"So you can come?"

"I'll come if Christiana's invited, too." It was more of a question than a statement.

"Do you think, I mean, will she be comfortable attending a stranger's birthday party on her first night in America?" I asked.

"Oh sure," Andie said. "She'll have a great time meeting you and Amy-Liz. Who else is invited?"

"Joy and Shauna are coming . . . and that's it," I said, thinking about Paula Miller, who didn't even know about the party. No way was the cat killer invited.

"That's six of us," she said. "It's best to have an even number at parties, my mom always says. That way no one feels left out."

I laughed. "My mom says the same thing."

"Should we bring anything?" she asked.

"Don't worry about it. We'll have everything we need here."

"I'll bring my new cucumber mask," she said. "You have to try it. It's organic and so earthy."

"I can't wait, now that you're coming. And guess what? Mom's hired a beautician for the party. We'll have our hair restyled after we experiment with makeup. Cool, huh?"

"Great! I want my hair straightened for a change," she said, laughing. "What about you? Gonna get your hair chopped?"

"Styled," I said. "Not cut."

"I've never seen you with short hair," she said. "Bet you'd look cute."

Here we were having this fabulous conversation, and she had to bring *that* up. She knew better. Never in a zillion years would I cut my hair.

"How long is Christiana's hair?" I asked, changing the subject.

"A little longer than chin length, according to her pictures. It's close to your hair color, Holly."

So that's why she mentioned getting my hair cut. She was thinking of her pen pal. Again.

"Guess what happened today?" I said.

"Something about your cat?" she asked casually.

"Yeah, Paula tried to kill him!"

"And you're upset."

"Upset, nothing. I'm furious at Paula. It's her fault."

"What actually happened?" Andie was all ears.

I told her about the daily bubble baths, how Goofey had swallowed lots of the soap, making him sick.

"Never heard of giving a cat a bath," she said. "Don't they lick themselves clean?"

"Of course. Anybody knows that."

"Well, Paula's different, you know."

"No kidding," I said, the anger boiling up again.

"Well, I'll see you tomorrow," she said. "I've gotta get my room ready for Christiana."

"Okay, see you."

I hung up, feeling both happy and worried. Andie would be at my party, but so would a complete stranger. One that I'd already decided to dislike.

Suddenly a new thought struck me. *What if Christiana doesn't like me?*

💜 💜 💜

Thursday after school, Mom drove me to see Goofey while Stan kept an eye on the other kids. Andie rode along, sitting in back with me.

"What'll happen to Goofey when he's released from the clinic?" she asked. "Who will take care of him then?"

I glanced at Mom. "Good question," I said, wishing I could persuade Andie to adopt him. "There's no way I want Paula getting close to him again."

"What's so bad about Paula?" Mom asked.

"Just because she's rich and gorgeous doesn't mean she can take care of cats," I mumbled.

"Now, Holly, please don't hold this against her," Mom said as she pulled into the parking lot behind the clinic.

Andie elbowed me in the ribs.

"Coming in?" I asked, unlocking the car door.

"You betcha," Andie said.

Mom waved as we headed inside.

Goofey had a tube in his stomach, so he couldn't have visitors. Besides, the technician probably didn't want to gross us out. "Your friend was here today," he said.

"Who?"

"Your friend Paula Miller. She came around lunchtime."

What gall! It made me madder than ever. But I covered it well. "Make sure you tell Goofey I love him," I said. "Say my name in his ear three times every hour."

His eyebrows shot up. "No problem," he said with a grin.

"You're crazy, Holly," Andie said on the way back to the car.

"So what? Doctors prescribe medicine in double and triple doses, don't they?"

She opened the car door. "Cats don't understand English, do they?"

I waited for her to slide in before I climbed into the back. "They're smarter than you think." I wanted to say, *Why don't you adopt Goofey and find out?* But I bit my tongue and decided I'd pray for an adoptive parent for him instead.

♥ ♥ ♥

After supper, Stan and I headed off to church with Uncle Jack.

When we arrived, Paula and Kayla were walking up the steps. "Go with me to the side door," I pleaded to Stan.

He frowned and turned on his John Wayne charm. "What's the matter, little sister?"

"Paula's pathetic," I muttered.

"Now, there's an interesting Christian attitude." He held the door as I trudged inside.

"If I never see Paula's face again, I'll be thrilled," I said.

And then . . . around the corner she appeared. "I have to talk to you, Holly," she said, reaching for my arm.

I backed away, ready to do battle.

Then Stan stepped in front of me. John Wayne's voice rang through the hall. "Listen here, pilgrim. This here's the sanctuary of God. I'd suggest you take your fight outside." He took Paula's arm by the elbow, guiding her away from my wrath. She looked up at him, smiling with all her teeth. "Well, missy, looks like I saved your hide," Stan said as they strolled down the hall.

I watched as Stan and the cat killer turned the corner in the foyer. Inching my way forward, I peeked around.

"Seems as though what we've got here is just a little misunderstanding," John Wayne droned on.

Paula, the cat poisoner, giggled just as Andie appeared at the top of the steps, face-to-face with Stan. With his arm around Paula!

Chapter 9

Andie's eyes popped. "Excuse me?" she demanded.

Not given to defeat, Stan came up with the perfect comeback. "Missy," he turned to Paula. "Like I said, life's full of little misunderstandings."

Gallantly, he offered his other elbow to Andie. "Well, pilgrims, let's go to church."

Sparks flew from Andie's dark eyes as she caught my glance. Stan was in for it now.

Paula's giggling diminished to a grin as she released her hold on my cousin. "Thanks for everything, mister. See ya at the roundup."

Some pathetic imitation, I thought, as she turned around and caught my eye.

"Holly, I really do need to talk to you." She was coming at me, full speed.

I stood my ground. "There's nothing to say." I pushed past her as Andie grabbed Stan and pulled him into the youth service.

After we sang some contemporary praise and worship choruses, Pastor Rob stood up. "Tonight we're going to divide into small groups, but first the devotional." He read the Scripture from Matthew 5:44. " 'But I tell you: Love your enemies and pray for those who persecute you . . .' "

Some text.

If I hadn't known better, I would've thought Stan or someone else had filled in Pastor Rob on what was going on between Paula and me.

He continued to talk about the verse, skillfully weaving the Scripture into his talk. When it was time to divide into discussion groups, Pastor Rob had us count off by fives. I was a two. So was Paula. Quickly, I disappeared into the girls' bathroom and stayed there till I was sure the small group stuff was over.

At last I came out, only to find Paula waiting beside the closed chapel doors. "I know you're angry at me," she said, "and I don't blame you. But I honestly didn't know bubble baths would harm your cat."

I couldn't look at her face. Those perfectly white, perfectly aligned teeth of hers could blind an innocent bystander. Innocent, that was me all right. I'd *innocently* allowed her to care for Goofey. What an ignorant mistake.

"Please?" she begged. "Please forgive me, Holly?"

I wasn't ready to discuss this. The anger in me was too strong. So strong I couldn't even begin to put Matthew 5:44 into practice. "I can't talk now." I turned to find my jacket.

"Can I call you?" she pleaded.

"No." I stormed down the steps, feeling totally out of control as I waited for Stan in the foyer.

A few minutes later, the rest of the kids poured out of the chapel. Andie invited me to go with her to Denver in the morning to meet Christiana. "Dad wants to leave right after breakfast, around seven-thirty. Your mom can call the school and get an excused absence for you first thing tomorrow."

"Thanks for asking," I told her, only because I wanted to be with Andie.

Not because I wanted to meet Christiana. Not in the least.

♥ ♥ ♥

On the way to Denver, Andie and I sat in the backseat, singing last year's choir tour songs. When we ran out of songs, we played alliteration games, making sentences with words that started with the same letter.

I started. "Pathetic Paula parades her perfect pose, posture, and clothes. She pampers pets par excellence with pink poodle pajamas."

Andie chimed in. "Paula ponders Paris, posh parlors, and Park Avenue!"

"With palette paint on her cheeks and purple powder on her eyelids," I finished, giggling.

Mrs. Martinez turned around in her seat. "Girls, are you making fun of someone?"

Andie and I looked at each other. "Not really," Andie lied. We smothered giggles behind our hands.

All too soon, we arrived at Denver International Airport. At least we had had two hours together before Christiana waltzed into our lives.

While Andie's dad parked the car, I looked at snapshots of Christiana. "Here's one," Andie said as we sat in the airport waiting area. "She's standing in front of Mozart's home in Salzburg. Can you imagine living in the same city as Mozart?"

"Bet you'd like to see it for yourself," I commented, studying the tall house with many windows.

Before she could answer, Andie's dad arrived, looking for the monitors posting departures and arrivals.

"There's one down there, Daddy," Andie said. We hurried to look at it.

"Let's see, flight 227 from New York . . . yep, it's on time." There was a certain amount of ecstasy in Andie's voice. I tried to overlook it. After all, this was a special moment for her.

Andie hurried to the baggage claim area. "I can't believe Christiana's almost here!"

I couldn't believe it, either. I was trying hard to squelch the green-eyed monster. It sure was causing me trouble.

Andie and I spotted the Austrian beauty right away. Being tall is an asset sometimes. She floated through the airport like some fairy-tale princess. A peaches-and-cream complexion graced her fair face, and she broke into a full smile at the sight of Andie. Hugging like old friends, the girls were quickly lost in conversation. For what seemed like several minutes I waited, rather impatiently, for Andie to introduce me.

At long last, Andie turned to me. "Holly, I'd like you to meet Christiana Dertnig. And Christiana, this is a friend of mine, Holly Meredith."

Immediately my ears perked up. In just minutes I'd been reduced to a mere friend. What about lifelong *best* friend?

Christiana extended her hand. "So very nice to meet you, Holly," she said. Perfect King's English.

I reached out, warming up my smile. "Same here" was all I could say.

"I've heard a lot about you from Andie's letters," Christiana said. "You're the girl Andie made up so you could fool your college pen pal, right?"

My face flamed. "Sort of," I mumbled. I disliked her instantly. Why'd she have to bring up one of the most embarrassing episodes of my life? And at our very first meeting!

Andie explained, "Christiana loves pulling tricks on people. They play jokes on each other all the time at her girls' school. She loved hearing about our plan to trick Lucas Leigh."

"That's nice," I said, fibbing through my teeth.

The entire trip home was spent discussing Christiana's hopes for her visit to America. One thing was clear: She wanted to attend a rock concert.

"Andie's never attended one," her mother said. "And I don't anticipate her father and I will change our minds about *that* issue."

Christiana's blue eyes widened. She was obviously shocked at the parental interference.

"There's a Mandee Trent concert in Denver next weekend,"

Andie's dad said. It was only a suggestion, but he seemed eager to steer the conversation away from rock concerts.

"Mandee Trent?" Christiana said. "Who's that?"

"She's a hot Christian pop singer," I volunteered.

"Oh," she said, like it was nothing.

"What about classical?" Andie's mother said. "I understand you enjoy Mozart."

Christiana the Great replied, "In Salzburg, we are surrounded by serious music."

"So maybe we should expose you to other types here," Andie said. She was beginning to sound like the Queen of England herself. I could hardly wait to get out of the car. Away from this strawberry blonde who seemed to affect everyone in her path.

Then Andie's mother mentioned my party. "Holly has a Valentine's Day birthday," she said. "And she's invited you both to a make-over party tonight."

Christiana had no idea what that was all about. Briefly, Andie explained.

I wasn't surprised when Christiana decided she would not be interested in a make-over. No doubt she was quite satisfied with her present look, thank you very much.

That afternoon Andie escorted Christiana around to the principal and all the teachers at Dressel Hills Junior High. They'd been expecting her, of course, so the reception was red-carpet.

I ate lunch with Jared, without Andie. "Everyone's freaking out over Christiana," I moaned. "Especially Andie."

"It won't last forever," he assured me.

"Even Danny Myers is following her around, volunteering his services."

"Hmm," Jared said. "Sounds serious. Are you jealous?"

"Are you kidding?" I laughed, and Jared grinned.

All day I avoided Paula as best I could. And it wasn't easy. She kept showing up at the most conspicuous places. Places like the stall next to mine in the girls' bathroom. And in the exact same section of the library—three books down. This was turning into a nightmare. Mostly because I refused to forgive her. How many times had she asked—begged—for my pardon?

Seeing her grim face only reminded me of that horrible tube in my cat's stomach. Poor little Goofey. His suffering had been caused by a senseless act, and it was totally Paula's fault.

When it came to prayer, I avoided the forgiveness issue with God. It was much easier to pray about a zillion other things, like Goofey's restored health and Christiana's quick return to her homeland.

There was one request I asked for repeatedly, however. "Dear Lord," I prayed, curling up on my window seat after school. "I need your wisdom and help as fast as you can send it. It's about Goofey's next home. He needs a new one—fast! Please let it be a place where I can visit him every day. Could you do something soon? Amen."

I reached for my journal and recorded my thoughts.

Friday, February 11: I miss Andie already. Every time I looked for her at school today she was tied up with Christiana. I want to disappear and come back AFTER Christiana leaves!

Chapter 10

The phone rang.

"Holly!" Mom called. "It's for you."

The vet was on the line. Goofey was being released tomorrow. A sad lump squeezed my throat.

"You'll need to monitor his eating and drinking for several more days," the vet reminded me.

I swallowed the lump. My heart was pounding. My darling Goofey was well, but for a cat without a home, this was horrible news. "Is there any way you can keep him a little longer?" I asked.

A short pause, then, "Is there a problem?"

Quickly, I shared my dilemma.

"We have a kennel of sorts," he explained, "but we can only keep him up to a week here."

"How much will it cost?" I thought of the birthday money I'd already started acquiring from relatives.

"About ten dollars a day," the vet said.

Mentally I tallied up my money. I had just enough to handle it. "Let's do that," I said. "Uh, only if I can visit Goofey every day."

"No problem. We'll look forward to seeing you. Good-bye."

I hung up the phone feeling a little better. But I wasn't independently wealthy, of course. And Mom must never find out about this. She wouldn't approve of using birthday money for Goofey's temporary housing.

When Uncle Jack arrived home, he took me for a quick visit with Goofey. My cat seemed much better, more energetic. And he licked my hand repeatedly as if to tell me so.

♥ ♥ ♥

When we returned home, I helped Mom set out the makeup and stuff for my birthday party. Together, we turned the kitchen into a beauty salon, complete with facial and beauty kits and hand mirrors for each girl. It was fabulous.

"The guests will be here in one hour," I said, thinking of the Patterson and Meredith family members. "Where are we gonna stash all our kids?"

"Well, let's see," Mom said, grinning. "Uncle Jack took Phil and Mark out for the evening. Stan's going to make himself scarce in his room, and Carrie and Stephie are planning their own party."

I sat down on a barstool, absently picking up a creamy-pink blush. "I hope this make-over thing is a good idea." Christiana's snide remark this morning had me worried.

Mom stopped arranging things for a moment and looked at me. She pushed a stray hair off her forehead. "Is everything okay, Holly-Heart?"

"Not exactly," I said. "I really miss Andie."

I heard her sigh. Extra loud. "This isn't about Christiana, is it?"

"Who else?" I muttered.

I ran upstairs to change clothes. By the time I freshened up and slipped into a clean pair of jeans and sweater, Mom was knocking on my bedroom door.

I let her in.

"How's my birthday girl?"

"Oh, Mom." I ran into her outstretched arms. "I love you!"

She hugged me bone hard. "Let's start getting the sloppy joes ready. Your guests will be arriving very soon."

I followed her downstairs. It was amazing; Mom could calm me down, no matter what. One of her many God-given gifts.

Speaking of gifts, Daddy sent me money from California, as usual. I wondered what my best friend would give me for my fourteenth birthday. As for Christiana, I would be lucky if she cracked her face to give me the slightest smile.

The doorbell rang, and I ran to get it. Shauna and Joy were first to arrive. A few minutes later Amy-Liz showed up. By the time I'd hung up their jackets, the doorbell rang again. This time it was Andie with her shadow—er, pen pal—Christiana.

"Happy birthday," Andie said, giving me a big hug.

"Thanks," I said. "Glad you're here."

Christiana reached out to shake my hand like she had at the airport this morning. Reluctantly, I held out mine.

Z-z-z-z-t-t! I shrieked and jumped back. Christiana had zapped me with a hand zinger.

"Ooh, she got you good, Holly," Amy-Liz exclaimed. The girls laughed.

"Are you all right?" Christiana said, trying not to smirk.

I nodded, forcing a smile.

Andie giggled. "Remember, I told you Christiana loves practical jokes."

Rubbing the zing off my palm, I led them into the kitchen. Christiana immediately launched off on entertaining my guests with her stories. She talked about Vienna and Mozart's *The Magic Flute*. I couldn't imagine Amy-Liz or Shauna or any of the others being half as interested as they looked. I was the one interested in classical music. They were diehard Mandee Trent fans.

"What's school like in Salzburg?" I asked.

"I attend a boarding school," Christiana said. "It's an all-girl school."

"You sleep over?" Amy-Liz asked.

Christiana chuckled. "It's great fun. We pull jokes on each other nearly every night."

I'll bet you do, I thought.

"Tell us some tricks you've played," Amy-Liz said.

"I'm sure you've heard of the hand-in-warm-water trick," Christiana said.

Everyone nodded, laughing.

"And there's the greased toilet seat," she said.

"We did that last year on choir tour," Andie piped up, glancing at me.

Christiana was all too eager to go on. And on.

Leaning against the kitchen bar, I decided it was time to divert the conversation away from Christiana's neck of the woods. "Did you hear? Mandee Trent's coming to Denver—one week from tonight."

"I already bought my ticket," Joy said.

"Me too," Shauna said.

"She sings like an angel," Amy-Liz said.

Andie spoke. "I heard she's dating some guy in her band."

Amy-Liz stood up and sauntered around, pretending to play the sax. "Wouldn't it be cool to travel together all over the country?"

"How romantic," I said, keeping my eyes on Christiana.

"What sort of professional training does she have?" Miss Austria asked, tilting her head.

I wanted to say, *Who needs training when you can sing like an angel?* but I stifled my thoughts and watched the reactions of the others.

Andie described Miss Trent's vocal training to a T. For Christiana's sake. As always.

Mom saved the day by announcing supper. We gathered around the dining room table where brightly colored name cards decorated each place setting. I spotted Andie's name beside Christiana's. Even my own mother was watching out for Christiana. Not for me.

Soon we were seated. "Let's pray," Mom said, and she began. First a special blessing on the birthday girl, then a joyful thanks to the Lord for "Holly's friends, each one of them," and last a food blessing. Everyone joined in with "amen" at the end. All but Christiana.

"Andie, start the buns and the chips around," I said.

Mom took the girls' soda orders and left the room while Andie began describing sloppy joes in great detail to Christiana. When she finished with the ingredients, she said, "My mom makes them every Monday night."

"Sometimes my mother sneaks leftovers into the hamburger mix," Amy-Liz complained. "It's disgusting."

"That's nothing," Joy said. "My mom uses ground turkey for our sloppy joes."

"Eeew!" the girls squealed.

After supper, Mom brought out the cake. The girls sang the birthday song while I contemplated my wish. Birthday wishes are supposed to be special. Very special.

Mom lit the candles. "Happy birthday, Holly-Heart."

I closed my eyes, wishing for the day when I would be number one again with Andie. Taking a deep breath, I blew out my candles. All but one.

"Don't worry, Holly," Andie said, eyeing the lone candle. "Today's not your real birthday, is it?"

I didn't know how to take her remark. I hoped she was being kind. But she sounded a bit catty. Anyway, my wish would never come true now. Thanks to one lousy candle.

For the gift opening, we converged on the living room and sat on the floor. I observed Christiana, noticing her shining eyes as she glanced at my gifts lined up on the sofa. She held hers tightly, fingering the pink bow in the center. Did she think her gift was more wonderful than all the rest?

I opened hers last, and soon discovered it was from both her *and* Andie. The gift was a jewelry box, which meant it probably wasn't Andie's idea at all. And by the sound of the Mozart tune, I was sure Christiana had chosen it.

To make things worse, when the beautician showed up,

Christiana suddenly developed a headache. Andie turned on her friendly charm and arranged for her mom to pick them up.

"Why can't you stay?" I cornered Andie, pleading with her.

"It's Christiana's first day here, and I'm her host," she reminded me rather coldly. "She probably has jet lag. It's two o'clock in the morning in Austria right now, you know." And with that comment, she flounced off to get their jackets.

We started the facials without them. Andie and Christiana sat in the living room, whispering and giggling while they waited for their ride. I sat in the kitchen with the rest of the girls while Joy smeared Andie's cucumber mask on my face. After it dried, I cracked it twice on purpose thinking about Christiana. She had to be so perfect. Every word, every gesture . . .

It was so disgusting. Besides that, she had Andie wrapped around her little finger.

Could my friendship with Andie survive five more weeks of this freak show?

Chapter 11

When Andie's mother arrived, I was polite. I thanked the girls for the birthday present and said good-bye. But in my heart I was crushed.

Passing through the dining room, I saw it: a huge black spider hidden in the crevice of a chair. I froze. I'd sat in that very spot tonight!

Inching my way past it, I gulped. Then I ran to the kitchen to get a broom.

"What's that for?" Joy asked, eyeing me suspiciously.

"Don't worry," I said. "Stay right where you are."

That brought all the girls running.

"Don't anybody move," I said as they huddled behind me, squealing. *Bam!* I came down hard on the monstrous insect. The girls leaned in, staring—holding their mouths.

"It's not dead!" Amy-Liz cried.

"Whack it again," Shauna screamed.

I raised the broom over my head, preparing for the kill.

"What kind of spider is it?" Joy asked.

"Indestructible," Amy-Liz said.

With broom poised, I inched closer, poking the spider with the wooden handle. The ugly creature didn't move.

"It's fake," I said.

That rotten girl, I thought of Christiana.

"Hey, good joke," Amy-Liz said. Joy and Shauna agreed.

I snatched up the lifelike critter and flung it at them. Screams filled the house, and Mom came running.

"It's nothing," I said. But it was. Christiana had arrived only a few hours ago, and already she was messing up my life. Stealing the show at my party. Stealing my best friend . . .

Back in the kitchen, I checked my facial mask in one of the hand mirrors lying on the counter. An alien-green tint covered my face. Cucumber facial masks are supposed to look like that. But I got carried away and imagined that my eyes were green as emeralds, too. *Green with envy,* I thought. *Look at me! I'm just a green-eyed monster.* But I didn't care.

Amy-Liz got brave and had her curly blond hair cut and styled. Joy and Shauna liked it so much they experimented with a new look, too.

Even without Andie, the make-over went pretty well. We made shy, sweet Joy look like a flirt with bright red, wet lipstick and tons of mascara. Shauna was grotesque with pale lips, dark eye shadow, and dark eyebrows. Amy-Liz went for the clown look with round circles of rouge on each cheek and on the tip of her nose. I wasn't much of a sport and opted for a more natural look.

When the girls left for home, I helped Mom clean up.

"You didn't have much fun tonight," she said, wiping the kitchen counters.

"It was fun, I just . . ." What could I say? Turning fourteen wasn't what it was cracked up to be. "I don't know," I said, twisting the lids on the foundation and cream blush. "Maybe it's just when you look forward to something so long, you have a mental image of how it'll turn out. Then when Christiana started telling her boring stories, I felt icky inside."

"I understand, honey." She gathered up the dirty napkins.

"Then Christiana said she was sick, which I seriously doubt, and Andie left, too." It was hard recounting the miserable evening. I didn't want to think about it. Writing my feelings secretly in my journal was much easier.

So I kissed Mom on the cheek and wiped my tears. "I'll be upstairs for a while," I said. "Thanks for everything."

February 11 continued: The party was weird. It was mostly a welcoming party for Christiana! Ick!

Goofey goes in the kennel tomorrow. Poor thing. I'll be broke by the end of the week. But I'll use all my allowance next month for my missionary project and the sponsor child for sure.

A strange sensation rippled through my scalp, down my shoulders, and into my spine. I shivered and stopped writing. It felt like someone was reading over my shoulder.

Slowly looking up, I half expected to see an angel, or . . . maybe God himself. But then, why would God need to read my words when He already knew them?

At that moment, Bearie-O fell off the shelf, landing in my lap. I stroked the top of his bald teddy head. The loving had worn it thin.

Bearie-O was symbolic of my friendship with Andie. Thinking back on the amazing bond we shared, I felt myself becoming even more jealous of Andie's attention to Christiana. I grabbed my journal and counted out the days. Thirty-four to go! March 17, St. Patrick's Day, was the day Christiana was scheduled to leave. I drew a giant smiley face over the date and wrote in big letters: *CHRISTIANA GO HOME!*

♥ ♥ ♥

Valentine's Day, my true birthday, came at last. A giant red envelope was stuck to my locker at school. I spotted it as I pushed through the crowded hallway.

"Happy Valentine-birthday," Jared said as I reached for his card.

I grinned back at him. "Thanks," I said. "Is it for Valentine's or my birthday?"

"Look inside," he said slyly.

I tore the envelope open. A card with red and pink hearts wished me a Happy Valentine's Day. The card behind it was homemade. Light pink construction paper, folded in quarters with pen and ink designs around the edges. The verse was without rhyme—free verse.

"This is incredible!" I said, referring to the homemade card and verse. "You're good, Jared. Thanks!"

"Thank you . . . for being born, that is." He bowed and rose with a grin.

I opened my locker, hiding my blushing face.

"Happy birthday!" I heard an all-too familiar voice. Andie's. But I kept my face inside my locker.

Jared leaned next to me. "You're being paged."

"Is she with Christiana?" I muttered.

"Who else?" he teased.

Both girls came right up to my locker. "You look the same," Andie commented. "Thought you were having a make-over."

I dragged up a smile.

Jared saved the day. "You girls going to hear Mandee Trent Friday night?"

Andie pulled something out of her jeans pocket. "Two tickets say we'll be there." She held them up.

Christiana smiled—at Jared. "I am dying to see what everyone is talking about," she chimed in, using one of Andie's expressions.

"I guarantee you'll enjoy yourself," Jared said. "The church is taking a busload to Denver."

Without missing a beat, Christiana said, "Oh, save us some seats, will you, Jared?" She flashed him a dazzling smile.

"Absolutely," Jared said.

I felt uneasy. He seemed just a little too friendly with the Austrian beauty.

♥ ♥ ♥

Later, Jared met me at lunch. "What's going on with you and Andie?" he asked, sliding in beside me at the table.

"I don't want to talk about it." I watched Andie and Christiana out of the corner of my eye.

"This doesn't have anything to do with Christiana, does it?" He was prying, and I didn't like it.

"Let's just say I'm sick of hearing about the Alps and Mozart's birthplace and fakey headaches."

Jared frowned. "Headaches?"

I told him about my birthday party and Christiana's sudden illness.

"What's so bad about a headache?" He grinned at me.

I sighed. "Maybe if you'd been there . . ."

Jared reached for his drink. "You're jealous," he said casually.

I sprinkled hot sauce on my tacos. "You could say that."

"It doesn't become you, Holly."

"Don't preach. You'll start sounding like Danny."

"I don't care who I sound like," he said. "Christiana probably isn't a Christian. At least, I get that impression."

"Well, if you're so interested, why don't you convert her?" I didn't mean to sound so harsh; it just tumbled out. Maybe because Andie and Christiana were heading toward our table right then. "Excuse me," I said, hopping up.

"Hey, where're you going?" Jared leaped up, leaving his tray behind.

"Enjoy your lunch. And your company."

But Jared followed me down the hall to my locker. He stared at me while I worked my combination lock. "Don't mess up your birthday, Holly-Heart," he said softly.

"Then don't bug me about Andie. She's *my* problem."

He ran his fingers through his hair. "If that's the way you want it."

Looking at his face, I felt lousy. Jared accepted me as I was, guilty or not guilty. He was only trying to help smooth things over with Andie. After all, it wasn't the first time she and I had fought.

"Hey, you're riding to Denver with me on the bus," he said, changing the subject. "Okay?"

I groaned. "I would, but my family's going skiing, and I just—"

"Just want to stay away from Andie," he interrupted.

"Skiing's a good excuse, don't you think?" I said, avoiding his eyes.

"But it won't be half as much fun without you."

"I'm sorry." I really was.

"I know."

That was another thing I liked about Jared. He wasn't pushy. He accepted things the way they were. For now, our friendship was comfortable, secure. Had Andie filled Christiana in on Jared and me?

I headed for PE. Andie and her sidekick would be there, sharing the same gym locker. It was hopeless the way Christiana finagled everything to her benefit. Why couldn't Andie see the light?

Chapter 12

Timed tests were scheduled for the last half of PE. And wouldn't you know it, Christiana and I were competing for first place. On ropes, no less!

Shaking uncontrollably, every muscle in my body straining with each pull, I did my best to block Christiana from my view. It was impossible. Her strawberry blond hair swayed as she slithered up the rope with her long, slender legs. Closing my eyes, I inched upward. Finally I reached the top.

The class was cheering . . . screaming. I'd made it! Opening my eyes, I saw the girls gathered around Christiana like she was a celebrity or something. Her smile of victory made me ill. I was wrong. She'd beat me hands down.

Sliding down slowly, I noticed Paula was waiting at the bottom of the rope.

"You almost tied her." She flashed her toothpaste smile.

I ignored her.

Andie was next for the test. I felt sick inside, helplessly watching her hang in midair, unable to get her chubby legs to assist in the climb. She barely made it to the first mark. *Whew, that hurt.*

I couldn't watch anymore.

Miss Tucker kept me after class. She said encouraging things about my rope time, but I still felt resentment toward Christiana. "You're good, Meredith," Miss Tucker said. "I'd like to see you get more athletically involved around here."

"Thanks." I glanced at the wall clock. She'd kept me too long. I had to hit the showers fast.

She patted me on the shoulder. "I hear you're having a birthday today. Hope it's a good one."

"Thanks." I headed for the steps to the locker room.

Paula was waiting. "How's Goofey?" she asked.

This girl never quits, I thought, mustering up two words. "Goofey's better." Of course, I avoided the kennel issue entirely.

"We can't be late for the math test," Paula said as we hurried downstairs.

I unlocked my gym locker and pulled out my clothes and a clean towel. Andie and Christiana were already dressing for class. I was really late.

"Is Goofey having visitors yet?" Paula persisted.

I was sick of the questions. "Only me."

"Well, I hope you have a happy birthday, Holly," she said, closing her gym locker.

"Yeah, right," I muttered as I undressed.

I stuffed my sweaty gym clothes into my locker, wrapped my towel around me, and headed for the showers, leaving my locker open. Time was running out. Our math teacher was a stickler for being prompt. Her pet peeve was kids who showed up late for class. She was known to knock a whole letter grade off a test for every five minutes a student was late.

I hurried into the shower room. Piling up my jeans, sweater, and clean underwear next to the wall near the shower, I hopped in.

Soaping up quickly, I relived Christiana's look of triumph when she had beat me on the ropes.

Poor Andie, short and chubby—what a nightmare the ropes had always been for her. If Christiana cared about Andie's feelings at all, she'd have been cheering her on instead of gloating about winning first place.

"Holly, hurry!" It was Paula. "We have five minutes to get to math," she hollered.

Peeking out of the shower stall, I saw Paula applying mascara with one hand while holding a compact with the other. Her hair was still damp from her shower. Could I never escape this girl?

Careful not to get my own hair too wet, I rinsed off quickly. Then, reaching for my towel, I dried off in record speed. Funny, it wasn't Andie reminding me about math. She was probably in class already, choosing a seat next to the Austrian Olympian.

I wrapped my damp towel around me and reached for my clothes. But the spot where I'd put them was empty. "That's strange," I said. Someone had moved my clothes by mistake.

Tiptoeing out of the shower, I looked around. My feet grew colder with each step on the wet cement floor. Scrambling over the full length of the room, I was frustrated. "I know I put them right here," I said out loud.

Wait a minute. Paula was just here, I thought. *What was she still doing here?*

That's when I saw the note. Leaning over, I picked it up. Someone had written: HAPPY "BIRTHDAY SUIT" in purple ink on the paper.

Was it Paula? I gripped the note and the corners of my towel. The clamor of the next class added to my confusion as they came bustling into the locker room.

I clumped toward my locker.

"You're late, Meredith," Miss Tucker yelled over the locker room noise.

"My clothes are gone," I said, but she was too busy to pay attention. Flinging my gym locker wide open, I looked inside. It was empty!

Where were my things? How would I ever make it to math?

Still clasping the note, I retraced my steps to the shower stalls, frantic to find my clothes. Where would a prankster hide them? In desperation, I choked the tears back. Wiping my eyes, I examined the handwriting on the note once again. I didn't recognize it. And, of course, it wasn't signed.

Clutching the note and the towel, I darted back into the locker area. I gazed up at the clock. Two o'clock. The math test was starting now.

Dizzy with rage, I stumbled to my open locker, pushed the note inside, and slammed the door.

"Holly!"

I spun around. It was Paula.

"What do you want?" I gripped the towel.

"I saw what she did."

"Who?"

"Christiana. She took your things and ran off before I could catch her. I even followed her to math class, but I didn't want to make a scene, so I came back to help you." She turned to open her locker and began to undress.

I stared at her. "What are you doing?"

"I'll wear my gym clothes to class. I always keep a clean pair in here just in case," she explained, tossing her sweater to me.

"I can't take your clothes," I muttered, dumbfounded.

"Why not?" she said, throwing her jeans at me. "That's what friends are for."

She slipped into some blue sweats and pulled a T-shirt over her head. "You can still make it if you hurry," she said as she fluffed her brunette locks and ran out of the locker room.

I was speechless.

Chapter 13

After school, Jared caught up with me at the bus stop. He whipped out a birthday present with a flourish. "Ta-da!" he announced. "Okay if I ride with the cutest girl in Dressel Hills?"

"Sure," I said, forcing a happy face as I pulled my jacket tight against me. Jared had noticed I was wearing different clothes. I could tell by the way he looked at me. After all, I didn't exactly fill out Paula Miller's clothes the way she did. But it was better than the "birthday suit" by far!

Out of the corner of my eye I noticed Andie and Christiana coming, half a block away. They were walking fast at first, but I was sure they'd spotted me because suddenly they slowed their pace. I kept my eyes on Jared, refusing to acknowledge their presence.

I vowed right there to begin the silent treatment. It was the ultimate punishment for their sin. Not that Andie had done anything wrong, but wasn't it her fault Miss Austria was here in the first place?

On the bus, Jared slid into the seat beside me. "Open your gift, Holly-Heart."

I gasped when I saw the CD—Mandee Trent's latest release. "I love it," I said. "Thanks, Jared."

"You're welcome." He winked at me.

"This is so cool. Now I can ski with Mandee Trent coming through my iPod while you watch her hit the stage in Denver." Such a romantic thought.

"Shall we synchronize the moment?" he asked.

I poked him. "Don't be silly," I teased, but secretly I loved the idea of listening to my new music at the exact same moment as Jared was experiencing the live performance. He reached for my hand and gave it a squeeze. *Fabulous.*

Downhill Court came up all too quickly. I thanked Jared again for the CD before getting off the bus.

"See you tomorrow," he called.

"Bye!" I held the gift close as I hurried across the snow-packed street.

Once in the privacy of my bedroom, I let my anger pour out in the safest place of all: my journal. First I recorded my intentions for the vow of silence. I would refuse to speak to Andie until she apologized. No, better yet, until she literally *pleaded* with me to return as her number-one best friend.

Next I removed Paula's clothes and tossed them in the hamper. What a remarkable thing she had done today. Something *I* might have done for a best friend.

Slipping into my robe, I popped my new CD into the player on my desk. Mandee Trent's voice wafted through the air. Perfect. I pulled a mystery novel off the shelf and curled up on my window seat, trying to forget the events of the day.

The harsh reality of my plan hit me hard when the phone rang. "For you, Holly," Carrie called to me from the hallway. "It's Andie."

"Tell her I'm not here," I said. Abandoning my book, I jumped up and headed for the stairs. "It's the truth . . . I'm not here." I raced down the steps, through the kitchen, and out the back door.

It was sub-zero cold out there and I counted, slowly, to thirty-five, shivering in my robe as I waited for Carrie to tell me she was off the phone.

But she never did, and I stumbled back into the kitchen, freezing half to death. "Carrie," I called to her.

Stephie, not Carrie, came running up the steps from the family room. "Carrie can't talk now, she's not here," she mimicked me, straight-faced. Then she burst into giggles.

"Get out," I said, chasing after her.

I found Carrie doing her homework. "What did she want?" I asked.

Carrie looked up, eyes filled with innocence. "Who?"

"You said Andie called." I leaned over the back of the sectional staring into her pixie face. "What did she say?"

"She said you're a goof brain."

I couldn't believe this. "You are so not cool." I left the room in a huff.

Wednesday after school Mom drove me to visit my cat. "How do you feel about missing the Mandee Trent concert?" she asked as we waited for a red light.

"I don't have to see her on stage. Besides, it'll be great skiing."

We stopped at an intersection, and she glanced over at me. "What does Andie think about it?"

"No big deal," I said. "After all, Andie's got Christiana. They'll have a good time together, she and the clothes crook."

Mom frowned. "What do you mean?"

I told her the horrible thing Christiana had done after gym class.

"I can't imagine Andie letting Christiana do that," Mom said. "Doesn't sound like her."

"No kidding."

She dropped me off in front of the animal clinic. "I'll be back in thirty minutes," she said.

It was fabulous spending time with Goofey. He actually smiled when he saw me, the way he always did—before Paula tried to poison him.

"I've been praying about a home for you," I whispered to him. "God must have something very special planned. He just hasn't let me know yet."

Goofey purred contentedly as if to say: Whatever you can do is fine, thank you.

"One day at a time," I said softly in his ear.

But deep inside, I was worried. Who in Dressel Hills could I convince to adopt my adorable cat? True, he wasn't the prettiest cat around. But beauty comes from within, after all.

Mom beeped her horn. I kissed Goofey good-bye and headed outside into the cold mountain air.

♥ ♥ ♥

At home, Carrie was waiting. Her bright eyes danced with delirious delight as she informed me of the numerous phone calls I'd missed. From guess who.

"Andie's dying to talk to you, Holly," Carrie said. "It's gotta be important."

"Yeah, well, that's too bad," I retorted, sticking by my vow.

"If she were my best friend, I'd at least ask my sister to take a message." Carrie's eyes danced with mischief.

"Look," I said, sitting her down. "Andie's not your best friend, and you can forget about lecturing me. Okay?"

"Mommy!" Carrie shouted, running out of the room.

"Fine, go tell Mom," I muttered, disappearing into my room. I slammed the door shut.

Settling on my window seat, I grabbed two pillows and leaned against the wall. The sun's rays made me drowsy as I relived the birthday-suit nightmare. . . .

I was in the shower again. At school. Reaching for a towel, I searched for my clothes.

"Put your clothes on," one seventh grader called.

The girls began to laugh. Echoing into a mighty roar, the laughter hurt my head, my ears. I cupped my hands over them, forgetting about the towel. It slipped away as I ran, naked, up the stairs.

At the top of the steps, I hid behind the door. I could see the math classroom just across the outside courtyard.

It was snowy and cold out there. I cringed. And then I saw her—Andie—my best friend in the world. She was waving something at me across the courtyard. "Hurry, Holly," she called. "You can still make it!"

I struggled to see what she had in her hands. Squinting, I peered through the snowy brightness. Then, for a moment, she stopped waving and I could see clearly.

My clothes! Andie had my clothes.

Whoosh! A blast of arctic air ripped through the courtyard, snatching them out of her hands. They flew at me, icy and hostile, sticking to my body. Covering me with their freezing, unfriendly fabric.

I looked down at the expensive clothes stuck to me. Labels and brand names I'd never heard of leaped up. M.A.D. Collection, Angry Jeans Co., and Bonjealous. I tried desperately to remove the tags, but my fingers were frozen.

Again, I struggled, clawing at the hideous labels. Anger . . . jealousy . . .

♥ ♥ ♥

"Holly-Heart, wake up!"

I opened my eyes. "W-wha-at?" I mumbled, still half asleep. "Where am I?"

"You're right here in your room, darling," Mom said, kissing my head.

I looked down. The tags on two throw pillows were pulled off. One of the heart-shaped ones had a hole in its seam.

My fingers must've gone to sleep. I let the pillows roll onto the window seat as I made a fist with both hands, limbering up my tingling fingers, still numb from the dream.

"You missed a long-distance call," Mom said, a hint of a smile playing around her lips.

"I did?" I yawned.

"It was Tyler, your stepbrother." She sat down beside me on my window seat, holding a cup of tea.

"Tyler? Oh yeah. In California."

"He asked when he should call again."

I stood up, stretching my legs. "What did you say?"

"That you'd be expecting his call around five-thirty our time."

I hugged her. "Why didn't you wake me?"

"You looked so peaceful in here, I just couldn't."

"But I was having a nightmare!"

"Well, you looked peaceful," she said, sipping her tea. "Are you anxious about going skiing?"

"What about you? It's your first time, Mom. Aren't you scared?"

"Oh, but Jack will be there," Mom said, a flush of color dancing in her cheeks. "He'll teach me just fine." And by that, I knew the honeymoon was still going strong.

When Mom left the room, I shivered, thinking about those horrible labels stuck on me. I couldn't get them out of my mind. Deep inside, I was still trying to rip the labels off my clothes.

Thank goodness it was only a dream.

Chapter 14

At four-thirty the phone rang.

"I'll get it!" yelled Carrie.

"I've got it!" shouted Stan.

"It's for me," I said.

Three of us picked up the phones in the house. Tyler was calling from California.

"Hey, Tyler," Carrie said.

Click. Stan hung up.

"How's California?" I asked.

"Fine, thanks," he said. "Happy birthday, Holly . . . a little late. Wait'll you see what I bought you. It's way cool!"

I laughed. "Give me a hint."

"Nope, you just wait. My mom's mailing it today."

"Is it nice there?" I asked.

"About seventy-five degrees, I think. Here, ask Sean, he's baby-sitting me."

Sean? My heart pounded. Why did *he* want to talk to me?

"Hang up the phone," I said to Carrie.

"Why?" she whined.

"Just do it!"

Before I could say any more to her, Sean was on the line. "Hey, Holly. How was your birthday?"

I'd forgotten how deep his voice was. "Don't ask," I said, laughing. No way was I telling him about the birthday-suit prank. "What's it like there?"

"It's great, as always, but I'm ready for a change."

Click. Carrie hung up. Boring weather talk does it every time.

"Your dad's thinking of coming to Denver on business next month," Sean continued. "If things work out, he'll bring Tyler and me along to ski." He paused. "Uh, I'd like to see you if we come to Dressel Hills."

Is this for real?

"You're coming here?"

"Over spring break," he volunteered. "It's the busiest time of the season, but school's out. Your dad thought it would be perfect timing."

I was suddenly shy again, like when I'd first met him on the beach last Christmas. "Sounds fun," I said. "Carrie will be thrilled to see Tyler again. They were quite a pair last Christmas."

"Well, I better let you go, Holly. But I'd like to write you a letter, if it's okay."

"Uh, sure," I said.

"Nice talking to you. Bye."

"Bye," I said, still shocked at his news. Coming to Dressel Hills? Next month?

I hung up the phone and ran to tell Carrie. Then I stopped cold. What was I thinking? She would blab this to everyone. The whole town would know about Sean Hamilton, the cute California surfer.

I decided not to record my conversation with Sean in my journal, either. Too risky. Especially with Andie teaming up with Christiana to do horrible things to me these days.

Somehow I kept things quiet about Sean through supper. And

Carrie never even asked why I wanted to talk to him alone on the phone.

♥ ♥ ♥

On Thursday Paula cornered me in the hall after school. Kayla was waiting for her several feet away. I noticed Paula's designer jeans and her new denim jacket. She looked completely different from her twin.

She probably wants her clothes back, I thought.

"How's Goofey?" asked Paula.

"Better."

"I'd love to see him again," she said, shifting her books from one arm to the other.

"I, uh, don't know," I stuttered. No way did I want to share my precious time with Goofey. Not with the cat killer.

Around the corner came Andie and Christiana, laughing and talking. No doubt they were staying after school again. Together.

"Hey," Andie said, smiling at me.

"Hey," Paula replied, wearing a flashy smile. "How are you doing on your science project?"

"It's almost finished," Andie told Paula. Then she looked at me. Almost sadly. "How's *your* project, Holly?"

Christiana butted in. "Andie and I are doing a joint project, you know." She was playing her "one-up" game again. And she didn't have to remind me Andie and I had planned to do the project together—before Christiana came and spoiled everything.

She continued her chatter. Several times, Andie made attempts to talk to me, but Miss Austria monopolized the conversation. I didn't care . . . the silent treatment was still in force.

I excused myself, turned, and walked away. When I was out of their sight, I fled from the building.

Paula caught up with me at the bus stop. "Holly, wait! I have to talk to you," she sputtered, out of breath.

"Forget it. I don't want to hear anything about *her,*" I snapped, referring to Andie.

"You have to," she insisted. "It's a matter of . . ." She stopped.

"What? Life and death?" I climbed onto the bus and pushed my way as far back as possible.

Paula followed me. "Please listen, Holly." Her eyes pleaded with me, serious concern written on her face.

Struggling with my curiosity and the vow of silence, I clunked my backpack on the floor and folded my arms across my chest.

"May I sit here?" she persisted.

"I need to be alone."

"But—"

"I *need* to be alone," I said.

A sad, lonely expression swept across her face. Hesitating, she turned away, searching for a seat. At last she chose the only other one available on the entire bus—beside her twin.

Torn between missing Andie and hating her, I dug around inside my backpack, looking for my mystery novel. Finding it, I opened to the bookmark and began to read as the bus made its lurching stops and starts.

Halfway down the page I glanced up, staring at Paula. *What's the message from Andie?*

I forced my attention away from her so-called important info, reading a few more pages in my book. Then the bus stopped in front of the doughnut shop and a bunch of kids got off, dashing inside to claim the Sweet of the Day.

Kayla crawled over Paula to get out, expecting her to come along. But Paula shook her head and stayed, gazing out the window as the bus doors whooshed shut.

I couldn't help watching her as the bus made its journey down the long stretch on Aspen Street toward Downhill Court.

Carrie met me as I came in the house. "Bad news," she announced, closing the front door behind me.

"The worst," Stephie added, sitting on a chair with her feet tucked under her.

"Now what?" I plopped my backpack on the sofa.

"We're staying home. The ski trip's off," Carrie moaned.

"You're kidding." I pulled my jacket off.

"Would I joke about this?" she whined.

I hung up my jacket. "So what's going on?" I noticed Mom's coat was missing from the closet. "Where's Mom?"

"She's at Uncle Jack's office," Carrie said, looking serious. "They got real busy."

"Yeah," Stephie said. "Looks like we're stuck at home." She shrugged.

"Are you sure? We're *not* going skiing?"

I went into the kitchen to hide my delight. Hurrying to the phone, I called Amy-Liz, telling her the news. It looked like I was going to the Mandee Trent concert after all!

"This is so cool, Holly," Amy-Liz said. "But you'd better hurry and get your ticket."

Just then, Stan burst through the back door. I waved at him, trying to get his attention. "Uh, I'll have to talk to you later," I told Amy-Liz, hanging up.

"Didja hear?" Stan said, his nose in the fridge.

"I know, the ski trip is off," I said. "Who told you?"

"I ran into Dad downtown after school. Something's come up with his business. It's booming." Stan poured a glass of milk. "But we're going for sure next weekend."

Oh no! I thought. *That's when Andie and Christiana are going skiing.* I slumped onto the chair in the corner beside Mom's desk.

"What's the matter with you?" he asked.

"Nothing much." I pushed away thoughts of bumping into Andie on the slopes.

"Here, go get yourself a ticket." He shelled out thirty-five bucks. "That oughta help you smile again, little sister." It was John Wayne again.

"Hey, what happened to your birthday stash?" Carrie demanded.

I glared at her. No way could she know my money was going

for Goofey's room and board. She wouldn't hesitate to tattle to Mom about it. I had enough problems without that, too.

"Are you broke?" Carrie asked.

I waved her off. "I just made an investment." I grinned my thanks to Stan, who grabbed a bag of potato chips and sat down at the bar. "Are you going to the concert?"

"Nah," he said. "I've got an appointment."

"Andie won't like it when she finds out," I said, sliding onto a barstool across from him.

"Aw, she'll get over it," he said, pulling a John Wayne video out of his pocket. I wished I could approach my relationship with Andie the way Stan did.

Eager to order a ticket, I picked up the portable phone. First one recorded message then another came on the line as I followed the directions, pushing the correct numbers for additional information. Finally an actual person answered.

"I'd like to reserve one ticket for the concert at McNichols Arena in Denver tomorrow night," I said, twitching with delight. Jared would be *so* excited.

"One moment, please," the woman said as recorded music greeted my ear.

I waited, visualizing the trip up and back on the church bus. It would be so fabulous, laughing and talking with Jared.

"Miss?" came the voice.

"Yes?"

"That performance is sold out," she said coldly.

My heart sank. "Thank you," I said as a wave of disappointment descended over my heart.

Chapter 15

I hung up the phone.

No tickets? Not a single one?

If Andie and I had been on speaking terms, I would have called her right then and cried on her shoulder. But no, she was busy doing her joint project with Christiana. Besides, it wasn't time for me to break my vow of silence.

Dejected and alone, I trudged downstairs and returned Stan's money. His eyes and attention were focused on his latest John Wayne video. He stuffed the money back into his wallet without saying a word.

It made me think of my missions project. I was eager to send the money, but I'd have to wait till Goofey was settled in a new home.

I shuddered at the thought. Heading for the kitchen, I heard the phone ring.

Carrie got it. She stuffed another cookie in her mouth. "Iths fer you."

"Who is it?"

She shrugged.

I took the phone from her sticky fingers. "Hello?"

"Holly?"

It was Paula.

"I can't talk now," I said and hung up.

"How rude," Carrie said, sliding off her stool.

"Just stay out of this."

The phone rang again. I let it ring and ring. At last, it stopped.

"What's wrong with you, Holly?" Carrie asked, staring at me.

"Brat," I said.

"I'm telling Mom," she hollered.

"Fine." I headed for a sink full of dirty dishes.

Carrie stomped off. "I'll be in my room, and I'm not coming out as long as you live in this house!"

"Perfect."

Stacking the dishes in the dishwasher, I thought about Paula. Why was she calling? Was the message from Andie *that* important?

Stan called from the family room. "Dad just phoned. They're on their way home. He said to take some meat out to thaw for supper."

I hurried to the freezer, thinking of the bone-thin child on the church bulletin board. Was it right for me to spend money to keep Goofey in the kennel when there were kids starving to death in the world?

I debated about staying in bed all day when Mom knocked on my door the next morning. "It's a beautiful day in the Rockies," she sang.

Groaning, I rolled over. Everyone in the world was going to hear Mandee Trent tonight. Everyone except me. I dragged myself out of bed and stared at my face in the mirror.

Hopeless.

Mom peeked her head into the room again. "Holly-Heart," she said, "let's plan to go shopping, maybe next week after school?"

I knew what she meant. Mom and I always went shopping after I'd accumulated birthday money from relatives in Pennsylvania and California.

I shrugged my shoulders. It was time to divulge my secret. I'd kept it from her too long.

"My birthday money's gone," I admitted, spilling out the whole story of Goofey's whereabouts.

Mom's mouth dropped open. "You used your money on a cat?"

I nodded ruefully, bracing myself for the lecture.

But she just sighed and said, "Well, it's your money. I guess you should spend it the way you want to." She frowned a bit, though.

Nothing more was said about Goofey, so I told her my plans for next month's allowance. "I want to sponsor at least one starving child," I announced, "and one of the missionaries on the bulletin board at church."

"But you shouldn't be giving away all your money," Mom said gently. "You need some of it to do things with your friends and family. And don't forget you need to start saving for college, too."

"I know," I said. "But I want to do something for other people."

Mom pulled me close. "You're all heart," she whispered.

Mom left, and I got dressed for the day. I felt better . . . at least about telling Mom where I'd spent my birthday money. But I kept thinking about the Mandee Trent concert I was going to miss. Nothing could make me feel better about *that*.

The phone rang during breakfast. Uncle Jack licked waffle syrup off his fingers and reached for the portable phone. "Meredith-Patterson residence. Jack speaking."

A short pause, then . . ."Holly, it's for you. Paula Miller's on the line." He passed the phone to me.

Carrie snickered at me across the table. She knew there was no way I'd hang up now. Not on Uncle Jack's business partner's daughter.

I took a deep breath. "Hello?"

"Please don't be mad, Holly," she began. "I had to call you early. Just listen—"

I interrupted, pretending to answer her. "Okay, I'll see you at school."

"But, Holly—"

"I have to go now," I said. *Politely*. For Uncle Jack's sake. And Mom's.

"I'll wait for you at your locker," she said before hanging up.

"Good-bye," I said, beeping the phone off.

"That was an early morning phone call," Carrie taunted, grinning at me.

"Must be mighty important," I muttered under my breath.

♥ ♥ ♥

I took my time getting off the bus and walking up the steps to the school. It was nearly time for the first-period bell when I arrived at my locker.

A yellow Post-it was stuck to my locker. *I HAVE TO TALK TO YOU! Paula,* it read. *Mission accomplished,* I thought as I peeled it off and crumpled it into my pocket.

Somehow I managed to avoid Paula all day. And I wouldn't have to see her after school because she and the other church kids had gotten permission to leave class early for the Denver concert—during sixth period.

Before Jared left math class, he whispered, "I'll call you tomorrow, Holly-Heart." I could see Billy Hill and a bunch of kids waiting for him in the hallway. My heart sank. I could've been out there with Jared. If only . . .

"There will be no assignment for the weekend," the math teacher announced as the classroom door closed, shutting out the view to the hall.

No assignment, big deal. A small trade-off for being left behind.

Deserted and alone, I plodded off to my locker. Feeling low

enough to crawl through the cracks at the base of my locker, I leaned against the door. Something poked into my forehead. I looked up. It was a note.

I pulled hard, finally retrieving it from its hiding place. Unfolding it, I discovered Andie's message in the form of a note.

Dear Holly,

Since you won't talk to me on the phone, I'm telling you straight. I had nothing to do with stealing your clothes on your birthday. It was Christiana's idea. I didn't even know about it till after school.

I don't blame you for being mad. I would be, too. Wish you were coming tonight!

Your friend,

Andie

I folded the note, feeling gloomy. Instead of riding the bus, I walked home in the freezing cold. The brisk air might clear out the cobwebs in my brain and the disappointment in my heart.

Jared was on his way to Denver without me. Tears sprang up in my eyes. Quickly, I wiped them away with my gloved hand. The wind chill was cold enough to freeze miniature icicles on my face. Another bus stop was two blocks ahead, but I chose to pass it up. Determined, I pushed my way through the ice and snow.

♥ ♥ ♥

The first thing I did when I arrived home was to gather up my dirty clothes. It had been days since I'd done my laundry, and the hamper was swollen and overflowing. Besides, I owed someone a clean pair of jeans and a sweater. The cat killer.

Sorting through the white and colored clothes, I remembered the crazy dream I'd had. I could still see the images of designer labels and my clothes flying out of Andie's hands, plastering themselves against me, cold and unfriendly.

I sat down in the middle of the floor, hills of laundry piled on either side of me like mountains closing in, smothering me. Christiana and her scheme to steal Andie, Paula driving me nuts, and poor homeless Goofey . . .

Goofey. What was I going to do about him? The clinic couldn't keep him any longer; I'd inquired about it. Even if they could, I was broke. I couldn't bear to think of losing my sweet cat. Tears rolled down my cheeks. What if nobody wanted him? What if he had to be put to sleep?

I brushed away my tears. Lost in self-pity, I gathered up the whites and carried them down to the laundry just off the family room. Stan and the rest of the kids were playing a computer game. I sneaked past them unnoticed.

Back upstairs, I rummaged through all my jean pockets, cleaning out junk. My fingers found old tissues, loose change, and a tube of lip gloss. In the last pair, I discovered a piece of blue stationery with golden flecks, folded in two.

I studied it. The paper wasn't familiar, so I held up the jeans. They were Paula's. *This must belong to her,* I thought, setting it aside, debating what to do with it.

My curiosity won out. Slowly, I unfolded the paper.

Dearest Grandma:

In response to your last letter, I have made no progress recruiting friends. Kayla seems satisfied with her one and only best friend—me.

Being nice to Holly Meredith just isn't working. She has only one thing on her mind. That's Andie and her foreign exchange student, Christiana.

Ever since we moved here, Holly has been upset with me. It was my fault, because I had a crush on the same boy she likes, Jared Wilkins. But even when all that changed, it didn't seem to matter to Holly. She won't give me a chance and it hurts.

Lately I've done everything imaginable to be nice to her, Grandma, hoping she'll change her mind. But she's not interested in me as a friend, and I'm so lonely sometimes I cry.

I could read no further. Paula felt left out because of *me*. My unkind words, snide remarks . . . all of it bored into my soul.

The letter shook in my hand as the realization of who I was and what I'd done pierced through me. I was treating Paula exactly the way Andie had treated me. Ignoring her, rejecting her . . .

Carrying the letter to my window seat, I knelt down on the floor as tears streamed down my face. I didn't want to read the rest of her letter. Paula Miller had painted a deft description of Holly Meredith. Pathetic as I was.

Chapter 16

I confessed my sins to God in prayer, then got up and recorded the event in my journal. I titled my entry and began to list the things I intended to change about myself.

MY "MOMENT OF TRUTH" LIST

I resolve to do the following:
_____ *1. Make friends with many different girls.*
_____ *2. Say only good things about others, even behind their backs.*
_____ *3. Forgive Christiana for taking my clothes—and my best friend.*
_____ *4. Invite Andie, Christiana, and Paula to go skiing.*
_____ *5. Trust God for Goofey's future.*
_____ *6. Forget the idea of a number-one best friend.*
_____ *7. Practice Matthew 5:44 every day of my life!*

That done, I felt like Ebenezer Scrooge in the scene where he flings wide his window on Christmas Day. If only my friends were in town, I might hire a Goodyear blimp to broadcast my news. HOLLY MEREDITH COMES TO HER SENSES it might say. Or, A FABULOUS COLORADO WELCOME TO CHRISTIANA DERTNIG.

I floated downstairs on a cloud of transformation, greeting and hugging my family, including Carrie, who gave me a wide-eyed, cynical reception.

"How can I help you with supper?" I asked Mom.

"You may set the table," she said, pulling out the utensil drawer.

My initial thought was to remind Mom that it was Phil's chore, but I squelched it.

At supper I made sweet alien faces at Mark.

"Stop it," he said. "That's *my* thing." But by the grin on his face, I knew he loved it.

I addressed each member of the family with endearing terms. "Precious Phil, please pass the salad," I said without smirking.

"Knock it off, fish lips," he said.

But that didn't discourage me. "Stephie, sweets, pass the salt."

"Call me Stephie-Heart," she teased.

Uncle Jack had to interrupt my flow of flowery expressions to announce the expansion of his business. "It's going to be big, and I mean *big*." He held up his water glass, proposing a toast.

Mom clinked her glass against his, beaming as she gazed at him. "And . . . it's a sure thing. We are definitely going skiing next weekend."

Phil and Mark cheered, Carrie and Stephie squealed, and Stan and I tipped our John Wayne "hats" at each other.

♥ ♥ ♥

That night, after I read my devotional, I recommitted Goofey to God for safekeeping. "Please don't let him see my tears tomorrow when I go for the final visit," I prayed. "That's all I ask. Amen."

Settling down in my canopy bed, I fell asleep, clean as a kitten after a bubble bath.

♥ ♥ ♥

The next morning I awakened to Mom's lovely singing. She sounded as happy as I felt. I looked at the clock. Ten o'clock. I'd overslept!

Bouncing out of bed, I raced downstairs in my pajamas, first hugging Mom and Uncle Jack, then running upstairs to kiss Carrie and Stephie.

"Lay off," Carrie said, pushing me away.

Stephie hugged me back. "What's with Carrie?" she asked.

"Beats me, but maybe we can sweeten her up," I said, skipping to the bathroom to find some spray cologne.

"Leave me alone," Carrie hollered as I sprayed the air around her.

Just then, the doorbell rang. I dashed to my room, grabbing my bathrobe. Scrambling to the front door, I looked through the peephole.

It was Andie.

I looked closer and saw Christiana beside her. My heart thumped. A feeling of overwhelming delight filled me as I flung the door wide.

Andie studied me cautiously. Noting my smile, she broke into a mighty grin. "Happy belated birthday, Holly," she said.

"Come in, both of you," I said.

"We have a present for you," Andie said. She pointed at the white wicker basket she held. "It's not a joint present like last time. It's just, well . . . we worked out a little surprise."

Christiana seemed nervous. When I turned to her, she said, "I'm sorry about the birthday suit joke, Holly. It was a really mean thing to do."

Then she flashed a rueful grin at Andie. "I've learned a hard lesson, thanks to Andie," she admitted. "She hid our science project from me for twenty-four hours. Practical jokes are . . . well, simply not very practical." She extended her hand. "Sorry about taking your clothes. Friends?"

I hesitated a second. Had she given up her hand-zinging days, too? Then I shook her hand. "Friends," I agreed.

"Okay, Holly," Andie said. "Sit down." She led me to the rocking chair. "It's time for your present."

Bending over, Andie picked up the basket. It was decorated with a pink ribbon, my favorite color. She placed it on my lap.

I accepted the heavy basket, wondering what on earth she was up to now. "Thanks." I held the basket firmly. What could it be?

I felt Andie's eyes on me as I slowly opened the lid. There was something crocheted inside. It looked like one of Paula's creations.

But wait! Something moved beneath the mound of creamy-white yarn. A little pink nose nuzzled through a hole in the crocheted coverlet.

It was my cat, Goofey.

Tears clouded my eyes. "Oh, hello, baby," I whispered. I looked at Andie, amazed. "You brought him so I could say good-bye?"

Andie chuckled as Christiana pulled another present from her pocket. By now, Stephie and Carrie had wandered into the living room. They were making over Goofey like crazy. Thank goodness Mom was still upstairs.

"You're going to need this today," Christiana said.

"But—"

"Try opening it before you say anything," Andie said in her silliest voice.

"Here, hold my baby." I handed Goofey over to her so I could open the package.

Inside the wrapping paper was a bottle marked AllerCat. I held it up. "What's this?"

Andie looked like she was ready to pop. But it was Christiana who responded. "If you apply this liquid to Goofey's skin as the directions recommend, your stepdad should have complete relief from his allergy."

"Really?" I looked at Andie. "Are you sure?"

Andie nodded. "Christiana told me about it. I tried and tried to call you and tell you, but, well, let's just forget about that."

Christiana stroked Goofey's neck.

"It's a miracle." I hugged them both. "Thanks for being my friends."

My birthday wish had come true after all.

"Mom," I called. "Come quick!"

The living room was already crammed with Stan, Phil, and Mark, who had wandered in, drawn by the commotion. Uncle Jack came wearing grubby jeans and a big grin. Carrie and Stephie took turns holding, stroking, and whispering to Goofey. And then Mom arrived, flying through the middle of them like Mary Poppins.

"Mom, this is so fabulous," I said. "Goofey's back home to stay." Before she could launch a protest, I quickly read out loud the directions on the back of the bottle.

"Well, why didn't *we* think of this?" Mom said cheerfully.

That's when I did it. I asked Andie and Christiana to come skiing with us the following weekend.

"Let's do," Christiana said.

"Love to," Andie replied, zipping her jacket.

"Thanks for the kitty surprise," I said, addressing both Andie and Christiana as they headed for the door. "It's the perfect gift." And I meant it.

I took Goofey from Stephie and followed my friends to the front porch. "How was the concert?" I asked.

"Mandee is amazing in person," Andie said.

"She really is," Christiana said. "I bought all her CDs."

"And that's not all," Andie said, grinning. "Christiana wants to know more about God."

"Hey, that's fabulous," I said, sorry I hadn't treated her better all along. I gave her another hug.

"I have a lot to learn," Christiana said. "But Andie has two Bibles."

Andie nodded. "And she's coming to church with us tomorrow."

"Cool. I'll see you there," I said as they turned to leave. Then I asked, "Did Paula have a good time last night?" I actually held my breath, waiting for an answer.

"I think so, why?" Andie asked.

"It's a long story," I said as they waved. "I'll tell you some-time."

Christiana floated down the front porch steps, turning to wave again several more times.

"Come again," I called to them.

Then, snuggling Goofey close, I went inside. "It's time to give you a bath in something very special." I reached for the bottle of AllerCat. "This will keep Mom and Uncle Jack happy. Besides that, you're going to have a very special visitor today."

Carrie and Stephie followed me to the bathroom. "Who's coming over?" Carrie asked.

I answered in a mysterious voice. "I'll never tell."

"But you have to," Stephie said, pulling my arm.

After applying AllerCat as the instructions directed, I wrapped the pink bow around Goofey's neck.

Then I marched to the phone in the hallway and dialed.

"Paula?" I said when she answered. It wasn't hard to imagine her smile. And for the first time, I didn't immediately think of a toothpaste commercial.

"This is your friend Holly, and there's someone here who misses you." I held Goofey up to the phone. He meowed twice on cue. Just the way a perfectly pampered and well-mannered pet should.

HOLLY'S HEART

Good-Bye, Dressel Hills

To

Barbara Birch,

my sister and friend,

who dots her *i*'s with hearts.

GOOD-BYE, DRESSEL HILLS

Chapter 1

I was brushing my hair before breakfast when I first heard the word. It hung in the air, like a dagger waiting to be hurled.

Tossing my brush onto the bed, I crept into the hallway, listening. Mom was in her bedroom, talking on the phone with Uncle Jack. I bristled when I heard the word again.

Moving!

"I'm not sure how I feel about it," Mom was saying. "Let's discuss it with the children first."

I gasped and stepped back into my bedroom, closing the door behind me. Moving! How could we leave the only home I'd ever known? Trembling, I pulled my journal out of the bottom drawer of my desk. I began to write: *Tuesday, March 22: News flash—Mom said something horrible today—something about moving!*

That was all I could write before my curiosity took over. I poked my head out the door and listened again. Mom was still talking. I headed for her open bedroom door and tapped.

"Come in," she called to me.

Quietly, I curled up on the foot of the bed and waited till she got off the phone. Trying not to eavesdrop, I glanced around the room. Things looked about the same as they had before Thanksgiving

Day—nearly four months ago—when Mom had remarried and her new husband, my former uncle Jack, and my four cousins had moved in. A gray leather case lay on the left side of the antique pine dresser, and a blue terry bathrobe hung on the hook inside their bathroom. Other than that, the bedroom still had Mom's feminine stamp on it.

Finally Mom said good-bye and beeped off the phone. A worried frown creased her forehead.

"Holly," she said, "I want you to listen before you say anything. Please?"

That's when she told me about Uncle Jack's consulting business and how well it was doing. So well, in fact, that he was thinking of opening an office in Denver.

"You mean we're leaving Dressel Hills?" I blurted.

"Well, it's a strong possibility." She tied the belt on her pink bathrobe. "But we'll know for sure on Friday."

"What's Friday?" I asked.

Mom sighed. "I'll let Jack explain it to you tonight."

"So my life is being put on hold for three days?" I whined.

"I know this must be disappointing for you, honey." She came over and kissed the top of my head. "Moving, especially to a big city, frightens me, too."

"I'm not scared to move, Mom. I just don't *want* to move," I said. "Dressel Hills is my life—yours, too!"

"Moving can be very complicated," she said, staring out the window. She had a faraway look in her eyes, as though she was remembering something painful.

I stood up. "Leaving fourteen years of your life behind—now, *that's* complicated. No way am I going to miss the junior high musical. Or summer church camp. Oh, Mom, can't you do something?"

I didn't mention my friends Andie and Paula. Or Jared. I couldn't bear to think of saying good-bye to any of them.

"Nothing's been decided yet," Mom said, turning around. "That was Jack calling from Denver. He'll be home tonight. We can talk more about it then."

I knew that Uncle Jack's consulting business had been taking him to Denver more frequently. And I knew that Mom didn't especially care for him being gone overnight. But those weren't good enough reasons to move. Were they?

More than anything I wanted Mom to say this whole moving thing was just talk. Something we would toy with and then discard.

"I'm going to be late for school," I said, scooting off her bed. Of course, I wasn't, but if I sat around arguing the benefits of staying in Dressel Hills, Colorado, I would be.

Hurrying to my room, I silently prayed that Friday's phone call—whatever it was—would cancel out this hideous moving talk.

♥ ♥ ♥

At school I kept the news quiet. Maybe by not saying anything the move wouldn't happen. But at suppertime, the reality hit me hard.

Still wearing his dress shirt, Uncle Jack sat at the head of the table. His suit coat and tie hung over the chair behind him. With a hesitant smile, he pushed his apple pie aside and leaned over to open his briefcase. Up he came with a flip chart. Then he reached into his shirt pocket and took out two packs of gum, distributing a stick to each of us.

I groaned silently. *Bribery.* He'd gone to great lengths to make points with us kids. The gum thing was clever, and I could see it already starting to work by the smiles coming from Carrie and Stephie across the table.

Uncle Jack flipped to the first card. "Okay, kids, we need to understand each other." He pointed to a cartoon picture of two big hearts and six little ones, complete with eyes and smiling faces. The girl hearts had long hair and the boy hearts had mustaches. There were mountains in the background. Our mountains.

Stephie and Carrie giggled, but Mom shushed them playfully. Mark and Phil wagged their heads, holding their hands around their faces, imitating the heart faces. Stan and I sat quietly, acting mature and civilized.

Actually, the drawings weren't half bad. Uncle Jack had always made special homemade cards for Mom when they were dating. "As you can see, this family is full of love for one another," he continued, glancing at Mom.

Phil made gagging sounds while Mark said "Yuck" at least five times. Uncle Jack waited, casting a hard eye on his younger sons. They settled down quickly.

Uncle Jack began again. "For the past few days, I've been driving to Denver to handle the new business accounts, and it looks as though I might open an office there." He paused. "The problem is, we have no one to run the Denver office except my partner or me."

I thought about Uncle Jack's business partner, Mr. Miller. He and Mr. Miller had been in business together in Pennsylvania before they moved to Dressel Hills. It was the Millers who'd suggested that Uncle Jack come here in the first place. They thought it would do him good, starting over in a new place after his first wife, my dad's only sister, died of cancer last year. So, from my point of view, it made more sense for Mr. Miller to take the Denver office.

I took a deep breath, scrounging up some courage. "Why can't Mr. Miller go to Denver?" I asked, suddenly realizing what I'd just said. If he moved, so would Paula and Kayla, his twin daughters and my good friends.

"You're thinking, Holly, but I'm the one who's established most of the Denver accounts," Uncle Jack explained. "So it seems that I'm the logical choice."

How could he be so unemotional about this? "Well, why can't you just get someone else?" I shot back.

Uncle Jack glanced at his flip chart. "We're trying. But there's only one other man we would entrust with this position. We've offered him the job, but we won't know his answer until Friday."

My uncle had all the answers, it seemed, but they weren't good enough for me. I argued, "But you just moved here. Doesn't that matter?"

Uncle Jack nodded. "Good point, but we never expected our Denver accounts to grow so quickly." He leaned back in his chair. "Sometimes that's very difficult to predict."

I swallowed hard. "Why'd you choose Dressel Hills in the first place?" It was a two-fold question.

"Now, Holly . . ." Mom had picked up my sarcasm instantly. She was glaring at me, her eyes squinting tightly.

Uncle Jack put his hand on Mom's shoulder. "At first it didn't matter where we based our company, since we set up computer systems all over the world."

I forced the tears back, slouching down in my chair.

Uncle Jack turned to look at Stan. "How do the rest of you feel?" His eyes scanned the table anxiously. All six kids stared at him, silent.

I couldn't believe it! He sounded like he was ready to pack up and ship out tomorrow. He didn't really care what we kids wanted. As far as I could tell, Jack Patterson was a much better uncle than he was a stepdad!

Mom glanced at me. A worried smile flitted across her face. I could tell she was concerned about my feelings.

Stan, Phil, and Mark, my brousins—I called them that because they were cousins-turned-brothers—continued to eat pie as though moving away was no big deal.

Ten-year-old Phil reached for a glass of milk. "I'm barely unpacked from moving here from Pennsylvania, so no problem," he said. "Denver sounds cool." His face lit up. "Hey, maybe Dad'll take us to watch the Colorado Rockies play!"

Mark stretched his lips wide with his pointer fingers, wiggling his tongue in and out of his mouth like an anteater. "Are dere juicy ants in Denber?" he blubbered.

"Stop it," I muttered, staring at my ridiculous nine-year-old brousin. Why couldn't he behave like a normal human being, especially at a time like this?

Uncle Jack ran his fingers through his wavy brown hair. The twinkle was gone from his eyes. "This won't take long, son," he said, giving Mark another serious look. Then he turned to the second card on his flip chart while I took another bite of dessert.

The next cartoon showed the big heart with the mustache waving good-bye to the other big heart with shoulder-length hair. The Denver skyline was in the distance. Little tears dripped off the mother heart's face. Six little hearts wore sad faces, too. Stephie was the smallest heart, followed by Mark, Carrie, Phil, me, and finally Stan, my fifteen-year-old brousin.

"Reason number one for moving," Uncle Jack began. "Your mother and I want to be together; we don't like being apart. We're newlyweds, after all." He squeezed Mom's hand.

I waited for Phil to gag and Mark to yuck, but they were busy stuffing their mouths with pie. Instead, eight-year-old Stephie spoke up. "I wanna stay here," she said. "We can't ride the city buses in Denver for free like Carrie and I do here."

Mom nodded, smiling faintly. "Denver's too big for little girls to do that by themselves, anyway. But that's a thought."

I could see Mom was trying to be democratic about this. By now, I didn't care what anyone was saying or how it was being handled. I just wanted to go to my room. Away from this nightmare of a stepfather.

Carrie, my nine-year-old sister since birth, sided with Stephie. "I don't want to leave Dressel Hills, either," she said. "The ski lifts are only five minutes from our house."

Ever since Mom and Uncle Jack got married, Carrie and Stephie had joined rank—usually against me. This time, though, the three of us were in agreement, but not for the same reasons. Not even close.

There was only one reason I couldn't begin to say good-bye to Dressel Hills. Only one. This ski town was my life—my entire life.

Fighting back the tears, I pushed my chair away from the table. "Excuse me," I stammered.

Without looking back, I ran from the room.

Chapter 2

Before fourth-period choir on Wednesday, I hurried upstairs to the music room and peeked in the door. Andie Martinez, my best friend, was sitting at the piano, arranging the music for rehearsal. She was the official pianist for choral union—the best of the seventh-, eighth-, and ninth-grade singers. Often during rehearsals, I watched Andie's fingers fly over the keys while her dark eyes studied the music intently. In fact, practices and concerts were the *only* times Andie was serious.

Today she wore denim jeans and a red-and-white shirt that set off her dark skin and dark brown curly hair. She ran her fingers over the keys, hit a wrong note, stopped, and frowned. Just as she began playing again, I opened the door and hurried inside.

Andie glanced up and immediately stopped playing. "Holly!" she said. "Ready for 'Edelweiss' today?"

For weeks we had been practicing the choral arrangements for the spring musical, *The Sound of Music*. Tryouts for the lead parts were April 11—only two and a half weeks away. Everyone was talking about who would get Maria, the female lead. But at this moment I had more important things on my mind, like my future and how I'd go on living without my Dressel Hills friends.

"Andie, we have to talk." I leaned against the console piano.

She looked at me and stood up. In two seconds her eyes changed from curious to concerned. "You look sick, Holly. You okay?" She reached for my arm.

"Oh, Andie, it's so awful," I burst out. "I think Uncle Jack's going to move us to Denver."

Andie's eyes grew wide. "What for?"

I explained the situation based on our family meeting last night.

"You can't move, Holly. I won't let you." She sat down hard on the piano bench. And then she was silent, like she was soaking it all in. It was a rare moment when my friend was speechless. But this wasn't just any news. This news could change our lives forever.

"It's such rotten timing," she said at last, hurling a crashing chord to the piano keys. "We *have* to go to high school together! After all, we're best friends. What about that?"

"I know, I know," I whispered.

"How can you move, Holly? I mean, this is your home. You'd hate a big city, stuck in some high-rise apartment building. Who knows, maybe you'd never see the sun again. And a new school and new kids. They might ignore you, or—worse—bully you if you don't fit in, or—"

"Just stop it!" I sat beside her on the bench. "I thought you'd be a little more sympathetic."

"I am. I feel sorry for you." She sighed. "For me—for us both." Andie frowned at her music. "How long before you know for sure?"

"This Friday."

"How could your uncle be so cruel?" Andie cried.

I stared at my feet. "He seems so selfish all of a sudden. I mean, he just waltzed into our lives and took over. And now this."

"I can't believe it." She shook her head. "It's so unfair."

A few kids were trickling into the room, and I didn't want to be caught crying, so I turned and headed for the alto section.

Andie played a mournful tune. It wasn't anything from *The*

Sound of Music. Watching her fingers on the keys, I sensed what Andie was feeling. I settled into a chair, worrying about the possible nightmare facing me.

"Holly? Are you, uh . . . *in* there somewhere?"

I looked up, startled to see my friend Paula Miller waving her hand in my face. Her other arm balanced a pile of music folders. "Oh, I'm sorry," I said, standing up to help her distribute them.

"Man, that was some trance, Holly," Billy Hill said, laughing as I tossed a folder to him. He flung it across the room to Jared Wilkins as he came in.

"Who's spacing out?" Jared asked, looking around comically, then catching my gaze.

"Holly. She must be dreaming about a new man," Billy teased Jared, elbowing him as he sat down.

"I seriously doubt that with a guy like me around." Jared flashed a grin at me.

I blushed, then wondered what would happen to our friendship if I moved to Denver.

"Up here, Holly." I turned to see Shauna holding her hands up for a folder. She sat in the back row with her best friend, Joy, who waved cheerfully.

Slowly, I moved to the back of the room, standing motionless as I gazed at first one friend, then another.

My eyes locked on Andie warming up at the piano. Her red Converse peeked out from under the hem of her jeans as she pressed the pedal. Our friendship went way back. During grade school, we'd written a set of Loyalty Papers and exchanged favorite teddy bears to seal the pact.

How . . . *how* could I leave Andie?

Jared hammed it up with Billy, laughing at his own jokes. He was every junior high girl's dream: gorgeous light brown hair, blue eyes, and a teasing wink that wouldn't quit. We'd jumped through a few hurdles, including my crazy month-long scrutiny test, to get where we were now. But I was comfortable with Jared—my first true guy friend.

Next to him sat Billy Hill, showing off his new letter jacket. I remembered the crazy antics he pulled at my thirteenth birthday last year. Where would I be without Billy?

Danny Myers wore one of his Sunday dress shirts. Long sleeves, buttoned at the wrist. He liked dressing up all the time. I smiled, recalling our short-lived close friendship—the gondola ride up Copper Mountain last summer and the afternoon at the library deciphering Uncle Jack's handwriting. Yes, I would miss Danny, too.

And there was Amy-Liz, a curly-haired soprano. Fun-loving and sweet, Amy-Liz was the life of the party. Her friends and mine, Joy and Shauna, whispered as they thumbed through their music folders. Probably looking for one of the best love songs in the musical so far—"Something Good"—assigned last week. What good friends they were.

My gaze rested on Paula. She sat beside her identical twin, Kayla. Paula was obviously attempting to establish her own identity these days. Her hair swirled around her shoulders in layers, while Kayla's was a mass of relaxed curls.

Thank goodness our feuding days were past. What a nightmare it had been since the twins moved to Dressel Hills last year. Their flirtatious ways had made me sick. On top of that, Paula had openly tried to steal Jared's attentions away from me. But things had changed between Paula and me. I actually considered her one of my very best friends now. Would she miss me enough to keep in touch by email?

Over the din of voices, I saw the door open. A hushed silence fell over the kids as Miss Hess, our choral director, marched into the room. Her black boots clicked across the floor like muted staccato notes. I hurried down the aisle and quickly slipped into the seat beside Paula.

"Miss Hess looks wiped out," Paula whispered.

"Maybe she had a late date," I said back. "Or maybe the musical's getting to her."

Young and pretty, Miss Hess had a positive outlook on life, but she was also quite a perfectionist. I knew she was concerned about the spring musical. In fact, I'd heard that she was getting a student drama teacher from a college in Denver to help her direct it.

I'll miss the musical if I move soon. The thought stabbed my heart, and I breathed deeply, watching Andie fidget at the piano. She glanced up at me, holding my gaze longer than usual. A lump grew in my throat as I thought about leaving this school, this town. Could I survive without Andie and Paula? Jared and Danny? Billy and—

"Good morning, class," Miss Hess said, interrupting my thoughts. "Today we'll begin with five-tone scales on *ah,* then on *oo.*" She gestured for us to stand. "Everyone ready?" She faced the piano, nodding as Andie gave the beginning note.

It was hard warming up your vocal chords when all you really wanted to do was cry. My voice sounded squeaky as we worked our way up the scale.

Paula must've noticed. She glanced my way after the first set of warm-ups. "You okay?"

"Barely," I said, making sure Miss Hess didn't catch me talking.

" 'Edelweiss' next, please," Miss Hess announced when we finished our warm-ups. "Altos first." She paused, glancing up at me. "Holly Meredith, will you perform the solo today?"

My heart sank, but I nodded. *Just my luck.*

Andie began to play the introduction.

"Go for it, Holly," Paula whispered.

I peered over at the tenors. Jared tugged on his Nike T-shirt, flashing his glorious grin at me. I swallowed the lump in my throat and counted the measures before my solo. Only eight.

Could I pull it together in time?

Jared's smile . . . those blue eyes . . . his sweet words . . . I might never see him again!

Tears sprang up, blurring the notes. I blinked my eyes, wiping the tears, trying desperately to see the music. Where were we, anyhow?

Struggling to find my cue, I listened to Paula next to me. My solo was coming up—only a few measures away. I coughed, trying to clear my throat.

When I opened my mouth to sing, nothing came out.

I tried again. It sounded squawky—perfectly horrid!

Miss Hess stopped the music and leaned her arms on the podium. "Holly?" Her soft hazel eyes expressed concern.

I froze in place as Miss Hess and the entire choir waited for my response. Coughing, I tried to speak, but a squeak emerged, "I can't . . ."

Paula put her arm around me. "Holly's not feeling well," she explained. She led me down the aisle. And a roomful of eyes pushed through the back of my head as we left the room.

Chapter 3

In the girls' rest room, I dashed to the first available stall. Locking the door behind me, I let the heart-wrenching sobs pour out.

"Holly, what's wrong?" Paula asked through the door.

"The worst thing in the world might be happening," I stammered.

"Are you sick?"

"Worse."

"Are you *very* sick?"

"It's not cancer, but it is terminal," I blurted.

"Open the door, Holly," Paula said. "You have to come out and talk to me."

I fumbled for the lock. "It's just . . . so hopeless."

By the time I emerged, Paula's face was ashen. "Is something wrong . . . at . . . at home?"

Leaning over the sink, I tried to rinse my face. The red blotches remained—hopeless. "Nothing's wrong between Mom and Uncle Jack, if that's what you mean. I've been through divorce before. Believe me, it's nothing like that."

"Well, then *what?*"

I hesitated, looking up at her. "We might be moving," I said softly.

Paula's eyes grew wide. "When?"

"We'll know by Friday."

"That's the day after tomorrow," Paula said. "Will you be completing the school year here?"

Sometimes Paula talked like she was straight out of another century.

"Wouldn't *that* be nice! The least Uncle Jack should do for me," I said. "He's completely unreasonable these days. All he thinks about is his dumb company. It's *so* annoying."

"I would think so." She looked at me with sympathetic eyes. "I wonder if this will affect my dad's part of the business. He never told us your uncle was thinking of moving."

"Maybe you'll move, too—at least it'll be nice for me if you do," I said. More tears.

"For me, too," she said with a hug. "We're friends now, don't forget."

It was true. Paula and I had come a long way since her family moved here last year. For the most part, Andie, Paula, and I were a threesome now.

After pulling gobs of toilet paper off the roll and dabbing at my eyes, I was ready to face the world again.

The practice for "Edelweiss" was over when we returned to the music room. The guys were working on an ensemble section of "The Lonely Goatherd." Miss Hess didn't comment as Paula and I took our seats. Thank goodness.

After class, things went crazy. "Holly, are you okay?" Jared asked, rushing over to me.

Danny followed on Jared's heels, his serious eyes surveying the situation. Billy and Andie came up to me. Soon, they and Amy-Liz, Joy, and Shauna circled me like a wagon train roundup.

I couldn't remember having been fussed over so much. It made me nervous. How could I stand here and discuss the possible move in front of all my friends?

Grabbing my arm, Andie spoke up. "We'll fill you guys in later." She ushered me through the huddle and out the door.

"Hey, wait up," Jared called.

"Later." Andie flung the word over her shoulder.

"Holly!" Jared tried again. He wouldn't give up, I was sure of it. I heard the sound of footsteps, then I felt Jared's hand on my shoulder, gently turning me to face him. "Look, if you're sick, Holly-Heart," he said, using the nickname Mom gave me because of my Valentine birthday, "I'll call your mom for you." He took out a cell phone.

"Does she look sick to you?" Andie asked.

"Well, her eyes are puffy," he observed.

"That happens when people cry. It's normal," Andie explained sarcastically. "She's having a mood change, that's all. When the sun comes out again, she'll tell you all about it." With that, Andie proceeded to pull me down the hall toward her locker, leaving Jared behind.

"Thanks," I said, waiting for Andie to work her combination lock. "You were sweet back there."

"You can't let these guys run you around, Holly," she said as she flung open her locker. "And Jared's way too possessive of you, in case you hadn't noticed."

I gasped. "He is?"

"Look at his eyes. You'll see it if you know what to look for." She reached up, stuffing a notebook inside her messy locker. "Remember what your dad told you in California?"

"I know, but—"

"Well, I've been watching Jared," she said. "I'm telling you, he's getting just a little too mushy, if you ask me."

"Shh! Here he comes," I said.

Jared came over and touched my hand. "Holly-Heart, let's talk."

Despite Andie's disapproving look, I nodded.

"Everything okay?" he asked as we walked to lunch.

That's when I told him my news. Half the school stared as we entered the cafeteria. By now, the choir had probably spread the word about my crying episode. That was one of the few disadvantages of attending a pocket-sized school—everyone knew everyone else's business.

Jared pulled out a tray, letting the excess water drip off before handing it to me. "Any chance you won't go to Denver?"

I shrugged. "My uncle has this wild and crazy idea. He thinks he's the only one who can run the office there."

We found a table and sat down without talking. Jared ate his cheeseburger and fries faster than usual. He seemed lost in thought.

Me? I was too upset to eat, so I picked at my food.

Finally I broke the silence. "How can we keep our friendship going with so many miles between us?" I asked softly.

His jaw was set; his eyes looked serious. "How many email messages can you write a day, Holly-Heart?"

"Zillions," I answered, looking away. His gaze was too intense for me. I didn't want to cry again.

"Oh, man," he groaned. "This is so bad."

"Let's talk about something else," I said. "How about the spring musical? What part do you want to audition for?"

Jared scratched his head for a moment, then blurted out, "If you won't be around, there's no way I'll feel like singing."

"I'm sorry." I pushed my tray away. "I don't know how to handle this, either." I leaned my elbows on the table, my hands on my face. "I can't believe this," I cried.

Jared cleared his throat. Maybe he was trying not to cry, too. "Look, Holly, we'll work something out." He paused. "I don't want to lose track of you. Never."

I sat up, looking at him. Andie wasn't kidding, he *was* serious!

"Maybe after I get my license I could drive to Denver on weekends." His eyes brightened.

"But that's two years away," I reminded him.

The light in his eyes faded. "Well, I'll call you every day, then."

"There's no way, Jared," I said, feeling as lousy as he looked.

"Holly," he persisted, "I'll get an after-school job to pay for the phone bill or something. I'm serious." By the look on his face and the tone of his voice, I knew he was.

Chapter 4

After school, Paula Miller met me at my locker. "Holly," she said hesitantly, "I don't have to come over today if—"

"I'm fine," I insisted, closing my locker. "You're coming home with me, just like we planned."

Paula grinned. "Great. I can't wait to discover the new me." She zipped up her leather jacket, blinking her mascara-laden eyes. "Maybe I can help you get your mind off moving."

"Sounds good."

Since I had tons of makeup leftover from my birthday party a month ago, I'd suggested to Paula that I do a make-over on her. She was really tired of looking like a clone of Kayla, her twin, and was eager to experiment with a new look.

We rode the bus to my house with Jared sitting directly behind me. He kept leaning over every other second with another new suggestion for our possible long-distance relationship. In a way, he was starting to bug me.

When Paula and I got off the bus a block from my house, Jared followed. "Mind if I tag along?" he asked as we picked our way over the snowy sidewalk toward my house.

I felt sorry about his pain, and I would have loved spending the afternoon with him. But I was ready to dump the moving thoughts for now. "Maybe another time," I said. "Okay?"

Jared seemed surprised at first, but then he slowed his pace. "I'll call you tonight, Holly-Heart." And he headed slowly back toward the bus stop.

Now I really felt bad. Turning Jared away like that was heartless. But having him around while Paula and I fooled with makeup wouldn't be any fun for him anyway.

"Jared's really nuts over you," Paula said as we clumped up the deck steps to my house.

"Well, I like him, too. It's just . . ." I sighed. "I don't know what our friendship will be like if I move." I opened the front door. "It's not fair to expect anything of each other at our age." I took off my jacket and hung it up.

Paula nodded. "Just be glad you're *not* older. What if you were dating?" She pulled off her jacket and draped it over the living room couch.

"For now, let's pretend I'm not leaving at all," I said, ushering her into the kitchen. "Let's talk about your make-over. I was thinking I'd give you a soft, new look so no one will even know you have an identical twin."

"Sounds terrific." She pulled out a barstool, all smiles.

Mom showed up just then. "Hi, Holly-Heart," she said, giving me a quick hug.

"Say good-bye to the old Paula Miller," I told Mom.

Mom chuckled, grinning at Paula. "Are you sure you trust Holly with your face?"

Paula laughed. "I must be pretty desperate."

Forcing nagging thoughts out of my mind, I washed my hands, then pulled out plastic bags of facial products and leftover makeup stored under the bar.

"Goofey, we're home," I called to my adorable cat. He came purring into the kitchen.

"Care for a snack, girls?" Mom asked.

"Sure, thanks," Paula replied.

"What about you, Holly?" Mom asked.

"No, thanks."

Mom's eyebrows shot up. "You mustn't be feeling well."

"Relax, Mom," I said. "I'm just not hungry." Usually I could eat everything in sight. Just not today.

Her eyes squinted a little as she pulled a couple of oranges out of the refrigerator.

"Besides," I said, "preparing to leave the only town you've ever known can bring on all sorts of eating disorders."

Now she really squinted her eyes. "We'll talk about *that* later." Mom cast a sideways glance at Paula. She took out some apples and began to peel and slice them into chunks, just the way I liked them.

Goofey spotted Paula and rubbed against her ankle. "Oh, he's so-o cute," she cooed, petting him.

I scooped up some cucumber-based facial gook and waved it in Paula's face. Lowering my voice, I said, "Your face is in my hands, Paula Miller. Are you ready for this?"

Her eyes widened. "Do you have any idea what you're doing?"

"You betcha," I said with great confidence. "You'll be absolutely delighted with the outcome. Guaranteed!"

She giggled, allowing me to glob the alien-green stuff on her nearly flawless face.

"You just wait," I whispered, thinking how funny Jared would look with the identical treatment. Lucky for him I'd sent him home. Besides, all the cucumber facials in the world wouldn't bring a smile to his face.

When it was time for Paula's facial mask to come off, I brought a hot towel over from the sink. She carefully patted the hardened green crust. In minutes, Paula's face was glowing and makeup free. I couldn't believe how much better she looked minus the dark eyeliner.

"Nice," she said as I held the mirror up to her. She puffed out her cheeks, gazing into the mirror.

"Now we can see your natural beauty," I said, admiring my work. "You have very clear, even skin, Paula, and if I were you, I'd go with only a little foundation and a touch of light blush. No eyeliner."

"You sound like a MAC saleswoman." She giggled as I applied a light base of foundation and a hint of blush. To accentuate her big eyes, I applied sable brown mascara and silky tan eye shadow.

"Hold still," I said.

Paula inspected her face again. "I . . . I don't know," she said hesitantly. "I don't look like myself."

"One thing's for sure," I said. "You look a lot less like your twin. You'll get used to less makeup. You'll see."

Mom brought over a plateful of apple and orange slices. Without asking, she poured a glass of milk for each of us. I noticed a little frown line. Was she upset about something?

"Enjoy," she said, taking a steaming cup of peppermint tea out of the microwave. "Nice seeing you again, Paula." She headed downstairs to the family room, where Stephie, Carrie, Mark, and Phil were supposedly doing their homework.

"Your mom is really sweet," Paula said. "You're lucky she's home all the time now."

"Yeah," I said, wondering what was bothering Mom. I settled onto the barstool across from Paula, reaching for an apple chunk. "It wasn't always that way. After Daddy left, she had to work all the time."

"I'm sure your uncle Jack makes things easier on the family's finances," Paula said.

"No kidding." I thought about my allowance. Uncle Jack had tripled it recently. At least that was one thing I could count on staying the same if we moved.

"Just think," Paula added, "if your mom hadn't remarried, you might not be leaving Dressel Hills at all."

"Probably not. But our family always sticks together, no matter what." What I really meant to say was: Mom, Carrie, and I always stayed together, no matter what. Uncle Jack could take a flying leap for all I cared.

Paula's voice grew softer, "Last year, when we first moved here, it was real hard making friends. For the longest time, Kayla was the only friend I had."

"What was it like moving away from your home in Pennsylvania?"

Paula looked up at the ceiling fan, as if doing so would help her remember. "Back east, my very closest friends and relatives lived within a few blocks of us. We grew up in the same neighborhood and attended the same school and church. When we told everyone we were moving, they promised to keep in touch. But I guess it's hard staying in touch with friends you don't see anymore." She paused for a moment, finishing off a piece of fruit. "There's one person who has never forgotten to write, though, especially by email."

"Really?" I leaned forward, eager to hear of Paula's secret love in Pennsylvania. Had she been holding out on me?

A broad smile danced across her shining face. "My grandma still remembers to write."

I slumped back, a little disappointed. "What about guys you knew?"

"Well, one of my guy friends emailed me every other day, but when school started, I was too busy to answer," she said with a grin.

I didn't need to be told who had distracted her. From the time she'd laid eyes on Jared Wilkins, *he* had been her focus. And I'd become furious. But everything changed drastically a month ago when Paula made repeated efforts to win my friendship. Now I knew in my heart that she could be trusted.

I offered her a choice of sheer lipsticks. She chose my favorite, for her coloring, at least: Cinnamon Toast. I watched as she held the mirror up to her face, applying the lipstick.

"Wow," I said, stepping back to view my handiwork. And hers. "You really look fabulous."

Paula gazed into the hand mirror. "I think you've missed one of your talents, Holly," she said. "You should consider becoming a makeup artist. You know, for movie stars and models." She reached down and hugged my cat good-bye.

We laughed together as we walked to the bus stop down the street. The way I always had with Andie. It was fabulous having more than one best friend!

"Thanks again for the new me," Paula said, waving as the bus screeched to a stop.

"Anyone who sees you will think you're the brand-new girl in town," I called to her.

She grinned as the bus doors swooshed open.

I hurried back to the house wishing a hearty farewell to my memory of the old Paula Miller. Inside and out.

When I closed the front door, Mom was sitting on the sofa, sipping tea. "Got a minute?" she asked. Her face looked drawn. Her eyes lacked their usual brightness.

Instantly, a knot formed in the pit of my stomach. I sat down. "What's up?"

"I need to talk to you." She placed her teacup carefully into the saucer on the round coffee table. By her precise movements and the tone of her voice, I knew trouble was brewing.

"Something wrong?" I asked.

"I'm not sure." She studied me. "I'm hoping you can fill me in, Holly-Heart."

"About what?" I felt the knot tighten.

Her fingers strummed the coffee table, and her eyes were squinty. "Exactly who is Sean Hamilton?" she asked.

Chapter 5

"Sean?" I repeated his name as Mom pulled something from her pocket.

"This came today." She held up a letter. "Your father will be skiing in town next week," she said.

I didn't tell her I knew all about Daddy's plans from Sean. The last I'd heard, though, Daddy was coming during spring break.

Mom continued. "Evidently, your father's bringing Tyler, your stepbrother, too."

I nodded.

"And . . ." She paused, rereading the letter. "A boy named Sean Hamilton."

I smiled, remembering the tall surfer I'd met last Christmas on the beach while visiting Daddy. "He's just a friend I met when Carrie and I were out in California," I explained. What I didn't say was that Sean had just started writing to me. I had talked to him on the phone after my birthday, when Tyler called, and he'd sent a letter soon after that. It was just a friendly letter, telling about his classes and his niece and nephew. Nothing heavy, though he'd asked to exchange email addresses.

She fingered the envelope from Daddy. "By the way your father refers to him, he sounds older than you. Is that correct?"

"A little, yeah." I set the record straight. "Sean's going on sixteen, and he baby-sits for Tyler sometimes. That's why Daddy knows him so well."

"Really? A *guy* baby-sitter." Mom wasn't making this easy for me.

"He's good with kids. He adores his niece and nephew," I volunteered, not sure why I was trying so hard to convince her. "Just ask Carrie. She really liked him."

Mom's eyes got squinty again. "Your father let Sean baby-sit Carrie?"

"And Tyler . . . just for one short afternoon," I said. Why was she making such a big deal over this?

"Well, I'd like to meet this boy before you go off skiing with him." She adjusted her earring. "Your father has asked permission for you to spend the day skiing with Sean . . . and Tyler and him, of course." She referred to the letter again.

"Well, it won't be like a date, if that's what you're thinking," I said quickly. I could hear Uncle Jack coming up the porch steps, and I didn't want *him* poking his nose into this conversation.

"I certainly hope not," she said with an air of finality. "Still, I want to meet him."

Uncle Jack was knocking the snow off his boots before he came in the front door. Quickly, I got up and left the room. He was the last person I wanted to talk to. My life, and possibly my future, lay in his hands.

I felt a blast of cold air as Uncle Jack came in. "Whoo-whee!" he said to Mom. "It's getting cold. The weather reports say there's a killer blizzard headed our way."

Who cares about blizzards? I thought, closing the door to my room. I snuggled down on my window seat and picked up my latest Marty Leigh mystery novel. But I had a hard time keeping my mind on the plot. I kept thinking about moving.

After supper, Jared called. He sounded depressed. "Hey," he began. "I couldn't pass up a chance to talk to you for free, you know." He chuckled a little, but he didn't sound like himself.

I sighed into the portable phone. "I know how you feel." I paused, hoping he wasn't hurt about this afternoon. "I'm sorry about today, it just didn't seem—"

He interrupted me. "It's okay, Holly-Heart. Honest." He was silent, then came the question I was expecting. "Have you heard anything more about the move?"

"Nothing."

He was quiet again.

"You okay?" I asked.

Sadly, he answered, "Call me the minute you know something."

"You'll be the very first," I reassured him. "I promise."

"I've been praying every minute, you know . . . that something will happen so you won't leave."

I smiled. "That's very sweet. And listen, Jared. I've been praying about it, too."

"That's good." He seemed to brighten a bit. "Isn't there a verse in the Bible about that?"

"Yeah, it's something about when two people pray for the same thing, it can happen." I swirled my hair around my finger. "Where's that verse found?" I asked, thinking of Danny. He would know.

"The Gospel of Matthew somewhere," Jared said. "Hold on, I'll grab my dad's concordance. Every word in the Bible is listed in it—linked to a verse."

"Perfect." I could hear the pages turning as he flipped through them, searching.

"Here it is," he said. "Listen to this."

"Hold on a sec." I walked to my desk, the portable phone still at my ear. I pulled out a pen from the center drawer and ripped off a piece of scratch paper to jot down the verse. "Okay, what is it?"

"Matthew 18:19," he said. "Wow. It says, 'If two of you on earth

123

agree about anything you ask for, it will be done for you by my Father in heaven.' "

"That's incredible," I said, switching the phone to my right ear.

"Keep praying, Holly-Heart," he said softly.

I shivered at his words. "See you tomorrow." Hanging up, I thought about what Andie said—about Jared getting too mushy over me. Maybe she was right. But for now, it was okay, I hoped.

♥ ♥ ♥

Sean's second letter arrived on Thursday after school. He wrote about how excited he was to come to Colorado to ski, and how much fun it would be to see me again. I'd been putting off writing to him because I really wasn't sure what to say. I didn't want to encourage him too much, especially feeling the way I did about Jared. But I didn't want to snub him, either. After all, he was coming next week. So I wrote:

Dear Sean,

Thanks for your letters. I'm sorry I didn't write sooner. I've been busy with homework and other things.

My sister can't wait to see Tyler again. He's coming along, right?

I was just curious—how well do you ski? I'm sure my dad will coach you if you need help. He's the one who taught me when I was little.

Dad wrote Mom a letter about bringing you to Dressel Hills with him, and now she wants to meet you. Mom's like that with all my friends, so don't worry, it's no big deal. Well, I better get going.

Your friend,

Holly Meredith

The doorbell rang as I finished rereading the letter to Sean. "Holly, it's Andie," Carrie called up the stairs.

"I'm coming!" I slipped my letter to Sean into the bottom drawer of my dresser and hurried to meet my friend.

She wore heavy black sweats and a purple ski jacket. "Did you hear?" she said, out of breath. "A blizzard's heading toward Dressel Hills."

I led her up the stairs to my room. "Yep, I heard," I said, thinking about Uncle Jack's announcement yesterday. I wished he would come home announcing something worthwhile for a change. Like that we were staying in Dressel Hills, for instance.

Andie plopped onto my four-poster bed as I closed the bedroom door behind me. "It's supposed to be the storm of the decade. And it's going to hit here tomorrow morning—before dawn."

"Perfect!" I said, getting excited now. "Just think how much fun it'll be getting out of school for a couple of days."

She nodded. "We haven't had off in ages."

I sat cross-legged on my window seat across from her. "Wanna spend the night?"

She lit up at my suggestion. "I'll call my mom and check."

I handed her the portable phone. "Want me to walk with you to pick up your clothes? Stan will be home soon."

Suddenly her eyes were ready to pop. "Uh, that's okay," she said, looking way too serious. "I'll catch the bus." Her words, and the way her face drooped, gave her away.

I gasped. "Is everything okay with you and Stan?"

"I can't talk about it."

"Aw, Andie," I pleaded. "You can tell me."

She stared at me. "You know, everything was absolutely incredible between Stan and me until your uncle started talking about moving to Denver."

I sighed. "Stan ended your friendship because of that?"

"Yesterday." She looked away.

"How rotten," I whispered. "Why couldn't you guys write or—hey, Stan could drive back up here to see you on weekends, when you're old enough to start dating."

She rolled over on my bed and propped herself up on one elbow. "Get over it."

I glared at her. "Hey, I just wanna help."

She sighed. "If you think a long-distance friendship with a boy can work at our age, you must be brain-dead." She punched in the numbers on the phone. Then she stopped suddenly, looking up at me. "I can't sleep over here tonight."

I understood perfectly. "Yeah, because it would be weird hanging around with Stan in the house," I sympathized with her. "Especially if we got snowed in tomorrow."

She pulled on a dark curl, sitting up. "He says we'll still be friends, but . . ."

"Yeah," I whispered. "It's never the same." I was thinking of Danny Myers. We'd been really good friends, too, before he'd asked me to be his girlfriend. Then, after I decided not to spend so much time with him, things were totally different, even though we still considered ourselves friends.

I stretched my long legs, yawning. "I'm worried that'll happen with Jared and me."

"Well, you have no choice, do you? Not if you move away," Andie insisted. "Besides, it's time Jared wakes up."

I studied her. "What're you saying?"

She let herself slide off the bed and onto the floor. "He acts like he owns you or something. You better check it out before you set up something long-distance. Maybe he thinks you and he, are, well . . ."

"What?" I demanded.

"Maybe Jared thinks he's going to marry you someday!"

"So, what's wrong with planning ahead?" I said, giggling, yet I was aghast.

Andie's one eyebrow shot up and her mouth gaped open. "You've got to be kidding."

"Well, we haven't discussed it, if that's what you mean, but I *do* think I care a lot about him."

It was Andie's turn to gasp. "Hey, Stan and I were humming

right along before he found out you guys were probably moving. But I never thought I cared *that* much for him."

"Mom says it's not something you always know right away," I said, still torn between hanging on to Jared and saying good-bye to our friendship.

Knock-knock.

We jumped. Someone was out in the hall! I hoped whoever it was hadn't listened in on our conversation.

I raced to the door. "Oh, hi." It was Stan. Frantically, I motioned for Andie to hide.

"Dad's calling a family meeting in a half hour," Stan said, looking quite serious. Then he leaned forward and asked quietly, "Is Andie here? Thought I heard her voice."

"Were you listening?" I asked, horrified.

"Not really," he said. By the mellow, sad sort of look on his face, I knew he was telling the truth. "I just wanted to talk to her before she leaves."

"Hold on a sec," I said, closing the door. I went to the closet and found Andie hiding there. "Hear that? Stan wants to talk to you. Maybe it's true love after all."

"In your wildest dreams," she muttered, pushing my clothes back and emerging from the closet.

I put my ear against the door, eavesdropping as they talked in the hall. Stan said something about accompanying Andie home. And, in a flash, she agreed to it.

Oh, sure, Andie could say all she wanted against the boy-girl thing, but when it came right down to it, she liked Stan as much as I liked Jared.

Chapter 6

When Stan returned from taking Andie home, Mom rang her dinner bell. It was a dainty white bell, a wedding gift from a friend at the law firm where she used to work.

"Family meeting," Uncle Jack called to us.

The sound of kids scurrying from one end of the house to the other reminded me of an old *Brady Bunch* rerun. But their "blended family" seemed to run much better than ours. After all, Mike Brady had never threatened to move *his* family to another city.

My stomach twisted in knots as I trudged into the living room and sat down. I glanced nervously at Uncle Jack. For the first time since his and Mom's wedding, I wished he had never fallen in love with my mother. Our cozy all-girl household had been just fine before he came along.

Phil and Mark came marching up from the family room, scowling. Had to abandon their computer games, no doubt. Carrie and Stephie carried American Girl doll cutouts into the living room. Stan sprawled onto the sofa. He folded his arms on his chest as a dimwitted smile played across his face. I couldn't help wondering: Had the trip to Andie's changed things between them?

The younger kids horsed around while we waited for Mom to

show up. Where was she, anyway? I groaned inside. Uncle Jack balanced a Bible and a family devotional on his knee. He seemed a bit nervous, too.

Finally, when I thought I'd burst with the build-up of suspense, Mom appeared. Stan moved his legs and sat up, making room for her on the sofa.

"Well," Uncle Jack started, "are all of us present now?"

We nodded.

He leaned back in his chair, looking at each of us as he spoke. "This has been a whirlwind week for your mother and me. As you all know, Patterson Consulting is simply bursting its seams." He paused, smiling at Mom across the room.

"So we're *moving*?" I snarled.

"Holly!" Mom said. "Please be polite about this."

"Tell your husband that," I shot back.

Mom gasped. Uncle Jack leaned forward, trying to smile cheerfully. "We need to work together on this, Holly. I know how you feel, dear."

Dear?

"Don't call me your sweet names," I shouted.

Over in the corner, Carrie almost lost it. Her eyes bugged out, and she put a hand over her mouth in shock. She'd never seen me freak out at an adult like this.

"Can we talk about this privately?" Uncle Jack said quietly.

I was burning inside, but from the look on Mom's face, I knew if I opened my mouth one more time, I'd be sorry later. *Very* sorry! So I put my head down, refusing to look at my horrible uncle-turned-stepfather.

Uncle Jack continued as if nothing had happened, telling us a few more details about the business expansion. Then he prayed. "Dear Lord, we ask for your help with our plans. We seek your direction and ask for a clear-cut decision tomorrow night. Be with the children if there is to be a move, I pray. Comfort Holly, especially, as she struggles with the idea of moving. I ask these things in your name. Amen."

What right did he have mentioning my name in our family prayer? It made me angrier than ever.

"Now," he said, turning the pages of the Bible. "I want to read chapter thirteen of the book of Numbers, where Moses sends spies out to Canaan to check out the land. My trips to Denver are a lot like spying, you know."

"Really, Daddy?" Stephie said. "Are we spies?"

Mom and Uncle Jack laughed. I slumped in my chair, sulking.

"Denver is a big place to spy on," Phil joked.

Mark started in with his alien face repertoire.

Uncle Jack snapped his fingers. "Let's have your encore later, son," he stated flatly. That meant to cool it. No questions asked.

Uncle Jack read about Caleb and Joshua and their investigation of the Promised Land. I imagined the eight of us eating wild honey, one of the foods the spies had found. Ick! It made me despise Denver more than ever.

♥ ♥ ♥

The next morning I awakened to the sound of the wind's voice, low in my ear. It moaned and whistled in the eaves and through the aspen trees in our backyard. Glancing at my clock, I realized it was very early. There was still plenty of time to lie awake, leisurely stretching, cuddling with Goofey.

Then I remembered—snow! I leaped from the cozy warmth of my bed and flung wide the curtains at my window seat to check. I stared down at the ground. Two inches, max.

Disappointed, I dragged back to bed. *So much for the storm of the decade,* I thought as I snuggled against Goofey's warm fur. A blizzard, made-to-order, would have been nice. Really fabulous. All of us home together, snowbound. Maybe Uncle Jack's important phone call would come early, before tonight. And I could celebrate if the answer was no. I shuddered to think about it being the other way around, so I quickly shoved that thought away.

Mom had us bundle up to go to school. Even though it had

stopped snowing, the forecast was for severe wind and sub-zero temps.

Stephie, Carrie, Mark, and Phil clumped off to the elementary school two blocks away, clad in snow boots and heavy jackets. The girls wore their new earmuffs and mittens to match; the boys had on their new ski hats.

I hurried down the street to the mailbox and pushed my letter to Sean Hamilton inside. Then I waited for the bus with Stan. I was dying to ask him about Andie, but decided to wait. Andie would be more than delighted to fill me in at school.

Not only could I see my breath as we waited, but it sort of hung in midair, turning to tiny ice crystals when I exhaled.

"Well," Stan said, his nose cherry red, "tonight's the night."

"Yeah." I turned my back against the wind. "I'd give anything if we didn't have to move."

"Maybe we'll return to Dressel Hills someday," he offered. He was only trying to make me feel better.

"I hope we don't have to leave at all."

"That's not too realistic by the sound of things," he said. "Don't get me wrong, Dad's not trying to mess up things here with you and Mom and Carrie."

"Could've fooled me," I whispered. I glanced at my watch. "The bus is late."

"Five minutes," he said.

Five seconds in this blustery cold and fierce wind was way too long.

"What time is the phone call expected tonight?" I asked.

"Seven-thirty." He turned toward me, shielding me from the wind blasts.

I wrinkled my runny nose, numb from the cold, trying my best not to sniffle. "I want to be right there when the decision comes."

"Well, don't hold your breath," he said.

I nodded, not wanting to open my mouth to speak again. My lips felt funny—like they were numb and nearly nonexistent.

"Here comes the bus," Stan said.

We huddled together, eager for the warmth of the bus.

♥ ♥ ♥

As usual, Andie met me at my locker. "News flash," she announced.

I grinned at her. "Okay, okay, let me guess. You're Stan's girlfriend again."

"How'd you know?" She eyed me curiously. "Stan?"

"Not a word," I said, struggling with still-frozen fingers to work my combination.

"So . . . what was your first clue?" Persistent. One of the many grand qualities I would miss about Andie. Depending on what was decided by phone tonight, of course.

I sighed dramatically. "His smile was different. Sort of, you know, sappy."

"Huh?"

"You heard me." And she had, because she began to giggle, quite pleased with herself as she turned to gather her books and notebooks for the first two classes.

"Careful about long-distance relationships," I teased, feeding her basically the same line she'd dished out to me yesterday.

She ignored my comment. "Hey. What happened to our blizzard, anyway?"

"Beats me." I piled my books into my backpack.

"Ladies, ladies" came a familiar voice.

I turned to see Jared. "Hey," I said, grinning.

"Today's our moment of truth," he said, referring to Uncle Jack's phone call. "You doing okay, Holly?" He leaned a little too close. Then he reminded me of Matthew 18:19.

"Thanks, Jared," I said, backing away slightly. "I remembered." In fact, I was banking on that Scripture.

Jared smiled. "I'll walk you to science."

I felt uneasy as he took my hand.

Andie shot me a strange look. It was a concerned, almost

parental look. She wasn't kidding. Jared was getting more possessive by the minute, and I was glad it wasn't too far to my first class.

Whew, this is getting heavy, I thought, finding my assigned seat and pondering my situation with Jared.

Slowly, I took out my notebook and pen. Glancing up, I noticed Mr. Ross erasing the board. He turned momentarily to answer a student's question. His thinning hair was brushed back from a broad but low forehead. He looked snazzier than usual. As he turned to greet the class, I saw it. A hint of pink on his chin. Squinting, I peered at his face. It was unmistakable. There was a smudge of pale lipstick on Mr. Ross's right cheek!

I wondered if Andie had spotted it, too. I kept watching her, tuning out Mr. Ross's words. Then I saw her shake her head slowly, back and forth, back and forth. It was a secret signal. She'd seen the lipstick, all right. I could almost hear her bursting inside: *Check it out, Holly-Heart,* she was thinking. Mr. Ross got smooched in the teachers' lounge!

Like I always said, love does strange things to people. Instantly I thought of Jared. His strong feelings for me were more and more obvious. Sure, I cared for him, too, but it wasn't like we were grown-up and twenty-two.

Funny, twenty-two was the magic number for me, the perfect age to meet someone, fall in love, and get married. Guess it was all Mom's fault. That's how old she had been when Daddy walked into her life. She'd told me so after Daddy left, when we sorted through old files. There were letters—tons of them—from Daddy after he and Mom had their first few dates. I was only eight, but I remembered helping her pack them away in a box. It wasn't a day I'd ever forget.

Mr. Ross and *his* love interest, our English teacher, Miss Wannamaker, had passed up that magic number long ago. Closer to fifty-two, Mr. Ross was a widower. Miss Wannamaker was an unclaimed treasure—or so Uncle Jack called women who'd never married. I preferred my label—ladies in waiting. It had such a regal grandness to it.

♥ ♥ ♥

Around fourth period, it began to snow again. I studied the line of menacing black clouds from my vantage point in the alto section during choir. By sixth hour, things grew dark. The north wind struck, blending the ground and sky together. Whiteout! The air was thick with furious flakes of snow.

"Students, please remain in your classes" came the principal's voice over the intercom. "A severe blizzard warning has been issued for the areas surrounding and including Dressel Hills."

"No kidding," whispered Andie, glancing at the windows.

"It's a little late for warnings, don't you think?" joked Billy Hill, seated in the desk across from me.

I nodded, mesmerized by the swirling whiteness. I'd seen blizzards before, but this . . .

"It's frightening," Andie said, coming over to watch with me.

"How will we get home?" I worried.

"You could get lost in this mess just by heading for the bus stop," she said.

Which was true. I'd read about people trying to walk even a few feet, like to the neighbor's or across the street, who were so blinded by the power of the wind and snow that they lost their way and froze to death. I shivered just thinking about it.

The principal's voice came over the intercom again. "Teachers, please report to the office immediately."

Our math teacher excused himself. Most of the kids had piled up against the windows by now, staring out at the roaring white beast.

"What if we have to spend the night at school?" Andie wailed.

"Are you crazy?" Billy said.

"This is the last place I want to spend the night," Andie announced.

"I *have* to get home," I whispered to no one in particular. Had to. My future was hanging by the single thread of a phone call.

GOOD-BYE, DRESSEL HILLS

Chapter 7

In a few minutes, big decisions were made. "No one is to leave the building," the principal announced. It was a semi-state of emergency. Students without cell phones could make one phone call. Two minutes per call.

I waited in one of the phone lines, dying to talk to Mom. Four phone booths were near the entrance, and several office phones were being used to accommodate students. Standing between Andie and Paula, whose cell phone reception was nonexistent, I agonized over the state of things.

"It's a perfect nightmare," I said, shifting my backpack to my other shoulder.

"Could be worse," Paula said.

"Oh yeah? Like how?" I said.

Andie began reciting a list of horrible things off the top of her head. "We could be buried in an avalanche, or stuck eating leftovers for a week, or . . ."

I stopped her just as Danny Myers came by. "Time to count our blessings, girls," he said, grinning. Yep, he'd overheard our conversation. "It's just a Colorado blizzard—probably won't last past supper."

"Past supper?" I wailed, thinking of Uncle Jack's life-altering phone call.

"My dad has a snowmobile," Paula said, grinning. "He'll come bail us out after the storm."

"Good idea," Danny said. "After you, I get first dibs on a ride."

We all laughed. Paula had gotten our minds off the worst-case scenario: an all-school sleepover.

The line for the phones inched forward. Suddenly Mr. Ross, our science teacher, made an announcement from the front of the line. "Sorry, kids, we'll have to try later. Phones are out. This storm is a big one."

Kids groaned as they broke up and headed for the corridor of lockers.

"Maybe that explains why my cell's not working," Paula said. "Doesn't look like we're going anywhere, at least not for a while."

"Yeah," Andie said. "We're stuck at school. What a kick."

"Trapped is more like it," I muttered.

As we strolled to our lockers, another voice came over the speakers. It was Miss Wannamaker, our beloved English teacher. "Students of Dressel Hills Junior High, meet me in the auditorium for an assembly in five minutes," she said. There was a strange, almost gleeful sound to her voice.

I got rid of my books and trooped off to the girls' rest room with Paula and Andie. "Sounds like Miss W's got something planned," I said.

"Leave it to her," Andie moaned. "I wanna go home."

"Me too." I yanked a brush out of my purse.

Paula stepped up to the mirror, primping.

"You look so good," I complimented her. And she did, now that she was minus the cat eyes from heavy black eyeliner.

"Guess who's experimenting with the natural look?" Paula said.

"I noticed," I said, referring to her twin, Kayla.

"Where is she today, by the way?"

"Sore throat," Paula said.

"At least she's home. Lucky for her," I muttered. "C'mon, let's see what Miss W's up to." I led my friends out of the rest room and into the deserted hallway.

Andie, Paula, and I shuffled into the auditorium, claiming three seats together. The period bell rang—end of sixth hour. School was as good as over. Now, what about getting home?

"Dear students," Miss W began the assembly. Her trademark. She started each class the same way, like a spoken letter. "It is an unusual situation we find ourselves in this afternoon. And we may as well make the best of it." She stood tall and plump, smiling at the audience. "You shouldn't worry. I will not be assigning essays titled, 'The Day I Stayed at School for Supper.' "

The kids cheered. Some applauded.

"Nor will I discuss the great blizzards of ancient literature," she joked.

I chuckled at her approach. She was really something. By now she had each of us in the palm of her hand.

"I will, however, propose an interesting activity," she said. "But first I need five volunteers."

Hands shot up around the auditorium. Miss W was an obvious favorite with students.

Andie was one of the kids chosen to go up on the stage.

"Now, then," Miss W addressed the audience as five students paraded toward her, "we will play a game involving the entire school."

Charades. The entire student body divided into five large groups. Not so difficult, because lots of kids were at home with sore throats and flu.

Miss W met with each of the five students. She told them to pick a favorite food and act it out.

Paula and I joined the group that had to guess Andie's imitation. For starters, she got down on the floor and slithered like a snake.

Someone called out, "Noodles!"

Next, Andie rolled into a ball and tumbled across the stage.

I called out, "Spaghetti and meatballs!"

Andie grinned. "That's right."

One by one, the other kids did their food routines. Soon Miss W asked for a new batch of charades contestants. I raised my hand, and Miss W motioned me onstage.

"This time, I will ask you to act out your *least* favorite food."

I glanced over my shoulder at Jared, Danny, and my other friends. Surely I could act out the charade so that *my* group would guess my ikiest food.

For some bizarre reason, the thought of honey stuck in my brain. It was one of the foods Joshua's spies had discovered in the Promised Land. I guess I paralleled their trip to Canaan with our possible move to Denver. Right now, for me, honey was the most hideous food I could think of. But how to act it out?

I started by lumbering across the stage like an old mama bear. Sniffing, I reared up on my hind legs, as if I'd found honey high in a tree. I scooped the sticky stuff from the tree with one paw, stretching it out like a rubber band. Then, *plop,* I dropped the wad of imaginary honey into my hungry jaws.

Jared called out, "Taffy!"

Miss W shook her head.

"Chocolate syrup," Andie guessed.

"Foods we *hate,*" Miss W reminded my group.

Danny Myers' voice was strong and clear. "It's honey," he said. "Holly is honey."

Our group clapped and cheered. Some of the guys whistled. And when I got back to my seat, Andie whispered, "I think Danny said, 'Holly is *a* honey.' "

I gasped, dropping my jaw.

She grinned at me. There was a mischievous light in her brown eyes. "He's stuck on you, Holly. Get it? Stuck?"

"No, he's *sweet* on her," Paula insisted, laughing.

I'd almost forgotten our dilemma. Here we were laughing, playing charades, while prisoners in our own school.

I checked my watch. Almost three o'clock. Four and a half hours before Uncle Jack would have some word on whether we were moving.

"Holly," Andie said, pulling on my sleeve. "Listen to this!"

Miss W was saying something about spaghetti. She and Mr. Ross were going to cook up a supper the kids would never forget. Right here at school.

"Don't forget," I said, poking Andie and Paula, "Miss W and Mr. Ross catered my mom's wedding reception. They're excellent cooks."

Just then Mr. Ross strolled onto the stage. He took Miss W by the hand—in front of the whole school. At first, I thought he was going to kneel down and propose marriage.

He began by saying, "All of you will be hearing about this sooner or later."

"What's he gonna say?" Andie whispered.

"Just watch," I said, eager to know.

"Your lovely English teacher is soon to become the bride of this old man," Mr. Ross boldly announced.

Most of us jumped to our feet, cheering. It was the announcement I'd been waiting for. Amid wild applause, Mr. Ross displayed the sparkling diamond on Miss W's plump white hand.

More cheers of delight filled the auditorium. But a wave of sadness swept over me. How could I ever say good-bye to this school? To these dear people?

Without a word to Andie, I slipped into the aisle, heading for the hallway. The school secretary was locking up the principal's office.

"Are the phones working yet?" I asked.

She shook her head. "I'm afraid not."

Disappointed, I glanced toward the main entrance. Wind rattled the doors. Whistling through the cracks, it created an eerie sound. And outside the snow continued to fall, wrapping our town in its layers of white fury.

Chapter 8

While Mr. Ross and Miss W did their culinary thing in the school cafeteria, the rest of the student body, about a hundred and fifty or so of us, were assigned to various places in the building. Like the music room and the library.

Andie chose the choir room to practice the piano, while Paula and I headed for the library. Paula worked on homework. I started writing a short story titled, "Good-Bye Whispers."

GOOD-BYE WHISPERS
by Holly Meredith

"Can it be?" asked Brett.

"It's true," said Roxanne. "We're moving and I know it's lousy for you . . . for me, too."

Brett shook his head, deep in thought. "But you're my life, my love."

Roxanne put her fingers to his lips. "Don't say another word, my darling."

I stopped for a moment, thinking about the plot and what should come next. Doodling, I wrote Sean Hamilton's name sideways in the margin. One week from today he'd be here skiing. Spending the day with me. I added curlicues around his name. It was hard to push away such excitement. Then I reminded myself we were just friends and marked out his name with an X.

Paula went to look for a book in the reference section. That's when it happened. Someone touched the top of my head.

I turned around and there was Jared, his bold, yet wistful eyes watching me.

My cheeks flamed with embarrassment. "What are you doing?" I asked.

"Just saying hi to my girl," he said.

I felt uncomfortable, even with the many students studying around us at desks and in chairs.

I moved my backpack off the chair next to me, and he sat down. "Whatcha studying?" he asked, glancing at the beginning of my story.

"Nothing, really," I said, twirling my pencil. "Just starting another story."

A strange look crept into his eyes as he stared at my writing pad. "Who's Sean Hamilton?"

Yikes! He'd seen the name in the margin.

Jared leaned over so that his pointer finger touched Sean's name, crossed out in the margin of my story. "Is he fact or fiction?"

Nervously, I cleared my throat. "He's just some boy I met last Christmas."

Jared's eyes registered jealousy. "What's this about?"

"It's no big deal."

"Are you going to tell me about him or not?" Jared asked.

By now, everyone around us was aware of the conversation. Jared's voice had inched up in volume with every sentence.

I wanted to crawl under the table. No, better yet, under the giant snowdrift outside the library window.

"Jared, please, not here," I whispered, glancing around.

He stood up abruptly and pulled me with him toward the hallway.

"We're not supposed to be out here," I said.

"Then you name the place," he said.

The only unpopulated place I could think of was the auditorium. I felt jittery as we headed there. "Jared, you're overreacting," I said as we settled into two seats near the stage.

Jared's eyes narrowed. "I think you'd better start at the beginning with this Sean thing."

"He's a friend of my dad's," I said. "I hardly know him."

"But you were thinking about him back there," he insisted.

"Only because he's coming with my dad to ski next weekend," I blurted without thinking.

"Oh . . . so that's it." Jared stood up, walking around with his hands smashed in his jeans pockets. He was scrutinizing me, making me feel guilty. Actually rotten.

I leaped out of my seat. "I've done nothing wrong!"

Jared's eyes bored into me. "Has Sean been writing to you?"

"And what if he has?" I shot back.

"Does he know about . . . you and me?"

Out of nowhere came the urge to slap him. For the pat on the head in the library. For his accusations. "It's none of your business," I snapped. "You don't own me."

"Is that how you feel?" He put his foot on the seat, leaning on his knee as he glared down at me.

Jared's frown, his words, made me even more angry. "I don't know *how* I feel right now," I said, sitting down again. "But I know one thing for sure." I took a deep breath. "It's too much. You and me . . . we're . . . way too exclusive."

Slowly, Jared sat in front of me, leaning over the seat. His face softened as the frown disappeared. Then he reached for my hand. "What are you saying, Holly-Heart? That it's wrong to like only one person?"

I stared down at our hands. "I'm not ready to be this serious," I said, fighting back the tears. "We're too young."

"Love doesn't know age barriers," he said. "Look at Mr. Ross and Miss W."

I should have known he'd use them. "Honestly, Jared, would you believe me if I said I want to be friends with lots of boys, including you?"

"Why don't you just say it, Holly," he said, minus the Heart. I could sense him backing off again. And not just because he pulled his hand away. "It's about leaving, isn't it? You want out because you don't think it'll work if you're in Denver."

"Even if we weren't moving, it might be a good idea to cool it . . . spend less time together," I said, avoiding his eyes, trying to be gentle about this.

He slammed his fist against the back of the seat. "Because of Sean? Or because you want to meet new people—big-city guys?"

I shook my head. "No, it's because of me."

"Well, consider it done," he said in a mocking sort of way.

I looked up at him, shocked.

"I really don't know how I feel about being friends with you anymore, Holly," he continued. "And don't expect me to follow that no-flirting rule of yours any longer." With that, he left me sitting alone in the semidarkness while the storm howled outside.

It was howling inside, too.

Crushed. That's what I was. Totally and completely crushed. "Will the real Jared Wilkins please stand up," I whispered.

I sat quietly, pondering the events of the week. *"I don't ever want to lose our friendship,"* Jared had told me. His plans to drive to Denver when he got his license and to call me long-distance still rang in my ears. So much for our prayer pact and Matthew 18:19.

My heart beat a zillion miles an hour. But my tears had dried up. Angry and hurt, I ran to the solace of the girls' rest room.

Chapter 9

I was washing my hands when Paula burst into the girls' bathroom. "There you are," she said, out of breath. "I've been trying to track you down."

"Jared and I needed to talk." I filled her in on the latest details of the Holly-Jared thing.

"Oh, wow, I'm sorry to hear that," she said, coming over to lean on one of the sinks. "I'm surprised Jared turned on you."

I pulled two paper towels out of the dispenser. "People say and do weird things when they're angry," I said, pushing the rumpled-up towels into the trash. "Besides, spending so much time with only one guy when you're fourteen . . . I don't know . . . my dad says it just doesn't make sense."

Paula nodded, touching up her shoulder-length hair. "Fourteen going on twenty-six, my mother says. But she explains it like this: From the time we're first attracted to guys, until we marry our life mate, females are more inclined to want special friendships with only one male at a time. It's one of the things God did when He created Eve."

I smiled at my reflection. Paula had a way of expressing herself like no other.

"That's how I felt about Danny, and then Jared. But now," I paused, pulling my compact out of my purse. "Now it seems like it was a mistake not to be friends with everyone, you know?"

She nodded.

Just then, Andie flew into the rest room. "Holly!" she called, running over to me. "Are you okay?" She flung her arms around me.

"I've had better days," I mumbled.

"You poor baby."

"I'm okay, really," I said. "It's Jared who's got a problem."

"I know." She flung her purse on the shelf above the sink. "He's not being too cool about this," she informed me. "He just told Stan and Billy you two called it quits."

"He did . . . already?" I said, amazed.

Andie sighed. "Jared's a macho male machine, in case you'd forgotten. Now brace yourself for this, okay?" She held on to my shoulders, looking into my eyes.

"I can almost hear it now," I scoffed.

"Jared's taking the credit for breaking up with you, like it's some big deal for him. But let me guess—you were the one who got this whole thing started, right?"

As usual, she was right on track. I nodded. "If that's the way he wants to play this game, let him," I said, resigned to whatever happened. It wasn't easy dealing with this kind of craziness when you were trapped at school.

"Supper is served" came Miss W's voice over the loud-speaker.

"Chow time!" Andie grabbed my arm and guided me into the hall. She instructed Paula to walk on the other side of me so Jared could see we were a unified force. "He's not gonna mess with your head anymore," Andie said, leading me to the cafeteria.

Andie was like that. She liked to take charge of things, especially when I was hurt. Maybe because, like me, she was the oldest in her family. Her twin brothers—at age three—were so much younger.

Stan came into the lunchroom and got in line with Andie. He

glanced out the windows at the vicious, swirling storm. "Tennis, anyone?" he joked.

Andie laughed.

"Has anyone heard the weather report?" I asked. "Sure would be nice to know when this blizzard will be over." I wondered what Mom and Uncle Jack were doing at home. Were they getting calls, or was *our* phone line dead, too?

Stan reached for a tray and handed it to Andie. "I heard Mr. Ross tell another teacher that the elementary schools closed at noon because of the severe windchill factor."

"That's good," I said, relieved that at least the rest of my family was home, safe and snug.

The cafeteria was a sight to behold. There were candles burning in glass holders on each table. And somewhere, they'd found plastic yellow daffodils for the centerpieces.

"Let's sit over there," Andie said, pointing to a table for four. Miles away from our usual spot. Paula and I followed Stan and Andie as they led the way.

I tried not to pay attention to Jared sitting with Danny and Billy across the cafeteria from us. Amy-Liz and her friends Joy and Shauna were eating with them, too. I didn't mind that the girls were there. It was their laughter that bugged me. Especially Jared's.

The spaghetti was great, and all of us concluded that Mr. Ross and Miss W were a good culinary team. When they got ready to retire from teaching, they could make extra money cooking for snowbound students.

Halfway through dessert, the principal made an announcement about phones being available for calls. "Students who have not had a chance to make a call may come to the office now," he said.

I looked across the cozy table at Stan. "Want to call home?" I asked.

He shrugged. "It's more important for you to find out what's happening. Go ahead." He was referring to Uncle Jack's phone appointment.

I glanced at my watch. Six-thirty. "It's still a bit early," I said. "What if the call hasn't come yet?"

"Then I'll call back later," Stan offered. "That way we'll know what happened with the move for sure."

"Thanks," I said, excusing myself.

Just as I got up, the lights went out. The kids *ooh*ed softly. I reached for the glass candle holder on our table. "Mind if I borrow this?"

Andie grinned up at Stan. "We can see just fine, can't we?"

Oh, puhleeze, I thought.

Paula looked uncomfortable about remaining at the table without me. I understood how she must feel. Especially since I kept hearing Jared's voice—and Amy-Liz's—drifting across the cafeteria.

"Come with me," I invited Paula, who jumped up.

We made our way by candlelight down the hall to the office phones. Only a few kids were in line ahead of us. Because there were fewer students this time, Mr. Ross allowed longer conversations than before. The office shone with soft candlelight. Three teachers stood around talking.

"Wouldn't you hate to monitor phone calls for a living?" Paula whispered behind me.

"Actually, I feel sorry for them," I said. "This has got to be every teacher's worst nightmare—stuck overnight at school with a bunch of kids."

"I wonder where we'll sleep," she said.

"Maybe we won't," I joked.

Mr. Ross paced nervously as each student talked on the phone. His eyes looked strained. He'd removed his sweater hours before, and the sleeves of his blue dress shirt were rolled up to the elbows. I could almost picture him stirring noodles in a deep pot of boiling water, with Miss W by his side. "Next," he called out as a girl hung up the phone.

Two more to go, I thought, dying for news about Uncle Jack's decision. Surely the phone lines hadn't been down all over Dressel Hills.

Paula asked Mr. Ross where we'd be sleeping if the blizzard didn't let up soon.

"We'll give the ladies the library since it's carpeted. How's that?" He smiled broadly. "Miss Wannamaker and Miss Hess will monitor the girls' side of the building. Lights-out will be ten-thirty." He said it as though he wished that were only a few minutes from now.

Paula flashed her perfect smile. "Bookworms unite," she said. "We'll have plenty to keep us occupied, if the electricity comes back on, that is."

"We sure hope so," Mr. Ross said. "We might easily run out of candles, and we don't have many flashlights."

Finally I held the phone receiver in my hand. I punched in my phone number. Busy. Quickly, I redialed. Still busy.

"I'll try again later," I told Mr. Ross, who was back to pacing.

Paula dialed her number next, since her cell was still useless. Her line was busy, too. We stepped out of line and let the student behind us go next.

"Maybe my dad's talking to your uncle," Paula said. "Maybe they know something already." She offered a comforting smile. Like she knew exactly what I was feeling.

Jared and Billy passed us in the hall, still joking around. I turned away. It hurt seeing Jared so jovial and carefree after what happened between us today.

When it was my turn again, I dialed my phone number. Again the line was busy.

Paula dialed next. She nodded her head, signaling she'd gotten through. "Hi, Mom. I'm still at school. We're stranded here, but I guess you knew that." She paused. "How's Kayla?"

A longer pause ensued as Paula listened to her mom chatter, no doubt.

"I miss you, too," she said at last.

Suddenly I had an idea. "Ask your mom if she's heard anything from Uncle Jack," I whispered.

Paula nodded. "Holly's here with me, and she's trying to get through to her house, but the line's always busy. Have you heard any news about the Denver move?"

I held my breath as seconds ticked by.

"Okay, thanks, Mom," she said at last. "I'll tell her." When she hung up, she turned to me. "Let's take a walk, Holly."

I held our little candle as we headed in the opposite direction of Jared and company—toward the library.

"What did your mom say?" I asked as the candle made leapfrog shadows on the walls.

"Evidently, it's been decided," she said, facing me. "I'm sorry to have to tell you this, Holly. But you're leaving Dressel Hills before school's out."

That soon?

My heart sank.

I stopped in the middle of the hall, still holding the candle. "This can't be happening!" I wailed.

Paula touched my arm. "I know," she said, fighting back the tears.

Someone came running up behind us. I hoped it wasn't Jared. He was the last person I wanted to see.

Turning around, I looked into Andie's face. "What's going on?" she asked.

That's when I buried my face in her shoulder. Paula took the candle holder from me and filled Andie in. Soon Paula's arms were around both Andie and me. And there we stood in the middle of the hallway, three best friends on the brink of separation—stuck in a blizzard, without electricity, and facing spaghetti leftovers for breakfast.

Sobbing like orphans, we stumbled to the girls' rest room, and once again I washed my tear-streaked face.

Andie couldn't stop crying. Probably because she was losing her best friend *and* her guy friend. "Someone's got to tell Stan," she muttered, blowing her nose.

"He'll know when he sees our faces," I said.

"He already said there's no reason for us to end our friendship," Andie said. "He'll email me, and there will always be plenty of skiing trips."

"But you two split up before," I said. "Are you sure it won't happen again?"

"We talked things out," Andie said confidently, blowing her nose. "We're fine now."

She sounded so sure of herself. Made me wonder if I'd been too hasty with Jared. Then I remembered his behavior—how he'd sneered at me, pounding his fist, stomping around. Did I really want to be friends with someone like that?

Miss Hess, our choir director, came into the bathroom just then. "Are you girls all right?"

Andie nodded solemnly.

Miss Hess looked at me. "Holly, are you?"

That's when I filled her in on my latest tragedy.

"I'm very sorry to hear this," she said. "I had hoped to see all you girls trying out for the female roles in our spring musical."

I sighed. "Me too."

Then Andie had an incredible idea. "Maybe Holly could stay with me till school's out."

"Really?" Paula was excited about it, too.

"Fabulous," I said. It was the best thing I'd heard all week. But could I get Mom and Uncle Jack to agree?

We followed Miss Hess to the library, where most of the girls had already gathered. Flickering candles on tabletops gave the place a charming, almost Victorian look. The smell of books, coupled with the brightness of white and wind outdoors, created a cozy atmosphere. I started to calm down. *After all, we haven't moved yet,* I thought. *Things could still change.*

Miss W and Miss Hess sat down with us and began to give instructions. "Think of this as an all-school sleepover," Miss Hess began.

We chuckled. In a strange sort of way, it was a comforting

thought. A much better way to look at things than being forced to stay at school.

"There will be an assembly at seven o'clock tonight," Miss W said. "After which we will divide the school with an imaginary boundary line. The hall just north of the office will be off limits to girls. And the hall running past the library is off limits to the guys."

Andie raised her hand. "What if the storm stops before then?"

Miss W glanced at the window behind her. "At this point in the storm, even if the wind and snow do die out, we would still have to wait several hours before the city could begin snow removal."

"Why don't we make the best of this time together?" Miss Hess said, smoothing her jean skirt. "Let's use it as a chance to get to know one another better." She leaned over and removed her calf-high boots. "I don't know about you, but my feet are killing me."

Several girls removed their shoes, from tall, city-style boots to hiking shoes. The atmosphere was peppered with conversation and laughter.

I looked on either side of me. Andie and Paula—my dear friends. What an amazing way to spend one of our last nights together. It was oddly fitting that we were together like this, surrounded by zillions of school friends from grade-school days.

Joy and Shauna joined us as Mr. Ross peeked his head into the library. "The city is working to get electricity restored as soon as possible," he said.

Cheers went up all around. I didn't clap, though. There was something terribly special about sitting in a beautiful library, candles glowing.

Miss W began talking again. "Girls, we'll have some free time here before going to the assembly. That is, if the electricity is turned on in time."

The doors opened suddenly and in marched Amy-Liz. She turned to say good-bye to someone in the hall. I knew it was Jared. I shut out the image by staring into the candle beside me. Jared was already back to his old ways. Why was I not surprised?

Amy-Liz worked her way through the maze of girls toward us. Sitting down, she handed me a note. "Here, Holly," she said. "It's from Jared."

"Give me that," Andie said, snatching it out of her hand. "Can't you see Holly's been through enough?" She began unfolding the letter.

"Wait," Amy-Liz intervened. "It's private stuff. And," she said, looking at me, "I think Holly oughta hear him out."

Andie got huffy in my defense. "What are you doing hanging out with Jared?" She turned her insufferable stare-lock on Amy-Liz.

Paula nodded. "Jared's not as trustworthy as you think."

Amy-Liz's face lit up like the candle flame on the table. "I think if you give Holly the letter, she'll understand."

Paula's eyebrows shot up. "How do *you* know what Jared wrote?"

"I . . . uh . . . he needed a friend," she said, turning to me. "Just like he needs you to read this, Holly. Read it," she urged. "Somewhere private."

Andie began to sound like my mother again. "Can you promise me this won't upset Holly?" she demanded.

"How should *I* know?" said Amy-Liz.

Reluctantly, Andie handed the letter to me. I took it from her, my heart in my throat.

Chapter 11

I abandoned Andie and Paula and the rest of the girls, searching for a quiet corner in the library. Settling into a comfortable chair, I opened Jared's letter. Slowly, I began to read by candlelight.

Dear Holly,

I can't believe what you did to us today. Bottom line—you'll never find a better guy for you than me. And after that ridiculous sixty-day scrutiny test you put me through. Let's face it, I'm ticked.

We were great friends—you'll have to agree. It doesn't have to end like this. Think it through. I won't wait forever for your reply.

—Jared

All I could do was stare at the letter. Who did he think he was? Part of me wanted to strangle him. And the other part . . . Well, I didn't know what to think.

I knew one thing for sure, Jared had treated me horribly this afternoon and again in this letter. The fact that he wanted me to overlook it—as though nothing had happened—smacked of pride.

No surprise there. Jared had always been full of himself. I couldn't allow him just to write me a guilt-letter and decide it would take care of everything between us. Everything was not okay again—no sir-ee!

Glancing at the letter again, my first reaction was to rip it to shreds. Jared had behaved like a perfect oaf tonight at supper, laughing loudly and flirting with Amy-Liz, who happened to be the cutest soprano in the school choir.

"Psst, Holly!"

I looked up. It was Andie. "You okay?"

"Not really." I stood up, folding the letter.

"What's Jared trying to pull now?"

"His usual." I handed it to her. "See for yourself."

"Man, what a jerk," she said, handing the letter back after reading it. "What are you gonna do?"

"I've got an idea. I'll tell you later."

We joined the other girls while Miss W got ready to do her storytelling routine. I stuffed the letter into my back pocket. "What happened to the assembly?"

"No lights," Andie said. "I think teachers want to keep kids from pairing up in the dark . . . you know."

"Yeah," I muttered, my mind on Jared's note. And on the raging storm outside. I shivered. "It's really cold in here."

"Go get your jacket," she suggested. "Only wait'll you hear what you have to do to get permission to leave the library." She snickered. Evidently, she'd eavesdropped on Miss W and Miss Hess. We sat on the floor, waiting for Miss W to do a final head count.

Still in her stocking feet, Miss Hess closed the library doors. "If you must leave the area to use the rest rooms or the phones," she said, "please sign one of these index cards." First she held a yellow-lined card up for all to see, then placed it on the pile on the desk. "Any questions?"

"They don't trust us," Amy-Liz whispered, grinning.

I bit my tongue. *Look who's talking!*

♥　♥　♥

After several well-presented tales by Miss W, we were given one hour of free time. For some of the girls that was tough. After all, what can you do in a school library with no electricity and candlewicks burning down to nothing fast?

No problem here. I had plenty to keep me busy sitting in the dark. First, I had to devise a plan—how to respond to Jared. I could almost envision the letter, no, the limerick, I would write.

I headed to the desk where the stack of index cards were kept. Miss W sat beside the desk looking fairly wiped out.

"May I please have a pass to get some paper out of my locker?" I fidgeted with the index cards.

"The eighth-grade lockers are on the opposite side of the boundary," she said. "It's off limits to girls."

"I'll be back in two minutes," I pleaded. "I promise."

She glanced at her watch, then looking up at me, she smiled. "For you, Holly, I'll allow it. Be back in two minutes."

I dashed out of the library and down the dark hallway. Feeling my way along the row of lockers, I discovered the futility of locating mine.

A faint glimmer came from the end of the hall. Rushing to investigate, I realized just how cold the school building had become. If only I could find my locker and get it open, I would have paper as well as my jacket.

Nearing the end of the hall, I discovered an array of communal candles and holders lying on the floor. Some were lit, some weren't.

I had to hurry. More than two minutes had passed! Miss Hess and Miss W would be sending out a search party any minute now. I lit a single candle off one of the others and, shielding the flame, I made my way down the dark corridor—locker hunting.

Finally I found mine. Balancing the candle in one hand, I spun my combination. Grabbing my notebook and jacket, I slammed the locker door. And just like that, the lights flickered on.

"Wow! I should've tried this earlier," I joked to myself. Blowing out the candle, I raced back to the library.

Miss W seemed delighted to see me. "Look," she said, pointing to the girls lined up near the windows. "The stars are coming out."

I ran to the windows and cupped my hands on the frosty pane. Monstrous drifts were everywhere, but the snow had stopped. I exhaled, leaving a ring of moisture on the glass. The blizzard of the decade had come and gone. So had my stormy bout with Jared Wilkins. Except the winds of war were still blowing. One pathetic letter from Jared wasn't going to stop anything.

Finding Andie and Paula, I whispered my plan to write a limerick in response to Jared's letter.

"How cool," Andie said.

"Want some assistance?" Paula asked.

"Perfect," I said, searching for a quiet table for three.

When we sat down, Paula and Andie announced their plans to throw a going-away party for me.

"It'll be one you'll never forget," Andie said.

"I'm afraid of that," I said, laughing.

"We're going to make the next few weeks count for a lifetime," Andie said, grabbing my elbow. "You'll see."

It was obvious she was trying to be brave. She didn't mention anything about my staying with her till school was out, like before. But we could make those kinds of plans tomorrow or the next day. After all, I'd have to get Mom and Uncle Jack to agree. Besides, the way Jared was acting, maybe several more weeks was long enough to hang around here.

I gave Paula and Andie a piece of paper. "Write a list of words that rhyme with Jared," I said.

A broad grin spread across Andie's face. "I've got one." She wrote the word, passing it across the table to Paula and me. We burst into giggles.

"It's fabulous!" I said, starting to write the limerick.

There once was a boy named Jared,
Whom everyone knew was an airhead.

I read it to them softly. "What do you think?"

Andie and Paula were in stitches. "You should do this for a living," Paula said.

Andie was laughing so hard she couldn't speak.

"Now for the middle part," I said. "Think of all the words that rhyme with *pride*."

Paula started her list. Andie wiped the laughter tears from her eyes, while I made my own list of words starting at the top of the alphabet. *Bride, cried, denied, dried, eyed, fried, hide, lied.*

Halfway through the alphabet I stopped. Now Paula was giggling so hard she could barely write. "Is this too much for you or what?" I laughed.

Paula nodded. "You should talk to the editor of the school paper. I hear they could use some help."

"But I'm moving, remember?" I said.

Sad recognition flitted across Paula's face. "I'm sorry, Holly."

When Andie and Paula were finished, we pooled our talents and finished the limerick.

> *There once was a boy named Jared,*
> *Whom everyone knew was an airhead.*
> *His problem was pride,*
> *"Forgiveness—denied,"*
> *Said Holly, who just could not bear it!*

"It may be a little rough," I said, "but this will state my point."

"Loud and clear," said Paula.

"Who's gonna deliver it to him?" Andie asked.

"What about you, Paula?" I pulled her up from her chair. "Fill out an index card," I teased. "Then go to the rest room, and on the way back, stick this in Jared's locker."

She read the limerick one more time. Laughing, she folded the paper and hid it in her pants pocket.

Andie and I went to the window, watching streaks of cirrocumulus clouds whip past the moon. She slipped her arm around my shoulder. "I'll never find another friend like you, Holly-Heart," Andie whispered. "Never in the whole world."

"Moving won't change things between us," I said, swallowing the lump in my throat. "I'll live in Dressel Hills again someday. You'll see."

And in my heart, it was the promise of a lifetime.

Chapter 12

None of us got much sleep on the carpeted floor of the library that night. At least we had heat. Thank goodness for that. Still, we bundled up in our jackets for blankets.

It was a typical sleepover, only on a larger scale and without the amenities of sleeping bags and DVDs. And instead of five or six giggling females, there were eighty-four of us.

At dawn, we woke up to the sound of snowplows and snow-blowers. Andie sat up next to me on the floor, rubbing her eyes. "Hallelujah—we're going home! I can't wait to sleep in my own bed."

"Sounds fabulous," I said, thinking about my cozy four-poster bed . . . and my beloved window seat. It seemed like weeks since I'd written in my diary.

Paula went with Andie and me to the rest room—nobody needed passes now. Andie peeked around each corner before we proceeded down the hall, making sure neither Jared nor his buddies were nowhere in sight.

In the rest room, I brushed my long hair while Andie groaned at her smashed curls. "I'd give anything to have your hair, Holly."

"I'll give it to you if you'll trade places with me," I teased, referring to the move to Denver.

Andie shot me a sideways glance. "I'd hate living in a big city," she said. And that was the end of that.

We made ourselves as presentable as possible. Then we headed to the office with Paula in the lead. She wanted to call home.

Stan was already waiting in the phone line. He looked a bit disheveled, with oily hair sticking out in places.

"Was your bed as hard as ours?" I asked.

"Worse," he grumbled. "You had carpet, remember?"

I gave him a sympathetic look. "Who are you calling?"

"Dad . . . again."

"Then you heard the news?"

"Yeah, I heard." I could see he didn't want to discuss things with Andie standing right there.

I changed the subject. "Paula says her dad'll bring his snow-mobile up to school if he has to."

"Good idea," he said. "Only it'll take him several trips to get us all home."

"Are the city buses running yet?" Paula asked.

"Most of the streets are drifted shut, according to the radio," Stan said, pulling out his MP3 player, which had an FM radio. "But the city crews'll be out all day."

"Some blizzard," Andie said.

"And poor timing," I said under my breath.

Stan heard. He shrugged his shoulders, forcing a sad sort of smile at Andie.

♥ ♥ ♥

By the time Stan and I got home, it was nearly ten o'clock. About the time I usually got up on Saturdays.

Mom threw her arms around us as we came in. Then Uncle Jack hurried down the stairs, looking mighty comfortable in his faded blue jeans and flannel shirt. I, on the other hand, was still unshowered and wearing the same clothes I'd slept in all night.

I held back when Uncle Jack bear-hugged me. He noticed, but he tried to act cool, as though it was nothing. But I had a right to be angry. After all, he'd railroaded his stupid move right through—and while I was stuck overnight at school. It wasn't fair. Not one bit.

"You'll have to record this event for posterity," Mom said, grinning. "I've never heard of being stranded at school all night."

Too tired and overwhelmed to talk, I grumbled a reply.

Mark rolled his eyes, grunting like a gorilla. "Better not happen to me. Oo-o-ga!"

"Go away," I snapped. Everyone was acting like nothing had happened. Like our whole world wasn't about to change.

Stephie jumped up and down when she saw me. "I slept with Goofey for you last night, Holly."

"That's nice," I growled.

Mom frowned at my response. "Come have some hot chocolate to warm you up," she said to Stan and me.

I didn't answer, but I followed reluctantly to the kitchen and sat on a barstool. Mom filled two mugs with the hot chocolate she'd kept warm on the stove. Stan took his cup and left the room, probably to veg out in front of the TV.

"Why can't we stay in Dressel Hills at least till school's out?" I whined as she handed me the steaming hot drink. Going to Denver was the only thing on my mind.

"I'm not comfortable with that," she said.

I set my cup down on the counter and stared at her. "What's that supposed to mean?"

"Just what I said, Holly." She was equally determined. "We—all of us—are staying together on this."

I had no idea why she was so adamant about something so illogical. "Where will we live?" I asked.

"Jack's already found several lovely rental houses to choose from," she said. "We'll buy a house later, when we've had a chance to look around."

"What about school?" I wailed.

"The schools should be fine," she explained. "If we aren't happy with the public schools where we live, we can always look into private, or homeschool till the end of the year."

I blew on my hot chocolate. It sure looked like Mom was calling the shots—right along with her new husband. So much for democracy.

"Well, why on earth do we have to move so soon?" I complained.

Mom sighed, obviously tired of my string of questions. "We have to set the office up immediately," she replied, "or Jack will lose several big accounts."

Mom seemed enthusiastic—and stubborn—about the move. I couldn't figure out why. She had never wanted to live in a big city. That was one of the reasons she and Daddy moved from Pennsylvania to Colorado after they were married.

I didn't tell her I wanted to live with Andie and finish out the school year. But I was dying to.

"It's going to be quite an undertaking getting this house packed," she continued. "Each day we'll do something big. Starting today."

I should have known. When Mom made up her mind, she pushed forward with all her might to attain her goal.

"After you shower and rest up, you could start sorting through your own closet," she said. "You'll find flattened boxes in the attic." She got up and went to one of the kitchen drawers. Pulling out a roll of packing tape and a scissors, she handed them to me. "The boys'll be around to help if you need it."

I won't cry—I won't, I thought as I trudged up the steps to my room, tape and scissors in hand. This house, and everything in it— well, almost everything—reminded me of Daddy. It had been over five years since he'd left. Still, I loved the memories. The nights he read to us till we fell asleep, the summer evenings we spent swinging on the front porch, the jokes he told around the supper table. All were memories he'd made with us here.

Gathering up clean clothes, I headed for the bathroom. As I showered, I thought of my short time in Dressel Hills. Fourteen years had come and gone. The water beat on my back as I cried.

No one could hear my sorrow. No one could see my tears. For the first time in my life, I felt totally alone.

After showering, I headed to my room. With a heavy heart, I stared at everything as if for the last time. My comfy bed. My droopy-eyed teddy bear, snuggled onto the lavender window seat next to a pillow. No room could ever be like this one.

I took out my journal, hoping that writing would help me to feel better.

Saturday, March 26—The worst thing happened to me yesterday after school, and it wasn't the blizzard. I found out that Uncle Jack's backup plan flopped. The guy he was trying to get for the Denver office turned down the job. So we're moving to Denver, and Mom's not even trying to do anything to stop it. I can't believe it. I always thought she loved Dressel Hills as much as I do!

More horrendous things: Jared and I are finished. Partly my fault, because I didn't handle things very well and Jared misunderstood. He got real mad and said some horrible things to me. The worst part is he sent a note to me (delivered by none other than Amy-Liz!), and he wants me to think about what happened—like I'm the one who should make the final decision. I really hate this!

I closed my journal. Whether I liked it or not, it was time to get started on packing.

I headed for the walk-in closet in Mom's bedroom. The ladder to the attic hung down from the ceiling in the far corner of the closet. I remembered hiding up there as a kid. Andie and I had written some of our first Loyalty Papers in our attic. Everything in this house seemed to call out to me—to remind me that I was leaving against my will.

At the top of the ladder, I pushed the wooden door open and poked my head through. The attic was cold, dark, and quiet—like a cave in the snow. Looking around, I shivered. Not much had changed, except there were a few more boxes stacked in neat piles against the wall. Probably Uncle Jack's stuff.

The attic floor creaked as I made my way to the pile of flattened boxes. A lopsided lamp, minus the light bulb, leaned against the wall, and a large gray trunk stood nearby. Kneeling on the dusty floor, I folded the cardboard along the indentations and made up three large boxes to take to my room.

As I finished the third box, I glanced up and noticed the initials SMJ just above the latch on the old trunk.

"SMJ . . . Susan Marie Johnson," I whispered. "Mom's initials before she married Daddy."

Almost reverently, I touched it. Mom had used the trunk to haul her clothes and books to college. It was special. Even doubled as a coffee table in the early years of Mom and Daddy's marriage before they had money for nice furniture. Before I was born. One of our scrapbooks showed them drinking tea on the floor, with a lighted candle perched on the trunk.

In the five years that had come and gone since Daddy left, this trunk had stored Mom's reminders of him and their life together. Along with scrapbooks and their wedding album, we'd packed up old love letters. Most of them were from Daddy while Mom was completing college. Even the slightest memory brought a veil of tears. Mom had nearly grieved herself sick.

I blew away some dust and slowly, gently, opened the lid.

The awful smell of mothballs brought back memories of the day we had packed this trunk. At age eight, I was too young to care much about love letters. But now, in the depths of my sadness, I wondered if they might hold the answer to The Question—that thing I could not bring myself to face. So deeply buried was The Question, that even though I felt close to my father last Christmas— and had been with him in the quiet of his study, the two of us, alone—I could not force my lips to shape the words.

Deep and dark, The Question stirred within me. *Find the answers,* it urged. But layers of pain concealed The Question. The pain of divorce, the lonely years without Daddy. Mom having to work full time while juggling office and family. The pain of an empty porch swing on cool summer evenings. Baking snicker-doodles without him.

The old days and Daddy—gone forever. And now I was facing another change. One almost as painful as my parents' divorce.

Reaching into the dim chasm of the trunk, I found three shoe boxes labeled according to month and year. Mom had allowed me to read a few of the letters kept inside. I opened the one on top and read it for old times' sake. Smiling, I folded it and slipped it into the envelope. My father certainly had a way with words. He could sweet-talk Mom into almost anything.

I put the letter back in the shoe box and spotted something new—a cluster of cards and envelopes secured with a rubber band in the far right corner of the trunk. Where had they come from?

I hesitated, almost afraid to delve into possible secrets of the past. Taking a deep breath, I lifted the stack out of the trunk, pur-posely holding it away from my eyes, struggling with the tempta-tion to snoop. Snooping was one of Mom's pet peeves. Mine too. I thought about Carrie and Stephie sneaking around, snooping in my journal, driving me crazy.

But my curiosity won out. I removed the rubber band and held the first letter up to the light. It was addressed to Susan Mer-edith; the handwriting was unmistakable. The letter was from my Grandma Meredith.

I sifted through several more envelopes to verify my suspicions. Sitting down on a torn hassock, I discovered that Mom had been corresponding with Grandma Meredith, Daddy's mother, after he moved out. But why? According to the postmarks, there were sev-eral years' worth of letters and cards here.

The Question raised its ugly head. And I trembled as I began to read the first letter.

Chapter 13

Dearest Susan,

We received your letter yesterday, and our hearts are deeply saddened by the news of your recent separation. How we pray something will stop this needless tragedy.

These many years, we have felt our son's work has been far too important. Insisting on you and the girls moving to the West Coast, especially when he knows how much you dislike big-city life, seems nothing short of insensible.

How are Holly and Carrie, our little darlings, handling the situation? We want to help you out in any way we can. Please let us know if you need anything. Tell our granddaughters how much we love them.

Take care of yourself. We love you, Susan.

—Mom and Dad Meredith

My heart pounded fiercely as I held the letter. The contents of Grandma Meredith's letter to Mom shook me up. It actually sounded like Mom had refused to move to California when Daddy wanted to be where the action was for his work. Somehow I was sure she would have followed a more submissive route if she'd been a Christian back then.

My thoughts wandered back to Uncle Jack and *his* career move. Wait a minute . . . Was this the reason for Mom's very supportive position?

Just then I heard footsteps. Someone was coming up the ladder. I hurried to hide evidence of my snooping. Fumbling to refold Grandma's letter, I slid it back under the rubber band without the envelope.

The footsteps were coming closer. I heard Stephie's voice. Was Mom with her?

Trembling, I threw the small bundle of letters into the trunk and slammed the lid. The envelope flew onto the floor.

Bam! I covered it with my foot.

"Whatcha doin' up here?" Stephie asked.

I peeked around her. "Where's Mom?"

"Sorting junk in the kitchen—some stuff we never use." Stephie pushed her chin-length hair behind her ears, then picked up a medium-sized box. "Can I have this?" she asked.

"Sure." My mind was still on Grandma's letter. Furtively, I wiped a tear away.

"What's wrong?" Stephie asked, putting her hand on my shoulder.

I forced a smile. "I'll be fine."

"But you're crying." She squatted down on the dusty floor beside me.

I ignored her comment, grabbing at a box. As I did, my foot slipped, revealing the envelope.

Stephie picked it up. "What's this?"

"Nothing much," I said. *Just what I don't need right now.*

Stephie opened the envelope. "Looks like something's missing." She eyed me suspiciously.

"Really?" I said, playing dumb.

Stephie stood up, her eyes dancing. "Are you snooping, Holly?"

I couldn't tell her, I just couldn't. She would tell Mom and . . .

"I did that once, after Mommy died," Stephie began. "Daddy let me help him pack some of Mommy's cards. She used to stick little notes on the mirror every morning. You know, love notes." She giggled.

"How sweet," I said.

"When we moved from Pennsylvania, Daddy put all of Mommy's stuff in special boxes. Even some of her clothes. And when he wasn't looking, I snooped." She turned around. "There they are." She pointed to the boxes stacked against the wall.

I was shocked. Aunt Marla's things were packed away in our attic. "Does Mom know about them?"

Stephie nodded. Her bright eyes sparkled for an instant, then suddenly turned sad. "I think so. But I wish Daddy would unpack some of it." Without warning, she burst into tears. "Because I can't remember my mommy's face anymore."

I wrapped her in my arms and hugged her tight. "It's okay, Stephie. It's okay," I said, trying to soothe her. "You have pictures to remember her by."

"I don't ever want to forget her," she cried. "I miss her so much. Why did she have to leave us? Why did she have to die?"

In the recesses of my being, a dam broke, spilling out the pain, releasing The Question. I began to sob along with the little girl in my arms. And with the little girl inside of me—that girl who, for five long years, could never bring herself to ask.

Into the dimly lit attic, I let The Question pour out of me. "Why did you have to leave us, Daddy?" I cried into the stillness. "Why?"

Chapter 14

My pain mingled with Stephie's, like the tears on our faces. And now that I had voiced The Question, I was determined to find The Answer—even if I had to snoop in Grandma's letters to find it.

Slowly, Stephie calmed down. She stopped crying and took some big breaths. I hugged her to me. "Are you okay?" I asked gently.

She nodded and rubbed her eyes. "Thanks, Holly." She looked up at me, her eyes still wet with tears. "I always wanted a big sister. It was no fun being the only girl in the house."

"Well, I love having another little sister," I said, suddenly realizing just how true it was. I *did* love Stephie. Like I loved my own birth sister.

Gently pushing me away, she got up to go. "You won't tell Daddy I was crying, will you, Holly?"

"I promise." I helped her down the ladder with her box.

At the bottom of the ladder she whispered up to me, "Don't worry, Holly. I won't tell your mom, either. About the letters—or anything."

"Thanks," I said.

For several seconds I stood silently, absorbing everything.

Sure, I had lost my dad. But Stephie and her brothers had lost their mother—to death. And think of Uncle Jack—he had lost his wife. . . .

But I wasn't ready to feel too sorry for him. Not yet.

Snapping back into action, I hurried back to the trunk. And to the empty envelope on the floor. My heart pounded as I reached for the lid on the gray trunk. I pulled, but it wouldn't budge. I tried again. Stuck!

Then I looked at the latch with Mom's old initials engraved on it. Unknowingly, I had slammed the lid when Stephie came looking for boxes. And now it was locked.

There was nothing left to do but stuff the evidence in my pocket. I figured if Mom was in the kitchen packing, it would be a cinch to find the trunk key in her bedroom. I thought about places she might hide a key like that and came up with several options. Mom had an odds-and-ends drawer in her vanity. Could be there. And the jewelry case on her dresser was another possibility.

Ready for the challenge, I descended the attic ladder. I peeked around the corner into Mom's bedroom.

All clear!

Hurrying to the door, I peered down the hallway. No one in sight. Perfect. Soon I'd have the key in my hand, and no one would ever know about my snooping.

First, I checked the junk drawer in Mom's vanity. Everything imaginable was scattered in there. Old thimbles, a paper clip, two pocket-sized Kleenex packs, and even some ancient postage stamps. But no trunk key.

Next, I searched her jewelry case. It was filled with dinner rings, bracelets, earrings, and necklaces. But no key.

Now what?

I dashed to my room to think. A backup plan—that's what I needed. As I contemplated the situation, the phone rang.

Mom called to me, "Holly, are you up there? It's for you."

I answered the phone in the hall. "Hello?"

"Holly, we have to talk." It was Jared. He sounded miserable.

"I don't know what to say to you," I replied quickly.

"Got your limerick," he continued. "You're angry with me."

"You got that right."

Jared didn't say anything to that. It was weird trying not to breathe too loudly into the phone. But I was really nervous. And, yep, still mad.

Finally he broke the silence. "Maybe we oughta talk face-to-face."

"I . . . well, maybe it's not such a good idea."

He pressed on. "How about after Sunday school tomorrow?"

"We'll see," I said. "You know we're definitely moving."

"Yeah, Stan told me." There was another long silence.

"Well, I've got to help my mom with the packing," I said. "Talk to you later."

We said good-bye, and I hung up.

Settling down on my window seat, I thought about Jared and what it would be like trying to hang out with him again. After all the things he'd said yesterday, and how he'd flirted with Amy-Liz, like it was no big deal. Why did he want to hang on to me like this? Moving to Denver with a cute boy to write to had its advantages—for me. But I couldn't see how it would benefit Jared.

I left the window seat to locate my journal. It was definitely time to record my true feelings about Jared. About Daddy, too.

Saturday afternoon, March 26—Even though I can think of all sorts of reasons NOT to give Jared the time of day, I think I know the true and only reason why I don't want to have anything to do with him. It's because Sean Hamilton is coming from California with Daddy and Tyler next Saturday. I want to be able to hang out with Sean—and other guys, too—without worrying how Jared might feel.

I glanced up from my journal. "That's it," I surprised myself by saying. "*That's* the reason. I really want to see Sean again." No way would Jared want me to spend the day skiing with another guy if he was my boyfriend again. Not in a zillion years.

I continued writing in my journal.

I think I found some answers to my questions about why Daddy left. It must have something to do with moving to California. According to Grandma's letter, it sounds like Mom purposely stayed here in Dressel Hills with Carrie and me. I know they were separated for a while before Daddy made it legal. I still don't know what happened to make him file for divorce, though.

Grandma Meredith's letters hold the answers somehow, I just know it. But now I've got to find the trunk key. Before we move. Who knows when I'll have a chance to snoop around again once we get to Denver.

I closed my journal and tucked it into its hiding place. Then I turned my attention to the mess in my closet. If I didn't hurry and get some of this stuff sorted, Mom might wonder what I'd been up to all afternoon.

Going through the closet shelves, I found piles of school papers, scrapbooks, old shoe boxes filled with embroidery floss from fifth grade when I was a cross-stitch junkie, and a bunch of other stuff.

By suppertime, I was finished. And even though Mom had made her fabulous meatloaf, I only moved it around on my plate. Uncle Jack's excitement bugged me, took my appetite away. Stubbornly, I tuned out his moving talk, refusing to make eye contact with him all the way through dessert.

♥ ♥ ♥

In the middle of the night, I felt icky. After a drink of water, I went back to bed. But by morning I felt even worse. Mom let me stay home from church, and it was a good thing, because I slept nearly all morning.

When I finally woke up, my first thought was of Jared. He'd probably think I was playing sick to avoid him. I hadn't planned it this way, but it did buy me some additional time.

I showered and dressed in a fleece shirt and clean jeans. I snickered to myself as I headed for Mom's bedroom and the walk-in closet. Perfect timing. Now . . . how to open that trunk?

Climbing up the ladder, I slid the wooden door open in the ceiling. The place was dark and dusty as before, but with a sense of purpose this time, I snapped on the light and made my way to the gray trunk.

Fooling with the latch, I made a surprising discovery. It was unlocked now. Someone had come up here yesterday after I left. I was sure of it.

Carefully, I lifted the lid. My eyes scanned the shoe boxes lined in a row. Scrapbooks—featuring Mom and Daddy, before Carrie and I were born—were piled up neatly, just as I'd seen them yesterday. But Grandma's letters were gone. I moved several scrapbooks, thinking they might have slipped down farther into the trunk. But no, the letters were missing. Someone had removed Grandma's letters from the trunk.

Soon the sound of car doors slamming and the voices of my family returning home from church floated up to the attic. Puzzled at the strange turn of events, I closed the lid, turned off the light, and climbed down the ladder.

I couldn't believe it. Had Stephie tattled to Mom?

Chapter 15

As soon as supper was over, I cornered Stephie.

"Come to my room," I whispered.

"What for?"

"You'll see," I said, taking her hand.

When we got to my room, I closed the door. "Did you tell anyone about yesterday? You know, when you caught me reading letters in the attic?"

Her chestnut hair flew back and forth as she shook her head.

"Are you positive?"

"I kept my promise," she said. "Carrie doesn't even know."

"Good girl," I said, more puzzled than ever.

"Can I go now?" she asked.

I nodded. What was happening here? I wondered about it as I headed down the stairs to the kitchen.

Carrie stopped me in the dining room. "Some guy at church gave me this." She waved an envelope in my face.

"Yeah," Phil said. "Jared misses you."

"Spare me," I groaned, snatching up the envelope.

"Holly, I could use some help," Mom called from the kitchen. "You too, Phil."

Phil complained. "It's not my turn."

Without looking up from the sink, Mom said, "Better check the duties chart."

Phil didn't bother to check, but I did. As always, Mom was right. Grumbling as usual, Phil carried dirty dishes into the kitchen from the dining room. When the last dish was on the counter and ready for scraping, he disappeared. Mom and I were alone at last.

I wimped out on the divorce question and asked permission to stay in Dressel Hills with Andie instead. "It wouldn't be for very long, really," I pleaded. "Only about two and a half months."

Not surprisingly, Mom countered my request. "Mrs. Martinez has her hands full with three-year-old twins. She doesn't need an extra person around."

I could see this was going nowhere fast. "You don't want me to stay and finish the school year, is that it?"

Mom wrung out her dishcloth. "It's much more than that, Holly-Heart," she said, turning to look at me. "I simply don't want to split up our family. We need each other—now more than ever."

Mom really loved her kids, all six of us. And she was giving me the only response I could have expected from a mom with a hang-up for nurturing. But it made me mad that she couldn't make an exception just this once.

She pulled her hair back into a ponytail for a second, then let it fall. "Could we consider this case closed, please?" She wasn't kidding. I could tell by the look in her eyes.

"Oh, Mom, I just wish—"

"Holly, please," she interrupted. "I'm sorry, but it's out of the question. We're leaving here *together*."

Silently, I loaded the dishwasher. None of this was fair. I could hardly wait to exit the kitchen and hide out in my room. Besides, Jared's letter was burning a hole in my jeans pocket.

Closing the dishwasher, I started the wash cycle. Then, without a word to Mom, I hurried off to my room.

Jared's letter turned out to be much more civil than the one at school. He said he was sorry I was sick and hoped I would be at school tomorrow *"so we can talk at lunch."*

But more than anything, I could read between the lines. He wanted me tied up with him the last weeks of my life in Dressel Hills. Why? It was easy to second-guess him. Sean Hamilton had to be the one and only reason.

❤ ❤ ❤

Early Monday morning, Mom knocked on my bedroom door. "Holly? Are you awake?"

I rubbed my eyes and tried to focus them. "Uh-huh," I grunted.

She came in and sat on the edge of my bed, holding up some jeans I'd thrown in the laundry. I looked closer. They were my jeans from Saturday. In the confusion of my first waking moments, I hadn't the faintest idea why she was here.

Then she pulled something out of those jeans. Wiping the sleep out of my eyes, I stared. It was the envelope to Grandma Meredith's letter. Was I in for it now!

"So . . . what do you know about this?" Mom asked.

There was no way I could talk my way out. So I told the truth right up front. "I was reading Grandma's letter to you."

"You were snooping in my things?" she asked. I was worried by the way her eyes squinted shut. It spelled trouble, with a capital T.

"I guess you could say that." This sure sounded worse than it had seemed on Saturday.

"Are you saying you didn't even attempt to control yourself?" Mom's eyes were squintier than I'd seen them in years.

I nodded.

"How many letters did you read?" It was a pointed question. She was worried, it seemed. Very worried.

"Just that one—I mean, just the one that was in there." I wasn't handling this very well. Mom was mad and had a right to be. But I wanted answers and deserved to have them. I took a deep breath and sat up.

Startled by my abrupt movement, Mom leaned back a bit.

"I've been dying to have this talk with you," I began. "It's time. I mean, I think I'm old enough to know certain things."

Mom's jaw was set, but slowly her eyes became less squinty. "To know what?"

I took a deep breath. "About what happened between you and Daddy."

Mom stared down at the envelope, tracing the edges with her finger. This discussion wasn't going to be easy for her, that was obvious.

Hesitantly, I voiced The Question. "Why did Daddy leave us?"

Sadness reigned as Mom spoke. "That's difficult to answer. It involves far more than you can imagine."

Visions of hideous things flashed across my mind. Had there been another woman? Was Dad unfaithful?

"In many ways, it was my fault as well as your father's," she began. "He had a wonderful career opportunity in California. I was stubborn—didn't want to leave our quiet town or our beautiful home. On top of that, I have always disliked big-city life. But your father was insistent upon moving. So I agreed that he should go to the West Coast by himself, hoping that after a few months there he'd change his mind and come home."

She sighed. "But it didn't work out that way. Instead, he found the business market stimulating and couldn't pry himself from it. Not even enough to come home when I had trouble with my pregnancy."

I gasped. "You were expecting another baby?"

Mom nodded slowly. "I wanted that child desperately, but I miscarried." She paused to wipe her eyes. "In the end, I blamed your father for what happened. It was a very tense time for us."

"Daddy didn't want the baby?" I asked timidly.

"He viewed the pregnancy as a power thing—a way for me to keep him in Dressel Hills."

It was hard to comprehend—Daddy treating Mom so poorly.

"I don't want you to worry about how your dad feels about you or Carrie. You had nothing to do with the divorce," Mom said.

Her words echoed in my brain. No wonder she didn't want me to find out about this in a letter. I was surprised that she'd told me at all.

Mom pulled me close. "Things could've been so different if I'd known the Lord back then. We could've been spared so much."

I looked up, fighting back the tears. "I pray for Daddy's salvation every day."

"I'm glad you do, honey."

That's when I told her about last Christmas Eve at Daddy's. "He read the Christmas story from the Bible to all of us. I was so excited." I went on to tell her about the man in his office who'd given Daddy a Bible. How he'd begun to read it—starting with Matthew's gospel.

A smile swept across Mom's face. Suddenly she looked years younger. "That's wonderful news," she said. "If he's reading the Bible and talking to his Christian friend at work, perhaps our prayers will be answered."

Mom hugged me hard and tiptoed out of the room, my dirty jeans in one hand and the empty envelope in the other. What had started out as an impossible conversation had ended up being the most incredible heart-to-heart talk ever.

♥ ♥ ♥

All day at school, I mulled the conversation with Mom over in my mind. Even when Jared wanted to talk about "us" during lunch, my mind was on Daddy and what had pulled him and Mom apart.

"I don't know how we can patch things up between us with you in never-never land," Jared said, leaning to look me square in the face.

"Oh, sorry."

"You okay?" he asked gently.

"Let's put it this way: I've had better days."

"Yeah, me too," he said, probably referring to the standoff between us.

"If we could just be friends and not so exclusive, how would you feel about that?" There. I'd put it to him straight.

Jared shook his head. "I don't know why I bother talking to you, Holly. You're impossible." And with that, he picked up his tray and left the table.

If that wasn't enough to ruin the afternoon, going home and seeing a For Sale sign stuck in our front yard sure as shootin' was!

Chapter 16

It snowed in the mountains Friday afternoon, the day before Sean was to arrive. A light, powdery kind of snow. Perfect for skiing tomorrow. I glanced up at the snowcapped mountains as I sat on my window seat, writing the final paragraphs of my story "Good-Bye Whispers." I decided not to have the hero and the heroine end up together. Anyway, it doesn't always happen that way in real life. Look at Jared and me. And . . . Daddy and Mom.

After I finished writing my short story, I pulled out my journal to record my thoughts.

> *Friday, April 1—Now that I know Mom's side of the story*
> *about the divorce, it's hard to think about hanging out with*
> *Daddy all day tomorrow. Thank goodness Sean and Tyler*
> *will be there. No way do I want my dad to suspect that I know*
> *what happened. Besides, it's in the past. Daddy is remarried*
> *to Saundra and might be moving closer to making a decision*
> *for Christ. At least, I hope so.*

Looking up from my journal, I stared out the window. The mountains seemed closer than usual. I could almost reach out and touch them. Would I be able to see these same mountains in Denver? I doubted it.

Tomorrow I'd be skiing on my beloved mountains with Sean. I couldn't help feeling nervous. The thought of seeing him again almost made me forget about the move. I could still kick myself for not meeting him on the beach last Christmas. But that was before I learned some hard lessons about boys. Now I felt more confident. Maybe even enough for a solid friendship with a soon-to-be sixteen-year-old guy. Like Sean.

I closed my journal and prayed. This had been a tough week for me—the mess with Jared, finding out about the reasons behind the divorce, trying to adjust to the thought of moving, and now getting ready for a visit from Daddy and Sean. I needed help sorting things out.

Just as I ended my prayer, a knock came at my door. Quickly, I shoved my journal under a pillow. "Mom, is that you?" I hurried to see who was there.

"Hey, Holly."

It was my uncle Jack. I stood facing him. Alone. For the first time since all this moving stuff started. I shifted my weight from one foot to another, completely speechless.

"Got a minute?" he asked.

I opened the door a little wider. "Sure."

He stepped into the room, looking big and awkward and a little out of place.

"Here." I pulled out my desk chair for him, then perched on the edge of my window seat. Waiting.

Uncle Jack turned the chair around and sat on it backward, his arms gripping the back. Looking uncomfortable, he began. "I know you've been angry with me about the Denver move, Holly."

I picked at an imaginary snag on one of the throw pillows. There was no point in talking. His decision had been made. So what did he want?

"I've been talking to your mother," he continued. "She says you asked to stay with Andie. We both agree that it would be a big burden on the Martinez family. However, we did talk to the Miller family about having you stay there till the end of the school year."

I looked up. "Are you kidding?" This was fabulous. At last, some good news!

He nodded. "Paula and Kayla are thrilled at the idea."

But he didn't smile. In fact, he didn't seem happy about it at all.

"How would you like that?" he asked gently.

I was close to shouting *yes* when something stopped me. His look. His eyes. Uncle Jack just wasn't Uncle Jack today. Where was the merry twinkle in his eyes? Where were the jokes and the laughter? Where was the man who Mom had fallen in love with— the crazy, silly, good man who'd survived the loss of his wife and who'd helped put our family back together again?

Looking at his face, I realized something. I had created all kinds of problems for him and Mom, throwing one tantrum after another, until finally I'd broken them down . . . gotten my own way. But was I happy—truly happy—now? Would I really want to stay with Paula, when I knew it would break up my family and hurt Mom and Uncle Jack? What was more important to me anyway—Dressel Hills and my friends . . . or my own dear family?

"Well, Holly?" Uncle Jack prodded.

Then I remembered what Mom had said about her and Daddy's divorce. *I was stubborn,* she'd said. *I didn't want to leave our quiet town or our beautiful home.*

I took a huge breath. Oh boy. Was I like Mom, or what?

Then I remembered Stephie. *"I always wanted a big sister,"* she'd said. But what kind of big sister? A spoiled rotten, selfish one? Or a sister who loved her and stuck with her no matter what?

"Holly, would you like to stay with the Millers?" Uncle Jack asked again.

With all the courage I could muster, I slowly shook my head. "Thanks, Uncle Jack," I said, "but no. I think I'll go ahead and make the move with the family."

At my words, the biggest grin I'd ever seen crossed Uncle Jack's face. "Are you sure?"

I nodded. Then I swallowed hard and went on. "I'm sorry about the bratty way I carried on. You really are a cool stepdad, in case you didn't know it." By now my eyes swam with tears.

They spilled over when Uncle Jack reached for both my hands. "You're quite a lady, Holly-Heart. Thank you for being so special." He paused. "I know this whole idea of moving has been difficult for you. Believe me, I'm going to do my best to make things easier for you."

I smiled back at him as the tears fell down my cheeks. I cried openly, not caring how I looked. My hands were resting in Uncle Jack's big, strong ones, and for the first time in days, I felt wonderfully at peace.

Chapter 17

The next morning at eight-thirty on the dot, Mom drove Carrie and me to the ski lodge at the base of Copper Mountain.

"Do you still have to meet Sean?" I asked Mom as she parked the van.

"Have to? I want to." She smiled knowingly.

"Come on, Carrie," I said. "Let's get this over with."

We headed for the ski racks, where we locked up our new skis till later. Then we climbed the wooden stairs to the lodge. My heart did a crazy tap dance when I saw Sean waiting just inside the lobby, with Tyler by his side. Sean's blue-and-green ski jacket reminded me of the Pacific Ocean, where we'd swum and built our sandman.

"Hey, Carrie," Tyler shouted, running to us. He pulled Carrie aside to show off his new skis and poles.

I introduced Mom to Sean. And he made it easy for me, shaking her hand and smiling. I'd forgotten how low his voice was. "So very nice to meet you, Mrs. Patterson," he said. He'd remembered Mom's new name. Perfect. Things like that always impressed adults.

"I've heard some nice things about you," Mom said. I hoped she

185

wouldn't launch off on something personal—like his baby-sitting skills or something else.

Sean glanced at me, grinning. "Holly's quite a letter writer," he said.

No way could I keep my face from blushing.

Tyler and Carrie dragged his equipment across the lobby. "Can you believe it?" Carrie told Mom, showing off her skis. "Tyler's got the exact same brand and color as mine."

"Well, isn't that nice," Mom said, running out of things to say, it seemed.

"Where's Daddy?" Carrie asked.

Sean pointed to the inside stairs. "He had a phone call to make. He'll be down soon."

Mom would surely take that as her cue to get going. I didn't think she'd want to have a face-to-face meeting with Daddy. Especially not in front of us kids.

Mom hugged Carrie and me. "Please be careful on the slopes, Carrie." Then she turned to me. "Take your time, and no stunts, okay?"

I assured her that we'd be safe. With a wave and a final good-bye, Mom left the lodge.

Sean and I sat together on a brown leather sofa in an alcove away from the doors. Several times my ski boots bumped his by accident. He turned to face me. His skin was as tan as I remembered. "Your mom reminds me of *my* mother," he said.

"She does?" It was hard to believe his mom was still babying him.

He nodded. "Boy, I would love to take my niece and nephew skiing here in Colorado," he said. It was obvious they were one of his favorite topics.

Ten minutes zipped by, maybe because Sean was so easy to talk to. Soon Daddy came downstairs.

"Hello, girls," he called to us. I stood up to greet him. But his hug stirred up strange feelings of resentment in me. It was still hard to handle—him leaving us behind just for a new job. I covered up by smiling and enjoying the scent of his spicy cologne as he held me tight.

"Let's hit the slopes," hollered Tyler.

"Yippee," Carrie shouted.

Sean held the door for us, and his smile warmed my heart. It was going to be a fabulous day after all.

While Daddy bought lift tickets, we unlocked our skis from the rack and snapped them on. Soon we were in the lift line, eager to ski down the mountain. Tyler and Carrie, Daddy and me, and Sean—alone—behind us.

At the last minute, the lift operator motioned for a girl to share the lift with Sean. That's when I wished I'd let Daddy ride by himself.

Up, up the cable pulled us toward the cloudless sky. The sun sent its rays, warming our faces, and just below us on the slopes, three guys were skiing in shorts, without their shirts.

"It's not *that* warm today," I commented. "Even for spring ski season."

Daddy seemed preoccupied with his own thoughts. A soft breeze tickled my face as I glanced at him.

"Your grandmother wrote to say that you're moving," he said. It was like he'd been waiting for just the right moment to bring it up.

Oh great. Not that.

"Yeah. Next weekend," I said, feeling my throat constrict. It was awkward discussing this. The exact same situation that had set him and Mom up for the fight of their lives.

"How do you feel about living in Denver?" He was probing, and I hated it.

"Nobody wants to leave best friends behind," I said, blowing air through my lips. "Especially not me. This place is my life."

"How is your best friend taking it?" Daddy asked.

"Andie hates the idea, too, but she's not my only best friend," I explained. "Paula Miller is also a close friend. The three of us do everything together."

"How's school?" Daddy asked.

"Fine." I told him about the blizzard and being stranded overnight last week. "Up here, the weather changes so fast."

I could see the lift landing coming up quickly. Thank goodness it was time to get off. I was tired of making small talk with Daddy. What I really wanted to say to him would have to be said in private. Someday.

Tyler and Carrie waited for us. Then, when Sean joined us, we split into two groups. Daddy went with Carrie and Tyler, leaving Sean alone with me.

The morning flew by as we skied down the blue runs together. My time with Sean actually seemed to evaporate as the day progressed.

Soon it was lunchtime, and Daddy treated us to a cozy dinner in the lodge—in the most expensive section—complete with candles on each table. He could afford it, all right. Like Mom said, his business out west had gone well. *Too* well, maybe.

♥ ♥ ♥

Sean seemed reluctant to say good-bye at the end of the day. "I hope we can ski together again sometime," he said with a warm smile.

"That'd be fun." I wished Carrie and Tyler wouldn't hang around so much then. "Let me know when you're flying out again."

He reached for a tiny blue address book from his inside pocket. "Mind if I get your phone number?" I told him, and he wrote it down quickly. "You'll have to send me your new address when you get settled in Denver."

I felt giddy, just the way I had when we'd first talked on the beach. I excused myself to call Mom to pick us up.

Sean was eager to talk again when I returned from the phone. "I want to be sure to keep you informed about your dad," he said, a serious look crossing his face.

"What do you mean?" I asked, suddenly concerned.

"I know you've been praying for him—Tyler told me you were a Christian."

"Then you must be, too," I said, excited at this tidbit of information.

He burst into a near-angelic grin. "I can hardly wait for your dad to accept Jesus."

"Do you know about Daddy's friend? The one at the office who gave him the gospel of Matthew?" I was dying to know more about that.

"You bet I do. He's my oldest brother, the father of my niece and nephew," Sean said, eyes shining.

"Wow," I whispered. "Small world."

"Sure is," he agreed. "I only wish Colorado were a little closer to California."

I knew I was blushing right through my sunburn about now.

And that's when Carrie waved me over. Mom had pulled the van up and was waiting outside for us, the engine running. Carrie and I said our good-byes to Daddy, Tyler, and Sean.

"We'll be in touch," Daddy called after us as we headed out the door of the lodge.

"Bye, Daddy," Carrie said. "Come back to Colorado soon."

As we hauled our boots and skis to the van, I hoped with all my heart Sean was right about Daddy. Was he really *that* close to making the all-important decision?

Chapter 18

I knew something was brewing as soon as I showed up for Sunday school the next day. The second I walked in, the kids clammed up. Even Jared and Billy, who were usually boisterous—till the teacher told them to cool it—were silent.

Things were winding down fast, with only six days remaining in Dressel Hills. Six days to say good-bye to lifelong friends. Besides all that, today was my last day at church. No wonder everyone was so solemn.

Jared was actually nice to me. Danny too. But then, Danny was always nice, and I was sure what Andie and Paula suspected was true: Danny Myers still liked me. I could tell by the way he kept smiling at me.

Things had changed so much in one year. Going from zero special guy friends to three—counting Sean—was like having to choose from three favorite ice-cream flavors at once.

After class, everyone except Andie and Paula headed upstairs, leaving us behind. "That's strange," I said. "They sure didn't hang around long."

"Oh, they'll probably say good-bye to you at school next week," offered Paula, no doubt trying to make me feel better. But it wasn't working. I felt sad.

We hurried upstairs to the sanctuary, where the organist was already playing the call to worship. I sat with Andie and Paula, since it was my last Sunday. At least for a while. Mom didn't know it, but I was already hoping to return to Dressel Hills someday soon.

The pastor's text was from Philippians 2:4. "Each of you should look not only to your own interests, but also to the interests of others." His sermon was titled "Poor Me"—about feeling sorry for yourself, conducting pity parties. I listened carefully, but wished he'd chosen Matthew 18:19 instead. Deep in my heart, I was still praying, along with Andie and Paula, that something would happen to change things around.

After church, Andie and Paula hurried off to catch up with their families. I walked toward the parking lot with Carrie and Stephie on either side of me. I already missed my friends. The friends I'd planned to grow up with.

❤ ❤ ❤

Mom's famous pot roast was extra juicy today. I ate heartily, instead of picking like I usually do when I'm depressed. There were scarcely any leftovers. Too bad for Uncle Jack. He loved them.

We had just cleared the dining room table when the doorbell rang. Carrie squealed, "I'll get it," and raced off to the living room

I stayed in the kitchen, rinsing scraps of food off the dishes. Next thing I knew, Carrie was tapping me on the shoulder.

"I think you'd better come with me," she said, wearing a sly grin.

I dried my hands, wondering what she was up to.

That's when I discovered a living room full of friends, including Jared, Andie, Paula, Danny . . . even our youth pastor.

"Surprise!" they yelled as I stood there, overcome with shock.

I turned to Danny, who happened to be standing nearby. "What's this about?"

He leaned over to whisper in my ear. "It's a surprise going-away party for you."

"Oh," I said, stunned. Then the tears started. "Excuse me a sec." I stumbled through the dining room and into the kitchen. "Quick, Mom! I need a tissue."

She led me to the desk in the corner of the kitchen. "Here, honey." She pulled several tissues out of the Kleenex box.

I blubbered, "I love my friends, all of them—even Jared." I surprised myself with that. But it was true. In spite of everything, I still cared.

After wiping my eyes and blowing my nose for the second time, I followed Mom into the living room, where everyone started clapping.

Andie stepped forward. "Holly," she began. "In case you don't know by now, we love you. A lot." I could see Jared nodding his head out of the corner of my eye.

"Pretty soon," she continued, "our moms will be arriving with some more surprise stuff."

I couldn't believe it.

"Sit right here," Paula said, making room for me on the rocking chair. "While we wait for the goodies, we each have a gift for you." She was starting to sound a little choked up, too. "We want to help you remember us forever."

Mom patted my shoulder, trying to comfort me. I took a deep breath and began opening cards and presents from all my friends.

By the time Andie's mom showed up with the other mothers, I already had a pile of gifts. Poetry from Jared. And a red rose. (Why was I not surprised?) A set of best-friend Velcro twin bears—give one to a friend and one to keep. From Andie.

Paula's gift was an adorable pink stuffed kitten with the name *Goofey-ette* written on the tag. Danny gave me a teen study Bible, complete with pen and notebook. It was signed with the date and his name on the first page.

Billy Hill's gift was a silver charm for my bracelet—a tiny

crutch—to help me remember the trick we'd played on Andie last year. Joy had wrapped a beautiful heart-shaped diary in music paper with hearts for notes. Shauna gave me a book about pen pals with a list of international Christian organizations.

Pastor Rob had a special gift from the pastoral staff. It was a gift certificate for a free lift ticket. "We want you to come ski with us," he said, grinning.

I looked around the room at my fabulous friends, some sitting on the floor, others standing around. "I promise not to cry if you promise to come visit me in Denver."

Andie waved her hands. "We'll come, all right. Two at a time," she said, looking at Paula.

I glanced up at Mom. She was wiping tears from her own eyes. That's when a giggle escaped my lips. Not because anything was funny; it was a burst of pent-up emotion. "Thank you so much," I said.

The kids applauded.

Mom rang her dinner bell, and all of us squeezed into the dining room. After a prayer by Pastor Rob, some of the kids spilled into the kitchen to make room. Pig-out time! Mrs. Martinez had brought several gallons of strawberry ice cream. And there were two angel food cakes—my favorite.

Over the din of the crowd, Jared made an announcement directed to me. "After this, we've planned another surprise."

I studied him. "There's more?"

He nodded, working his way through the group toward me. Then, pulling me aside—actually all the way into the living room— he began apologizing. "Holly, I'm sorry about everything. You were right. It doesn't really matter whether you call yourself my girlfriend anymore," he said. "I just want you to know, before you leave, that I'll always miss you."

I smiled. "I'll miss you, too, Jared."

He winked at me. "Friends?"

"Forever," I said, taking his hand and leading him back to the festivities.

After multiple desserts, Jared and Andie directed me and the rest of our friends out the front door and down the street. All of us made a human friendship chain with our hands. People driving by gawked, but we didn't care.

At the bus stop, we waited together, including Stan, who had just arrived home from the library. Andie looked mighty glad to see him again.

My big surprise turned out to be a city bus tour of Dressel Hills. A clever way to say good-bye to my beloved town. Jared even moved to let Danny sit beside me from the Explore Bookstore back to Downhill Court. Incredible.

When we arrived at my house again, it was hard to say good-bye to everyone. One by one, the kids went home, until Andie and Jared were the only ones left.

I walked with them to the driveway, where I threw my arms around Andie. She hugged me like never before, clinging to me and sobbing in my ear.

"Maybe it won't work out in Denver," she cried. "Maybe you and your family will be back in a few weeks."

Poor Jared stood there sort of embarrassed while Andie and I gushed about our loyalty to each other.

And then they were both gone.

Thank goodness I had five more days of school before the final good-byes. Otherwise, I probably would have gone upstairs and fainted on the spot.

♥ ♥ ♥

By Tuesday night, I had packed nearly all my personal belongings except the clothes I planned to wear. The big stuff, like beds and other furnishings, was scheduled to go out the door on Friday morning. The movers could do their thing without us kids around. Thank goodness for small blessings.

Paula Miller's dad, Uncle Jack's business partner, had invited us to spend our last night in their home. They, of course, would remain in Dressel Hills, and Mr. Miller would run the downtown office for Uncle Jack.

I tried to share my feelings during family devotions after supper, but tonight I could hardly speak. *We're moving. We're actually moving. We have to leave Dressel Hills* were the thoughts going through my mind. The hideous chant tumbled over and over in my brain. How could Carrie and Mom and the rest of the family be so calm about this? So glib? I couldn't bear to think of our remaining three days here.

Some way, somehow, God would have to work a miracle. Either that or give me the grace to bear this. I was afraid it would be the latter.

Paula had told me at school that she'd invited Andie to spend Friday night with us. It would be our final farewell.

♥ ♥ ♥

Wednesday after school, Andie came home with me. Homework was the excuse, but actually it was a way to spend extra time together before the worst day of all—moving day.

We hopped off the bus and walked the half block to my house. Andie jabbered about plans to visit me in Denver during spring break. "It'll be so cool," she said. I knew she was trying to make me feel better. "Let's go to Casa Bonita and pig out on Mexican food" was one of her ideas.

"And don't forget the Imax theatre," I said, referring to the giant screen near the Natural History Museum.

We walked on in silence. There seemed to be nothing left to say.

Turning the corner, we headed up Downhill Court. There was my beloved home: the tan split-level house Daddy and Mom had designed and built. I would miss the beautiful view of the mountains from its windows. And the deck where we'd spent so many warm summer evenings. And my beloved window seat . . .

As I stared at the house, it looked lonely, empty . . . like something was missing.

"Something's different," I said, pausing in the driveway.

Andie stood still. "What is it?"

Surveying the front yard, my eyes spotted something weird. I walked across the grass, over the melting snow piles, and peered at a hole in the ground. My heart sped up as I turned to Andie. "Someone's ripped out the For Sale sign. Come on!"

We dashed up the steps and into the house. "Mom!" I shouted. "What's happened to—"

Just then Uncle Jack emerged from the garage, carrying the sign. "Someone looking for this?" A mischievous smile danced across his face.

"What's going on?" I said, and Andie started screaming and hugging me at the same time.

Uncle Jack explained, "The partner we had in mind for the Denver office changed his mind. He's going to take the job."

"So we're staying here?" I asked.

"For the time being," he said.

I danced around the room, shouting for joy. Mom came downstairs, grinning. "Looks like someone's very happy," she said. "Thank goodness the house didn't sell out from under our noses."

Andie took my hand and pulled me upstairs. She closed my bedroom door and made me sit on my window seat. "This is so cool," she gushed. "It's *fabulous!*"

"I can't believe it," I said. My mind was racing to catch up.

Snatching my Bible off the nightstand, she giggled. "Read it and weep," she said, opening to Matthew 18:19. "Man, did this work, or what."

"Thank you, Lord," I said, my hands clasped heavenward. "You were almost too late."

"Hey, you oughta know better than that," Andie scolded. Then a smile burst across her face. "Good-bye, Denver," she shouted.

I laughed. "Hello, world!"

HOLLY'S HEART

Straight-A Teacher

For my dear readers,

especially those who share

heart secrets with me.

STRAIGHT-A TEACHER

Chapter 1

I was late for fourth-period choir. Really late. Today Miss Hess, our choral director, was auditioning students for the lead role of Maria in *The Sound of Music*. And I was competing against all my girl friends for the part.

Holding on to my notebook, I heaved the rest of my books into my locker and slammed the door. Then I dashed down the hall, past the principal's office, and spun around the corner.

Whoosh! I plowed into someone. My notebook flew out of my hands, creating a fan of loose papers all over the floor.

"I'm sorry," I gasped, looking up. And there he was: The cutest guy I had ever seen. Soft gray eyes. A flash of a dimple in his smile. And just a hint of a five-o'clock shadow.

"Are you all right?" His gentle tone took my breath away.

I mumbled a pathetic apology. "I'm really s-sorry." Stuttering wasn't my style, but this guy . . . My heart flipped and fluttered like some poor, unsuspecting fish dragged up on the sand.

"Are you sure you're all right?" he asked again, his eyes still concerned.

I managed a nod.

"It was my fault," he insisted, leaning over to gather up my papers.

Slightly dazed, I reached for my notebook. It was then I noticed the navy blue sleeve of his sweater and his nicely pressed khakis. This guy was too young to be a parent, he was certainly not a teacher, and he was too old for junior high. In fact, I'd never seen him around Dressel Hills before.

Slowly standing, he handed the pile of papers to me, glancing at the one on top. "Holly Meredith," he remarked as he studied it. "Are you a teacher's assistant?" His eyes twinkled as he spoke.

Surprised, I shook my head slowly. Again his eyes met mine.

"I'd better hurry," I heard myself say. With a fleeting smile, I scurried off to the stairway and up to the music room.

As I pushed open the choir room door, Miss Hess stood behind a music stand, organizing her music folder. She wore a blue skirt and funky shirt. More fashion conscious than the older teachers, Miss Hess had a wardrobe that just wouldn't quit.

Jared grinned at me from the tenor section, and Andie and Paula motioned for me to sit between them in the alto section. I hurried to take my seat.

"You're late," Andie whispered. It wasn't just a statement; she wanted details.

I fidgeted, not ready to divulge my encounter with the sweater-and-pressed-khakis guy. Just how old was he, anyway? I called up his face in my imagination. The hint of a beard and the way he dressed told me he was in his late teens—or early twenties. I still couldn't believe he'd actually mistaken me for a grown woman!

Andie jabbed me in the ribs. "Snap to it, Meredith," she whispered.

Still giddy, I tried to pay attention as Miss Hess gave instructions for the tryouts. "To cut down on after-school time, we're having auditions during class," she began. "*The Sound of Music* is a classic, as all of you probably know. The roles of Maria and Captain von Trapp will involve major commitment on the part of the girl and guy who win the leads this year." She paused, studying the competition perched on the risers around us.

Commitment? Dedication? Shoot, I'd ingest frog legs for the part of Maria! But then, so would Andie on my right and Paula on my left. I sighed.

Behind us, little sevies sat in clusters of four or more, exchanging nervous whispers and frantic looks, while we sophisticated female students of Dressel Hills Junior High—eighth graders, of course—sat poised and calm. As always, there were a few top-of-the-heap ninth graders acting disgustingly pert and casually cool on the back row of the risers—the Pinnacle of Pride. The truly cool ninth graders, like Danny Myers and my friend Paula's twin, Kayla Miller, sat closer to the front.

Miss Hess began to hand out copies of the script, a stack to each row. Danny offered to help her. When he passed my row, he made a point to catch my eye. "Break a leg, Holly," he said. The twinkle in his eye was hard to ignore. That was Danny, a super-serious Christian and a very encouraging guy.

I returned his smile. "Thanks. You too." But secretly, my heart sank. What if he *did* get the part of Captain von Trapp? And what if I was Maria? Yikes! We'd have to act like we were in love. *That would add fuel to the fire,* I thought, remembering what Andie had said last week. She thought Danny still liked me. We'd had our chance at a special friendship last summer. But now the redhead—well, auburn, really—was merely my good friend. End of story.

Andie poked me again. "Who's that?" she whispered, staring at a tall, good-looking guy conferring with Miss Hess across the room.

The sweater triggered my memory. I jerked to attention as Miss Hess introduced him.

"Class, I'd like you to meet my student teacher. Mr. Barnett will assist me as drama coach throughout the remaining weeks of the semester," she explained. "We are truly fortunate to have this talented young man on board."

The student teacher smiled as we applauded. "Thanks," he said, glancing around the room. "I'm looking forward to working with each of you to make this the best performance ever." With that, he picked up his notebook and sat on the risers with the tenors, like one of the guys.

My heart thumped as I watched him pull a pen out of his shirt pocket, underneath his sweater. His hands moved with such purpose. Like a seasoned professor of drama, he was prepared to eliminate the competition, narrowing us down to the choice few. Mr. Barnett clicked his pen, and unexpectedly, he turned and caught my stare. Embarrassed, I looked down at the script portion in my lap. If I was to try out for Maria, I'd better focus on things at hand. This audition could be tricky.

After giving us several minutes to study scripts, Miss Hess asked for volunteers to read parts. Amy-Liz, a spunky, curly-haired soprano, raised her hand. Mr. Barnett met her alongside the piano. He leaned on the console piano and briefly discussed the scene. Then Amy-Liz stood tall and began the scene without ever refer- ring to the script!

But an even bigger surprise followed. Mr. Barnett began play- ing the part of Captain von Trapp. It was a romantic scene, where he tells Maria he loves her.

Miss Hess stopped the scene, encouraging Amy-Liz to act more in love. *So that's what she wants,* I thought, carefully scanning the script. A super-romantic female lead? I fidgeted as the scene progressed.

"I can pour on the mushy stuff, if that's what it takes," Andie whispered in my ear.

I really wanted to tell her: *Please mess up!* But all I said was, "Better be careful, Stan's watching." Stan, my fifteen-year-old cousin- turned-stepbrother, was her longest-running boyfriend ever.

Soon it was Andie's turn. She hardly waited for Amy-Liz to sit down before she started. She was doing fine until she totally blew it by giggling halfway through the scene. It was the most immature thing imaginable!

By the end of the hour, most of my friends had auditioned

for the part of Maria, including Paula Miller and her twin, Kayla. Jared Wilkins, my former guy friend, kept staring at me from the opposite side of the risers, trying to get me to try out next. Even though we were simply friends these days, he still liked to flirt with me a little.

Danny watched me, too. Was he worried I'd get the part, opposite some other guy? He kept crossing his legs, first the right, then the left. It was obvious he was restless. Maybe he wasn't so sure about watching me audition the part. Of course, there would be no real romantic stuff, just the script.

"Well, are you gonna audition or not?" Andie asked.

I could tell by the gleam in her eye that she hoped I'd back out.

"Of course!" I answered, thinking Andie would make a better von Trapp *kid* than Maria.

Miss Hess called my name. "Hurry, Holly," she said, glancing at the clock. "We have time for one more."

It should be easy now, after observing so many girls audition the part. I made my way down the risers, feeling comfortable with the text and the action. . . .

But there was Mr. Barnett's face again. His eyes seemed to search out mine, of all the possible Marias in the room. It was as though he could see me, look through the layers of me . . . into the real Holly Meredith.

Breathing deeply, I began.

Chapter 2

From the moment I opened my mouth to speak, it was as though Mr. Barnett and I were alone in the room. Alone, except for the rhythmic interplay of dialogue and drama. Effortlessly, I blocked out the observers. To my thinking, the two of us quickly became the actual characters we portrayed. He, the older Captain Georg von Trapp, and I, the younger, innocent Maria. When he said his lines, his face seemed to light up.

The applause startled me as the scene came to an end. "Encore!" I heard Jared yelling.

"Go, Meredith!" Stan hollered.

Sad that it had to end, I relished the applause.

We were fabulous together, Mr. Barnett and I. *Too bad he isn't a student,* I thought. But then the maturity he possessed would be missing. That thought settled over me as the clapping swelled to a roar. I was careful not to expose my true emotions as I returned to my seat between Andie and Paula.

Paula made a circle with her thumb and pointer finger. "Par excellence," she said. But her weak smile gave her away. I knew how badly she wanted the part.

Andie grabbed my arm, a bit harder than usual. "Hey, you

missed the giggling part!" she teased. I could tell she was afraid she'd blown it with her laughter.

"Yeah, right." I pulled away from her viselike grip.

Danny's serious gaze caught my eye as I glanced at the tenor section. What was *he* thinking?

Miss Hess grinned from her desk. "A stunning performance," she said, looking first at Mr. Barnett, then at me. Had she forgotten the other prospective Marias in the room? Quickly, she composed herself and announced, "We've had many wonderful Marias today. And Mr. Barnett and I will post the winner on Friday. Tomorrow, we'll be on the lookout for our best Captain. Get ready, guys!"

Jared raised his hand. "Who's playing Maria for *our* auditions?"

"You're looking at her." Miss Hess curtsied comically.

I felt someone tap my shoulder and turned to see a folded note on the floor behind me. I picked it up and read it.

Dear Holly,
Will you sit with me at youth group this Thursday? I'll call you soon.

Very sincerely,
Danny

Andie wasn't kidding! Danny *was* interested. No wonder he'd watched my every move today. No wonder he seemed to have a tough time while I pretended to be in love with Mr. Barnett . . . er, Captain von Trapp.

"Better watch out," Andie whispered, eyeing the note. "Next thing you know, you'll have Danny Myers running your life again."

"Fat chance." I stuffed the note into my pocket and grabbed my notebook just as the bell rang. Hurrying to my locker, with Andie at my side, I replayed the audition in my mind.

♥ ♥ ♥

After school, at home, I trembled as I wrote in my journal.

Monday, April 11: What a fabulous day! Today was the begin-ning of something incredible and new. Miss Hess introduced us to our gorgeous student teacher: Mr. Barnett. I ran into him in the hall on the way to choir. And then he auditioned with me when I tried out for the part of Maria. To think that when we met, he thought I was a student teacher, like him!

I put my pen down and read my journal entry, thinking. And then it came to me—the perfect way to get to know Mr. Barnett better. Why hadn't I thought of this before? I would interview him for the school paper. Fabulous idea!

Writing for *The Lift* was something new for me. I had just seen my first article in print—a lighthearted interview with the cafeteria cook. It had taken lots of work, including the actual interview, the rough draft, and the rewriting—three or four times. But for Mr. Barnett, I was more than willing to put in the required additional work.

I picked up my pen and twirled it between my fingers, reliving the collision in the hall, how his eyes met mine. . . .

Thoughts of Danny crept into my head. Could I handle him in a diplomatic fashion? I didn't want to hurt him. Not again.

It all came rushing back. Last summer, Danny and I had been good buddies. He'd even rescued me from a horrid-smelling out-house at the top of Copper Mountain! But it had taken all summer for him to finally ask me to be his girlfriend. Of course, we were both too young to actually date, but we enjoyed our special friend-ship for a while, with things coasting along fine between us. But soon he was trying to run my life. With the Bible, no less!

It was a nightmare. And finally I had called it quits by storming out of the Soda Straw during a church ice-cream social. Danny had been humiliated, and I felt lousy. Eventually, we worked things out between us so we could be friends again—just the way we were now. The way we were going to stay.

I went to the hall phone and called him. He answered on the first ring. *Too eager,* I thought.

"Hi, Danny," I said. "Got your note."

"That's good." He sounded nervous, really nervous.

"You know, we've discussed all this before," I began.

"I know, still—"

I interrupted him. "It won't work, Danny. You're one of my best friends. Can't we keep it that way?"

I could hear him breathing. Sort of. "You okay?" I asked, feeling sad for him.

"Sure, Holly, I'm fine. But think about it, okay?"

I hated being so hard on him. For one thing, I knew it had taken loads of courage to send this note. For another thing, he was a year older, and I wanted to look up to him, to respect him. But his pleading like this bugged me.

Sounding a bit dejected, Danny hung up. Hopefully the boy-girl issue was behind us now.

I sat down and pondered the selection of male students at Dressel Hills Junior High. "Boys my age are a waste of time," I said to myself.

♥ ♥ ♥

Tuesday after school, I stopped off to see Marcia Green, the student editor of *The Lift*. Peeking over her long desk, I noticed a few of the memos she'd written. My name appeared several times on yellow stickies posted on the wall near her desk. By the looks of things, she had other article ideas for me to pursue.

Marcia looked up from the manuscripts she was proofreading. "Hey, Holly. What's up?"

That's when I volunteered to interview Mr. Barnett for the April issue of *The Lift*.

"Great idea." Marcia picked up her pen and tapped it on the desk. "Thanks for the suggestion." I turned to leave, but she continued, "Stop by Thursday after lunch, Holly. I'll have some preliminary stuff for you on Mr. Barnett."

"Okay, thanks," I said.

She nodded, already preoccupied with her work, completely oblivious to what this article—and this interview—meant to me.

♥ ♥ ♥

At lunch on Wednesday, talk of the leading roles for the school musical buzzed everywhere. In hot-lunch line, at the tables . . . It hovered in the air. The guys were split on their personal choices for Maria. It appeared to be a close contest between Amy-Liz . . . and me. But Miss Hess was notorious for being unpredictable. At this stage, it was anyone's guess who'd be chosen for the female lead.

I sat in the cafeteria with Paula and Andie, at our usual spot next to the windows. Settling down with a bowl of chili smothered in cheese, I gazed out the window. Time and place disappeared as I daydreamed, staring at the mountains, the new foliage. Spring was here. New beginnings . . .

"Holly, you're doing it again," Andie's voice careened into my private thoughts.

"What?" I turned away from the window and dipped my spoon into the cheesy chili.

"You know what." She sounded exasperated.

"It's called daydreaming," Paula intervened. "Pure and simple, and there's no crime in it." She flashed her million-dollar smile.

"Thanks for your insight, Paula," I laughed.

"So . . . what's on your mind?" Andie was pushing.

I ignored her, sipping some milk.

"Oh, let me guess," Andie said. "You're dying for the part of Maria, right?"

It would've been so easy to agree with her, just to get her off my back. In fact, landing the role of Maria took only second place to what was really on my mind. The way I figured it, the girl getting the part of Maria would have the most time with Mr. Barnett.

"Maybe it's a secret," Paula offered, defending my right to privacy once again.

Andie snorted. "Could be, but if it is, Holly always breaks down and tells all. That's how she is." Her dark eyes danced with mischief.

It felt weird hearing her discuss my faults right under my nose.

Paula studied me with sympathetic eyes. She actually looked

prettier these days without the inch-thick mascara. "At this age, we're changeable," Paula said. "Holly will tell us what's on her mind when she wants to. It's our job as friends to be here for her."

Quickly, I changed the subject, before Andie had a chance for a comeback. Knowing her, she'd have one eventually. "Who do you think will get Captain von Trapp?" I asked.

Paula spoke up. "Danny's taller than most of the ninth-grade boys, but he can't act."

"He can memorize fast," I commented. "But you're right, Jared's the better actor and singer."

Andie chimed in. "I could see Jared and Amy-Liz onstage together."

"How can you *say* that?" I shot back. What a low blow! And from my best friend!

"Well, what do you want to hear?" she said. "I'd give anything to put myself in Maria's shoes—next to Jared's. How's that?"

I shook my head, not letting her get to me with her dumb remarks. "Let's just see who Miss Hess and Mr. Barnett pick for the part, okay?"

"Miss Hess seems fair enough, but I don't know about Mr. Barnett," Andie replied. "He's got his teacher's pets picked out already. I noticed it right away."

Gulp! What had Andie noticed?

Paula pulled on her brunette locks. "I don't think Mr. Barnett plays favorites. He's just super nice."

"Maybe you're right," Andie said without looking at me. She pushed her chair out and went to get more soda.

When Andie was out of earshot, Paula asked, "Do *you* think Mr. Barnett has favorites?"

I shrugged my shoulders, pretending not to care.

Jared came over and sat down. I breathed a sigh of relief as the conversation made a complete turn. Away from Mr. Barnett.

Chapter 3

Thursday during choir I did my best to avoid eye contact with Mr. Barnett. He sat on Miss Hess's desk, arms folded across his burgundy sweater, waiting for everyone to arrive.

Restless chatter filled the room as students, eager for tryouts, jostled and hooted back and forth. Today, auditions were being held for the abbey nuns, Sister Berthe and Sister Sophia, Franz the butler, and some of the older von Trapp children. I blocked out the noise, imagining my upcoming interview with Mr. Barnett. I, with my notebook and pen, poised to ask thoughtful, intelligent questions. *Just the two of us.*

"Earth to Holly," Andie whispered.

I jumped. "Huh?"

"You look dazed, girl," she said. "I think we better have a talk."

My cheeks grew warm as the lingering vision slowly faded. "About what?"

Andie's finger poked my enflamed cheek. "About that."

The din of chatter subsided as Mr. Barnett stood, notebook in hand. He cleared his throat. "Okay, students. This is home stretch."

Here, he scanned the room with his eyes. Once again they found mine, if only for an instant.

Heart thudding, I wondered how I'd ever find the courage to arrange my interview with him. After all, I would have to speak to him to set it up.

I stared at Miss Hess sitting at the piano. She listened intently as Mr. Barnett made announcements. Was she grading him mentally? Isn't that what supervising teachers had to do—grade their student teachers based on performance and progress? I couldn't imagine Mr. Barnett getting less than straight *A*'s.

The pink floral pattern in Miss Hess's below-the-knee skirt caught my attention. I stared at the shimmery oranges and swirling pinks. What was it like, spending each school day, every day, from now until the end of school with someone like Mr. Barnett? I envied Miss Hess.

After class, I took my sweet time gathering my things, hoping the classroom would clear out in a hurry. I didn't want Paula or Andie to know about the interview I was planning. So far, at least, my secret was safe.

"Hurry, Holly," Andie called over her shoulder, rushing for the door with Paula. "We'll save you a seat at lunch."

Lunch or not, I had to talk to Mr. Barnett about the interview. But now Danny was in my way—discussing props and stage management with him. Glancing over at the piano, I noticed that Miss Hess had already left for lunch, too. Fabulous timing! Now if only I could get Danny to disappear.

Eavesdropping on Danny's conversation with Mr. Barnett made me jittery. I shuffled my feet and self-consciously watched the clock on the wall. Its second hand jerked rhythmically, reminding me of how little time I had left for lunch.

Shifting my books, I gave up and headed out the door.

Danny caught up to me in the hall. "Holly, I'm finished," he said. "Thanks for waiting around."

Oh no, I thought. *He thinks I waited for him!*

"Can we eat together?" He followed me down the hall to my locker.

"I, uh . . . Andie and Paula . . . I think . . . are saving me a place."

"I don't mind sitting with your friends. If it's okay with you."

Of course it wasn't, but I nodded my consent anyway. It was the only decent thing to do after the way I'd treated him on the phone.

Andie's eyes nearly popped when Danny and I showed up together at lunch. I shot her a warning with my eyes. She caught the secret message—every bit of it. Andie knew better than to make some dumb remark about Danny and me.

We spent most of lunch discussing Mr. Barnett. Danny got it going. "What do you think of our new student teacher?"

"He knows theater, that's for sure," Paula said. "Did you see how he marked off the floor in the music room when Billy auditioned for the butler? I tell you, he's good."

"He wants me to be stage manager," Danny said.

"No fair. You know what you're gonna be before us," Andie teased, pretending to pout.

How childish, I thought, watching Andie mope. But deep inside, I was secretly relieved to know Danny was out of the running for the male lead.

"What do you think of Mr. Barnett?" Andie asked me. She leaned forward on the table, balancing herself on her elbows, her impish eyes flashing. She seemed to suspect something, and I resented her for asking me right in front of everyone. It was another one of her childish, more immature traits.

"Mr. Barnett?" I said casually, willing my pulse to slow. "I agree with Paula. He seems to know his stuff."

"That's it?" Andie said.

Danny stopped eating his spaghetti, which featured chunks of yellow-green mystery meat mixed with off-white worms, er, noodles.

I forced my gaze away from the worms of the week and focused on Danny's eyes, which were so close I could see gold flecks in them. It was as though he—and Paula and Andie—were waiting to pounce on my secret.

"What's there to say?" I responded. "I think Miss Hess should have a student teacher every year for the spring musical." I reached for my napkin.

If my friends only knew . . .

Danny excused himself from the table. "Nice having lunch with you, Holly." He turned beet red, no doubt realizing he'd eaten with all three of us.

"Any time at all," Andie piped up.

"See you, Danny," Paula said, smiling and waving.

It was a strained moment, all right. But the second Danny was out of sight, we burst out laughing. It wasn't fair to make fun of him, but Danny had it coming. He'd literally set himself up by acting like a love-sick toad.

I hurried off to the girls' rest room to wash my hands and check my hair. My plan was to intercept Mr. Barnett somehow. I needed to set up the interview with him. Not because I had a pressing editorial deadline, but because it was part of my plan. Besides, I was dying to talk to him. One mature soul to another.

I dried my hands, glancing at my watch. Time was running out! Hurrying into the hall, I scoped out the area for signs of Andie or Paula. Danny too. No way did I want them spying on me.

All clear. I dashed upstairs, heading for the music room. Tiptoeing up to the door, I peeked in the window.

Yes! He was there. Taking a deep breath, I knocked.

"Come in," he called.

Trembling, I turned the doorknob and let myself in.

"Oh, hello there, Holly," he said, looking up from his desk. He remembered my name! I nearly hyperventilated on the spot.

"Is something wrong?" A slight frown played across his brow.

"Oh, nothing's wrong," I said, trying to regain my composure. "I just wanted to talk to you about—"

Suddenly Miss Hess breezed into the room. "Andrew," she

called. "I need to see you in the teacher's lounge." A flirtatious smile played across her lips as she turned and left as quickly as she'd come.

Andrew?

"I'm very sorry, Holly," he apologized, standing up. "Can we talk later?"

I wanted to ask when but only nodded, standing there in a daze, watching the most wonderful guy in the world disappear through the choir room door.

I sighed. "His name is Andrew," I whispered reverently. In a fog, I stared at his cluttered desk, piled with papers and the open notebook. Suddenly the image of Mr. Barnett's precious notebook leaped out at me. There were students' names listed beside names of characters.

I froze, trying not to entertain the thought of snooping. Yet I was tempted. Tempted with one of my greatest weaknesses.

Think how easy it would be to take one quick look. One secret look. No one will ever have to know. . . .

It was the Garden of Eden all over again—Eve listening to the voice of the tempter. And just like Eve, I inched forward and reached for the forbidden fruit.

Chapter 4

I scanned the list. There was Danny Myers as stage manager, Stan Patterson, my stepbrother, as Rolf Gruber. Andie was listed beside Mother Abbess. I could almost hear her singing "Climb Every Mountain." I couldn't picture her, however, as the Reverend Mother of Nonnberg Abbey!

Laughing out loud, I ran my finger halfway down the list, searching for my name.

Br-ring! Br-ring! The fire alarm rang out. Startled, I ran out of the choir room. I couldn't see or smell any evidence of fire or smoke. Quickly, I headed for the nearest exit, slipping in line with other students. I was disappointed about not finding my name. Now I'd have to wait, like everyone else, till tomorrow morning.

Andie fell in line with me outside. "Probably just another silly drill," she said. "We've had twenty-five of them already this year."

"Not even close," I said, wondering why she had to exaggerate like that. Another sign of her lack of maturity.

Suddenly I spotted Mr. Barnett. He was hurrying out of the building with Miss Hess and several other teachers. I watched the way he walked, the way he interacted with them. I watched Miss

Hess, too. She seemed quite attentive to Mr. Barnett. Was it her way of being a good supervisory teacher, or was there more to it?

Jared joined us, his voice interrupting my thoughts. "This is some cool way to spend a lunch hour."

"Yeah," Andie said, eyeballing me. "What happened to *you*? One minute you were primping in the rest room, next thing, you were gone." Her eyes twinkled with a zillion questions.

Jared grinned, elbowing my arm. "Sounds like you've got a second mother here."

"I'm her guardian angel," Andie retorted. "She's sneaking around, up to something." She twisted a curl around her finger.

I tried to visualize Andie draped in the robes of the Mother Abbess. I couldn't help myself; I snickered.

"Now what?" she demanded.

"Oh, nothing." I waved my hand, flipping my long ponytail.

"You're hopeless," she said. "But I'll get to the bottom of this sooner or later." She probably would, too.

Several more minutes passed before the all-clear bell rang and we filed inside. Fifth hour was pending, so we headed like a herd of cattle to the rows of lockers.

♥ ♥ ♥

After school, I dropped in to see Marcia Green about the interview stuff. I held my breath as she thumbed through her notebook. "Let's see," she muttered to herself. "I know it's here somewhere."

Pulling up a chair, I waited impatiently for Marcia to find my new assignment. I twisted my hair and bit on the ends. Crazy as it seemed, I was actually going to interview Mr. Andrew Barnett!

"Here it is." Marcia held up the file at last. "I'll need good copy by next week." She looked at the calendar. "Next Thursday, a week from today. Think you can squeeze it into your schedule?"

"No problem," I said, taking the file. The name in black marker leaped off the file at me.

Andrew Barnett.

His name alone made my heart jump. Could I still it long enough to conduct a reasonably intelligent interview? The thought flamed my cheeks. I dashed down the hall, hoping to create a breeze strong enough to fan my flushed face. Had to before Andie saw me and pumped me with questions.

"Holly, wait up!"

It was Andie. But I kept going, blowing air out my lips. Another couple of seconds and maybe, just maybe, the red would drain from my cheeks. . . .

"Listen, girl, if you don't slow down, you'll attract Coach Tucker's attention for sure," Andie hollered.

She had me.

I turned around. "Miss Tucker better not nab me for track try-outs," I muttered. "I despise running."

"But it's that time of year," Andie sang, "track and field." Then she searched my face. "You're blushing again. *Now* what's going on?"

We'd had this conversation before. "It's nothing, really." No way could I tell her. I shoved Mr. Barnett's file down, out of sight.

We pushed through the crowded hallway. "Holly, you're avoiding me," she said.

"Right." I laughed. "That's impossible."

The sound of slamming lockers and the bustle of scurrying students interrupted my thoughts. When we stopped at Andie's locker, she flicked through her combination and pulled on the door. I hurried to my locker, opened it, and stuffed the file safely behind another notebook just as Andie came over.

Although I was usually perfectly content to be in Andie's company and was comfortable with our ongoing friendship, I was discovering more and more that I didn't want to expose my heart for examination with her like I used to. Andie was developing a high-and-mighty way about her. *Evolving,* my mother had said. Well, whatever it was, Andie was establishing a know-it-all attitude that made me uneasy.

Stan showed up and Andie beamed at him. Andie turned to

me with that all-too-familiar glint in her eye. "We're off to the Soda Straw, Holly. But I guarantee you'll tell me your little secret, sooner or later." She accented her words with a bang of her locker and a rambunctious wave.

Overconfident. That described Andie, all right. It seemed she was forever rehearsing the part of an outspoken, self-assured woman. Hopefully, by the time she grew up, Andie would learn not to fire shots that pierced the soul of her friends. Maybe she would learn something from the role of Mother Abbess.

I began sorting my books as I analyzed my relationship with Andie. It had never been easy keeping secrets from her. She was absolutely right; I always poured out my heart to her . . . eventually. Came from years of growing up together in Dressel Hills, Colorado. In a tiny ski village like this, it was easier to opt for one or two best friends over gobs of casual ones. At least for me.

Still, I needed to share my secret with someone. It was so warm and fabulous. Such a beautiful secret should be shared with some-one like Andie. I knew she'd be straight with me. I'd never known her to hold back if she felt strongly enough about something. And that's what I needed now, someone who could think clearly about this—whatever it was—that I was feeling for Mr. Barnett.

Danny met me on the stairs as I took two at a time, still hoping to catch Mr. Barnett. His eyes lit up when he saw me. "Are you coming to youth service tonight?" he asked.

I stopped and leaned against the wall, catching my breath. "I think so, why?" Then I remembered his note and my phone call to him. It irritated me. I thought this matter had been settled between us.

Danny hesitated. "We're grouping up for Bible Quiz Team. And . . . I hoped you'd be my partner."

"Me?" I shrieked. "Danny, you've got to be kidding. You can memorize whole chapters of the Bible in one shot. There's no way I can keep up with you."

"I'll help you," he said softly.

That's what I was afraid of. He wanted to tutor me—one on one.

Much too cozy. Besides, if I were in the musical, I'd need tons of extra time to memorize my lines. "I'm sorry, Danny. I really can't." I thought of suggesting Paula's twin sister, Kayla, or someone else for him to team up with at church, but I didn't.

Slowly, Danny nodded. "Well, see you around," he said and left.

I was determined not to let his reaction get to me. After all, it was only quiz team.

Thankful the Danny encounter was over, I raced upstairs, hoping to find Mr. Barnett. I thought about casually wandering into the choir room, pretending to sort music or something. Maybe he'd notice and strike up a conversation. But as I approached the door, I knew the mature thing to do was simply knock.

"Come in," he called. His voice sounded much lower than Danny's. Or any other guy's at school, for that matter.

I hesitated, then took a breath for courage and walked in.

"Hi again." He was seated behind the keyboard, and something about the way he looked up to greet me startled me. Shafts of light from the late afternoon sun streamed through the long, vertical windows behind the choir risers.

I peered round the room. Empty. At last, a chance to talk. The hustle-bustle of the school day seemed distant somehow as I returned his smile. With all my heart, I wanted to hold this moment close—memorize it for always.

Still seated behind his keyboard, he motioned to a chair. "Please, sit down." I noticed nut shells strewn on top of his keyboard. "I'm a pistachio nut junkie. Here, have one."

The sheer joy of being here might have left me wordless and clumsy, but like the time of my audition, I felt a strange openness and sense of ease with him. "Thanks," I said, surprised at the way the words spilled out so easily. I took a few nuts and cracked them open.

"So . . . how are things?" he asked. Cool and easy.

"Fine, thanks," I said. *Would it shock him to know I think of him nearly every waking minute?*

"I'm working on a new song," he remarked. "Tell me what you think." And he began to play. The minor melody drifted down like a mountain brook in June. And when it found a resting place in a gentle broken chord, it took my breath away.

"It's beautiful," I said, longing for more. "It reminds me of a bittersweet book I read once."

"This song is in memory of my grandmother," he said.

I was surprised and pleased that he was sharing such personal information.

"I wish she could hear it." I paused, wondering when I should ask about the interview.

He glanced up at the skylight, neck tilted back slightly. "Sometimes I think she does."

I nodded, smiling. "For me, music paints word pictures. I listen to it when I write."

"My sister's a writer," he said.

"Creativity must run in your family," I said without thinking. "It shows up in the way you teach."

His hands slid off the keyboard and into his lap, and he leaned back. "You are a very perceptive young woman, Holly."

I felt my cheeks do their usual cherry number, but he looked so pleased with my statement, I didn't let it embarrass me. I pulled out my tablet and pen and asked if he had time for a quick interview. "It's for the school paper. I'm one of the reporters."

"Absolutely," he said. At that moment, I couldn't have been happier.

Chapter 5

The interview sailed by, smooth and easy. I asked the usual journalistic questions, prompted by the five *W*'s. Things like why he'd chosen to major in education, who were his mentors, and what he hoped to do when he graduated from college.

Only once were we interrupted. The janitor came in to empty the trash. Later, I thought I heard the *cre-e-ak* of the door, but when I turned to investigate, no one was there.

Satisfied that the interview was complete, I stood to go. "Thank you for your time, Mr. Barnett. It was nice getting acquainted with you." *If he only knew . . .*

"I've heard you have an excellent way with words, Holly," he said, smiling again. "I'll look forward to seeing your story in *The Lift*."

"Thanks." I reached for my notebook.

He seemed reluctant for me go. "Above all," he added, "I hope you keep working at your creative goals."

"Thanks," I said again. Slipping my pen into my backpack, I looked up. That's when his eyes met mine. And I knew, sure as anything, that I had hopelessly fallen for this student teacher.

♥　♥　♥

That night at youth service, a bunch of kids signed up for the Bible Quiz Team. By the looks of the quiz team T-shirts sales, it was a big deal.

"Who're you going to study with?" Stan asked as we came in together. Before I could respond, Andie walked over to him.

"Got a partner yet?" she asked Stan.

He sat down, crossing his long legs. He leaned back and merely grinned.

Here comes John Wayne, I thought. But I was wrong. Today it was Stan Patterson himself. "I'm thinking about it," he said.

Andie giggled, probably holding her breath for him to pick her as his team study partner.

When Danny showed up, I scooted down in my chair. No way could I survive a repeat performance with him. Paula and Kayla Miller arrived just in time, and I waved them over. Paula had established a strong identity all her own. I noticed it as she fluffed her soft shoulder-length curls. Kayla, her twin, seemed content minus the look-alike aspect.

I sighed with relief as I glanced down the row of chairs. *Good, no room for Danny to barge in.*

Pastor Rob made an announcement. "If you didn't get a Bible Quiz Team card when you came in, please take one home. I'd like each of you to prayerfully consider being on the team or at least help with one of the fund-raisers. We'll be traveling to Denver and Grand Junction for regionals, so it's going to cost us some bucks."

I felt a twinge of guilt as I thought back to the flippant answers I'd given Danny this afternoon. It wasn't the idea of studying and memorizing Scripture that kept me from signing up. It was Danny himself.

Before the youth service ended, I slipped a card into my purse when Danny wasn't watching.

♥ ♥ ♥

The next day was Friday. Audition results! Bypassing my locker, I ran toward the stairs. Had I made it? Was I Maria? Halfway up the stairs, I remembered that I was much too mature to race around the school like this. Slowing to a more sophisticated pace, I made my way toward the music room.

The area was crammed with clusters of kids jockeying for position in front of the music bulletin board. I watched Andie's expression change from curiosity to horror when she saw her name beside the character of Mother Abbess. She'd wanted Maria. Who didn't?

Paula clenched her fists and shook them back and forth with glee when she discovered her name beside Liesl, the oldest daughter of the von Trapp family singers. Liesl, along with Mother Abbess, was a strong supporting role. She'd be playing opposite Stan. Wouldn't Andie die over that matchup?

I could hardly suffer the suspense any longer and pushed through the crowd. Head and shoulders above most of the girls, I could see my name clearly at the top of the list. *Holly Meredith— Maria.* I grinned with delight. This was so perfect.

Just below my name, Jared's name was listed. He was Captain Georg von Trapp. Talk about a nightmare!

Grabbing Andie, I bear-hugged her. "Can you believe it? I'm Maria!" I shouted amid the din of excitement.

She pulled back, glaring. "I should've known."

"Known what?" I demanded, trailing after her.

"C'mon, Holly. Are you brain-dead?" Her tennies slapped against the waxed floor as she hurried toward our lockers.

I grabbed her arm, like *she* usually does to me. "Spell it out, Andie."

She scrunched her face. "Teacher's pet," she snarled. "I saw what you did."

I swallowed hard. Had Andie spied on me doing the interview?

"You thought I was at the Soda Straw with Stan, didn't you?" Her dark eyes flashed with anger. "Well, you were wrong."

"I don't get it," I said, still puzzled.

"I came back to school yesterday to get my math assignment.

That's when I ran into Danny, looking pretty lousy. It's none of my business, but what did you say to him?" She took a quick breath. "Never mind. Danny told me you'd gone upstairs. And when I looked for you, there you were in the choir room, shooting the breeze with Mr. Barnett." She wouldn't let me toss a word in edgewise. "How does it feel to bribe a teacher into giving you the lead role?" Her accusing stare made me angry.

"You've got it wrong, Andie," I stated flatly. "You don't know what you're saying."

"Oh yeah?" She slammed her locker. "Guess again."

I couldn't believe it. "Please, don't do this," I said. "You're wrong—it was only an interview."

She didn't hang around to hear more. Off she flew, down the hall to first period. I opened my locker, refusing to let her childishness spoil my moment.

Maria! I'd actually landed the female lead. I could hardly wait to start working with Mr. Barnett.

♥ ♥ ♥

In science, Mr. Ross droned on about the number of neutrons in a given nucleus. I tried to listen, but this wasn't exactly my favorite subject. It came in a close second to getting my foot stuck in the toilet—unfortunately, a real-life occurrence.

I doodled while the less-than-fascinating lesson continued. *H.M. and A.B.* I wrote calligraphy-style complete with swirls and curls all around.

I proceeded to assess the age difference between Mr. Barnett and myself. Fourteen from twenty—only six years. Not bad. In a few years, say, when I was eighteen, he'd be twenty-four. And someday we'd both be in our twenties. That seemed appropriate enough. The older you get, the less the age thing matters. But . . . how could I be sure he'd still be around when I grew up?

Instead of taking notes, I pulled out my tablet from the interview yesterday. I'd have to be careful not to let anything too obvious slip, especially since Andie was on my trail. So far, she'd only accused me of being the teacher's pet.

After science, Captain von Jared met me at my locker. "Hello-o, Maria," he sang out, leaning against my locker.

I couldn't help wondering what Mr. Barnett was like when *he* was a junior high student. Surely he had more class than to sing in public, which is what Jared began to do. "How do you solve a problem like Maria?" Right there in the hall with everyone listening. Well, not really listening. Just really staring.

"Knock it off," I said, playfully pushing him aside. "I need to dump some books."

He spied my interview notes. "Hey, what's this?"

I snatched it back. "None of your business."

"Oh, aren't we cute," he teased. "I suppose you expect me to wait till it shows up in *The Lift*."

"It's hardly a rough draft," I shot back.

He leaned over, reading my notes again. "Hey, you're right, this *is* rough. But what can you say about a wimp like Mr. Barnett, anyway?"

I spun around. "A what?"

"You heard me. Barnett's obviously not very good with the ladies, or he'd have latched on to one by now. I mean, what is the guy, twenty-something going on—"

"That's rude," I shot back.

"Okay, so judge me." He ran his fingers through his wavy hair.

"Look, Jared," I huffed, "I've had it with your attitude. Miss Hess thinks we're lucky to have someone like Mr. Barnett helping with the musical this year. And so do I." There, now maybe he'd back off.

"Oh, man," Jared whispered, coming closer. He touched my cheek. "I think you're—"

"Get back!" I jerked his hand away.

"I'm sorry, Holly. I didn't mean to—"

"Yes, you did," I retorted.

His voice grew softer. "Look, we'll never pull this musical off if we can't work together."

Jared wasn't kidding. Whether I liked it or not, he and I were stuck with each other. I let go of my sophistication for only a second and groaned audibly, piling my books into my locker.

"C'mon, Holly, give me a break." He grabbed my hand. "It'll be fun, you'll see."

"Right," I muttered, thinking of Mr. Barnett again. Was *he* this immature in eighth grade?

I controlled myself and closed my locker without slamming it. And with as much maturity as I could muster, I walked away from Captain von Disgusting, thinking of a zillion drawbacks to playing opposite him in the spring musical.

Chapter 6

I fumed my way into creative writing class. It was going to be horrible—Jared and me together onstage, playing like we were in love. Three weeks ago it wouldn't have been a problem. But now?

Finding my desk, I sat down with a thud. What a nightmare! Jared sat across the aisle to my left, staring at me. I tried to ignore him, but it was hard. Unless I wore blinders, I couldn't help seeing him.

I tried to zero in on Miss Wannamaker's talk. She was discussing humor techniques in writing.

"By bringing two unrelated entities together," she said, "it is possible to surprise the reader. The element of surprise is essential for humor. For instance," and she paused to think. "Ah yes, here's a good example. 'My mother's feet are so big, they have their own zip code.' Feet and zip codes are totally unrelated. So it creates the unexpected, and a good laugh."

She continued giving various examples of surprise twists. I was distracted, however, by Miss W's big, beautiful diamond, her engagement ring from Mr. Ross. It caught the light, nearly blinding me.

Rumor had it their wedding was to be held in the auditorium on the last day of school. A fitting place for two middle-aged teachers to be married, since they'd met here at Dressel Hills Junior High. Visions of white silk, candlelight, and flowers flitted in my brain. *Miss W and Mr. Ross.* True love breaks age barriers, no matter where, no matter when.

Jared startled me by holding out a sheet of paper. I shook my head, thinking it was some mushy note of his. But he looked serious, pointing to the words at the top of the page. I felt mighty embarrassed when it turned out to be one of Miss W's handouts. Slipping it into my notebook, I went back to daydreaming about weddings. This time it was mine. And Andrew Barnett's. Someday . . .

I didn't dare close my eyes in class, but staring at the clouds would do. Zipping through time and space, I was now twenty-two, the perfect age for a girl like me to say "I do." It was, after all, the age of my mother when she married my father. Andrew, at twenty-eight, had eagerly, but patiently, waited for me to graduate from high school and finish college. Now, the proud owner of a degree in English, I planned to write scripts for Andrew's musicals once he and I had united our hearts in wedded bliss.

I stood by his side in front of an altar flanked with white roses. All shimmery in white organza and lace, I gazed into my groom's eyes. On cue, he went to the keyboard and played his lovely song, written especially for our wedding. Strains of the haunting love song filled the sunny mountain chapel.

Soon the minister posed the important question. "Do you, Andrew Barnett, take Holly Meredith to be your wedded wife?"

"I do," Andrew answered. He smiled sweetly.

The minister turned to me and asked, "Do you, Holly Meredith, take Jared Wilkins—"

Jared Wilkins?

Inwardly, I shrieked as Jared's boyish face appeared before me, in front of the flower-draped altar.

"Jared Wilkins," Miss W was calling his name.

Snapping to attention, I jerked back to reality as Jared stood at the front of the class, preparing to read. By the looks of things, we'd had an assignment while I was planning my future.

I listened carefully as Jared read, trying to decipher the assignment. The class laughed as he read his clever combinations of unrelated entities. Maybe, just maybe, if I hurried, I could catch up with the class before someone called on me.

I searched through my notebook for the handout Jared had given me earlier. By the time I found it and read the assignment, it was too late to put anything on paper.

Miss W called my name. "Holly, will you please read your work to the class?" Startled and completely unprepared, I looked up at her. She adjusted her glasses, studying me. She knew.

"I'm sorry, Miss Wannamaker," I confessed. "I'm not ready."

She cast her angelic smile my way. "Holly, this isn't like you." She walked toward my desk. "Do you understand the assignment?"

I understood, all right. I'd been caught daydreaming, and she was making a point of it. Being the wonderful teacher she was, Miss W didn't embarrass me, but she did pat my arm in a concerned sort of way as she called on Marcia Green, the smartest student in school.

Jared slid into his seat, motioning to me with his hands, palms turned up. "What's going on?" he whispered.

I turned away, ignoring him as I stared at the blank sheet of paper in front of me. My daydreaming had just put a black mark on my record. I hoped Miss W wouldn't count it against me when it came time for the semester grade.

When the bell rang, Jared waited for me by the door. "I heard we're having the first read-through on act one today after school."

"We are?"

"Mr. Barnett said to pass the word." Jared held the door for me as we headed for the hall. Reluctantly, I walked with him through the halls toward history class. On the way, I saw my mom with Stephie, my stepsister, heading upstairs.

"What are you doing here?" I asked, surprised.

"Miss Hess is having tryouts for the younger von Trapp children this morning," Mom said. "Stephie's dying for a chance at it, so I took her out of school."

Stephie nodded. "I'm going to be Marta." Mischief danced from her eyes.

I blurted my exciting news. "And *I'm* going to be Maria."

Mom threw her arms around me in front of Jared and everyone. "That's absolutely wonderful, Holly-Heart."

Jared grinned, waiting for me to tell *his* news, no doubt.

Stephie came to my rescue. "Aren't you supposed to tell me to break my foot or something?"

Jared nodded. "Close enough."

Mom remembered Jared. "Hello, again," she said to him. "Are you in the musical?"

Is he ever!

"Yes, ma'am," he replied. "I'll be playing the part of Captain von Trapp."

Mom's eyes twinkled as she put two and two together. "Oh, Holly," she said. "So this is your leading man."

I glanced at my watch. "Well, I better get to class." I was eager to end this cozy conversation between Mom and Jared. "See you after school. Good luck on your audition, Stephie."

"Bye, Holly," Stephie called after me.

Jared seemed more than anxious to keep up with me. "Mind if I walk the leading lady to class?"

I tossed my hair. "I'll walk myself, thanks." My pledge to abandon the boys my age was still in force. Besides, what if Mr. Barnett met up with us?

♥ ♥ ♥

Jared was right; Mr. Barnett began spreading the word to everyone involved in act one of the play. If possible, we were to meet in the choir room after school. I told Andie about it when I saw her at lunch. "It's going to be so-o fabulous," I said.

Still fuming, she pretended not to pay attention.

"Okay," I said. "Have it your way. But I thought nuns took the vow of celibacy, not silence." That got her going.

"Holly Meredith, you think you're so smart because you got Maria's part," she retorted, looking to Stan for moral support. But he only made matters worse by waving Paula over to their table.

Andie made a face, but Stan laughed it off. "After all, if Paula's going to be my girlfriend in the musical, don't you think I oughta get acquainted with her?"

Leave it to Stan to get himself into hazardous situations. Andie began twisting a curl around her finger. Man, was he in trouble now!

"Just relax, Andie," I heard Stan say as I turned to go. "It's only a play."

Only a play? I thought. It was much more than that. It was the path that led to time with Mr. Barnett. And nothing—not Andie, and certainly not Jared—could keep me from walking it.

Chapter 7

A bunch of kids showed up for the read-through of act one. Students took turns sitting around a long table. I sat at the opposite end, away from Jared. Characters who appeared in later scenes sat on the risers, observing.

When it came time for the third scene, where Andie portrays the Mother Abbess, we cracked up. She really hammed it up, especially when she came to the part about Maria being a good choice for a governess. "Look here, Sister Maria twit," she ad-libbed. "I'm sick and tired of the way you're causing problems around here, trying to catch clouds, flibbity-jibbiting your way through morning prayers . . ." Andie crossed her eyes and looked down her nose at me, raising her voice to a ridiculously high pitch. "Are you catching my drift?"

"Andie," Mr. Barnett cut in. "Please read your lines more carefully."

I snickered, watching his face, serious and drawn, loving every second of his putting Andie on the spot. She so deserved it!

When it was time for my lines, Mr. Barnett stopped me numerous times. Not likely because he had a problem with what I was doing, but because he wanted to interact with me. Why else?

On one occasion, he even acted out Jared's part of the scene with me. I watched his face light up as we exchanged dialogue. Genuine interest seemed written all over his face. Was this the beginning of my dream come true?

♥ ♥ ♥

Mr. Barnett gave final instructions before we left. "I want lines for this act memorized in two weeks." I wondered how I'd juggle homework and a zillion lines between now and then.

I headed for the bus stop with Andie, Paula, and Kayla. That's when Andie jumped all over me. "It's really too bad you and Jared broke up, you know. This could've been so-o romantic," she crooned.

Paula wasn't quite as direct, but she had an opinion, all right. "I have a great idea. Why couldn't you and Jared act a little friendlier offstage, at least for the sake of the play?"

Some nerve!

"Look, you two," I said, irritated beyond my limits of mature behavior, "if you think Jared's so fabulous and wonderful . . . well, have at him." Boiling with anger, I pulled on my hair clasp, and my hair came pouring down. "He's all yours."

I halfway expected Paula to take me up on it. Not too long ago she'd been crazy over Jared. Now that he was free for the taking, though, she didn't even seem interested.

I sat in the back of the bus by myself, while Andie and Paula crowded in with Kayla. Periodically, they turned and scowled their disapproval.

Fine, I thought, staring at the backs of their heads. *Go ahead, behave like the children you are.*

♥ ♥ ♥

At home, Stephie met me at the front door, squealing her excitement. "I'm going to be in *The Sound of Music!*"

"That's perfect," I said, swinging her around. "We can practice the 'Do-Re-Mi' song together."

She nodded, taking my hand and pulling me into the kitchen. Mom looked up from her desk in the corner.

"Mommy made snickerdoodles for us to celebrate," Stephie announced.

"I think she's become an addict," Mom said, laughing. "Like you."

I picked out three extra-round cookies before settling down at the bar. "Mmm, perfect."

"Thought you'd be ready for something sweet," Mom said, handing me an envelope. "This came in the mail today."

I recognized the handwriting. "It's from Daddy."

I hurried to the knife rack and sliced the envelope open.

"Careful Maria doesn't cut herself," Stephie teased.

"Yes, Marta," I answered.

Stephie seemed pleased with herself as she snatched up a handful of cookies and disappeared downstairs.

Letters from California were coming more frequently these days. Especially since Daddy's visit to Dressel Hills a few weeks ago. Carrie and I had spent the entire day skiing with him, making happy memories. About time. More than five years had passed since he and Mom split up. We had some major catching up to do.

I pulled the letter out slowly, curious about Daddy's life in California, as always.

> *Dear Holly,*
>
> *Thanks for your letter. I always enjoy hearing from you. Carrie too. Please share this letter with her.*
>
> *My reason for writing is to tell you some wonderful news. When you were here last Christmas, we talked about my investigation into the New Testament. Well, after many weeks of reading the gospels (several times, I must say), I've been pondering the teachings found in them.*
>
> *Last week, I accepted Christ as my Savior during a Christian businessmen's luncheon. I wanted you to be one of the first to know.*

I stopped reading and looked over at Mom, who was sorting coupons at the kitchen desk. "Daddy's become a Christian," I said solemnly.

Mom leaped off the chair, coupons scattering everywhere. She peered over my shoulder.

"See?" I pointed to his words.

"That's wonderful," she said. Her smile warmed my heart.

I finished reading Daddy's letter.

Many times I recalled your words, Holly, the ones you said that night in the Los Angeles chapel, nearly a year ago. Do you remember?

I stopped reading, thinking back. He and Saundra, his new wife, had come to hear me sing while I was on tour with the church youth choir in California. After the concert, Daddy and I talked quietly on the second pew of the sanctuary while the risers and sound equipment were being carried out to the bus. He'd held my hand as we discussed his sister, my aunt Marla, and her death. For a precious moment I had felt close to my estranged father.

I continued reading:

I'll never forget what you said, Holly: "I've been praying for you all this time," you told me. How grateful I am that you never gave up on your terrible old man.

What did he mean, terrible? He had no way of knowing what I knew about his and Mom's divorce. In fact, it had only been a few weeks since Mom and I had the mother of all heart-to-heart talks. Shocking as the truth was, it boiled down to two major problems. Daddy had been determined to move to California. Wanted to uproot the family to pursue his career in another state without taking Mom's aversion to big cities into consideration. She was stubborn, too, and wouldn't agree to go. Ultimately, she sent him on ahead, by himself, secretly hoping he'd get his fill of the mad-dash executive lifestyle in a few months. But Mom's plan backfired. Daddy had thrived on the fast pace and never returned.

At that time, neither of them was a Christian, and Mom found it difficult to give in to Daddy's desire to move. But that wasn't the only problem. My father was proud and sorely hurt. When Mom had a miscarriage and asked him to come back to Dressel Hills while she was hospitalized, Daddy refused. Evidently he wasn't interested in having more children anyway, and his selfish reaction to her request was the straw that broke the marriage.

Stubborn and angry, they agreed to divorce, leaving Carrie and me without a father. And with a hollow ache in our hearts.

Of course, I didn't know all this at age eight, but now I was much more mature. Was I mature enough to forgive Daddy for leaving? I sighed, thinking back to the many years of nightly prayers. For Daddy . . .

For all of us.

I folded the letter and carefully slipped it back into the envelope. Daddy was a Christian now—the answer to my dearest prayer. So, why wasn't I dancing for joy?

I joined Mom at the sink. She whittled away at a long, fat carrot, flicking curly shavings into a bowl.

"The Lord answered my prayer," I said softly.

Mom nodded, and letting the peeler fall into the sink with a clatter, she reached out to me. For a long, sweet moment we held each other. Mom stroked my hair, whispering "Holly-Heart" over and over. Her soothing voice and her gentle perfume erased my worry. If only for a moment.

In a strange sort of way, the timing of his conversion upset me. It had taken all these years to find out the truth, and just when I was ready to unload on him, ready to fire questions at him about the rotten way he'd abandoned us, he decided to become a follower of Jesus Christ.

God had forgiven Daddy. Wasn't I supposed to do the same?

Chapter 8

Supper was plain boring. Not because the Spanish rice and fixings weren't delicious. It had to do with living in limbo, waiting for the weekend to melt into Monday, when I would see Mr. Barnett again.

Grabbing my journal, I let Carrie do kitchen cleanup while I headed for the porch swing to record my thoughts. The last rays of the sun warmed my back as I drifted back and forth, thinking through the amazing events of the past week. My attraction to Mr. Barnett was more than a silly crush. I was sure of it.

I opened my journal.

Friday, April 15. If my friends knew my secret, they'd die laughing. Especially Jared. Danny too. I'm sure Danny would think my feelings for Andrew Barnett are totally illogical. But so what? I don't care!

I looked up, staring at the clouds. Logical or not, my feelings were strong. They'd been growing since Monday, when Andrew Barnett's world collided with mine.

I lay down on the swing, letting its gentle swaying lull me into a daydreamy place where it was safe to concoct elaborate scenes. Warm, cozy scenes featuring Andrew and me. He looked into my eyes, sharing the secrets of his life, his dreams, his goals. Yet he seemed to see how wonderful I was, too.

Then we walked together, in a wooded area near a pond, talking about nature and life and God. He listened, admiring my adult view of life, and my faith. Beneath the moonlit sky, he held my hand, clasping it warmly in his.

Andie's loud whistle caught me off guard. The daydream tumbled down as she plopped onto the chaise lounge across from me. "Whatcha doin'?" she asked, smoothing her Capri pants.

I sat up on the swing, stretching, surprised to see her. "Nothin' much." I held my journal close.

She glanced at me, wistful eyes acknowledging her curiosity. "Anything going on?" She pulled her knees up under her chin.

"Nope," I said, wondering if now was a good time to test my secret on her. "Just catching up on my journal, that's all."

"Oh," she said, her voice trailing off. "Thought I'd come over. Nothing's happening at home. I tried to call . . . your phone's tied up."

"Stan's hogging it," I commented without thinking. Now she'd probably launch off on her jealous routine.

"Who with?" I was right, she *had* to know. "Better not be Paula. She gives me the creeps being Liesl in the play. You know she has that long, lovey-dovey scene with Stan."

This was so childish. Why wasn't I surprised?

"What do you think of Mr. Barnett?" I heard myself saying.

"Him?" Andie shrugged. "He's okay, I guess. Might make a good teacher someday."

"Might?" I snapped.

"He's so . . . so serious. Kinda like you've been lately." She was using one of her best tactics to get me talking.

"What's wrong with that?" I crossed my legs and pulled them under me.

"It's not like you, Holly."

"You're wrong. I *am* serious," I said. "Much more than you know."

Andie cocked her head, studying me. "This is about something else. Mr. Barnett, right?"

Hearing his name took my breath away. "I think he's a wonderful teacher," I said softly.

Andie raised her hands to the sky. "Not another crush, and on an older guy, no less! Didn't you learn anything from your fiasco with that pen pal, Lucas Leigh?"

"This is different," I answered. "I didn't have these feelings for him."

Andie put her hands behind her head. "Well, I've got all night." She leaned back. "So . . . Mr. Barnett, huh?"

"He's pretty fabulous," I said defensively.

"Of course you'd think so—you're the teacher's pet!" She wasn't taking me seriously.

I turned my head and looked at the front yard, gray in the fading light of dusk. Cunningly, I steered the conversation away from Mr. Barnett by telling her about Daddy's conversion.

"That's so great, Holly. It's what you've been living for all these years," she said. "What about his wife?"

"He didn't mention her in the letter, so I don't know."

Andie leaned forward, her eyes boring a hole in me.

"You're not so thrilled about this. How come?"

"Are you kidding?" I said, hoping Andie would drop it, now that she knew. After the way she acted about Mr. Barnett, I wasn't eager to tell her anything else personal.

Mom stepped out on the porch with a glass candle holder and matches. "It's getting dark," she said. "Thought this might be more fun than a porch light."

"Thanks, Mom." I watched her light the candle and set it on the white wicker table beside the chaise.

"Is anyone using the phone now?" Andie asked her.

Mom glanced through the screen door. "I believe it's free, but you'd better grab it quick."

Andie excused herself and went inside. When she came back, Stan was with her. "We're going for ice cream, wanna come?" she asked.

"Not tonight," I said, getting up. "I have tons of lines to memorize."

"Did you sign up for the car wash next weekend?" she asked as they hurried down the steps. "We could use some more help."

"Sure, I'll help," I said.

"See you at church Sunday," Andie called to me before getting into the family van.

"Okay, see ya," I said, hugging my diary tightly.

♥ ♥ ♥

On Saturday, I took a break from learning lines and rode my bike downtown. Paula and Kayla were out jogging around the courthouse grounds.

"Holly, hey!" called Paula when she saw me. Her hair was pulled up in a loose updo. Kayla waved as she matched her pace with Paula's. Their long legs moved in identical motion, glazed with sweat.

I pedaled hard to catch up with them, then coasted, free and easy, careful not to crowd them or throw off their rhythm.

"Looks like you guys are serious about this," I said as we made another lap around the courthouse.

"It's Miss Tucker's idea," Kayla said. "She's desperate for runners this season."

We circled the grounds again. Aspen leaves rippled, robins sang in chorus, and the Miller twins panted, out of breath.

At last we slowed our pace, coming to a stop. I dropped the kickstand down on my bike and sat on the courthouse lawn. Paula jogged in place, puffing spurts of air, slowly lowering her pulse rate. Kayla swung her arms wide around her, back and forth, running in place, creating a human windmill.

I pulled *The Sound of Music* script out of my backpack. "Sometimes I wonder why I ever wanted to be Maria," I complained, watching the twins do their stretches. "I didn't realize how much work it would be."

"You should join the track team if you think sitting around memorizing lines is tough," Kayla said.

"Track's not for me," I confessed. "But I can't wait to read through act two on Monday." I pulled on a blade of grass.

"Anxious to see Mr. Barnett?" Paula teased.

I bit on the end of my hair. "What do you mean?"

"That you have a thing for him," she said, flashing her perfect pearly whites.

Kayla perked up. "Is it true?"

"Where'd you hear such a thing?" I asked.

Paula's eyes widened. "I can't imagine Andie making up something like this."

A cold shiver swept over me. "Andie told you that?" *Some friend!*

Embarrassed at our conversation, Kayla looked away, digging into her shorts for a ponytail band.

I stood up, brushing the grass off my shorts. "Look, I don't know what kind of info Andie's feeding you, but what I told her was I think Mr. Barnett's a wonderful teacher. That's it."

"Okay, okay," Paula said. "It's no big deal then, is it?"

No big deal when you've just discovered your best friend can't be trusted? How could Andie do this to me?

Chapter 9

I ignored Andie as much as possible the next few days. Every single minute I had my head buried in my script. Besides that, after-school rehearsals and the article featuring Mr. Barnett kept me super busy. Because of a slight lull in homework assignments, I managed to turn *The Lift* story in well before the deadline.

My feelings for Mr. Barnett continued to grow. Not only had I included his name on my prayer list, he was showing up in my dreams, too.

♥ ♥ ♥

Car wash day, Saturday, April 23, dawned sunny and hot, so I wore my jean shorts. By helping to raise money, I was doing my part for Danny and the quiz team. No way could I be Danny's partner and still be true to my feelings for Mr. Barnett.

Danny showed up first thing, before any of the others. "Need some help?" he asked as I searched in Pastor Rob's pickup for an extension cord.

"I'm sure it's around here somewhere," I said, hoping I wouldn't be stuck with Danny all day. Not surprisingly, he didn't take the hint, and scurried around searching for it anyway. Finally he located the longest cord the church owned.

"Good, we're in business," he said.

Then Jared showed up. Now it was the three of us. Working as a team, we washed cars and vacuumed their interiors. By midmorning I was wiped out. "Can you cover for me?" I asked the guys.

"Glad to," Danny said, wiping the perspiration from his forehead.

"Take your time," Jared called to me.

I chuckled at their childish attempts to impress me—something I couldn't imagine Andrew Barnett doing in a zillion years. Digging into my shorts for some cash, I headed to the nearest pop machine. I poked the appropriate selection and waited for the machine to do its thing. Nothing happened. Gently, I tapped on the selection button again.

"Kick it."

I turned to see Andie. "Where'd you come from?"

"My dad just dropped me off," she said. "Still mad at me?"

" 'Course not." I pushed the coin return. Coins clattered down and I picked them up to try again. "But I still can't believe you told Paula about our private conversation." I glanced around, hoping no one was listening. "It was supposed to be confidential."

"What, that you think you-know-who's wonderful? I thought you meant it was like some little crush. I mean, it's nothing like the real thing, is it?"

My face felt hot. "Well, no. I'm not in love, if that's what you mean." The defensive words slipped out, even though they felt an awful lot like a lie. "It was a private matter, Andie, and I expected you to act grown-up enough to keep it to yourself. I mean, hey, if I can't trust you, who can I trust?"

Andie grabbed my arm. "Look, I'm sorry. Paula's the only one I told, honest."

Could I believe that?

"It's the truth, you can ask anyone here," she said with a straight face.

"Why, you!"

Just then my pop can came rumbling down.

"Saved by a Pepsi," she said, laughing.

I couldn't help myself, I laughed with her. It dispelled the anger I'd bottled up inside me all week.

As I drank the soda, two more customers drove in. "Guess we'd better get busy," I said, spotting a baby-blue Thunderbird.

"Wow, would you look at that," Andie said, staring at the 1957 classic Thunderbird sports car. We stood there watching as Danny and Jared ran over to inspect the beautiful old car.

"Perfect, maybe now I can work in peace, without Danny breathing down my neck," I muttered. I tilted my head back and took a long, slow drink of the ice-cold soda.

"Only if you're lucky," Andie snickered and ran over to check out the T-Bird.

Still sipping my soda, I straddled the log bench. That's when the door on the car opened. Out stepped Mr. Barnett!

I swallowed my pop too fast and the fizz went up my nose. Coughing, I ran inside the gas station to the ladies' room. I yanked on the toilet paper and blew my nose. Before I left, I checked my hair. It was no use. Embarrassed and nervous, I headed back outside.

"Holly," called Danny, motioning to me. "Can you vac this one out?"

"Sure," I said, hurrying over to the T-Bird.

Mr. Barnett was under the hood, showing Jared and Billy the engine. Danny, conscientious as always, began soaping up the car with his giant sponge.

I pressed the button on the vacuum canister and began to clean the inside of Mr. Barnett's glorious old car. The two-seater had been refurbished, by the looks of things. Nothing *this* ancient could still be in such good shape. Pieces of lint and pebbles of dirt had found their way onto the floor of the driver's side. Other than that, the interior was immaculate.

I balanced my pop can in one hand and gave the passenger's

side a going-over even though it looked spotless. It was obvious no one had sat there recently. *Must mean he doesn't have a girlfriend,* I reasoned.

I could hear Mr. Barnett talking about the V-8 engine and how it could get up and go on the road. It struck me as special—taking time to introduce the guys to the mechanics of a fifties sports car.

Peeking through the crack in the hood, I could see Mr. Barnett's face. Gentle, sweet. I leaned against the dash, sighing. Not wanting him to see me, I pretended to put my pop on the dash as an excuse for being so close to the windshield.

That's when it happened. I accidentally pressed the button for the glove compartment, and it flew open.

"Oh no," I whispered, fumbling to pick up its contents, hoping Mr. Barnett wouldn't choose this moment to close the hood. As long as it was up, with him under it, showing off the engine, I was safe.

Hurriedly, I stuffed a note pad and pen, several maps of Colorado, and an address book back into the roomy compartment. I checked under the seat to make sure I'd found everything. Two snapshots had strayed from sight, and I reached to rescue them. Pulling them out of hiding, I stole a quick look.

Mr. Barnett and a beautiful woman posed on an arched bridge over a small stream. Willow trees draped their branches around the smiling couple. I swallowed hard as I shuffled the second photo on top. The people looked the same, but this time Mr. Barnett had his arms around the slender woman, hugging her playfully.

Ka-whack! The hood came down. Startled, I jumped, dropping the pictures. Mr. Barnett was coming around the driver's side. He'd catch me snooping for sure.

Without thinking, I slammed the glove compartment and bent the pictures just enough to let the vacuum hose suck up the evidence.

"Holly!" Mr. Barnett called over the noise of the vacuum. "I had no idea you were in here." He leaned on the window, smiling warmly.

Forcing a smile, I punched the Off button on the vacuum, thinking only of the swallowed-up pictures, deep inside the cavernous cleaner. "I like your car," my boring words came out. It's hard to be eloquent when you're frantic with worry, not to mention having to deal with the pain of coming face-to-face with your competition. Snapshot or not.

"Who's collecting the bucks for the wash job?" Mr. Barnett asked, admiring the work Danny had done.

"You can give the money to me," Danny said. "I'll see that it gets into the Bible quiz fund."

Mr. Barnett came around to my side of the car, where I was securing the vacuum cleaner attachments, preparing for the next job. He reached into his pants pocket and pulled a ten-dollar bill from his billfold. I couldn't help noticing the face of the woman in the front of his billfold, safely snuggled in the little wallet window. The *same* woman.

I drew a faltering breath as I looked away, enduring the heart pain. Why hadn't I suspected something like this before?

Andie came over just then. "You look tired," she said. "Why don't you take a break?"

"I need to check the vacuum cleaner." I rolled it away from Mr. Barnett's car. Andie followed me as Danny and Mr. Barnett stood talking. I whispered to Andie through clenched teeth, "Stand in front of me and don't make a big deal about this."

Her eyebrows gathered into a frown. "What's going on?"

I wanted to cry. "Just don't say anything," I warned her, reaching inside the canister's cone and pulling out the snapshots. "Whew, that was close." I wiped the dust off the pictures with my shirttail. "They're only slightly bent."

I heard Mr. Barnett start his car and let the engine idle. Without rehearsing my words, I dashed over to the passenger's side of the car, waving the pictures.

He leaned over and wound down the window, looking puzzled.

"These got vacuumed up, accidentally." It was the truth. Sort of.

"That's weird, but thanks." A slight frown appeared.

"I'm really sorry, Mr. Barnett. I'll be happy to pay you for reprints, or whatever," I offered.

He took the pictures from me. "Don't worry about it, Holly." He looked up at me, smiling, and I felt even worse about what I'd done.

"I'm sorry," I said again, wiping my forehead on my sleeve.

Andie called to me, "Who was supposed to pick up hamburgers for everyone?"

"Oh, *that's* what I forgot," I said. "I'll run down to McDonald's and be back in no time."

"Why do that?" Mr. Barnett said. "I'd be glad to drive you." He leaned over and opened the car door. "What about you, Andie?" He looked at her. "Ever ride in an old jalopy?"

Andie shook her head. "We're a little shorthanded here. But thanks." She waved, grinning from ear to ear. I knew what was going through her mind. She'd declined so I could be the one to ride with Mr. Barnett. And I loved her for it.

One of my daydreams had come true. Maybe Mr. Barnett would whisk me away, dump the other girl, of course, and we'd live happily ever . . .

I hesitated, leaning on the car door.

"The jalopy's safe, Holly," he teased. "I rebuilt the engine myself." He opened the glove compartment and pushed the pictures out of sight.

My heart skipped a beat. And without another thought, I stepped into Mr. Barnett's Thunderbird.

Chapter 10

The breeze from the windows blew my hair as we rode toward Aspen Street. The Golden Arches was only a mile or so away. I tried to imagine what it would be like to someday go on a date with Mr. Barnett, maybe with the convertible top down, the wind blowing our hair, his arm resting on the back of my seat.

He glanced at me as we stopped for a red light. "What do you think of my great-aunt's Thunderbird?"

"Well, I've never really seen one this close before," I said. "But I think your aunt has good taste in old cars."

"Better than that," he said with a smile. "She left it to me in her will. I doubt she knew the value of it, though."

"Looks like she took good care of it."

"Aunt Edna was like that. She hung on to all kinds of things. My sister does the same thing." He chuckled softly. "Those pictures you rescued," and he pointed to the glove box, "are of my sis and me outside Aunt Edna's place, before my aunt died last year."

"Your sister?" My heart sang. "She's beautiful," I said, certain I would never have admitted that if she'd turned out to be his girlfriend.

"Janna's five years older than I am. She's finishing up a double master's program this quarter," he said proudly.

"I'm impressed." I pushed a strand of hair back behind my ear, wondering how I was doing holding up my end of the conversation.

He leaned his arm out the window. "She's a very special girl." He paused. "You remind me of her when she was your age."

Things were so comfortable between us, like we'd known each other all our lives.

"How's it feel having an older sister?" I asked.

"Oh, things aren't much different than if she and I were close in age. At least not now. I guess that's the way it is . . . as people grow up, the age barriers drop away." He signaled to turn. "I see that Danny fellow is hanging around," he continued.

I knew what he was getting at. "Yeah, Danny and I were pretty close last summer," I said.

"Looks to me like he's still interested."

I sighed, wanting desperately to change the direction of our conversation. "Actually, Danny and I are just good friends now." I had to let Mr. Barnett know, in no uncertain terms, the status between Danny and me. I relaxed a bit as we pulled into McDonald's.

"Danny's older, right?"

"Only a year," I said, wishing we'd get off this subject.

"Well, I have a question for you, Holly. What do you think of age differences . . . when someone likes the other person but isn't totally certain the feelings are mutual?" He paused, turning off the ignition, looking at me.

Could it be he was thinking of us, our age difference?

"I've read about relationships where one person's lots older." I hesitated, trying to remember the book I'd read. "I think it helps if one of them gives the other a sign."

He looked blank, confused.

I tried to explain. "You know, a sort of message . . . from one heart to another." It sounded corny, but it sure worked in the book. Besides, it gave me a fabulous idea.

We walked into McDonald's together, and when he held the door for me, I felt more grown-up than I ever had. In fact, I was so busy thinking about what Mr. Barnett had said, I could scarcely manage to answer when he asked how many hamburgers to order.

On the way back to the car wash, I clasped the large sacks of warm cheeseburgers and fries. My mind felt numb, paralyzed by a desire to let Mr. Barnett know how special he was to me. But how?

He turned on the radio to the only oldies station in Dressel Hills. His smile made my heart leap. "So what do you think, riding in a hot old T-Bird?"

I shook my head, not quite able to look at him, but the warm, easy way about him unlocked my brain and I heard myself say, "Thanks for driving me to McDonald's." It wasn't what I really wanted to say. Not even close.

"My pleasure." He turned onto the street where the rest of the car wash crew was probably dying of starvation. Precious seconds were slipping away as Aunt Edna's classic Thunderbird sports car purred down the tree-lined street.

"When do we start blocking the musical onstage?" I blurted, longing to fill each remaining moment with the sound of his voice.

He nodded. "Very soon. And we've got such a fantastic cast," he said, flashing his grin at me. "You're perfect for Maria, you know."

I blushed. "Thanks. I really like this musical."

We drove into the car wash area, and Danny and Jared came running up like raving maniacs before Mr. Barnett could stop the car. So typical of boys their age. By the way they were salivating, you'd think they hadn't eaten in days. They grabbed several sacks overflowing with cheeseburgers and fries and headed for the shade of the gas station. Andie, Paula, and Kayla came dashing over as I got out of the car. Amy-Liz, Joy, and Shauna were close behind.

"Thanks again, Mr. Barnett," I called, keeping things businesslike, hoping no one would accuse me of being teacher's pet today.

"I hope your church makes a lot of money for the quiz team."

"Good-bye," I said.

"I'll see you Monday," he called, honking his car out on the street. All of us waved as he sped away.

"I'll see you Monday" still echoed in my brain as I handed three sacks of food to the girls. "There should be plenty for everyone," I said.

"What, no ketchup?" Andie asked, digging into the sack.

"It's in there somewhere," I said, following her over to the grassy area behind the gas station.

We girls sat together, gobbling down our lunch. Several parents from the church took over the car wash operation while we ate. And Danny, eating with the guys, kept glancing over every so often. *Now* what was he thinking?

After we finished eating, I dragged Andie into the ladies' rest room. "We *have* to talk," I whispered.

"I'm dying for details. And don't tell me your brain froze up and you forgot them."

"There's no way I'll ever forget," I said, locking the bathroom door behind us. "I've stored his words away forever." I patted my heart.

"Spare the dramatics," she said. "Get to the facts."

I told her everything, even what Mr. Barnett had said about age difference not being a problem.

"You've got to be kidding! You're sure he was talking about you two?"

"Cross my heart, and hope—"

"Don't say that, Holly. Grow up," she said.

"I have." At that moment, I felt sure Mr. Barnett and I would be together. Someday.

Chapter 11

It didn't take long to think through my plan once I arrived home. In the safety of my bedroom, a deliciously warm feeling settled over me as I wrote in my journal.

> *Saturday, April 23: This is the best day of my life! Something fabulous happened today. I rode in Andrew Barnett's beautiful baby-blue Thunderbird, just the two of us. Even more amazing, Mr. Barnett brought up age differences in relationships—ours, of course. I must let him know that I agree that our age difference won't always be a problem. Wouldn't it be wonderful if he waited for me? I have the most fabulous idea. More later . . .*

I tucked my diary safely away in my bottom dresser drawer. That's when I heard Mom's little dinner bell.

"Supper will be ready in fifteen minutes," she called.

I grabbed some clean clothes and raced to the bathroom, hurrying to clean up. While in the shower, I decided I would compose my written response to Andrew Barnett after supper. It should be anonymous. Besides, he'd surely know it was from me.

♥ ♥ ♥

After supper, Carrie and I brought the leftovers from the dining room into the kitchen. "Have you written back to Daddy yet?" she asked.

"I've been too busy," I said, not eager to talk about it. "Haven't had time with all the rehearsals for the musical."

"Mommy told me that Grandma Meredith says he's going to church every Sunday."

"That's good." And it really was, but I still couldn't deal with my hidden anger toward him. He'd hurt my mother big time, and now that I knew exactly what had happened to cause the divorce, I couldn't just overlook his sins and forgive him. Only God could do that.

"Saundra goes along to church with him sometimes," she continued. "Tyler too."

"Really? That's great." I'd been hoping my stepmother might open up to spiritual things. And I wasn't surprised about Tyler. He'd been full of questions about God and creation and the Bible ever since day one—since last summer, when I first went to California to visit Daddy.

Carrie headed back into the dining room, nearly bumping into Mom, who looked slightly peeved at Uncle Jack. He was piled high with plates. Dirty napkins were scrunched under one hand. He tossed a strained grin at Mom. "Here comes the other partner in the Share the Housework Team," he said.

"After nearly five months of marriage, it's about time," she said sarcastically.

With great fanfare, he balanced the dirty dishes, placing them carefully on the counter. Hurrying over to the freezer, he pulled out the ice-cube trays. "Aha, just as I thought. Empty again!" And with boyish delight, he rushed to the sink and filled the trays with water, as though he were doing something very important for the family.

Mom looked like she wanted to continue scowling, but when Uncle Jack closed the freezer, with the newly filled ice-cube trays safely tucked away, he tiptoed over to Mom and gave her a hug. She giggled as he planted a kiss on her neck, and I knew their tiff over household chores was past.

I didn't see what the big fuss was anyway. After all, I'd seen Uncle Jack helping around the kitchen occasionally, fixing meals. If you can classify meals as something involving important ingredients like peanut butter and jelly. I'd seen him help in the kitchen at least three or four times since they'd married. So what was the big deal?

Maybe the honeymoon stage was starting to dissipate. Maybe now they would start acting normal. Like other married people.

I heard Mom say, "Can we talk?" while smothered in Uncle Jack's arms.

It was my cue to disappear, dishes or not. Thrilled at the chance to exit, I ran to my room.

Closing the door, I wished for a lock, but the lack of one didn't keep me from pulling out my prettiest stationery and settling in at my desk. Important stuff like this must be thought out carefully, so I wrote the first draft on scratch paper.

At last, I was ready to transfer my words to my flowery paper, which just happened to have hearts scattered all around.

Dear Andrew, I began. It was important to address him by his first name since I wanted to respond on his level, to reassure him just how mature I already was.

What a fabulous job you're doing on The Sound of Music. *Thanks for working so hard to make it a success.*

I couldn't work my way into the nitty-gritty without some sort of compliment.

Also, thanks for sharing your thoughts with me Saturday. It meant a lot.

I have a great idea. Let's get together sometime and discuss things further. Maybe over coffee or tea?

I chose coffee because that's what adults usually say when they want an excuse to tie up a restaurant booth for at least an hour. And tea? That's what Mom drinks when her nerves are frayed. The peppermint variety. For sure my own nerves would be a little on edge if Mr. Barnett agreed.

In keeping with my original plan, I decided not to sign my name, but wrote: *Most sincerely, You-know-who.*

Ecstatic about my plan, I folded the stationery and slid it into a matching envelope. I didn't lick it. Not yet. It was only Saturday night and Monday seemed far away. Who knows? I might want to read the note again—so I hid it in Marty Leigh's latest mystery novel, replacing the bookmark.

♥ ♥ ♥

Sunday, the next day, was both strange and sweet. Danny *and* Jared expected me to sit with them in Sunday school. And on the chair right between them, no less. Paula and Kayla snickered into their Bibles, while Stan shot Andie a knowing look.

It was a good thing Andrew Barnett was nowhere in sight. He'd think I was just another silly eighth grader, trying to juggle more than one guy friend at a time. I was poised first on one edge of my chair, and then the other, trying to keep my arms from touching either Danny or Jared, depending on how close either one leaned at any given moment. Most girls would have been flattered having two cute guys vying for their attention, but not me. My sights were set higher now.

♥ ♥ ♥

Monday came at last and, lucky for me, Paula was working as a student-aide in the office before school. I was in a big hurry, as usual. Motioning her over, I whispered my intentions. "Can you put this in Mr. Barnett's box for me?"

Her eyes brightened. "What's this about?"

"I'll tell you at lunch."

She took the envelope, and I turned around. Holding my breath, I waited outside the office. When I was sure she'd had time to sneak off to the faculty mail area, I peeked my head around the doorway. She grinned at me. It was the only sign I needed.

Feeling mighty smug, as well as eager for his response, I sailed off toward my locker.

Jared was waiting.

"You're not going to sing to me today, are you?" I teased.

"How about we practice our duet, you know the one—'Something Good'?" He leaned against the locker door.

"Oh no, you don't," I said, pushing him away. That song was supposed to end with a long kiss. At least, that's how it was in the movie. We still didn't know what Mr. Barnett wanted us to do there. And I wasn't about to ask.

"You're not worried about that scene, are you?" he asked, a silly frown on his face.

"I, uh, guess not."

He pushed his hands into his jeans pockets. "Funny, isn't it?"

There was an awkward silence.

"What's funny?" I said.

"There just aren't enough girls like you to go around, Holly-Heart." There was a sober ring to his voice.

I broke the spell. "Don't be weird." I found my books for science and closed my locker.

"I mean it." He fell in step with me as I headed to first period. "Danny thinks so, too."

Oh great, I thought. Now they were conferring with each other about me.

"C'mon, Holly. Don't be mad. I mean, what's a guy to do? We can't ignore you."

"You could try." I waved him on as I opened the door to Mr. Ross's class, thinking only of the note I'd written to Mr. Barnett. And his response to it. What would it be?

♥ ♥ ♥

After school, we met for play practice. Today we were going to work through the speaking parts onstage. Excited and very nervous, I hurried into the auditorium.

Danny and his stage crew sat on the edge of the stage, waiting for instructions from Miss Hess and Mr. Barnett. I sat between Paula and Andie, hoping to escape Jared's attention, but he squeezed in next to me, making Andie slide over.

Mr. Barnett passed out a rehearsal schedule. I glanced over it, wondering how I'd ever survive the next few weeks. While he gave instructions for blocking, I wondered if he'd checked his mailbox yet, or read my note. If he had, he wasn't letting on. Not by a secret smile or even a look. Maybe that meant he hadn't had a chance to check.

"Okay, let's start with act one, skip to scenes two and three," he said, cupping his hand over his mouth to amplify his voice. "Everyone pretend we're in the Nonnberg Abbey, back in the thirties, in Salzburg, Austria."

Andie, Kayla, Joy, and Shauna took their places in the imaginary abbey, pretending to be solemn and nunlike. Andie's face was so solemn it was actually funny as she took her place behind the Reverend Mother's desk.

My throat felt dry as I took my place onstage. In the scene, Maria had just come in from singing and frolicking in the hills of Austria when the Mother Abbess calls her into her office for a chat.

Things went well with that scene. Andie behaved herself, trying to act holier than anyone onstage. It was a kick. She actually folded her hands and walked around looking rather stuffy.

When it came time for me to meet Captain von Trapp in the great hall at the von Trapp villa, I kept spotting a nose and a pair of eyes peeking through the curtains in front of me. Very distracting. I motioned to the person, whoever it was, to close the curtain. "Go away," I whispered while Jared said his lines. It was in the middle of the captain's dialogue, where he instructs me how to call his seven children with a whistle.

Suddenly Mr. Barnett came up onstage. "Holly?"

"Yes?" I answered, glancing at his shirt pocket, wondering if my note had been tucked away for safekeeping.

"Are you practicing lines while Jared is speaking?"

"Oh no. It's that." I pointed to the gap in the curtains. Quickly, they sprang shut.

"Carry on," Mr. Barnett instructed. And we did.

Later, during the romantic scene between Maria and Captain von Trapp, the nose and eyes appeared through the curtains again. This time, a wisp of auburn hair showed, as well. The hair gave him away. It was Danny, spying on scenes where Jared's and my character were supposed to be romantically involved.

♥ ♥ ♥

After practice, I located Danny backstage. "Have fun snooping today?"

He ignored me, shuffling around with props and things.

"You really could be watching from the audience," I suggested. "Why'd you take this stage manager job, anyway, if you're just going to gawk?"

He shook his head innocently, but I was sure I knew the answer. Finally he left, and I was searching for my script when I overheard Miss Hess and Mr. Barnett talking together.

"You could've signed your name," he was saying to her.

"I'm not sure what you're talking about," Miss Hess answered coyly.

I held my breath as I eavesdropped backstage.

His smile gave way to a grin. "Oh, you can deny it, but I'm telling you it was a nice surprise."

I peeked through the curtain as he continued. "I think we ought to discuss things further over coffee, or is tea better for you?"

I nearly choked. Andrew was totally mixed up. He thought Miss Hess had written the anonymous note—*my* note. It was all I could do to keep from leaping through the curtains and setting the record straight.

As Mr. Barnett planned their rendezvous for tomorrow after school at the Soda Straw, Miss Hess smiled back at him, obviously delighted. There she stood, just outside the orchestra pit, letting him think whatever he wanted. Letting my note do the job she'd probably hoped to do all along!

I gripped the folds of the curtain. End of act two, scene two. So much for my crazy little scheme. The curtain had come crashing down around me, without any applause.

Chapter 12

I waited, watching as they left the auditorium together. The custodian came in to turn out the lights before I could muster the strength to come out and face the empty chairs. People or no people, there would be a grand musical here, and I was Maria, the star of the show. Mr. Barnett had thought I was the best choice for the lead. He'd said I was the perfect Maria.

Was that all I was? Just a talented drama student? With a heavy heart, I trudged down the steps and walked the long aisle to the back doors, replaying the conversation in his car.

What was all his talk about age differences? Was he actually referring to Miss Hess?

Andie and Paula waited for me at the bus stop. Running to meet them, I nearly tripped, but I caught myself.

"Watch out," Paula called.

"I'm okay," I said. And I was—on the outside. Inside I was a wreck.

The bus arrived and its door screeched open.

"Good practice today," Andie said, jostling for a seat in the back of the bus. She and I sat together. Paula sat in front of us, saving a place for her twin, who was running down the street, frantically flagging the driver.

Andie giggled. "Look at Kayla go."

"You should see her jog around the courthouse," I said. "You too, Paula. You guys are fast." It almost made me wish I'd gone out for track instead of the musical.

"You look terrible, Holly," Andie offered.

"Thanks, I needed that."

Paula turned around just as an exhausted Kayla slumped into the seat next to her. "Holly, you okay?"

I sighed. "The note I sent Mr. Barnett backfired," I said, feeling more foolish than ever. "Guess I should've signed my name."

"Are you crazy?" Andie said. "No way!"

"What happened?" Paula asked.

I told them the conversation I'd witnessed between Miss Hess and Mr. Barnett.

"You're kidding." Kayla turned around, suddenly coming to life. "Miss Hess likes Mr. Barnett?"

"Sure seems like it," I said. "Now what should I do?" I felt like crying.

"You could always write another note," Paula suggested. "Just tell him you wrote the first one and sign your name this time."

"No, no!" Andie was emphatic. "Holly can't be stupid about this. There's a better way."

"If he really does like me, like he said on Saturday, then what's to lose?" I said. "Why couldn't I write him another letter?"

"Wait a minute," Andie said. "Try to remember everything he said on Saturday."

What was she getting at?

Andie took a deep breath. "Here's the deal. If there's the slightest chance that Mr. Barnett was thinking about Miss Hess, or some other older woman, you've simply misread him. But if he was actually talking about you and him, well . . . that's what we've gotta find out."

"And as soon as possible," I said. "Or else Miss Hess could move in on him."

"You might have another problem," Paula said. "What if he *is* interested in you, and he's not a Christian. What then?"

"Yeah," Andie said. "You know the verse in the Bible about not being yoked together with unbelievers. Besides, your mom won't let you date till you're fifteen anyway. He'd have to wait a whole year."

"More than that, since he's already in college," I said, wishing I could ignore that fact.

"Plus he's our student teacher right now. There's no way he could go out with a student." Paula sighed.

"Do you think he'll wait for you if it turns out he's . . . well, you know, interested in you?" Andie asked.

"Why not?" I said. "The way I see it, he'd have a chance to finish his degree and get settled into a good teaching position, maybe even here in Dressel Hills."

Kayla giggled. "Looks like you've got it all worked out . . . in your head."

"Wait a minute," Andie said, looking serious. "When's your article coming out?"

Kayla gasped. "You mean she interviewed Mr. Barnett for the school paper?"

Andie nodded slowly. "You betcha. This girl doesn't waste time. When's it coming out?" she repeated.

I said, "Next week, I think."

"That's good," said Andie excitedly. "Because when it's out, here's what you do. You take your copy to Mr. Barnett and ask him to sign it. You know, get his autograph, since he'll be leaving at the end of the school year."

I groaned. "What'll *that* do?"

"Hold on a minute," Andie said as Paula and Kayla looked on, wide-eyed. "It'll give you a chance to talk with him again. We'll even guard the choir room doors, won't we, girls?"

The Miller twins nodded in sync.

"Sounds ridiculous," I said, thinking I was in way over my head.

Andie got huffy suddenly. "Well, Holly, if you don't like that, you could always try the direct approach. Just blurt it out—ask him what he meant by all that age stuff."

"Now, *there's* a thought," I whispered sarcastically. But I had a better plan. One I wasn't going to reveal. Not in a zillion years.

When Downhill Court came up, I prepared to exit through the back door of the bus. I could see that Andie was over the worst. She was talking a mile a minute to the Miller twins. That's how she was. Mad one minute, best friends the next.

"See ya," I called to them.

"Call me," Paula said.

"Me too," Andie said.

"See you tomorrow." I stepped off the bus and headed across the street, intercepting the mail truck. I waited for the mail carrier to sort our mail, noticing Daddy's handwriting on one of the envelopes. Feeling guilty about not responding to his good news earlier, I hurried into the house with the mail.

Uncle Jack and the younger boys were doing math at the dining room table. Uncle Jack looked up as I came in. "Late practice?" he asked.

"It'll be this way from now till opening night." I handed the mail to him but kept the letter addressed to me from California.

He spotted the envelope in my hand. "I hear your dad recently became a Christian."

"Uh-huh."

"That's terrific," he said, running his fingers through the top of his hair. "I've been praying for him since before I married his sister twenty years ago."

"Wow," Phil said. "That's a long time."

"You're not joking," Mark piped up. "I prayed for a boy at school, you know, back in Pennsylvania, and he just got worse."

"But you didn't give up, did you?" Phil asked soberly.

"Not really, but I got tired of being bullied. I prayed the Lord would make him move away or turn him into a Christian." Mark bit the eraser on his pencil.

"What happened?" I asked.

"God didn't answer either of my prayers, but He did do something else."

Uncle Jack grinned like he knew the answer.

"God moved us out here." Mark blinked his eyes, smiling.

"Our Lord works in mysterious ways," Uncle Jack said. "Right, kiddo?" He looked at me. And somehow I felt he understood my struggle about my father becoming a Christian.

"People are mysterious, too, sometimes," I muttered, heading for the stairs. What I really meant to say was: Why did Daddy's decision for Christ upset me so much? It was wrong for me to hang on to something that had happened five years ago.

In my room, I sat on my window seat, letting Goofey curl up beside me. Slowly, almost fearfully, I opened the letter from sunny California.

Chapter 13

Daddy's letter was a rundown of church-related activities. He was even attending a businessmen's prayer breakfast every Saturday. He didn't comment about the fact that I hadn't answered his last letter, but he'd heard about our school musical and that I had been chosen to play Maria. The news of the musical had come from Grandma Meredith, his mother, who still kept in close contact with Mom. In fact, Mom talked on the phone with her several times a month. She and Grandpa had always said we were still their family in spite of the divorce. And now even more so, since Mom had married their former son-in-law, Uncle Jack.

I held the letter in my hands, letting the late afternoon sun beat on it. Tears filled my eyes as I remembered the years of my prayers for Daddy. The man who'd abandoned us. God had forgiven him; so should I. But when I prayed, I could only say, "Thank you, Lord, for answering my prayers about Daddy." The forgiving part would have to come later. If at all.

Picking up Goofey, I gave him a hug. "It's time to invite someone very special to come see *The Sound of Music,* junior-high style," I told my cat.

Goofey began licking his paws, giving himself a bath on the

sun-dappled window seat. I went to my desk, pulled out some plain stationery, and began writing.

When I finished, I read the letter. "Daddy probably won't come, you know," I said over my shoulder to Goofey, who was now sound asleep. "He's too busy with his work. That's how it's always been. But at least he knows I want him to come."

I added a P. S. to the letter: *I'm up to my eyelids in scripts and rehearsals. That's why I haven't written.*

I walked out to the mailbox to mail my letter, wishing with all my heart he'd arrange his schedule and come see the performance. But knowing Daddy, I wouldn't hold my breath.

♥ ♥ ♥

By fourth period the next morning, Andie had heard some strange rumors about Jared and me. "Everyone's talking about the romantic scene in the play," she said. "I've heard that Jared plans to kiss you for real."

"Just let him try," I said, boiling mad.

Andie giggled. "C'mon, Holly, it's not like you haven't thought about what it would be like."

"That was then, this is now." I was thinking about the months he and I had spent so much time together

"Maybe today's the day to talk to Mr. Barnett about what he wants you guys to do." She lowered her voice to a whisper as we walked into the choir room with a bunch of other kids. "Maybe he'll say to just fake the kiss. Watch his face when he tells you."

"How come?"

"Think about it, Holly," Andie insisted. "It'll give you some insight, you know, into how he might feel about you."

"Oh," I said. Once again, Andie was on top of things.

After class, Andie nudged me. "Don't forget to watch his face, especially his eyes. You can tell how someone feels by their eyes."

"Okay, okay." I waited till the choir room was empty. Andie left just before I approached Mr. Barnett's desk.

"Ah, it's you, Maria herself," he greeted me warmly.

"I've been thinking," I began. "That scene outside, beside the gazebo, uh, where Captain von Trapp proposes to Maria, what should Jared and I do there?"

He looked down, twiddling his pen. "That's a good question." He leaned back in his chair, looking me straight in the eye. "How do you feel about it?"

Not fair! I wanted *him* to tell *me*.

Mr. Barnett stood up. "You know, Holly, you could talk it over with the leading man."

"But what do *you* think we should do?" There, the ball was back in his court.

"Well, to tell you the truth, my feeling is to leave out the kiss and just fake it. Most of the audience won't be able to tell the difference. Okay with you?"

I was relieved. Could he see it in my eyes?

"Thanks, Mr. Barnett, I'll tell Jared what you said." I turned to leave.

"Oh, Holly, before you leave, I've been wanting to talk to you."

"Yes?" I was hyperventilating for sure. What was he going to say?

"It's about your church," he said. "I was impressed with the kids from your youth group last Saturday."

"Thanks," I said, not sure how to respond.

"I've been looking for a good church. Maybe I'll visit yours sometime. Do you go to the early or late service?"

"Usually the early," I said, barely able to get the words out.

"Good." He smiled warmly. "I'll see you there."

I scurried out of the choir room and off to lunch, my heart in my throat. Wait'll Andie heard *this*!

♥ ♥ ♥

Backstage that afternoon, things were crowded. I found Jared ready to go with script in hand. It was the day to rehearse the romantic scene.

"We have to talk," I said, pointing him to a quiet corner near the makeshift dressing rooms.

He looked worried. "Everything okay?"

"I talked to Mr. Barnett today about this scene."

"Yeah?" He seemed concerned.

"He wants us to leave off the kiss." I said it firmly, without hesitation.

He looked a little disappointed. "Whatever you want to do is fine."

I couldn't believe my ears. I honestly thought he'd fight for the kiss.

Later, during the actual scene, Jared seemed distant. No, guarded. Like he didn't want to offend me or something.

Mr. Barnett stopped us. "Jared, you're going through the motions. Think about this moment," he said. "You're declaring your love to Maria." He glanced at me. "The captain's been a lonely man since his wife died years ago, and all these children . . . think of trying to raise seven kids by yourself. Now, can you warm up to this pretty Maria of yours a little more?"

Mr. Barnett stepped back while Jared said his lines again.

"Still not enough feeling," Mr. Barnett interrupted. He pulled Jared off to the side. "Look, have you ever been in love?"

"I think so," Jared said, glancing at me.

"Well, terrific," Mr. Barnett said, clapping his hands. "Can you transfer those feelings to Holly here, er, Maria? Isn't she lovely? Don't you want to let her know how much she means to you? She's going to be your wife, for pete's sake!"

That did it. Jared warmed up, all right. Too much. I could see the emotion practically oozing from his eyes.

Finally Mr. Barnett was delighted with our performance. He called it quits earlier than usual, probably because he had that date scheduled with Miss Hess.

I fooled around backstage, making sure everyone was gone

before I made my move. Then I snuck into the props room to set the wheels of my perfect plan in motion. First, I found Andie's Mother Abbess habit, complete with robe and wimple. Then I located some pillows to fill me out a bit. I shivered with excitement as I slipped into the habit and looked at myself in the mirror. Fabulous! No one would ever know it was me.

With another quick glance at the mirror, I was off to the Soda Straw to spy on Mr. Barnett and Miss Hess.

Chapter 14

I couldn't remember ever having seen Catholic nuns in the Dressel Hills area, but I guess there is always a first time. Solemnly, deliberately, I made my way out the backstage door, hoping to bypass teachers and other students. Most everyone had gone home for the day, so I didn't see a single soul as I took short, reverent steps to the Soda Straw.

I pushed the door open gently, wishing the jingling bell didn't have to sound every time someone entered. And there they were—Mr. Barnett and Miss Hess, looking too cozy together in a corner booth. They never even turned around when the bell jingled. A bad sign. A sign that they were too deeply involved in conversation to care.

I chose the booth next to them, careful to sit with my back to Mr. Barnett. I wanted to hear *his* remarks.

The waitress came around, smiling politely. "What can I get for you today, sister?"

I glanced at the menu and saw precisely what I wanted. "This looks good," I said, disguising my voice.

"A banana split?" She seemed surprised. Had I done something wrong? Something out of character for a righteous woman?

"Yes, please," I said. "With extra strawberries and whipped cream, if you don't mind."

She jotted down the order and scurried off. I stared at the stools lined up at the aluminum counter as I eavesdropped on the conversation directly behind me. So far it was rather boring. Nothing like the things Mr. Barnett and I had discussed last Saturday. Or before that, in the choir room, the day he played his composition for me.

"Teaching on the junior high level is very challenging, but I have to admit that I do enjoy it," Miss Hess was saying.

"So far, it's fun," Mr. Barnett agreed. "But what I'd really like to do is get my doctorate and teach at a college."

"What about coaching drama?" she asked. "You're so good at it."

There was a slight pause. "I've been involved with summer stock since high school," Mr. Barnett said. "But it's very different coming from the other side of the orchestra pit, if you know what I mean."

Miss Hess sighed. "Getting students to loosen up onstage takes some doing. Especially young teens."

The waitress came back with my banana split with strawberries and extra whipped cream. "Here you are, sister."

I nodded, smiling, relinquishing the opportunity to speak. The less I used my vocal chords, disguised or otherwise, the safer I would be.

My ears perked up when I heard my name in the booth behind me. "Holly sure has a feel for the stage," Mr. Barnett said. "Has she had parts in other plays at school?"

Miss Hess said, "I think this is her first play. But her composition teacher says she has a vivid imagination and does quite a lot of writing."

Mr. Barnett chuckled. "She sure knows how to conduct a good interview. I can't wait to see what she wrote about me in the school paper."

Suddenly Miss Hess changed the subject. Was she jealous?

"How long have you lived in Colorado?" she asked.

"My folks moved here from Seattle when I was a kid," Mr. Barnett said. "What about you?"

Boring small talk.

"I'm one of the few natives around," Miss Hess said, almost boastfully. "Ask me anything about Colorado—its music, its culture—"

"Its anonymous letter writers?" Mr. Barnett interrupted.

I almost choked on a banana. No, not that!

Miss Hess actually giggled. *Now* she was enjoying the conversation.

"I didn't write that note to you, Andrew. Honest."

Would he believe her this time?

"C'mon, Vickie," he said. "Tell the truth."

It sounded like he wished she *had* written the note!

"I told you," she said coyly.

"Are you sure about this?"

I could almost see the mischievous twinkle in his eye. Why wouldn't he listen to Miss Hess?

Confused, I spooned up a bite of ice cream. It sure seemed like Mr. Barnett was flirting with Miss Hess. He even called her Vickie! Was he just a fun-loving tease?

I thought about his other wonderful words. *"Holly sure has a feel for the stage . . . she knows how to conduct a good interview. . . ."*

I heard Miss Hess talking again. "Looks like you have a thing for pistachio."

Although I didn't dare turn around, I could visualize a mountain of pistachio ice cream.

Mr. Barnett chuckled softly. "One thing's for sure. The woman I marry better not mind a few pistachio shells around the house."

The woman? Where did that leave me?

The door jingled, and Andie and Paula waltzed in with Stan and Billy Hill. Yikes!

I flew off to the ladies' room. Not very holylike, but, oh well.

Inside one of the stalls, I undressed, thankful I'd left my own clothes on underneath. *Love does strange things to people,* I thought, trying to figure out how to smuggle Andie's costume out of here.

Just then, Andie flew into the rest room. "Holly," she called to me in the stall.

I waited silently. Without breathing.

"I know you're in here," she continued. "And I saw you in that nun's habit. What on earth are you doing parading around in my costume?"

I tried to stifle the giggles, but it was no use. They came pouring out, a little at first, then out came a full-fledged burst.

"You're so-o immature," Andie said. "Now come out here and talk to me."

Slowly, I emerged from the bathroom stall. "How'd you know it was me?"

"How'd I know?" She nearly collapsed with laughter. "You left your hair hanging out, that's how! Your hair's a good three inches longer than the wimple, you know."

I gasped. "Really? Oh, Andie, this is horrible. What if Mr. Barnett saw it, too?"

She shook her head, raising her eyebrows. "Why didn't you tell me what you were doing? I could've advised you . . . helped you."

"You still can," I pleaded. "Get your school bag or your purse. Anything." I began folding the habit.

"I don't have anything with me that'll hold the costume," she said.

"Just please try." I stood there holding the costume and looking in the mirror at my hair as she left. How stupid of me! Why hadn't I taken time to plan this more carefully?

Andie said to wait here—"I'll be right back!"

And she was. She flew in the door, and we began to stuff the habit into her school bag. Then, attempting to hide the bulging evidence, we returned to the booth where Paula, Billy, and Stan were waiting to order.

I slid in next to Paula. Glancing over at Mr. Barnett and Miss

Hess, I hoped they hadn't noticed my blond hair earlier. Then I spotted my perfectly good banana split waiting to be devoured. My heart sank. Which was worse? Wasting a delicious dessert or making a total fool of myself?

Shortly, Mr. Barnett and Miss Hess left via the jingling door. I dashed back to my table, rescuing my banana split just as the waitress came to remove it. She wore a vague, puzzled look as I told her, "Don't worry. I'll pay for it. The sister won't be back."

At least, not if I could help it.

I ate the remains of my sweet treat, rethinking my amateur spying attempts. While Billy and Paula bantered back and forth, I came to this realization: I was not nearly as mature as I'd thought. The truth was, I'd made a major blunder, forgetting to hide my hair under the wimple.

STRAIGHT-A TEACHER

Chapter 15

Two days later, on Friday, I was still trying to live down my ill-thought disguise. At least with Paula and Andie.

"You don't have to be perfect to be mature," Andie said, waiting at my locker for Paula. They were coming for a sleepover at my house.

"I know, but it's so humiliating." I closed my locker door.

"What about Mr. Barnett?" Andie asked. "Do you think he saw your hair hanging out?"

"Nah, I can tell by the way he acts around me."

Andie waved as Paula came down the hall. Then, turning to me, she said, "I'm so glad you're having us over. It'll be so cool practicing our lines together. Maybe we can get one of your younger brothers to read the guys' lines."

"Don't forget, Stan'll be hanging around," I said. "He might fill in some of the parts for us."

"Just so he and Paula don't get any ideas and rehearse that romantic scene of theirs," Andie snapped.

When we arrived at my house, Mom was tossing a gigantic salad and putting the finishing touches on a homemade pizza. Leave it to Mom to make the perfect food for a party.

♥ ♥ ♥

After supper, we headed for my room, scripts in hand. Since Stan was busy with Phil and Mark, playing the final level on a hold-your-breath computer game, I suggested we take turns filling in the parts of the male leads. Things went smoothly for over an hour, but soon our dry throats were ready for something cold and soothing. Mom offered to make root beer floats, and she brought them up to us on a tray.

Handing me a frosty-cold glass, she said, "Holly, your father called this morning. He's coming to Dressel Hills . . . for your play."

"He is?" I gasped. "Oh no, hand me my script."

I caught it as Andie tossed it to me.

After Mom left, we started all over again on Act One. After two more times through, we stopped practicing lines, and Andie got up and went to my closet. She pulled out a yellow sweater and tucked it inside her oversized T-shirt. Marching around the room, Andie took ladylike steps, the way Mr. Barnett had instructed her to as the Mother Abbess. Paula and I laughed hysterically as the long yellow sleeve dangled down her back—the way my long hair had under the nun's wimple.

"It's not very funny, when you think about it," Paula said, recovering from giggling. "I remember having a huge crush on a teacher back East, before we ever moved here."

Andie stopped cold. "Really?" She looked horrified, then began to laugh.

"It happens," I said, eager to plan my next move with Mr. Barnett. It was time to come forward and let him know how I felt.

Andie quit laughing and pulled my sweater down out of her top. She lowered her voice and checked the door. "Huddle up," she whispered.

By the look in Andie's eyes, I knew this was going to be good. Secrets were dancing in the air tonight.

"Promise not to tell anyone?" she began.

Paula and I nodded.

"Not a soul?" she demanded.

"You've got my word," Paula said.

"Ditto for me," I said.

Andie leaned in close to us on the floor. She opened her mouth to speak. Then she caught herself.

"Quick, Holly. Turn on your radio," she said.

I frowned. "What's the secret?"

"Hurry," Andie insisted. "We need music to drown this out."

I did as she asked, finding a contemporary Christian music station. "How's that?"

She nodded as I scurried back to my place like a mouse hungry for a morsel of cheese.

When our heads were close enough to tell who'd brushed teeth after pizza and who hadn't, Andie began. "Remember when Pastor Rob first came to Dressel Hills?"

I remembered. Andie and I had been only eleven.

"Well," she continued, "I had this enormous crush on him. It was like every time I saw him at church, it got worse. I can't believe I ran around asking to help him with church stuff. He must've known. Especially after I told him I'd put his name at the top of my prayer list."

I gasped. "You *told* him that?"

"Give me a break." She grinned broadly. "I was in fifth grade back then."

"How come you never told me?" I asked.

"Because I thought you liked him, too."

I grinned. "I did, but I didn't want you to know."

"This sounds like true confessions night," Paula said.

"Yeah, right," I said, thinking of Mr. Barnett.

♥   ♥   ♥

The next day, after the girls' parents picked them up, I hopped on my bike and rode downtown. I now had the perfect plan—with pistachio nuts at the center of it. Mr. Barnett had a weakness for pistachios; he'd said it himself.

I locked up my bike in front of Explore Bookstore and hurried a few stores down to the drugstore. Every kind of nut imaginable could be found in large bins. Locating the pistachio variety, I told the clerk I wanted enough to fill the plastic container on display.

"One moment, please." And he disappeared behind the counter.

Soon, I was the proud owner of two pounds of pistachio nuts, the perfect answer to my dilemma. I couldn't wait to present them to Mr. Barnett on Monday.

♥ ♥ ♥

Sunday—*gasp!*—he showed up at my church wearing a dark suit and classy tie. Since I'd never seen him dressed up that much, I nearly fainted on the spot.

Andie spotted him, too. "Would you look at that," she said, gawking at him across the foyer.

"Quiet," I whispered.

"He's come to take you away," she teased.

"Yeah, right," I said. "Go sit with your mother."

"See ya." And she turned and headed toward the inside doors, with a quick glance back at me.

Just as I was reaching for the church bulletin, Mr. Barnett came up to me. "Good morning, Holly. What's on the program for today?"

Program? Was he for real?

I shuffled through the bulletin, aware of my increasing anxiety—maybe because Mr. Barnett was standing so close. "Here. It looks like our senior pastor is speaking. You'll like him," I said, smiling.

Mr. Barnett hesitated slightly. Then he said, "I thought I'd sit with Stan if he won't mind."

"No problem. Follow me," I said, giddier than ever. I led him down the aisle, to our family's pew. Stan was sitting on the end. I poked him. "Hey, cuz."

He looked up.

"Mr. Barnett is visiting our church, and he'd like some company," I whispered, gesturing toward our teacher.

Stan smiled and said hello to Mr. Barnett, then slid over to make room. Thank goodness he wasn't making a big deal of this.

I caught Andie's glance across the church as I sat down at the end of the pew—next to Andrew Barnett. I wasn't sure, but it looked like—for once—she was close to fainting.

♥ ♥ ♥

If sitting in church on a springtime Sunday with the main focus of my affection wasn't enough, on Monday during choir he asked me to stay after class. He needed to see me about something. Fabulous! Maybe that would be a good time to give him my gift.

Gingerly, I set my school bag down on the riser as we warmed up for sectionals. Neither Andie nor Paula asked about the obvious bulge. My Pistachio Plan was perfect, and in just fifty minutes, Mr. Barnett would know the truth.

After class, Mr. Barnett had a question about my style preference for a wedding gown. For the wedding scene in the musical, of course.

"Footloose and Fancy Things has some fabulous gowns," I said. "In fact, they might loan one to the school just for the play."

"In exchange for free advertising, perhaps," he said. "Good thinking, Holly."

Billy Hill and some other boys stood at the door just as I was about to present my gift. Mr. Barnett went over to them; his back was turned to me.

Without hesitation, I pulled out the plastic container filled with his favorite kind of nuts. I glanced at the gift card I'd found for him at Explore Bookstore. It was signed: *Love, H.* Gently, I placed the nut-filled bowl on his desk.

The door closed and Mr. Barnett came smiling back to me. "What's this?" he asked, obviously delighted.

"I, uh . . . I brought this for you." Butterflies played tag in my stomach.

"Incredible." He reached for the card.

For a moment, I waited, dying for his reaction.

When he had read the card, he glanced up, grinning. "That Miss Hess! Did she put you up to this?"

"I . . . er, I—" It was hopeless, the words were stuck. And this might be my last chance to tell him, face-to-face, how I felt.

For what seemed like a never-ending moment, we just looked at each other. Then suddenly the intercom crackled. "Mr. Barnett, you have a phone call. Can you take it in the office?"

He turned to face the speaker high on the wall. "I'll be right down." Then, beaming at me, he said, "Thanks for taking time to play delivery girl. You're really very sweet."

After he left, I stood there, stunned. Staring at the Pistachio Plan—make that Total Flop—on his desk, I felt numb. Sick.

Not again!

Chapter 16

The next four weeks were a total nightmare. Everywhere I turned, Mr. Barnett was there. At practice every day. In my dreams at night. And, as before, in my daydreams. But I didn't dare make an attempt to tell him how I felt. Not after two plans had so totally failed. I'd be testing fate to try again.

To make matters worse, the practice schedule escalated to every day after school and three evenings a week! Lines had been memorized, but now came the emphasis on facial expressions and body movements. Mr. Barnett got right in there and worked us through all the important inflections.

Character dynamics were essential, too. Stephie, my stepsister, was a superb little Marta—my youngest charge as the governess, Maria. Our interaction onstage reflected the close relationship we had at home. Same with Stan. Andie, Paula, and I were close friends, so working together onstage was a cinch for us, too.

With the constant practicing, even Jared and I were actually developing a good working relationship. And offstage, he hardly ever flirted with me. Well, not much, at least.

As for Mr. Barnett, I couldn't summon the courage to tell him the truth about the pistachio nuts, but it was obvious by the trail of shells on his desk that he was enjoying them.

♥ ♥ ♥

Finally it was the afternoon of May 27: dress rehearsal. We performed in front of the elementary school down the street from my house. Carrie and our stepbrothers, Phil and Mark, sat in the audience with their respective classes. From their talk at breakfast that morning, I knew they were as excited as Stephie and I.

I peeked through the curtains, looking for my brothers and sister, hoping to dazzle them and their friends with my rendition of Maria. More than anything, though, I intended to impress Mr. Barnett.

At the end of each scene, the kids clapped loudly. They seemed to like Jared's introduction of his children with his weird whistle calls. But Jared had seemed a little out of it. And his face looked awfully pale.

Backstage, before final curtain calls, Mr. Barnett said this was our best performance yet. "Now tonight, keep your audience in mind as you say your lines." He was a stickler for enunciation. "If they can't understand you, we're toast."

Danny nodded. He ought to know, after the tons of eavesdropping he'd been doing on our performances. Guess that's the way it had to be as stage manager, though. Knowing who was where and what was what. He was good.

Still, I had eyes for only one person. And as Mr. Barnett talked, I longed for a way to share my true feelings. A foolproof way—one that wouldn't flop.

♥ ♥ ♥

After a quick taco salad for supper, Mom flew around the house getting Stephie ready for our big production.

"I'm really scared," Stephie said.

"You'll be fine," I said, squeezing her around the waist.

Carrie helped Stephie carry her things to the van. The rest of the family planned to come later, in time for the best seats.

When I arrived at the dressing room, Andie was all aflutter. "What if I forget my lines?" she worried.

"It'll never happen," I said. "You think so fast on your feet, Andie, you could make it up if you forget."

"How's it feel getting married to Jared onstage in front of everyone?" Paula asked with a grin.

"You would ask that," I said. "How's it feel kissing my cousin?" I thought about Stan and Paula onstage as the love-struck couple, Liesl and Rolf.

Andie jerked away from the mirror, horrified. "Who's kissing?"

Paula giggled. "Don't worry, Andie, we're only faking it."

"Yeah, well, don't get too close." She wasn't kidding.

"Don't worry," Paula said. "Billy asked to take me to the cast party tomorrow night."

I leaped up, hugging her. "Really? You and the butler?"

Andie smiled. "You'll like him. We were close friends for a while last year, before Stan moved here."

"Hello?" someone called through the dressing-room curtain.

I looked around. "Everyone decent?"

"Go for it," Andie called.

I moved back the curtain, poking my head out. And there he stood, looking absolutely fabulous in his tan business suit—even the silk hankie matched his tie. "Daddy!" I cried, letting the curtain go as we hugged.

"This is your big night, Holly," he whispered. "I couldn't miss it for the world, could I?"

I grinned with excitement. "I can't wait till you see the show!"

"Well, the place is filling up fast," he said. "I'll be praying for you."

"Thanks, I need it."

He held my hand, and for a moment I thought of the pain he'd caused our family. The lousy way he'd treated Mom . . .

His eyes searched mine. "What is it, honey?"

Instead of launching my questions, probing into the pain of the past, I reached out and hugged him again. Bone hard, like Mom hugs me sometimes. "I love you, Daddy," I whispered. "That's all. Just . . . I love you."

In his arms, the need to confront him disappeared, and my heart overflowed with forgiveness and joy for his newfound faith in God. Slowly, I pulled away. "I'd better get my makeup on."

"Break a leg, Holly-Heart." Smile lines creased his face.

"Thanks."

♥ ♥ ♥

The musical might have been called *The Flight of the Butter-flies*, the way my stomach flip-flopped before curtains. Packed to capacity, the auditorium was a sellout. And to think my father had come all the way from California to see me!

My hands felt damp and my heart pounded as I listened to the buzz of the crowd. If only Gabriel would blow his trumpet right now.

Then the overture began, with gentle woodwinds setting the mood, followed by the fuller sound of strings. The joyous melody swelled to a crescendo, soothing me. As I took my place onstage, waiting for the rush of rising curtains, I sent up a silent prayer.

Act one, scene one, the hills of Austria. Exhilarated by the excitement of the crowd, I spun around at center stage, swinging my arms wide and singing the theme song, "The Sound of Music."

Mr. Barnett watched from the orchestra pit. His face, the way it shone in the stage lights, spurred me on to greater heights. *Oh, if only I could tell him my true feelings before he leaves,* I thought as the orchestra played my interlude. Time was running out. Student teachers don't stick around forever. School would soon be out for the year. How could I pull it off?

The audience applauded as I sang the reprise, then the curtain fell, ending the first scene. I ran into the wings, awaiting my next cue.

But, just then, a commotion broke out backstage. Andie grabbed my arm. "Jared's real sick; he's going home," she said.

"He's what?" I rushed to the chair where he sat with his head down. Leaning over, I placed my hand on his shoulder. "Jared, are you okay?"

He looked at me momentarily. A weak smile flitted across his deathly white face. "I'm sorry to let you down like this, Maria, my love."

It was the sweetest thing he'd ever said. On or offstage.

Suddenly Mr. Barnett showed up. "What happened?"

"He's been throwing up," Andie explained while Paula and Kayla and all the others looked on.

Jared moaned. "I nearly blacked out."

Quickly, Mr. Barnett turned to Andie and me. "You girls go ahead with the next two scenes. The captain isn't on till scene four."

Andie and I hurried for the stage, passing Danny in the wings. "The walking microchip could play your leading man," Andie whispered in my ear.

"He knows the lines all right," I agreed. But we both knew he could never pull it off. Besides, no one could run ship behind the curtains as well as Danny.

Worried about Jared, I took my place onstage, and the curtains rose slowly. It was hard to concentrate on my lines with the part of Captain up for grabs.

At the tail end of scene three, the music swelled as I headed for the von Trapp villa—eager, yet worried about the job of being governess for seven children. But I was *more* worried about my leading man, sick and trembling, backstage.

The audience clapped as the curtains fell again. Dashing backstage, I found the janitor cleaning up the floor near Jared's chair. I didn't have to ask why.

"His parents took him home," Stan said solemnly.

"So now what?"

Stan stood up. "Better ask Mr. Barnett."

Danny motioned to me from the wings. "Take your position, Maria," he whispered. His flashlight led me to the floor marks. Next came Billy as Franz, the butler.

Not knowing who would play the male lead, I waited, jittery and tense. Next to passing out at the seventh-grade musical, having my leading man get sick was the next worst thing. I felt sorry for Jared, missing his opening night. But I was also sorry for myself and possibly the audience, depending on who was appointed the role of Captain von Trapp.

Then, suddenly Mr. Barnett strolled onstage. Wearing a navy blue sea captain's uniform, he was as handsome as ever. Danny pointed with his flashlight to an easy chair on stage left. And the new Captain von Trapp sat down.

Mr. Barnett smiled. In the semidarkness my heart danced off beat. And together, we waited for curtains.

Chapter 17

I remembered Miss W's words the day she'd described how to create an element of surprise during creative writing class. *By bringing two unrelated entities together* . . . How right she was. Mr. Barnett and Holly-Heart acting the leads together? Now, this was some fabulous surprise!

Standing on the other side of the curtain, Miss Hess was explaining to the audience the necessary substitution of characters. The orchestra played a soft interlude as she spoke.

My mind raced ahead to the upcoming scenes. First, I would be introduced to Captain von Trapp at his Austrian villa. Then, several scenes later—the moonlit gazebo scene!

Then it hit me. I knew the perfect way to show Mr. Barnett my true feelings. Thinking ahead, I felt strangely calm. Like this was supposed to be. Fate had brought us together, and now we were here, onstage together, performing in one of the greatest romances of the century.

Slowly, the curtains rose. When the applause died down, I rang the gold-painted doorbell on the prop representing the double doors of the von Trapp villa. The butler, wearing his wig, opened the door to the grand hallway. Maria mistook the butler for the captain, and the scene was under way.

Once again, the incredible rhythm of dialogue and drama began to unfold. It took me back to the day I auditioned, when Mr. Barnett and I had played our parts as if we'd been born to them. Tonight, wearing his dazzling uniform, sparring verbally with me onstage, Andrew Barnett *was* Georg von Trapp. And I, his Maria.

♥ ♥ ♥

In the silvery blue moonlight, two lovers sat beneath a gazebo, trees casting dim shadows across their faces. "I can't marry the baroness when I'm in love with someone else," the captain said after a long, endearing look. "Can I, Maria?"

Slowly, coyly, I shook my head.

"I love *you*, Maria," he said, reaching for my chin.

I held my breath as he drew me close. Then, to make the audience think we were kissing, he turned the back of his head toward them, just as Jared and I had practiced. We held the stance while the crowd *ooh*ed softly. And as they did, I gently kissed his cheek.

There. Now he knew.

The orchestra played the introduction of "Something Good" as arms entwined, and eyes filled with tenderness, we sang our beautiful duet. It was surprising how well our voices blended.

At the end of the musical, we bowed repeatedly. Separately, and then together. We were a dynamic hit, Mr. Barnett and I. Quite obvious by the thunderous applause.

Afterward, people rushed onstage, presenting me with flowers. Mom and Uncle Jack were some of the first. Miss Hess was full of compliments, and so was Miss Wannamaker, who held hands with Mr. Ross as she carried on about the performance.

Later, when the audience thinned out a bit, Daddy came up to congratulate me. More flowers. I introduced him to Mr. Barnett, who stood nearby.

"Have you thought of studying drama?" Daddy asked me. "You are a wonderful actress."

"I agree with you," Mr. Barnett said. "Holly seems very comfortable onstage."

"Thank you," I said, blushing. But under all that stage face-goop, who would notice?

"I'll call you from my hotel later," Daddy said, hugging me.

"You made this night extra-special for me, Daddy," I said. "I'll never forget it."

He waved and turned to go. As his figure disappeared into the crowd, I started to cry.

Touching my elbow, Mr. Barnett guided me backstage. "Can I help?" he asked.

I shook my head. "It's a long, sad story."

"Your father certainly loves you." He smiled as I wiped my eyes. "Everyone does."

It was a sweet thing to say. But did he include himself in the comment?

"You'll be leaving soon," I said. "And I'm going to miss you around here."

"I'll miss you, too, Holly," he said kindly. Like a big brother. Then he smiled. "Well," he said, his voice brightening, "if you were little older, I'd take you out for a banana split with extra strawberries and whipped cream."

Instantly, his words struck home. "You *knew*?" I covered my mouth. "You knew it was me at the Soda Straw that day?"

"Hey, young nuns with flowing blond hair are few and far between," he said, trying to suppress a grin.

We both burst out laughing. It was a welcome relief—especially after the pressures of seeing Daddy and being alone with Mr. Barnett like this.

"Thanks for keeping quiet about my stupidity," I said, setting my flowers on a chair. "Did Miss Hess know?"

His eyes sparkled with mischief. "If she did, she never let on."

I sighed. "Thank goodness." Then I shot him a sly glance. "Are you and she . . . ?"

He actually blushed, I thought. But he dodged my question. "About that banana split," he said, turning on the charm again. "Where will you be four years from now?"

His friendly teasing made me laugh. "Four years from now? Oh, that's hard to say," I said, playing along. Now that I'd revealed my true feelings, I could relax and just be myself. Besides, I was beginning to see Andrew Barnett for what he really was—a good-looking, older, over-grown Jared.

Mr. Barnett glanced over at Danny and Billy organizing props for tomorrow's show. "There *are* some pretty terrific guys your own age around here, in case you haven't noticed."

Just then Paula came out of the dressing room, carrying a large bouquet of red roses. "These are for you, Holly," she said. "Someone left them during the last scene."

I glanced down at the card. It read: *When the Lord closes a door, somewhere He opens a window. Always, Jared.*

It was a line directly from the musical, where Maria tells Mother Abbess she feels called to work with the von Trapp children instead of staying on at the abbey.

Leaning my face into Jared's roses, I breathed their fragrance deeply. "About those guys my age," I said, smiling up at Mr. Barnett, "maybe you're right."

♥ ♥ ♥

Jared's illness turned out to be a twelve-hour flu, so we performed together the second night. Of course, we were fabulous together, but never would I forget my shining moment—the night I shared the stage with Mr. Barnett.

The last few days of the semester flew by, and my feelings for our student teacher began to change. For the better. I started to see him for who he was—instead of who I'd daydreamed he could be. A very cool teacher. A good friend. But not future husband material.

Of course, I never knew if he took Miss Hess out again. I decided it was best if I didn't. Funny how that goes.

♥ ♥ ♥

Before long, Miss W's wedding day arrived. The faculty and the student body filled the auditorium during the final hour of the school year.

Miss W surprised everyone by wearing a full-length white gown with a six-foot train and a long white veil. Her smile was as sweet as a young bride's.

"I better not be that old when I get married," Andie whispered as "The Wedding March" came over the sound system.

Step by step, the matronly teacher made her way down the long aisle toward Mr. Ross, who was looking mighty spiffy in his long gray tuxedo.

"She's really beautiful." Tears welled up in my eyes.

We turned and watched as she stood beside Mr. Ross at the front. The minister motioned for us to be seated. As he began with "Dearly beloved," I glanced down the row of seats.

My friends, each one, were within hugging distance. Jared and Danny sat directly behind me. Andie and Stan sat on one side of me, and Paula and Billy on the other. Amy-Liz and all the others filled up the seats in the row. Together we witnessed the blending of two lives in holy matrimony.

Next year, Miss W would be known as Mrs. Ross. Not only that, Andie and I would be at the top of the heap—ninth grade. We'd come so far, so fast. Where had the years gone?

Stan, Danny, and the Miller twins were heading off to high school. So many things were changing.

Mr. Barnett was leaving Dressel Hills to graduate from college, taking his fabulous T-Bird with him . . . and leaving behind a trail of pistachio shells.

Special days, special moments don't last forever. Anyone knows that. Breezes of change blow hard and fast. And before you know it, skinny figures fill out. Kids grow up. Journals burst with top-secret information. Prayers get answered.

I smiled through my tears as the minister pronounced the happy couple husband and wife. We gave Mr. and Mrs. Ross a standing ovation as they walked down the aisle.

♥ ♥ ♥

Back at my locker, I gathered up my books and papers for the final time. Then I headed toward the front doors. Ahead of me was another fabulous Dressel Hills summer. And behind me—all of eighth grade.

As the glass doors of the school swung shut behind me, I thought of Jared's note. *When the Lord closes a door, somewhere He opens a window.* God was closing a chapter in my life. But by trusting Him, I knew that, in time, a window would fling wide.

And I could hardly wait.

HOLLY'S HEART

No Guys Pact

For one of my fans,

Lisa Lease . . .

she knows why!

Chapter 1

"I can't believe it. Are you sure?" I asked my best friend.

Andie Martinez nodded. Her dark eyes looked all too serious as we corralled her three-year-old twin brothers near their backyard jungle gym. "Amy-Liz told me herself. She's definitely not going to church camp this summer."

I helped Jon climb the monkey bars, steadying him as he scrambled to the top. "But Amy-Liz *always* goes to camp," I insisted. "She's never missed a summer."

Andie gave Jon's twin, Chris, an under-duck in his swing. "The way I heard it, Amy's dad's been laid off, and they're cutting back on everything."

"Wow," I said softly. "Even Amy's voice lessons?"

"Those too."

I felt sorry for Amy-Liz. Sounded like things were perfectly rotten at her house. "Isn't there anything we can do?" I asked, watching closely as Jon jumped off the bars into the sand below.

Andie frowned. "Like what?"

"I just thought we could help. Maybe a bunch of us could pitch in some money."

Andie sat at the bottom of the slide. "You've gotta be kidding,

Holly. There's no way Amy-Liz Thompson is going to accept charity. You oughta know that."

"But," I insisted, "we should try, don't you think?"

Leaning back against the hot slide, Andie shook her head, shielding her eyes from the late afternoon sun. "Nope, not a good idea."

"Then . . . *what?* What can we do?"

Unexpectedly, Jon threw a handful of sand at his brother's face. Chris squealed and rubbed his eyes. Andie leaped off the slide and ran to Chris, lifting him from the swing. "No, no, Jon," she scolded.

"No!" Jon yelled back at her. "No!"

Andie hauled Chris into the house. He kicked against her bare legs as he screamed in pain.

I scolded Jon. "Never, ever throw sand or dirt in someone's face. You could hurt your brother's eyes."

He squatted in the sand, making a circular motion with both hands like he was thinking hard. He wouldn't look at me.

I reached down and patted his arm. "Let's go inside and say sorry to Chris."

Jon stared at the ground, patting the sand with both hands. "No. I make sand cakes. Mushy sand cakes." And with that, he ran to get the garden hose near the house.

I wanted to say, "Forget it, kid," but that's not exactly the best way to get a three-year-old's attention. Little kids always seem to do the exact opposite of what you ask them to. At least that's how it was with these twins. Jon and Chris—just recently out of the terrible twos—had minds of their own. I shouldn't have been surprised. After all, their fourteen-year-old sister was consistently hardheaded.

Jon ran across the length of the yard in his bare feet, talking to himself as he headed for the house. He reached for the outside faucet and it squeaked on. Seconds later, water shot out of the hose. I wondered if I should let him make his silly sand cakes, but my mind was really on Andie, inside with Chris. She probably needed my help.

"Come here, Jon," I called, but he ignored me. I walked across the yard to turn off the water when a mischievous look slid across his face. Suddenly he ran toward the nozzle.

So did I.

"Whoa! Stop right there," I shouted, hoping to scare him into submission. But he didn't stop, and both of us ran toward the end of the hose—the nozzle that lay innocently in the middle of a patch of thick green grass.

Jon kept running, giggling unmercifully. Fortunately, my legs were longer and my grip tighter. Man, did he change his tune fast when I threatened him with a cold blast of H_2O.

"Now, go over there and turn the water off," I insisted in my most authoritative baby-sitter voice. Holding the hose high, I pressed my thumb against the edge of it. Water gushed out in a fanlike spray.

I inched it closer and closer to the little shrimp's body as his pleas for mercy rose higher and higher into the warm June breeze.

He hollered, "I'm thorry, Howwy. I'm tho-o-o thorry!"

"You better go tell your brother that." I tried to keep from laughing—wondering how he'd look soaking wet. But being the fabulous baby-sitter I am, I removed my thumb from the end of the hose and let the pressure fizzle out.

Jon stared wide-eyed at the hose. The rushing, roaring Niagara had become a steady stream once again, and Jon's face looked mighty relieved. "Pwomise you won't spway me?" His lower lip quivered.

I pushed the hose behind my back, feeling bad about what I'd done. "I promise. Now, be a good boy and go turn off the water."

"Uh-huh." He nodded his head sheepishly and turned and ran to the spigot. "It's off!" he shouted, hands in the air as though he'd done something really terrific.

"You're right, it is." I dropped the hose and followed him into the house. How many more willful standoffs would I encounter before Andie's parents returned home? It was anyone's guess.

As for Andie, I wasn't going to let her talk me out of my fabulous idea. Amy-Liz deserved to go to camp this summer. End of discussion!

Chapter 2

When Jon and I went inside, we found Andie in the kitchen, kissing the top of Chris's head. He sat dangling his chubby legs from the kitchen counter. Apparently Andie had successfully washed out his eyes.

"Everything okay?" I asked.

Andie nodded. "He'll be fine." She turned to look at Jon, who stood staring down at his toes.

I knelt down beside the little terror and put my arm around him. "Would you like to say something to Chris?"

Jon's head rose slowly. "I'm thorry, Cwis," he said softly.

Andie lifted Chris down off the counter, and Jon put his arms around his twin's neck. "Aw, how sweet," I cooed as the fiercesome twosome hugged and made up.

"Don't hold your breath," Andie whispered to me.

Suddenly the boys lost their balance and fell onto the floor in a heap of look-alike arms and legs. Giggles too.

At last we got the boys settled down and cleaned up. It took some doing even for both Andie and me to get things under control with these live wires. It made me appreciate the way Andie's mom seemed to handle things every day. And my own mom, who was not only a mother to me and my sister, Carrie, but was now—with her marriage to Uncle Jack, who was a widower, having once been married to my dad's sister—stepmom to four of my cousins, too.

While the twins watched a cartoon DVD in the family room, Andie and I sat on the sofa behind them, arguing about Amy-Liz and how to help her.

"C'mon, Andie. It's a great idea," I said.

She shook her head, making her dark curls dance. "How would *you* feel about receiving charity?"

"Get over it, Andie. Can't you see? Amy's gonna miss out if someone doesn't do something, and fast."

"Yeah? Like what?"

Finally Andie was ready to listen.

I sat up against the back of the sofa, eager to share my absolutely fabulous idea. "We could have a bake sale."

She cackled at my idea. "Coming from someone who hates to bake, that's nuts."

"I don't mind baking; it's cooking I despise."

"Whatever," she muttered, waving her hand at me like I was suggesting something outrageous. "So, who're you gonna sell this baked stuff to?"

She'd caught me off guard. "Oh . . . just some people."

"What people?"

I should've known she'd question me every step of the way. Taking a deep breath, I said, "People like neighbors . . . uh, you know, and friends. Lots of people."

"Sounds cool." She leaned back against a soft plaid pillow.

Andie was like that. Unpredictable . . . and frustrating beyond belief. I never knew what to expect from her.

"So you'll help me, then?" I asked.

She flashed one of her serious stares. "Whatcha gonna bake?"

"What about my Super-Duper Snickerdoodles?"

Andie's eyes brightened. She actually smiled!

"And what about you?" I asked. "Don't you have a special Mexican cookie recipe or something?"

Andie gasped playfully, clutching her throat. "You mean our *secret* family recipe? You can't be serious."

I laughed.

"I'd be crazy to let our recipe for *polvorones* fall into the wrong hands, Holly Meredith." She leaned close, her dark eyes shining. "It's top secret."

"Well, if it's so hush-hush, why don't *you* just make them . . . whatever they are. I'm not interested in selling the recipe, anyway."

"Oh, you'll want it after you taste the results," she replied. "Wait and see." She had a weird dreamy look on her face. "So, that settles it. We'll have a bake sale."

I sat up. "Let's start taking orders."

"Not until after my mom gets home," she said.

"I didn't mean this second, silly." I leaned back into the couch and sighed. "Thank goodness we're not going to earn Amy-Liz's camp money by baby-sitting."

Andie frowned. "What . . . don't you like my baby brothers?" She picked up the pillow and punched it hard.

"Course I do. Nothing against your brothers." I paused, trying to think how I could get out of this gracefully. Andie wasn't making things very easy. "I really love Chris and Jon." I glanced over at them. "You should know that."

"Yeah, right." She sniffed and turned a cold shoulder.

"You know perfectly well I'm serious, Andie. I like helping you baby-sit your brothers." I turned away from her glare, looking over at the darling boys on the floor. Jon sat chewing on his pointer finger, totally entranced with the cartoon characters and their antics. Chris rocked back and forth, humming softly to himself, also transfixed by the tube.

"What you mean is, you love getting *paid* for helping me with my brothers." She said it with a straight face and a tinge of anger. What was going on?

"Andie, I don't get you!" I stood up abruptly.

Jon turned around, startled. "Howwy not go bye-bye," he said, shaking his slobbery finger at me. "Not go."

Andie started to laugh, not her normal cackle. No, this laughter was new. A sort of midrange laugh with an eerie staccato bounce to it. And it sounded like she wasn't really laughing at all. She had caught me in one of her crazy pretend conflict setups. Caught me flat. And what had I done? Fallen for it. I just stood there watching her have her giggle game.

"I really had you, Holly . . . I can't believe you fell for . . . this." She stopped laughing long enough to breathe, holding her sides. "How could you think I was actually serious?"

"Guess I'm gullible, that's all."

"Gullible, mullible," she chanted. More laughter.

Finally, when the giggling ended, Andie settled down to normal—whatever that was—and we planned how to arrange getting the money from our baked-goods sale into the church scholarship fund.

"I'm sure Pastor Rob will agree," I said, thinking how lucky we were to have such a cool youth pastor. "I'll call him first thing tomorrow."

"Make sure he keeps the bake sale a secret." She grabbed my arm. "If Amy finds out, the whole thing will backfire in our faces."

"Okay, I'll tell him to keep it quiet," I promised, amused at her sudden interest. But I was glad to know Andie was supportive of this project, because funding Amy-Liz's camp trip wasn't going to be all that easy.

Chapter 3

The next day, even though it was summer vacation, I got up early. Before the sun. I grabbed my journal from its special place in the bottom drawer of my dresser and hurried to my window seat with pen in hand.

> *Friday, June 17: I can't wait to get started on a fabulous new top-secret project with Andie. If everything goes as planned, we're going to raise zillions for the church camp scholarship fund. Actually, the money's going to Amy-Liz Thompson because her dad's out of work. And since she'd never accept our money any other way, this is a perfect plan.*
>
> *I can't wait to see her face when she finds out she's going to camp after all!*

A quick glance at the calendar told me Andie and I had a lot to do in a short time. The church bus was scheduled to leave for a camp in the San Juan Mountains next Thursday. That left only five days to take orders, bake goodies, deliver them, and get the money into the church camp account. All without Amy-Liz ever finding out.

Five days!

It would be tricky, but I was confident we could do it. With my organizational skills and Andie's baking ability, not to mention that secret family recipe of hers . . . surely we could pull it off in time.

The first thing I decided to do to speed up matters was call Pastor Rob. I waited till seven o'clock, though. Didn't want to wake him too early. I figured unmarried youth pastors like to sleep in on lazy summer days.

I tiptoed downstairs to the kitchen, took the portable phone out of its cradle, and hurried to my room. Safe inside, I closed the door. Had to make sure no one overheard this conversation.

The phone rang four times before the answering machine came on. After the beep, I left a message and wondered where I'd gotten the crazy notion that single youth pastors slept in on summer mornings. The machine said he was out playing racquetball and could be reached at the church office later in the day. Ten o'clock, to be exact.

I looked at my watch. Yikes! That was three long hours from now. I let myself freak out for a while about wasting those precious hours, then my thoughts turned to Andie. Maybe I could get things rolling with a quick phone call to her.

But wait. Knowing Andie, she'd still be in bed. I couldn't risk upsetting her. She might get mad and dump the whole mission in my lap. Without her top-secret recipe.

Snuggling against the pillows in my window seat, I tried to figure out a way to make the time pass more quickly. Goofey, my cat, purred loudly, and I reached for him, holding him close.

Minutes dragged as I stared at the clock on my dresser and Goofey lazily washed his paws. Then an idea popped into my head. I could use the time to contemplate my life. On paper, of course. The usual way.

I began to write in one of my many spiral notebooks, marked *Secret Lists*. This one was a skinny red notebook, perfect for making a single list down the left side. Today, I decided, the list would chronicle the major accomplishments of the last school year. Eighth grade.

I, Holly Meredith, age 14 years, 4 months, and 3 days old, with the help of God, have accomplished the following:

1. *Passed eighth grade with mostly B's, a few A's, and one C+.*
2. *Played the part of Maria in* The Sound of Music.
3. *Made room in my heart for more than one best friend.*
4. *Survived a huge crush on a student teacher . . . Mr. Barnett.*
5. *Learned what true love certainly is not.*
6. *Found out that God waits, sometimes till the very last possible minute, to answer prayers.*
7. *Discovered that having a stepdad can be fabulous.*
8. *Helped pray my father into the family of God.*
9. *Made strides in getting along with my three brousins (cousins-turned-stepbrothers)—Stan, 15, Phil, 10, and Mark, 9.*
10. *Showed big-sisterly love—most of the time—to Stephie and Carrie. (And may the Lord continue to assist me on this one!)*

I put my pen down and reread my list. Sounded good. I read it again. Something was definitely missing. Oh yes, I'd sponsored an overseas child.

Number 11. Quickly, I added that to my list.

Leaning against my heart-shaped pillows, I thought back over the last school year. Sometimes it was easier, more comfortable, remembering the past than looking ahead to the future. Maybe deep down I understood, but I shrugged the thought away. Next year—ninth grade—was going to be so different. Too different.

I refused to think about it. After all, nearly the whole summer lay ahead. And in just five days . . . summer camp. A whole week of fun. There would be hiking, swimming, craft classes, horseback riding, camp choir, a talent night . . . and those cozy campfires with s'mores!

Our church owned a large mountain property in the San Juan Mountains just outside of Ouray, Colorado, three hours from Dressel Hills, our tiny ski town. Ouray, pronounced you-RAY, was the perfect place for a camp, and I couldn't wait. Not only was the camp in a fabulous setting, everyone in our church youth group was going.

Last I'd heard, Jared Wilkins and Danny Myers planned to share a cabin with Billy Hill, my stepbrother Stan, and two other guys.

Andie, Paula Miller and her twin, Kayla, and I would definitely be together in one cabin. Joy and Shauna, inseparable friends, knew we expected them to join us. Counting Amy-Liz, there would be seven girls crammed into a cabin set up for six girls plus a counselor. It would be tight, but hey, what fun!

Oblivious to the time, I slid off the window seat and stretched for a few minutes. Then I went to get my devotional book and Bible off the lamp table beside my four-poster bed. I wasn't exactly sure how long I sat reading, but suddenly I was aware of footsteps in the hallway. Probably Mom going downstairs to start coffee for Uncle Jack. I leaped off my window seat and opened the bedroom door. "Psst! Mom?"

The top of her blond head appeared as she inched backward up the stairs. "Why are you whispering?" she asked.

"Didn't wanna wake up the whole crew," I said, referring to my five siblings.

Mom smiled, her blue eyes twinkling. "Everyone's already up."

"They are?"

She nodded. "We thought you were sleeping in."

I laughed, glancing over my shoulder at the notebook lying on the window seat beside my cat. "Guess I just got a little carried away."

"Well, come down when you're ready. We're having waffles."

"Didn't miss devotions, did I?"

"Uncle Jack left an hour ago," she said, wiggling her fingers into a tiny wave and heading down the steps.

"I'll be right there." I gathered up my pen and the Secret Lists notebook, putting it away for safekeeping. I could almost taste Mom's blueberry waffles as I pulled on a pair of shorts and T-shirt. Now, that's what I call a good way to start the day.

♥ ♥ ♥

After breakfast and after the kitchen was cleaned up with the help of Carrie and Phil—it wasn't my turn, but I pitched in and helped anyway—I ran upstairs to call Andie in the privacy of my room.

"Hey," she answered softly. "It's too early for intelligent conversation, in case you didn't know."

"Just be glad I didn't call you when I first got up," I said, visualizing a disheveled Andie on the other end of the phone. "So you're not officially up yet, huh?"

"You could say that."

"When should I call you back?"

"What's the rush?"

"Well, you know . . . remember what we talked about yesterday? About the money thing, for Amy-Liz?"

"Is that why you called?"

"I thought since we only have five days to raise the bucks, we oughta get started."

I could tell Andie wasn't in the mood for fast-moving conversation, let alone actually getting out and knocking on doors, taking orders, and stuff like that.

She sighed into the phone a little too heavily. Was she upset?

"Sure, that'll work," she said finally. And then—"You're really serious about this, aren't you?"

I held my breath. She wasn't backing out on me, was she? "Uh, yeah. It's important, you know, for Amy's sake."

Andie yawned into the phone. "I'm on my way. Don't start anything without me."

I beeped off the phone. I figured she'd be over in a half hour or so—plenty of time to brush my hair and braid it. I reached for the wooden box on top of my dresser. My hair accessories were inside.

Pulling my waist-length hair over my left shoulder, I began brushing. When the long, thick braid was secured with a hair tie, I went downstairs to the kitchen in search of my recipe box.

Our kitchen was a large, sunny room with the refrigerator and pantry at one end and a built-in corner desk at the other. The pantry was almost a walk-in closet, although I couldn't exactly stretch my arms straight out and still close the door. To me, a real pantry was one where a person could actually move around comfortably. Or hide from the world.

As a kid, I had declared this spot the perfect hiding place from my sister, Carrie, now nine. Of course, I was much smaller then. That was long before my parents divorced and Daddy moved to California.

Standing in the doorway, I scanned the shelves for my recipe box. The recipes had been an assignment for seventh-grade home ec. Probably wouldn't have one to this day otherwise.

Cooking was Andie's thing, not mine. I'd much rather write stories or read mysteries than keep track of recipes and ingredients. Reflecting on that fact, it suddenly hit me that Andie was actually right about my plan. Recommending this baking thing really was out of character for me.

Now . . . where was that silly recipe box?

The doorbell rang just as I spotted the hot-pink file box. I reached for the top shelf. "Could someone please let Andie in?" I called to no one in particular.

"I'm in," she said, right behind me.

I whirled around, almost dropping the box. "Don't do that!"

"Do what?"

"Sneak up like that. You scared me half to death."

Andie snatched the file box out of my hand, grinning. "So this is your famous seventh-grade recipe fiasco."

"Give me that!" I grabbed for it, but she ran across the kitchen.

"Why'd you always hide this from me?" Her eyes danced mischievously. "You were so secretive about it."

I could've easily retrieved the box. My arms were much longer than hers, and I was lots taller. "Go ahead, have a look," I said, relinquishing it.

She looked up at me, "You sure?"

"Uh-huh." I nodded, staring out the window and acting disinterested. That's when I noticed someone coming through the side yard.

I hurried to the window. I couldn't believe my eyes.

"Lousy timing!" I muttered, aghast. Amy-Liz was hurrying to the back door. I felt sorry for her—about her father losing his job. And worried, too, that Andie's and my plan might fail.

"What's wrong?" Andie asked.

I whispered, "Amy-Liz is here."

Smack! Andie dropped the file box on the island bar. She zipped over to the window.

"You don't think she's heard anything, do you?" I said. Without waiting for Andie's response, I turned and snatched my recipe box off the bar, returning it to the pantry.

Andie's eyes were transfixed on the window. Silently, I closed the pantry door behind me. The recipe box was safe. At least for now.

"What'll we do?" I said, tiptoeing to the window beside Andie. "I mean, she might discover the plan, and then she won't accept the money if she knows—"

"Relax, Holly," Andie interrupted. And with an impish grin, she turned to look at me. "Just go open the screen door. Leave the rest to me."

I cast a disapproving glance at my friend as I took baby steps across the kitchen.

Andie shooed me to the back door. "Go on," she whispered. Her eyes danced with mischief.

What did Andie have up her sleeve?

Chapter 4

Cautiously I headed to the door, which stood ajar to let in the fresh breezes of summer. I unlocked the screen door and let Amy-Liz inside.

"You're right on time!" Andie told her.

She looked completely startled. "For what?"

Amy-Liz glanced first at me, then at Andie, who marched right over to the pantry, flung the door wide, and . . .

Stop! I said with my eyes. Sending messages that way to Andie was a common occurrence. What was she thinking? How could she spoil our fabulous plan?

Andie ignored my facial warnings and brought out my pathetic recipe box, displaying it on the bar. What scheme was she cooking up now?

Andie motioned to Amy-Liz. "Here, pick out something, anything, for Holly to make for supper tonight. She wants to surprise her mom." She glanced over her shoulder and shot me a weird look.

I didn't say anything, mainly because Amy-Liz didn't seem a bit interested in my recipe box.

"Uh, I'm sorry." Amy-Liz backed away from the bar. "I really can't stay. Sorry, Holly"—she turned to look at me, her blond curls dangling—"I wish I could help, but I've gotta go. I only stopped by to see if I could borrow some of your sheet music."

Andie smiled, obviously relieved. "Well, you came to the right place, because Holly has tons of it."

I closed the lid on the recipe box and stood in front of it—hiding it—facing the girls. "Borrow whatever music you'd like," I told Amy-Liz. "Miss Hess let me keep some of the scores from the school musical, you know, just for the summer. I don't think she'd care if you borrowed them."

"Could I?" Amy-Liz seemed delighted.

"Wait here; I'll be right back." I hurried through the dining room to the stairs, leaving the recipe box behind.

When I returned with the music folder, I found Andie and Amy-Liz huddled over the kitchen bar, laughing. They stood up quickly as I came in.

"What's so funny?" I clutched the bulging folder.

"Just this," Andie said, holding up a recipe card. "How do you make meat loaf?"

I felt humiliation setting in. "Why . . . what does it say?" Although I didn't remember much of anything I'd written on those file cards, I did know one thing: Part of the home ec assignment had entailed creating recipes out of thin air. In other words, we were to simply make up whatever we thought would be delicious concoctions.

Andie waved the recipe in my face. "I can tell you one thing—nobody puts baking soda in meat loaf," she announced through a stream of giggles.

Amy-Liz frowned and pursed her lips. "Hey, give her credit for something," she said. "Maybe Holly likes her meat loaf light and fluffy."

I couldn't hold the laughter in. "Yeah, that's it. Puffy meat loaf." Reaching for the file box, I closed the lid. When it was resting safely in my hands, I smiled apologetically. "I think recipe analysis class is over now, girls." I stared at Andie, who caught my meaning instantly. I knew she did because she watched in total silence as I handed Amy-Liz the folder of music.

"Thanks, Holly," Amy said. "This'll keep me busy." She thumbed through the folder without mentioning her family's financial problems or the fact that her voice lessons had been axed. "I'll take good care of this, I promise."

"Have fun." I walked her to the back door. "And keep it as long as you want."

"Thanks again . . . and oh, sorry about your meat loaf recipe."

"No problem."

She waved good-bye. The screen door slapped shut.

"Whew, was that close or what?" Andie muttered when Amy-Liz was gone. "Think she suspected anything?"

"How could she?" I opened my recipe box and flipped through the index cards until I found my Super-Duper Snickerdoodle recipe under the tab marked *Cookies and Pastries.* And not once did Andie comment about the ridiculous meat loaf recipe the rest of the day.

♥ ♥ ♥

Aside from Carrie and Stephie showing up every five minutes to get something to eat, things went rather smoothly. We started work immediately on our money-making project by creating an order form on the computer, a kind of chart. Andie's cookie orders were on the left side and mine on the right. When we'd finished creating the form, I returned my recipe box to the pantry.

I checked to see that Carrie and Stephie were safely out of earshot. Then I called Pastor Rob to tell him our idea. He was delighted but reminded me of the short time remaining. I assured him that we could pull this fund-raiser off.

That done, Andie and I pranced out the back door, eager to take on our first street. My street, Downhill Court.

Probably anyone who saw us standing in front of Mrs. Hibbard's house next door would have thought we were just two girls out visiting the neighbor lady on a lovely summer day. But I felt nervous about this whole money-making thing. What if no one wanted to buy our stuff?

"Well, well, if it isn't little Holly Meredith," Mrs. Hibbard said, peering over her reading glasses. She glanced at Andie. "And who do we have here?" She lifted her head to get just the right angle, finding the bifocal line on her glasses as she reached out to touch Andie's shoulder.

"Aren't you Holly's girl friend? I believe I do remember the first time the two of you came to visit this old woman. Yes sirree, you were just about this high." She leaned on the screen door with one hand while she held out her other hand, trying to find the correct height in the air.

Andie grinned. "We're taking orders for snickerdoodles and Mexican wedding cookies today, Mrs. Hibbard," she said in her most pleasant voice. "You like delicious sweet and nutty treats, right? How many dozen would you like?"

Mrs. Hibbard gasped. "Dozen? Why, my dear, it's only me all by my lonesome. What could I possibly do with a dozen of anything?"

I sighed. Why had we come here first?

"Well, if you don't mind, Mrs. Hibbard," Andie continued, "maybe you'd like to purchase a dozen of each and give them away to the children in the neighborhood. Or freeze them ahead for the holidays." Before Mrs. Hibbard could interrupt, Andie said, "After all, it is for a worthy cause. You see, Holly and I are helping one of our girl friends go to church camp this summer. Because her father—"

"Well, why didn't you say that in the first place, little dear?" And with that old Mrs. Hibbard disappeared and went to get her purse.

"Why didn't you say that in the first place?" I whispered. "We can't forget this fabulous approach, okay?"

Andie wrinkled up her nose at me playfully. "I think it's time for *you* to get your feet wet with this door-to-door sales business. You may have the privilege of the next house."

"Oh, Andie," I moaned. "You're doing so well. Can't you keep—"

"Here we are, girlies," Mrs. Hibbard said, flashing a ten-dollar bill as she came to the screen door. "I don't care what it costs, just keep the change. It's for a worthy cause." She adjusted her glasses and looked at us both. "Now, when can I expect those snickerdoodles?"

My eyes darted to Andie's. Whoops! We hadn't discussed this important angle. "Uh, we'll have them ready by Monday," I said. "Is that all right?"

"Quite all right," the woman said, nodding.

Yes, that'll work, I told myself. *Tomorrow's Saturday—we'll bake up all our orders then. Sunday isn't a good day for deliveries because of church.* Monday was perfect.

"So . . . Monday it is," Andie said, thanking my neighbor for her donation and the order. "Have a lovely weekend, Mrs. Hibbard."

Together we scampered down the steps to the sidewalk like schoolgirls on a picnic. We'd made a sale—our very first!

The sun beat down hot on my head as we headed to the next house. I wished I'd worn a hat.

"Okay, it's all yours," Andie reminded me as we made our way to the next house.

"Please don't make me do this," I pleaded. "I'll do everything else. The cleanup, the baking . . ."

"Not my polvorones, you won't," she said. "That recipe does not leave my house!" Her eyes twinkled mischievously as I reached for the doorbell.

The neighbor's oldest son showed up at the door wearing his iPod. I waited for him to remove the plugs from his ears, but he didn't. He just stood there in a half daze, caught up in whatever he was listening to.

"Hey, Bryan," I said, a little too loudly. "Wanna order some—"

"Huh? What'd you say?"

I pointed to his ears.

"Oh, yeah," he mumbled. "Sorry."

I repeated myself, completely forgetting to say the perfect sales pitch that had worked so well with Mrs. Hibbard.

"Nah, s'too hot for baked stuff," Bryan said and put his ear-plugs back in.

"See," I told Andie as we reached the sidewalk, "you're much better at this."

"I see what you mean." But that isolated incident wasn't enough to get me out of doing my share of the sales soliciting. Nope. Andie wasn't one to give up so easily.

♥ ♥ ♥

After an hour of taking orders, we were hungry and really thirsty. We ran back to my house for some lunch and a tall, cold glass of lemonade. Mom had just finished making a pitcherful when we showed up.

"Well, hi there, Andie. Nice to see you," Mom said. Then she asked me, "Have you seen Carrie or Stephie lately?"

"Last I saw them was after breakfast. Why?"

"Well, they were just here a minute ago rummaging through the pantry," she said, looking puzzled.

I looked at Andie, who was frowning like crazy. "Uh-oh," I said. "You don't think—"

"Let's go," Andie said quickly.

"We'll be right back," I called to Mom as I followed Andie through the living room and out the front door.

"What's up?" I asked Andie, letting the door slam acciden-tally.

"I have a funny feeling we're being watched," she said as we began to scour the neighborhood, "and possibly followed . . . if you know what I mean." She sounded like a bona-fide detective.

We followed Downhill Court, with its bricked sidewalk and tall aspen trees. Turning at the end of the block, we hurried down another whole block before coming to Aspen Street, the main drag in our Colorado ski village.

The elementary school was located on the corner. I knew that my sister and stepsister often hid in the playground area behind the school. Mainly to discuss private things, they would say.

I stood in the shade of a clump of aspen trees, searching for signs of them. "See 'em anywhere?"

Andie groaned. "This is so bizarre. Haven't you taught your sisters good manners?"

"What's that supposed to mean?" I glared at her.

"You know. About snooping and stuff."

"Of course I have. I threatened both of them with their life last time they snooped around my room."

Suddenly I caught sight of Carrie's long blond ponytail. "Look! There they are. Behind the swings."

The long wooden play area with steps and levels, where kids played during recess, was like a fort. I could see Carrie's hair peeking out from behind the wooden slats.

"Let's scare 'em," Andie whispered. "It'll teach them a good lesson."

Perfect!

So, like slithery lizards, we crept across the playground, not making a single sound. Quietly, we inched our way closer and closer.

I could see Stephie leaning over, looking at something with Carrie. Her chestnut hair hung around her pixie face as she read out loud. We were only a few feet away from them when Andie spoiled everything by hiccuping.

Carrie turned around, startled.

Andie and I ducked out of sight behind the fort.

"No one's there," Carrie's tiny voice rang out, probably attempting to reassure Stephie.

But Stephie stood up and brushed the sand off her knees. "Something's spooky. I'm getting outta here!"

Another one of Andie's hiccups cut loose. I stood up just as

Carrie came around the corner. "Hey! What're you two doing spying on us?" she demanded.

"Well, well. How's it feel?" I glared at the stolen recipe box in her hands.

"Uh . . . it was Stephie's idea, honest," she insisted.

"Stephie's only eight," I said, implying that she wasn't smart enough to come up with something like that on her own.

"But I can read every word in that recipe box," Stephie said, innocently defending herself.

"Mom's gonna be ticked when she finds out you ripped off my stuff," I said.

Slowly, dramatically, Andie twirled a curl around her finger and moved in for the kill. "Exactly what are you two doing with Holly's recipe box in a school playground, two blocks from home?"

Stephie looked at Carrie and then back at Andie.

"You there . . . Carrie," Andie said, turning on the not-so-charming side of herself. "Speak up."

Carrie lowered her eyes, avoiding Andie's gaze.

I thought she was going to cry.

"Wait a minute," I intervened. "They can explain all this to Mom later. I'm starved."

"Hold on a minute," Andie bossed me. She moved closer to Carrie. "I want an answer, little girl, and I want it straight."

Man, did she sound like John Wayne today. Not so much the way she said it, but her words sounded like something out of one of those Westerns my oldest stepbrother liked to watch. Except Stan could really turn on the old John Wayne charm when he talked.

Carrie's bottom lip quivered. She was a pro at making it do that. Andie had met her match.

Finally, when Carrie had waited long enough to get the right amount of sympathy from Andie, she confessed, "We just wanted to do something like you big kids."

"Aha!" Andie shouted. "So you were snooping!"

I was worried that our entire mission was in jeopardy now. "Hey, time out," I said to Andie, giving her the eye.

"All right, you two," Andie said, wagging her pointer finger in Carrie's face. "Don't move. Wait right there!" And we left them looking mighty worried.

Andie and I made our huddle several yards away from the girls. I figured we were far enough from the fort area where Carrie and Stephie stood waiting. No way could they hear us over here.

I spoke first. "Whatever you do, Andie, don't tell them about our project being top secret."

"Why not? We'll just bribe 'em to keep their mouths shut or something."

"No, it doesn't work that way. We have to make sure they don't tell Amy-Liz what we're doing. They could spoil everything."

"So don't you at least wanna know how much of our plan they overheard?" Andie hiccuped again.

"Let's just drop it," I suggested. "The more we make of it, the more likely one of them, especially Carrie, might spill the beans at church."

"Okay, have it your way," Andie said, and we grinned at each other, ready to handle the situation in a very diplomatic manner. We turned around, ready to reason with the enemy.

But Carrie and Stephie were nowhere in sight!

"Why, those little . . ." I muttered.

"Look what you did!" Andie wailed at me.

"*I* did?"

"Whose idea was it to leave the scene of the crime and huddle up?"

I rolled my eyes. Andie was so good at turning the tables.

"Look, we need to work together on this problem," I said. "Let's try and stick up for each other for once."

That did it. Andie spun around and stormed off for the fort. She climbed up the chain steps and sat up there sulking like a little kid.

"What're you doing?" I called to her.

"Count me out of your benevolence project, Holly!"

I didn't like the sound of this. "But, Andie—"

"You heard me," she shot back. "You're on your own."

The last thing I wanted was to go door-to-door selling my baked wares alone. Andie was the expert spokesperson. I wasn't! Besides, we didn't have time for this crazy immaturity—summer camp was just six days away.

Chapter 5

"Fine, have it your way!" I called back to Andie.

Turning, I headed toward the street, trying to look confident. Inside, I was a total coward. In fact, if Andie didn't hurry up and have a change of heart and fall for my bluff and come running, like *now,* I was in big trouble. How could I possibly fill all those orders from this morning's door-to-door work, let alone whatever I would get this afternoon?

The sun was bright. A gorgeous day. Perfect for going home, bawling out Carrie for taking my recipe box without asking, giving Stephie the evil eye in hopes that she'd start thinking for herself, and last but not least, heading down the street to peddle my cookies. Alone.

I couldn't allow myself to worry about making Andie's wedding cookies without her. At least not at the moment. For now, I'd just have to pitch my Super-Duper Snickerdoodle cookies and hope someone would buy them.

Over and over, under my breath, I chanted Andie's winning phrases: *This is for a worthy cause. A friend of mine can't afford to go to church camp.*

By the time I reached the front porch of my first prospective buyer, I'd worked up a sweat, not so much from the sun's rays but from stress.

I rang the doorbell and waited.

Two preschoolers accosted their mother with begging and pleading after I told them what I was selling. Exactly the kind of assistance I needed!

The young woman literally had to pull one of the kids off her knee. "Can you wait for just a minute, miss?" she asked.

"No problem." I watched as the kids tore off after her. When she came back with the money for her order, I thanked her and headed to the next house.

Not bad, I thought as I reached for the next doorbell. By explaining Amy-Liz's dire situation first, I was saving myself time . . . and getting the customers' attention.

When I had acquired twenty additional orders, I decided I'd better cool it. If I got too many orders, I wouldn't be able to fill all of them by Monday. Andie and I had racked up seventeen sales earlier this morning. All totaled, I had thirty-seven orders. Nine of them for Andie's polvorones!

I raced home and found Mom and the boys folding laundry downstairs in the family room. Carrie and Stephie were hustling piles of clean clothing off to the respective bedrooms.

Maybe I'll get Mom to help me, I thought. But how to approach her . . . and when? Since becoming stepmom to four more kids, she was lucky to have even a couple of free minutes in her day. I really didn't want to bother her with my problems.

And Andie? Well, I could hardly believe it. She'd actually given in to her madness and stayed angry this time. All afternoon!

I went to my room, straightened it up a bit, and then wrote in my journal.

Friday afternoon, June 17: I can't figure Andie out anymore. She's really changing. I wonder sometimes if we aren't grow-ing in different directions. I guess it's really no one's fault, but things feel real lousy between us.

*I still can't understand why she didn't want to follow
through with my fund-raiser for Amy-Liz. And after all the
work she did with me this morning. I know she likes Amy-Liz
as much as I do. Maybe her heart just isn't in it. Well, nothing's going to stop me! Not now . . . not ever!*

Closing my diary, I glanced at the list of orders.

I hadn't taken a single order for Andie's recipe this afternoon.
Still, I had tons of work ahead of me. I nearly shook thinking about
coming up with twenty-eight dozen snickerdoodles by Monday.
Not to mention the nine dozen—that's 108—polvorones, which I
had no idea how to make!

"Lord, help," I whispered. "This is for a very worthy cause."

After supper the phone rang. I almost dropped the receiver
when I heard Andie's voice.

"So . . . how'd you do?" she asked.

"How'd I do what?"

"You know, the orders?" she said. "You went back out this
afternoon, didn't you?"

Not to be pushed into a corner, I said, "Hold just a minute,
Andie," and went to the kitchen to get a drink of water. A long,
very slow one.

"What's going on?" she asked when I came back to the
phone.

"What do you mean?"

"C'mon, Holly, don't play games with me. I've got something
very cool to tell you."

I tried to sound disinterested. "Like what?"

"You won't believe it," she went on like she was really excited.
"After you left, I went around to a bunch of houses, and I just got
done counting my orders."

"Wait a minute, did you say—"

"Yep, you heard right," she said. "I rounded up orders for twenty
dozen more Mexican wedding cookies."

I gasped. "You did what?"

She was laughing hysterically. "We're really in business now!"

"No kidding." Wow, what a bizarre turn of events. Maybe Andie wasn't changing so much after all.

"So where do you wanna do the baking?" she asked. "My house or yours?"

"Sounds like a project bigger than both of us," I said, suddenly feeling a little lightheaded and overwhelmed. I could just see us trying to get things done at her house with little Chris and Jon running around, snatching cookies off the table. And here? Well, it could only work if Uncle Jack took all the kids out of the house and left Mom home to help bake.

"I say we grab the Miller twins and some other girls in the youth group and bake at the church," she suggested. "What do you think?"

It was nice hearing Andie ask me for my opinion for a change. Actually, I was still too stunned to comment. I mean, just five minutes ago I was convinced that Andie had dumped the entire project.

"Well?" she persisted. "Any ideas?"

"Short of hiring out some help, we don't have much choice, do we?" I sighed. "The church kitchen is the perfect place. How many dozen did you say again?"

Andie giggled. "It's okay, Holly, really. I think we'll probably end up funding more than one needy kid with the proceeds from this project."

"You're right." We said good-bye, and I hung up the phone. Whew—what a day tomorrow was going to be!

♥ ♥ ♥

Not only did Paula and Kayla Miller show up to help, their mother came along, too. So did Shauna and Joy. Even Mrs. Martinez, Andie's mom, came to help supervise for a while.

When it came time to make Andie's recipe, she acted as though none of us should even see the recipe card. "It's been passed down for three generations," she bragged, holding it close.

"Andrea, for goodness' sake," her mother said, frowning.

I sneaked over when Andie wasn't looking and saw part of the ingredients. "Hmm, yummy," I said, reciting the first three items on Andie's index card.

"Holly!" She spun around. "Keep away!"

Her mom shook her head as she chopped away at a pile of pecans. "Share the recipe, will you?"

Andie stuck the recipe down her T-shirt, grinning.

"Aw, Andie, just *one* little peek?" I pleaded. "Ple-e-ase?"

The Miller twins, Shauna, and Joy inched closer, surrounding Andie.

"What shall we do to bribe her?" I asked.

"Girls, girls," Mrs. Miller called to all of us. "We have lots of work to do. Better get started."

"Call your daughters off me!" Andie hollered, now giggling.

"We'll leave you alone if you let us see the recipe for thirty seconds," Paula suggested.

"Ten," Andie said, holding her hands against her chest.

"That's not even long enough to focus," I said.

"Okay, okay." Andie finally gave in. "Twenty seconds." She pulled the recipe file card out of her T-shirt, then held it in front of her while she counted out loud.

"Looks easy enough to me," I said, playing it down in hopes of defusing the situation.

"Anybody can bake these," Kayla said. "What's the big deal?"

Andie's face broke into a broad smile. "Wait'll you bite into one. Just wait!"

We set to work sifting flour, mixing confectioners' sugar, and mashing butter.

♥ ♥ ♥

Stan stopped by at lunchtime with sandwiches for everyone, made by Mom. Wow, what an angel. (Mom, not Stan, although sometimes he could qualify, I guess.)

Andie started talking about delivering the orders.

"We haven't really worked out all the details yet," she said, glancing at me for moral support.

I nodded. Andie was right. This thing had mushroomed into such a monstrous mission, we might need two days for the deliveries.

Then, out of the blue, Stan offered to help us haul the cookies around Dressel Hills on Monday and Tuesday. "I can use the bike trailer."

"That'll be perfect," I said, giving Stan a playful hug before I went back to chopping pecans with Andie's mom.

"Hey, what about Billy and Danny?" Stan suggested. "Betcha they'd help us."

Paula smiled at her twin.

"Good idea," Kayla said.

"Then it's settled," I said, explaining where we'd meet and who would do what.

Paula and Kayla chattered about Billy and Danny and what an asset to this project they'd be. "I'll call Billy right now," Paula said, reaching for the phone.

"Remember to tell him to keep things quiet," I said in her ear. "This can't get back to Amy-Liz."

Paula nodded her head. "Oh, you don't have to worry. Billy can keep a secret."

It was interesting watching the relationships evolve between Paula and Billy and Kayla and Danny. Toward the end of school the foursome had been seen hanging out together around town. I'd seen them at our favorite hangout, the Soda Straw, several times.

I honestly felt good seeing the Miller twins, who were still rather new to Dressel Hills, spending time with some of the church guys around here. And, surprisingly enough, Danny seemed to be making his friendship with Kayla work. As far as I could tell, there'd been no evidence of Bible-thumping yet. Danny had a tendency to get preachy with his friends, something that became intolerable during the short time he and I were close.

It really didn't bother me seeing him with someone new. Danny Myers and I were history, and I was sure he felt the same way.

The baking was finished by suppertime thanks to all our fabulous help—an assembly line of workers. We'd even made extra cookies for the fun of it and shared them all around before everyone left. And Andie wasn't kidding. Those polvorones were out of this world.

♥ ♥ ♥

Sunday school and morning and evening services came and went, and miraculously, Amy-Liz was still completely in the dark about our secret project. Andie and I were giddy with excitement early Monday morning as we anticipated the many deliveries we planned to make.

"It's so cool, this whole thing," Andie said to me as we sipped orange juice on my front-porch swing. "I'm glad you thought of this project."

"What a job, though," I said, reaching for a cream-filled doughnut. "I hope I never see another snickerdoodle for as long as I live."

She laughed. "Ditto for polvorones."

We sat around relaxing as we waited for Stan to get back from downtown. Between the two of us, it seemed we could rope him into just about anything these days.

Andie and I laughed about it.

"We've got Stan wrapped around both our little fingers," I said, holding my hand up.

She glanced at her watch. "Hey, where is he?"

"Give him time," I said. "Mom said he had to run an errand for Uncle Jack first thing today."

"Is he wearing a watch?" Andie asked.

"He usually does."

"Yeah," Andie said softly. "So what's keeping him?"

I shrugged my shoulders and tightened the purple hairband holding my braid. "He'll be here sooner or later; you'll see."

But at nine-thirty, Stan still hadn't shown up.

"What'll we do?" Andie moaned. "If we don't get started soon, we'll never get done." She studied her list of names and addresses. "It'll take us forever."

I hadn't counted on Stan being this late. Surely he hadn't gone off fishing or something else with his buddies. I got off the porch swing and went inside.

"Mom!"

When she didn't answer, I went downstairs and checked the laundry room.

The house was quiet. Too quiet.

Quickly, I ran upstairs. She wasn't in her room. Not in any of the kids' rooms, either. I opened the door to Carrie and Stephie's bedroom. Both of them were sound asleep.

"That's strange," I said, closing their door. "Mom's gotta be around here somewhere."

Determined to locate her, I went back downstairs, through the kitchen, and out to the new addition. Phil and Mark were also sleeping when I tiptoed into their room.

Stan's room, however, was alive with sound. I dashed into his bedroom, through the maze of car mechanics magazines and a pile of underwear, and turned off his radio. Then I glanced around, looking for clues as to his whereabouts.

I knew he'd be furious if he found out I had rummaged through the junk on his dresser. But when I saw the note with Jared Wilkins' phone number and the words *video arcade—tomorrow,* I leaped for joy. Of course Stan was probably down at the old arcade. He probably just assumed that there'd be plenty of time to hang out with Jared—play a few games—before helping me and Andie.

But his irresponsibility had put us behind by a whole hour. How rude.

Guys!

Chapter 6

When I told Andie the news, her face scrunched up. "We'll just call the arcade and roust him outta there."

I could see it now, the place crammed to the seams with kids exhibiting that glazed-over look in their eyes, while the phone rang and rang off the hook. If there even was one.

Andie stood up, empty doughnut plate in hand, and headed for the kitchen. "So where's your phone book?"

"Where is my mom is a better question." I told her how I'd searched the house and found nothing but sleeping children everywhere.

"Maybe she went for a walk."

"Maybe."

Andie put her plate in the sink while I dragged the phone book out from the drawer. "I'll look up the number for the arcade," Andie offered.

I handed it to her. "Be my guest."

"Hmm, let's see . . ." She flipped through the book, found her place, and slid her finger down the page. "This oughta be it."

I pressed the numbers while she called them out. And just as I had anticipated, the phone rang and rang. And rang.

No one even bothered to set foot outside their individual game worlds. Reality-based worlds such as telephones and girls waiting for promises to be kept were lost in the mind-numbing maze of sight and sound and the challenge of defeating monsters. What could be more important?

"Okay, now what?" Andie closed the phone book and placed it on the countertop.

"Don't ask me. This is so typical," I muttered. "You just can't count on males."

Andie ran her fingers through her dark, wavy locks. "Okay, calm down." She was thinking it through. "What if we hop the bus and head downtown?"

I sighed. "That'll take too much time. We've got to think of another way."

She pulled out a barstool and sat down, leaning her elbows on the bar. "So, what's your plan?" She stared at me.

I'd thought of a Plan B, all right, but I knew Andie wouldn't be thrilled about it. Standing up, I took a deep breath. "We could make our own deliveries."

"Like how?"

"With a little help from Carrie and Stephie."

She tugged on the sleeve of her T-shirt. "You're joking, right?"

"Ever hear of wagons?"

She pretended to fall off the barstool. "Wagons? Are you crazy, Meredith? Do you know how long it's gonna take to pull loaded wagons around to all those houses?"

"Do you have a better idea?" I said.

"Hey, wait a minute. Whatever happened to Billy and Danny helping us? Weren't they supposed to show up today?"

"You're right." I drank the rest of my juice. "Paula called Billy from the church on Saturday, remember?"

She nodded. "Maybe Stan was supposed to remind them."

"Guys have a way of forgetting." It was true. Right now— when they were supposed to be over here assisting us with our noble mission—Stan, Billy, and maybe even Danny were probably shooting the breeze somewhere. Or hanging out at that ridiculous arcade with Jared.

Finally, after another glass of cold orange juice, Andie gave in. "If this is the best we can do, let's go for it." She mumbled something pretty nasty about Stan—and boys in general—before helping me get two red wagons down off their hooks in the garage. We loaded them carefully with stacked boxes of cookies.

I was actually amazed. We looked like we knew what we were doing as we wheeled our goods down the driveway and onto the bricked sidewalks of Downhill Court. Andie continually checked our lists as we made one delivery after another. One customer wasn't home, so we placed the order carefully inside the screen door. The main door behind it bumped open, revealing a snoring man on the living room floor!

Later we encountered a bulldog running loose in the neighborhood and freaked out for a while. Andie suggested we feed him a box of cookies to wipe the fierce look off his forbidding face. I said we couldn't spare any and suggested we ignore him. And we did . . . for three whole blocks!

Our problem was finally solved when we spotted my mom chatting with a neighbor down the street. She had been walking and said she'd lost track of time. Like someone else we knew!

"Will you take this dog home for us?" I whined, dumping my woes on her—about Stan not showing up, and the heat, and this miserable beast following us around.

She called to the ferocious fellow. He must've sensed the nurturing nature in her and went right over to her. Mom checked his collar and located his home address and phone number. "I'll call the owner," she said, heading into the neighbor's house.

"I hope Mom gets on Stan's case for not showing up," I mumbled to Andie, wiping the sweat from my face.

♥ ♥ ♥

Hours later, when Andie and I were in the middle of our own

personal heat strokes, Jared Wilkins rode by on his bike. He actually had the nerve to snicker at us. "Well, what do you know—it's the little red wagon brigade," he taunted.

"Beat it," Andie shouted. "It's all your fault."

"Yeah," I said, fanning myself with my hand. "Yours and Stan's."

Jared looked baffled. "I don't get it. Could you two be a tad more specific?"

I spun around, dropping the handle of my wagon. "You spent the morning with Stan, right?" I said, exasperated.

He shook his head.

"At the arcade, remember?"

"No, I just got up." He ran his fingers through his hair as he thought it over. "Hey, wait a minute, I was supposed to meet Stan downtown." He turned and smiled. "Thanks, Holly. Almost forgot."

I called after him frantically, but he kept pedaling down the street in the direction of downtown.

"What a nightmare!" I said.

I turned to see Andie opening one of the boxes, searching for eats. "I don't know about you," she said, "but I'm going to die right now if I don't grab a bite."

I pulled her away from the opened box. "No, no, you can't eat up our orders. If you're that hungry, let's just go back home."

She looked up at me, frustration in her eyes. "Here's the deal," she said, clutching her throat for effect. "If I leave now and take a break, you'll never, I repeat, *never* get me back out here in this heat again today."

"But what about our customers? We promised."

"Promises are made to be broken—isn't that what Stan and the rest of the guys did to us?"

I could see she was on the point of collapse. It was hot. So hot that I wished my hair were shorter instead of waist length. Thank goodness for one fat braid on a day like this.

"Look, Andie," I said. "I know it's hot and you're wiped out, but we have to finish this. Here, I'll take your orders while you go back to my house for lunch. Just leave your wagon parked here and I'll keep working."

"What about you?" She wiped the perspiration off her neck with a tissue.

"I'll manage. Besides, Mom should be home by now. Maybe she'll bring you back with something to eat and drink."

Andie huffed her response.

I could see this was asking too much. "Okay, okay, just fill up two sports bottles with ice water. That'll work. Oh, and bring the sunscreen."

She smiled weakly. "You're really something, Holly. Thanks."

"Don't worry about it," I said. But nobody else was out here in these blazing temperatures without a canteen of water or ice-cold pop, getting sun fried. "Hurry home," I called to her as I made my way up a set of very familiar steps, carrying two square boxes. One very frazzled mom and two clingy preschoolers came to the door.

The thrill of surprising Amy-Liz with a camp scholarship began to be crowded out by a zillion negative things such as hot temperatures, a parched tongue, and a growling stomach. Either that or my brain was cooked and no longer functioning.

Anyway, I was back on track—I kept telling myself—forcing polite smiles for the customers as I made each delivery, pushing myself onward.

One more block. Just one more . . .

And at the end of that block I repeated the same thing again. Over and over I pushed doorbells, keeping my promise to make the deliveries. No one would've even remotely suspected that I was secretly dying for the moment when Mom might pull up in our gloriously air-conditioned van.

Just when I thought I'd conquered and suppressed the desperate urge for a cool, refreshing drink, some guy came walking his white toy poodle, guzzling a can of pop. He must've seen my desperation as I stared longingly at the pop, because he stopped and started talking to me. "Man, you're wiped out," he said.

I stumbled over to an aspen tree. I felt dizzy as I sat down, leaning my head against the trunk's white bark.

Unexpectedly, he held out his can of what I thought was ice-cold pop. "Here, want some V8?"

In spite of my thirst, I didn't feel comfortable drinking from the same can as a complete stranger. Besides, a yucky vegetable drink made with tomatoes and celery and other hidden healthy stuff didn't exactly sound thirst quenching. And after being held in the sweaty palm of some stranger, the juice was probably lukewarm and congealing.

I shook my head and declined, which was probably a big mistake, but at this point, I didn't care. "Thanks anyway," I whispered.

He shrugged, said something to his dog, and off they went.

As I sat beneath the aspen trees, my tongue thick with thirst, I realized why the rich man in the Bible had pleaded with Lazarus to cool his tongue with a single drop of water. Vegetable juice just didn't cut it.

Now, I'm not saying Dressel Hills, Colorado, is like hell in any sense of the word. It's just this heat . . . this unbearable heat . . . this . . .

I closed my eyes, praying for relief, not caring about the wagon still half filled with cookies waiting to be delivered. All I could think about was how hot and thirsty I was.

Until now, I'd never really thought about the Lake of Fire. Our pastor's sermons weren't hell-bent like some ministers' sermons. In fact, he hardly ever mentioned the place. For some reason, our pastor was more into heavenly things when it came to preaching sermons. Maybe he thought people ought to choose God's Son out of a desire for divine, unconditional love, not because they were scared silly. Or . . . maybe that wasn't the reason at all. Maybe it was a lot more fun to preach about a perfect, fabulous place created by our heavenly Father than a hot, miserable pit prepared for the devil and his angels.

"Hot . . . pit," I muttered, fanning my face with my limp hand. "Horrible."

Waves of heat surrounded me. I sank into them.

"Holly-Heart." A familiar voice spoke my name.

I was too weak to respond, but I felt a cool palm against my feverish brow. Lightly, gently, she pushed back wisps of my hair, and the touch of her hand made my eyes flutter open.

"Oh, Mom . . . it's you."

Nearly incoherent, I thought I'd died and gone to heaven. The way her hand felt against my forehead—like the brush of an angel's wing. And then the sudden stream of cool water on my tongue. It was heaven, all right. Heaven on earth.

"Andie, help me get her into the van," I heard Mom say. She said it with the sweetness of one who could be trusted to take care of me. Mom was like that. I could count on her.

I strained to hear her voice. But it came and went like a poor phone connection.

"Holly, can . . . you hear . . . me?"

I tried to let her know I could, but my voice wasn't working. Nothing was.

She was talking to me again, but she sounded frightfully distant. As hard as I tried, I knew in my foggy state her voice was fading fast.

And then . . . it was gone.

Chapter 7

I drifted in and out, slightly aware of a plastic straw being propped between my parched lips. "Here, try to take a sip, Holly."

Straining to look up at the source of the voice, I was surprised to see Stan. Where had he come from? I sipped some cool water as I tried to get my bearings.

"Next time, why don't you use your brain and come in when it gets too hot," he scolded.

"Wha-at?" I mumbled drowsily, looking around.

Strange.

I found myself lying on the living room sofa. "Where's Mom?" I asked, pushing stray strands of hair away from my face.

Stan squatted beside me. "She and Andie are out delivering cookies."

I sighed. "What time is it?"

He glanced at his watch. "One-thirty. Why?"

"Guess I oughta eat something."

"You're right; you should." He got up and hurried off to the kitchen like he was the big man in charge.

He shuffled around with utensils and things, and that's when I decided he should make my lunch every single day for the rest of the summer. I wanted to punish him for the miserable way he'd abandoned Andie and me this morning.

While I waited for lunch, I thought about asking him why he hadn't shown up earlier. But I decided it was the wrong time. I wouldn't bring it up. Instead, I'd play the noble martyr and make him feel like the heel he was.

Stan himself brought up the subject when he returned, balancing a paper plate filled with chips and a tuna sandwich. "Uh, sorry about this morning," he said rather feebly, handing me the lunch. "Got a little sidetracked."

I avoided his gaze and picked at the chips, fuming inside.

"Hey, I said I was sorry . . . what do you want me to do, bleed?"

Then I blurted out what I hadn't really wanted to say. "Well, if you'd helped us like you promised, instead of spacing out at the arcade, I wouldn't be feeling so lousy right now."

There, I said it.

Silence reigned for a moment. Then he got up and started to walk away. "Look, girl, from now on make your plans without me," he sneered.

I nearly choked. "It was your idea to help make deliveries, remember? *Your* idea!"

His only response was silence. Some stepbrother he was. But I figured, par for the course. After all, he couldn't help it; he was a guy!

♥ ♥ ♥

Much later, when Mom and Andie returned, I was still peeved at the way the day had turned out. I wasn't very good company. Not for Andie, not for anyone. And my sunburn felt hotter than ever.

When Mom cornered Stan in the kitchen, I heard every word between them. "I want you to get out there and finish up those deliveries for Holly," she said sternly. "And when you get back from camp, you will be grounded for one week."

"But, Mom," he whined. He sounded just like Carrie and Stephie.

I snickered, scrunching down in the sofa next to Andie.

Mom continued, "You have an obligation to fulfill your promise to your sister and Andie." She wasn't budging on this, and I secretly applauded. "Now, I don't want to hear anything more out of you, or I'll add another day to your grounding."

When the kitchen encounter was over, Stan turned things around and acted like some kind of hero. Probably for Andie's benefit. Not for mine. I couldn't care less about his sudden change of attitude except that it meant our baked goods were going to get to our customers as promised.

My veins pulsed with anger. The idea to raise money for Amy-Liz Thompson had been my idea. Now Stan was waving like a valiant soldier before he headed out the door to make the rest of our deliveries. His schizoid behavior was back, for sure!

"Who does he think he is?" Andie said as we watched from the living room window.

I scowled at Stan even though he couldn't see me. "He's so-o disgusting."

"Worse," Andie hissed.

I turned to look at her. "You two still together?"

"Barely." She shrugged flippantly. "All he wants to do is play those mindless arcade games and brag about 'the virtues of virtual reality.' I really wonder whether it's worth being tied down to such a shallow guy."

"Especially since camp's almost here." I giggled, starting to feel much better just thinking about the possibility of the male options at Camp Ouray.

"Exactly," Andie agreed.

Carrie and Stephie showed up just then. "How much money did you make?" Carrie asked, eyeing the leather money pouch Uncle Jack had loaned us for the occasion.

"Let's count it," Andie said with a sparkle in her smile.

"Hey," I said to Andie, "sounds like you're actually excited about this project after all." After my words slipped out, I realized how insinuating they sounded.

"Don't give me that," she shot back. "Just because I didn't nearly sacrifice my life and die on the blazing sidewalks of Dressel Hills doesn't mean I didn't do my part!"

"Okay, okay." I dumped the dollars out on the coffee table. Then I handed the loose change to Carrie and Stephie, who spread the coins out on the living room carpet and took turns counting it.

Together, the four of us tallied up the proceeds. By the time we subtracted the money for all the ingredients and the boxes we had to buy at the uptown baker, there was enough money to send not only Amy-Liz to church camp, but one more!

That, of course, is when Carrie got the not-so-bright idea to pass herself off as a teenager. "I could go to youth camp, don'tcha think?" She pulled her hair up and strutted around the room.

"Don't think so," Andie sang. "Besides, you don't want to go to camp—there'll be boys there."

Carrie sassed back, "Maybe that's why I wanna go."

"Well, you'll just have to wait," Andie replied quickly. "Pastor Rob wants kids to be thirteen before they join youth group."

Carrie moaned.

"What's your hurry?" I asked, remembering Mom's typical response to me when it came to the subject of dating.

Carrie sat on the floor, letting her blond hair cascade down her back. "There's a cute boy in the group."

I gasped. "You're kidding, right?"

"Nope," she said with a straight face. "I'm ready to start dating."

I nearly choked. "Better not say that around Mom."

"And besides," Andie piped up, "boys aren't as cool as you think." She looked at me with her all-knowing grin. "Right, Holly?"

After a zillion and one hints, Carrie and Stephie finally left the room so Andie and I could talk privately. Not only were we thinking identical thoughts where the guys were concerned, but her finger was doing its twirly thing with her curls, which meant one thing: The male church youth population was in very big trouble!

♥ ♥ ♥

The following morning I boarded the city bus, the money pouch safely in hand. Andie and I had agreed to meet Pastor Rob at the church. He would see to it that the money we'd earned got to the church treasurer in plenty of time. Then he would notify Amy-Liz and her folks about the church scholarship, allowing us to remain anonymous. It was perfect.

Andie joined me several blocks down. The minute she boarded the bus, I could tell by her face that she had bad news.

"What's up?" I asked.

She bounced into the seat. "More boy trouble," she said. Then she proceeded to tell me the latest about Paula Miller's hassles with her guy friend, Billy Hill. "She says he's forgetting to show up when they have plans, and other stuff."

"How rude!"

"I know," she said. "But the worst thing is he's paying more attention to her twin than to her."

"Sounds perfectly awful," I said.

"Wanna know my theory?" She frowned. "The guys around here are simply spoiled rotten. Spoiled brats—that's what."

"But Billy Hill . . . I thought—"

"Better think again. He's turning out to be just like the others." She lowered her voice. "And just for the record, I called it quits with Stan last night . . . for leaving us in the lurch yesterday. And for making you faint dead away from heat exhaustion."

I stared at Andie, shocked. "I wondered why he was hoarding the phone too long last night."

She shrugged, acting like she didn't care. But her words told another story. "Did he say anything?" she said, almost too casually.

"What do you care?" I teased. "You're the one who ended it, right?"

She sighed. "Sometimes it's just nice to know the other person feels some of the pain, too." She sat up straight and as tall as she could for being inches under five feet. One thing for sure, though, she looked fired up and determined to follow through with her decision.

I tried to encourage her. "It's really much better this way. You need to be available—without a guy friend—when camp starts. You just never know who might show up."

"Maybe . . ." She took a deep breath. The situation between her and Stan wasn't quite as simple as she'd tried to make it sound.

"Sounds to me like the whole youth group's falling apart," I said, "at least in the boy-girl department."

Andie nodded pensively, and I knew by her silence she wasn't wild about discussing anything pertaining to guys.

♥ ♥ ♥

When our church came into view, we got off the bus. I clutched the money pouch as we strolled up the sidewalk toward the administrative wing.

At the corner, waiting to cross the street, we spotted Kayla Miller. Instead of looking fabulous, as usual, she looked rather pathetic. And even though I'd once used "pathetic" to describe her sister, Paula, this time I meant the word in a completely different way. Something was very wrong with Kayla.

It didn't take long for Andie to notice. "Hey," she said, giving me a quick nod of her head when Kayla wasn't looking. The gesture meant we should hang around and talk. Cheer her up.

"Hey, yourself," Kayla said, forcing a smile. "Are you pleased with the outcome of your pastry sales?"

The Miller twins always talked like they were fresh out of another century. But Andie and I were used to it; it was no big deal anymore.

"Fabulous results," I responded, more interested in finding out why she had wet mascara streaks down her usually perfectly made-up face. "Are you okay?"

Kayla reached for her shoulder bag and groped for a tissue. "Danny's completely unreasonable," she sobbed.

I might've predicted she and Danny Myers would end up like this. "So, which chapter and verse did he quote this time?" I blurted out.

She actually looked a bit stunned, but after she blew her nose she made no comment, so I didn't push for details. If she didn't want to talk about it, fine. It was her choice. Besides, she might get the wrong idea if I pursued the matter.

Kayla's face said far more than a batch of angry words. Her attitude toward Danny, and guys in general, permeated the air. She was one more innocent victim of some unthinking guy's lousy behavior.

Andie finally spoke up. "So, did you call it quits?"

"Absolutely," Kayla said between nose blowing and eye patting.

"Join the club," Andie said, not pompously but almost militantly.

"You too?" Kayla said.

Andie nodded. "I think it's time for a major change around here."

I registered exactly what she was thinking. "No kidding," I said, thinking of yesterday's lineup of miserable males: Stan's irresponsible attitude, Jared's glib "little red wagon" comment, and that goofy guy with the can of tepid V8.

Kayla dabbed her tissue up and down her cheeks. "It sounds to me as though too many of us have suffered the ill effects of having devoted too much time to our male counterparts," she said.

We agreed, consoling her by inviting her to accompany us to the church. When she'd composed herself, we walked up the steps to the main doors, camp scholarship money in hand.

Pushing open the church door, we headed inside like three musketeers. Down the hall, past the senior pastor's office suite and the secretarial offices, to Pastor Rob's little home-away-from-home.

He smiled, looking up from his desk as the three of us came

breezing in. "Morning, girls." He looked relaxed in light gray casual slacks and a striped golf shirt. "Whoa, somebody's got a sunburn," he said, looking at me.

"For a very good cause." I placed the camp money proudly in front of him on his desk.

"Thanks for your hard work," he said. "I know Amy-Liz will appreciate this."

I spoke up. "But you can't tell her where it came from, okay?"

"I won't breathe a word." He grinned.

The feeling I had as we skipped down the front steps of the church was excitement, pure and simple. Amy-Liz was going to camp. And her friends had made it happen!

Chapter 8

Thursday, June 23: Yikes! It's five in the morning! I can't believe I'm writing this early. It feels more like the middle of the night than the crack of dawn. This'll be the last time I write for one whole week.

I wish I could take my journal along to camp, but it's totally impossible—someone could find it and read it. No sense risking that. Besides, I'll be too busy.

I looked at my watch. Time to shower and get dressed for the day.

Seven days. A painfully long time to go without writing. Somewhat reverently, I placed my pen and journal back in my bottom dresser drawer. But before I finished packing, I slipped a blank spiral notebook into my overnight bag, just in case. . . .

♥　♥　♥

The church parking lot was crowded with parents and kids when we arrived. I couldn't remember seeing so many bags of luggage piled up, except maybe during choir tour last year.

The Millers' van took forever to unload. Looked like Paula and

Kayla had brought along their entire wardrobe and eight sets of shoeboxes to boot!

Danny Myers was carrying a mountain of books, and I was sure several of them were Bibles. I wondered if Pastor Rob was going to have Danny lead some of our devotions. He was good at it, all right. If only he could learn to temper his Scripture quoting away from the pulpit.

Amy-Liz and her girl friends Shauna and Joy stood around talking with one another's parents. I noticed the funky tie-dyed tights Amy-Liz was wearing under her shorts. Weird, but the fashion statement was definitely hers. But most of all, I was thrilled she was coming to camp.

I rushed over to her. "Hey, Amy!"

She smiled. "I can't believe this. I'm really here!"

"I'm so glad you're going. We'll have a great time in our cabin."

After we said good-bye to our bleary-eyed moms and dads, Andie, Paula, Kayla, and I found seats together on the bus. We settled in for the three-hour drive to Camp Ouray, smack in the middle of the rugged San Juan Mountains of southwestern Colorado.

Unlike the wild and crazy camp bus scenes so often depicted in books and movies, our bus ride was fairly sane. Most of the guys on board had wadded up a pillow and dozed off. I could see Jared and Stan toward the back of the bus sawing logs. Danny and Billy Hill were out of it, too.

Amy-Liz sat toward the front with Shauna and Joy, singing songs in harmony from *The Sound of Music.* I watched Amy's face as she sang one of Maria's songs, obviously ecstatic about getting to go to camp. Tiny tears of joy came to my eyes, but I brushed them away before anyone noticed.

On our church bus trips, girls were supposed to sit with girls, and guys with guys. So everywhere the girls sat, you could see two heads stuck close together, either whispering or giggling. A few of the guys, those who were not already asleep, were munching snacks.

Andie, Kayla, Paula, and I passed the time by discussing everything from how to keep sneakers deodorized with sprinkles of baking soda to how many outfits we'd packed for camp.

"How many outfits did you bring?" Paula asked me.

"Five."

"That's all?" Kayla looked dumbfounded.

I explained my strategy. "I read a book once about packing light and still being able to bring along lots of different looks."

"Like how?" Kayla chirped in disbelief.

"The trick is to layer, you know, like for weather changes and stuff. You never know what might happen in those ominous San Juan Mountains," I answered.

Kayla looked worried. This was her first trip to Ouray. "What do you mean, ominous?"

"For one thing, lightning storms can come up out of nowhere, and sunburn is always a problem at such high altitude," I said, remembering my own overexposure to intense heat three days ago. "And . . . it's even possible to encounter a freak blizzard this time of year."

Andie groaned. "Oh, spare me. Let's not talk about snowstorms."

Paula nodded sympathetically. "You must be thinking about the night we spent at school in that blizzard last March."

"Uh-huh," Andie said, glancing at me.

I remembered the blizzard. People had called it the storm of the decade. But it wasn't the lousy weather that stuck in my mind. Jared Wilkins had shown his true colors that night, and we'd ended up having a terrible argument. The worst ever. Trapped inside the school with the wind howling and the snow falling, I'd ended our special friendship.

Andie must've sensed my reminiscing. "So back to the wardrobe thing," she prompted me. "Tell us more."

I shifted gears mentally, letting the image of Jared's and my fight fade a bit before continuing. "You probably know all this stuff already," I said. "It's real easy to cut down on bringing lots of clothes just by learning to mix and match."

Paula nodded, smiling at her twin. "Kayla does that sort of thing automatically, don't you, sis?"

Kayla brightened, glancing down at her matching tan camp shirt and tennies. "I don't mean to boast, but it does seem to come quite naturally to me."

On that note, Andie inched down in her seat, pulling her legs under her. "I'm gonna snooze for a little bit now if you don't mind."

Snoozing sounded like the perfect solution to getting up much too early, along with being a good way to survive the long ride ahead of us. Except for one thing. I loved the mountains, and for me, experiencing a glorious sunrise while touring the Rockies was a fabulous way to begin a week of church camp. While my friends slept, I savored a pink and purple celebration of sunlight, a kaleidoscope of my favorite colors.

At that moment, I had a strong desire to record my feelings. I missed my journal already. Staring lazily out the window, I let my thoughts go. Let my body relax, too. The tensions of the week— convincing Andie to help with the baking project, organizing the fund-raiser, and surviving my fainting spell—crowded my memory. I escaped by imagining that I was sitting on my window seat back home.

I had always loved the way the sunlight filtered into my room above my cozy spot. Sometimes the light sprang in like a spotlight; other times it was like a warm, sleepy "hello." The comfy padded seat ran the length of the window, which was longer than it was tall. Because Daddy built the house back before I was born, I always figured he'd had some secret insight into my future snugglings there.

My window seat stood for many things, but the most important were privacy and the feeling of security I had when I sat there, journal in hand, with Goofey, my cat, purring nearby. Just a few of the amenities writing freaks like me had to sacrifice in order to go to camp. It would be 168 long hours before I could register my thoughts about life. And God.

♥ ♥ ♥

After stops for refueling and rest rooms, we arrived on the outskirts of Ouray, a picturesque relic of old mining days. Surrounded by towering rock cliffs, some pinnacles as high as five thousand feet, the place was hopping with tourists.

Among other things, Ouray offered all-day jeep trips and hot springs, which the Ute Indians had called sacred long ago. It also had high mountain meadows and herds of wildlife, not to mention Box Canyon, with its five-hundred-foot walk to a thundering waterfall.

Outdoor adventure, here we come!

The bus wound its way through an alpine meadow via a dirt road dotted with zillions of wild flowers—blazing orange Indian paintbrushes and blue and white Colorado columbines.

When we came to a clearing, the bus jolted to a stop. Instantly, sleepers awakened, yawning and stretching. I leaped out of my seat and crawled over Andie, drowsy from her nap, picking my way through the maze of passengers.

I was first off the bus. Outside, I breathed in the clean, pine-scented air. Even in June, the mountain air was crisp. Perfect weather, warm and breezy. And skies bluer than blue. Birds sang their welcome—a chorus of them. I felt the warm sun on my back and closed my eyes for a moment, realizing how very tired I was.

Behind me I heard a twig snap. I turned around to see Pastor Rob stretching his arms and legs. He walked up the slope toward me, gazing in all directions at the rustic campsite, nestled in a secluded pine forest. "Sure beats the city any day," he said.

"This is definitely God's country," I agreed.

"Yeah, and now it's our country, too—for seven days!" He clapped his hands. I turned and headed back down toward the bus, waiting for my friends.

The luggage war had begun, and I didn't have the energy to

fight it. I wished now that I'd slept on the bus. When I looked at my watch, I discovered it was only nine-forty. Seemed like forever since I'd crawled out of bed to shower and throw last-minute things into my suitcase.

Kids began spilling out of the bus. I spotted Andie and Kayla, and they motioned to me, whispering to each other. Suddenly Stan was right there talking to them. Danny too.

I rushed to Andie's side just as I heard her ask him—no, *tell* him—to please disappear.

Bravo!

And Kayla, well, I could see by the frown on her pretty face that Danny was definitely history. Only it hadn't quite registered with him. Maybe because she was being so cordial to him due to the fact that Pastor Rob was nearby.

But soon Pastor Rob got involved in helping kids find their bags, and it was just us. That's when Kayla got up her nerve and told Danny to hit the road. "It's over," she said, quietly yet firmly.

Danny wasn't giving up. "If something's wrong, Kayla, I'm sure we can work it out," he implored.

Billy called, "Yo, Danny!" and pointed to a pile of luggage. "I need your help over here."

"Coming," Danny called back. But before he left he looked at Kayla and made an attempt to apologize. "Look, I'm real sorry about whatever it was that—".

"Danny, are you coming?" Billy interrupted.

Danny shook his head, then looked at me. "Holly, can we talk later?"

"Me?" I squeaked, feeling extremely awkward about being stuck in the middle.

Andie grabbed my arm. Kayla's too. "C'mon, girls, let's not overexert ourselves." Danny's eyebrows shot up as she pulled us away.

Pastor Rob whistled for silence and began to distribute maps of the campground, as well as the schedule for the week. We stood around in clusters, trying to pay attention to his instructions. It wasn't easy, though. Danny and Billy kept gazing over at Kayla and Paula. Stan, on the other hand, completely ignored Andie. And me.

As was previously planned, Pastor Rob assigned Amy-Liz to Cabin B, already packed to capacity. "Hey, which of you girls is going to sleep on the floor?" Pastor Rob joked, eyeballing Andie and me.

"I will," I said, not certain how hard the floor of a log cabin might be.

"Let's locate an extra sleeping bag for Holly," Rob said. "She'll need it for the padding." He signaled for Jared to check for an extra one.

Jared ran down the hill to the bus. He poked his head into the luggage chamber and was still rummaging around searching for the elusive sleeping bag when I caught up with him.

"I'll get it," I said. No way was I going to let a guy help me with something so simple.

"No trouble, Holly-Heart." He flashed his biggest grin.

"No, I mean it, Jared. Let me do it!"

He threw up his hands and stepped back. "Fine, have it your way." And he left without another word.

Andie showed up, looking for her stuff. Paula and Kayla had very little trouble spotting their things. Their luggage looked like something fresh out of a department store catalog.

"Hey, this is camp, not Paris," Andie said, laughing at the elegant black suitcases and the accessories to match. Just then another church bus pulled into the parking area.

"That's probably the group from Buena Vista," I said. "Isn't our counselor supposed to be on that bus?"

"What's her name again?" Andie asked.

"Rhonna Chen."

"Just pray that she's not some mopey, stringy-haired biddy," Andie teased.

"Andrea Martinez!" I scolded.

Paula and Kayla blinked their eyes in synchronized rhythm. I guess that's what happens with identical twins—even if you don't have the same interests, your eyelashes can still blink to the same beat.

I couldn't help noticing some exceptionally cute guys getting off the Buena Vista bus. A boy wearing faded blue jeans and cowboy boots, his hair the exact same color as mine, stepped out of the bus. His T-shirt had the words *Rugged West* printed across it, and he was carrying a guitar case.

"C'mon, Andie," I said, leaning over and pulling her out of the luggage compartment. "We can do this later."

Pastor Rob whistled for us to gather around for bunk assignments. We hurried back up the hill to join the group.

♥ ♥ ♥

After orientation, Pastor Rob introduced a lineup of all the camp counselors and staff. Mr. Boyce, the camp director, was first, followed by the cooks, custodian, and lifeguard. There were two older men, one of them bald, assigned to two of the boys' cabins. I held my breath when I spotted the women counselors. Some of them looked as old as our mothers! But none of them looked Asian.

So where was Rhonna Chen?

Pastor Rob called out, "Cabin B." For a split second I had visions of the week turning out to be a total bomb. Maybe we'd get a super-strict mother type and never get to have a bit of fun. *Shoot, for this I could've stayed home. At least I'd still be keeping my journal going.*

Then . . . a Korean girl stepped out of the crowd. She had delicate features and a sparkling smile. Her Mickey Mouse T-shirt and red camp shorts were perfect. She even wore a red newsboy-style hat atop her shoulder-length black hair.

I wanted to dance. Andie did . . . sorta.

Rhonna Chen was not only cool, she was young. Not a day over twenty.

"Man, did we luck out, or what?" Andie said later as we lugged our things up the pine-covered slope to our cabin. Counselors and kids seemed to be running everywhere with their camp gear and luggage.

"Think she's gonna be strict?" Amy-Liz asked, stopping for a breath.

"Nah." Andie shook her head. "You can tell by looking at her."

Pine needles crunched under our feet as we took the dirt path, an uphill slope all the way. We followed the path across a log bridge that arched over a rippling stream, and then a few more yards to Cabin B—our home for the week.

All of us were a little out of breath when we arrived. I held the door open to the log cabin.

Amy-Liz trailed behind with Joy and Shauna. "Are you sure you wanna sleep on the floor, Holly?" Amy-Liz asked as she dragged her bags up the wooden steps. "After all, I was the last to sign up."

"I don't mind," I said. "It's important for all of us to be together in one cabin."

"Maybe we can trade off," Shauna volunteered.

"Good idea," Amy-Liz said.

"Count me out," Kayla said, glancing around the room. "I have trouble sleeping on a firm mattress, let alone on a hard floor." Paula nodded to verify her twin's remark as Kayla darted to claim the only bottom bunk left.

From the doorway, I could see our counselor crossing the narrow log bridge. She bounced as she walked, swinging her arms, yet there was a pained expression in her eyes. I stepped away from the door as she approached.

"Good morning, girls." She took off her red cap and spun it on her finger. We said good morning back.

Rhonna's face broke into a beaming smile as she leaned against the log doorjamb. Quickly, she scanned a list of names on her clipboard. Then, looking up, her dark eyes studied the three sets of bunk beds. "Looks like there aren't enough beds to go around." There was a question mark in her voice.

"It'll be okay," I spoke up. "Several of us are going to trade off sleeping on the floor." Shauna and Andie nodded.

I had to make sure I thought through what I said next. No way did I want to let on what Andie and I had done to get our friend here. I explained, "Amy-Liz just found out she could come, and we wanted her to be with us in Cabin B."

The girls cheered.

Rhonna held up her hand, grinning. "Okay, okay," she said, trying to quiet us down. "I get the picture."

She motioned for us to sit down. Joy climbed up with Shauna on one of the top bunks. Andie and I sat on the floor near Paula and Kayla, who sat side by side on Kayla's lower bunk.

Rhonna glanced around the room at each of us. "We have seven days to get acquainted with each other, but if you've been to camp before, you know how fast the days zip by."

We nodded in unison as she filled out the cabin roster.

"Well," she said, looking up, "let's not waste a single minute. Let's find out who's who."

It took us more than a half hour to go around the room telling our names, ages, favorite hobbies, and why we'd come to camp this summer. I knew almost everything about my friends, but I listened with interest when Rhonna told us about herself.

"This is my first summer as a full-fledged camp counselor." I couldn't believe she'd admit something like that. She was inviting all sorts of trouble—at least with any other bunch of girls. Us? Well, we were seven little angels!

Rhonna continued, "Last year I was a junior counselor in Grand Junction. I've always wanted to work with kids." Here she glanced at us. "I guess I should say *teens*."

We laughed.

"We're in this thing together," she said, emphasizing *together*. "And I'll be as easy to get along with as I can, but I won't stand for pushing the rules. If there's one thing I have a problem with, it's rule breakers. And bad attitudes." Her face took on a serious look. Not stern. Just serious . . . like she wasn't kidding.

"My college degree will be in political science when I gradu-ate next year, but I'm leaning toward working with young people. So—impress me, okay?"

Rhonna was charming. Not a pushover, but a fun-loving person who would probably bend over backward to get along with us this week. But there was something special about her. I felt drawn to her. Why?

When Rhonna led us in prayer, I felt very close to God. Almost as close as if I were at home, sitting on my window seat, having a private conversation with Him. "Dear Lord," she began. "Guide us by your tender hand. Keep us safe . . . and in the warmth of your love. Thanks for bringing all of us together in this fantastic place—in the middle of the tallest mountains around. Let us feel the majesty of your creation and the gentleness of your love. In Christ's name, amen."

After prayer, we had some free time to unpack and clean up for lunch. I couldn't help sneaking looks at Amy-Liz as she unfolded her clothes and made her bed—the bunk above Andie's. She giggled with Shauna and Joy as they unpacked. Seeing her here, and happy, made up for the sunburn and the near-heatstroke I'd suffered.

Even though I was dragging from lack of sleep, inside I felt absolutely fabulous.

"Check this out," Andie said, showing off the iron-on name tags on her stuff. Her mom had made her put them on everything—underwear, towels, even socks!

"Did you carve your name in your soap, too?" I teased.

"Yeah, right." She threw her pillow at me, which launched the first of many pillow fights. One of the true glories of summer camp.

Rhonna pitched in and helped make beds and get our linens and things in order. It was like she was really one of us. Why had I worried about who we'd get for our counselor? At this moment, things couldn't have been more perfect.

NO GUYS PACT

Chapter 9

Lunch was sloppy joes, potato salad, fruit cup, and chocolate chip cookies. We met in the long, rectangular-shaped log cabin that served as both a dining hall and a chapel area, as well as classrooms for several of our daily sessions throughout the week.

At one end of the hall, a white banner with the words *CAMP OURAY . . . HIP, HIP, HOORAY!* hung over a massive fireplace.

Even without air-conditioning, the all-purpose area was comfortable, probably due to plenty of open windows that allowed the mountain air to circulate. Outside temperatures were typically in the low eighties this time of year, but the low humidity was a big factor in maintaining the comfort index.

And no mosquitoes! Not even a common housefly survived at such high altitudes. No wonder tourists flocked to Ouray in the summer.

At the opposite end of the dining area, the kitchen and serving line were well laid out and quite suitable for a room this size. Andie and I, along with our friends, quickly found a table together.

Amy-Liz started telling about last Tuesday, when Pastor Rob had called with the news about the camp scholarship. "I could hardly believe it," she exclaimed, her face shining with happiness.

We shared her excitement, but no one uttered a word about the zillions of cookies we'd made and sold to make her camp dream come true.

Halfway through the meal, Jared came over and started talking and flirting with Amy-Liz. Since he and I were ancient history, it was no big deal—at least until he grabbed my braid. Just like that, he slid the hair tie off the end of it.

I spun around. "Hey! Give it back!"

But Jared was already out of reach, dodging two guys carrying lunch trays.

"Jared!" I shouted as my braid came undone. As thick as my hair was, no way would it stay braided through lunch without the pink hair tie. Luckily, I'd packed extras.

"Oh, Holly, your braid," Paula said sympathetically. Then, turning around, she glared in Jared's direction.

I squinted my eyes like Mom does. "Why'd he do a dumb thing like that?"

"Only one reason." Andie straightened up to her full height. "He wants your attention. He hates it when females ignore him—no matter who they are."

"Yeah, we know how he operates," Amy-Liz piped up.

"And to think I'd believed he'd changed." I thought back to the way things turned out between us at the end of eighth grade. Jared had actually seemed more settled. More mature.

Guess I was wrong.

"Once again, Wilkins snookered us." Andie rolled her eyes in disgust. "This is so-o grade school!" she observed.

"Well . . . immature or not, he's got no right." I slid out from behind the bench as my hair continued to unwind.

Andie stood up, too. "I'm coming with you, Holly."

"Me too," Amy-Liz said.

Kayla wiped her lips delicately with the napkin before getting up. "Count me in."

"Make that two of us," Paula said, raising her hand like she was in school or something.

We abandoned our lunches in order to catch the culprit. "Where'd he go?" I stood in the midst of kids chowing down all around me.

"Wait a minute. There he is!" Andie pointed toward the kitchen, and we hurried to nab him.

But Jared had spotted us. He pushed open the swinging doors leading into the camp kitchen, bumping into a lady with a large basket heaped with sloppy joe buns. Up . . . and out of the basket they flew. Buns everywhere.

"Hurry, let's help her," Amy-Liz said, and all seven of us raced to assist the bewildered cook.

I glared at Jared, who was acting disgustingly innocent. "Don't ever touch me again!" I shouted at him while scrambling around on the floor, gathering up sloppy joe buns.

"Sorry," Jared managed to mumble amidst the chaos.

I leaped up. "No, you're not!"

Unexpectedly, he showed me both of his hands, palms open. Empty!

"Where's my hair tie?" I demanded.

Jared began pulling the lining out of his pockets.

"Give it back!"

Jared turned tail and ran. "Later," he called.

"Why, you . . . !" I shouted, but by then the camp director had come to see what the commotion was about.

"Holly? Is everything all right?" Mr. Boyce asked.

I didn't know what to say. If I tattled on Jared, he'd have it in for me for the rest of the week. Yet if I didn't tell on him, I'd probably never see my pink hair tie again.

"I can handle it," I said, playing down the incident. Lucky for Jared.

Mr. Boyce looked at his watch. "You girls don't have much longer for lunch."

"C'mon," I said to Andie and the rest of the girls. "We better finish eating."

"I'm starved," Joy said.

"Me too," Andie said.

We hurried down the narrow aisle between the rows of fold-away tables. I wound my hair around in a makeshift bun as we headed back to our table. Then I snatched a clean fork out of the utensil tray and stuck the long end into my hair, securing the thick wad.

Wouldn't you know it, that's precisely when the Buena Vista cowboy caught my eye. Feeling suddenly shy, I smiled and rolled my eyes to show that this fork thing wasn't usual with me. His face lit up in return, surprising me.

I quickened my pace and caught up with the others. While I ate the rest of my lunch, my cabinmates shared again the woes of their past associations with males.

"I've had it up to here with Stan," Andie spouted off, touching her eyebrows. "He's a living, walking, breathing nightmare!"

Kayla spoke right up about how horrible she thought Danny Myers had been treating her. And Paula could hardly wait to launch off on Billy Hill.

I thought we'd taken this guy thing as far into the ground as possible when Amy-Liz pushed her plate aside. "I can't believe this is happening to the rest of you. I mean, I thought I was the only one suffering from male burnout." She muttered something about being sick of that flirt Jared.

Not surprised, I asked, "Is Jared bugging *you* now?"

"He's been calling nearly every day, talking sweet and all . . . then Shauna and I wised up and started comparing notes." Here she glanced down the table at Shauna, who nodded coyly. "We found out he's calling her after he says good-bye to me!"

"It's true," Shauna said. "Jared's doing what he does best—playing one girl against another." She looked sympathetically at Amy-Liz. "The thing is, he doesn't think he'll get caught."

"Well, he's got another *think* coming," Andie said.

Andie's comeback got the giggles started at our table. But across the dining hall, Stan was heading toward us, wearing a determined look.

Andie spotted him, too. "Oh, this is great," she muttered. "What's he want?"

I glanced up as Stan approached our table.

"Hey, Andie," he said. "Thought I'd pick up that magazine you borrowed."

Andie shrugged like she couldn't care less.

Stan kept looking at her like the magazine was real important. "It's the one with the article on John Wayne," he explained.

"I know which one it is, and I didn't borrow it; you gave it to me," she said.

"Well, I want it back."

"Fine," Andie snapped. "It's over there with my music folder." She pointed to a row of shelves near the entrance. And without another word, Stan left.

"If you wanna know the truth, I never really liked John Wayne," Andie whispered.

"Too bad Stan's obsession with his Old West movie hero hasn't rubbed off on him," I said, laughing.

Andie snickered, too. "Yeah, John Wayne could teach Stan Patterson a thing or two about women."

Kayla held her fork in midair. "Our church guys treat us with essentially zero respect."

"Who needs guys, anyway," I announced, forgetting about the cute blond cowboy four tables away.

"I'll say amen to that," Kayla blurted out.

"Not a-men," Andie giggled. "Not any-men." And once again, we totally lost it.

When all of us finished eating, we waited at the door while Andie went to get her music folder. I happened to glance over to where she was standing. By the frustrated look on her face I figured there was a problem. I told the others I'd be right back. Rushing to Andie's side, I discovered her plight.

"I'm gonna be in such trouble for this." She gestured wildly. "My piano music for choir practice is gone."

I looked around. "Where could it be?"

"I put it right here before lunch." She pointed to the lower shelf next to the window. "Mr. Keller won't be happy about this." She looked at her watch. "And choir's in two hours!"

I felt her rage. Probably because Andie and I had been best friends forever. The way I figured, she had a right to be angry. After all, Andie shouldered the sole responsibility of accompanying our camp choir. And she was good . . . the best around.

Today was our first scheduled rehearsal. Mr. Keller, the youth choir director from our church, expected promptness and perfection. Nothing less.

"Do you think Stan took it?" I asked, remembering the thing with his movie magazine.

Andie's countenance changed from frustration to pure anger. "That rat!"

I groaned. "Why did God have to give me such a louse for a brousin?"

Andie frowned. "What's brousin mean again?"

"It's the combination of cousin and stepbrother—"

"Never mind!" Andie was freaking out. "What's Stan want with my music, anyway?"

"He's probably ticked because you dumped him."

Her face turned a rare shade of bright purple. "Well . . . serves him right."

To top things off, Danny flagged us down as we were about to leave the dining hall. "Holly! Andie!" he called.

"Make it quick," Andie said.

"I saw what happened with your music," Danny said.

"We know—we know. Stan took it," Andie said sarcastically.

Danny's auburn hair was neatly combed, as usual, and he wore one of his button-down Sunday shirts. He looked like he was ready to claim the nearest pulpit.

"Calm down, girls. 'A gentle answer turns away wrath, but a harsh word stirs up anger,' " he said.

"Save your breath, Danny," I replied. "It's too late for soft answers or whatever. Stan's a toad." I almost added, "and so are you," but bit my tongue.

Once again, Danny had found one of the many proverbs stored in his vast memory bank and used it against us. Some friend.

Without looking back, Andie and I joined the girls from Cabin B, leaving Danny in the dust.

Chapter 10

Andie told the girls about Stan and her missing music on the walk to our cabin. "I've got to have it back before choir," she insisted.

"Well, it's quiet time now," Paula commented. "Stan's probably off trying to be quiet somewhere like a good boy."

I smiled at her insightful remark. Coming from Paula's lips the comment was hilarious.

"Well, it won't be quiet around here for long when I get ahold of him!" Andie exclaimed.

Shauna had an idea. "Maybe he'll just bring the music along to choir."

"Right, like *that*'ll happen," I said. "Not unless Andie begs him first."

Andie fussed. "Well, I'll just have to go track him down."

"I'll go with you," I offered. So did the rest of our cabin-mates.

A sudden breeze came up, making the aspen leaves rattle. I noticed that the sky had darkened; clouds were rolling in from the south. A summer storm was on its way.

Reaching back, I pulled the fork out of my bun and twisted my hair into an even tighter knot, hoping it would stay.

"Why don't you just let your hair hang free?" Amy-Liz suggested. "It's so long and thick."

"And glamorous," Kayla added.

Andie disagreed. "What she really oughta do is trim it—about ten inches worth."

"Don't you wish," I said. Andie was always hinting that I should lop off my locks.

"I know, I know, your hair is your best feature, right?" Andie said. I knew she was still fuming over Stan, so I overlooked her cutting remark. A loud clap of thunder and a burst of wind sent us scurrying up the path to the safety of our cabin.

Inside, I dug through my luggage and pulled out my bag of toiletries. Lip gloss. Sunscreen. Deodorant. Toothbrush . . . I groaned as the truth set in.

"What's the matter?" Andie asked.

"I forgot to pack my hair ties," I moaned. "Anyone have some I can borrow?"

I looked around. Everyone had that sorry-can't-help-you look on their faces. Paula and Kayla usually wore their hair down. Andie was definitely not into hair clips and things. And Shauna, Joy, and Amy-Liz didn't wear their hair up, either. I was sunk.

"Maybe someone from another cabin might have one you could borrow," Amy-Liz suggested.

"I can't ask a complete stranger." I couldn't believe this. At home I had zillions of hair ties—at least two for every day of the month. But in my early morning rush, I'd forgotten to pack extras. How could I have been so stupid?

Wrong, I corrected myself. *How can* Jared *be so stupid.*

I stood up, a frown of determination on my face. "It's time we women unite," I declared.

Kayla looked up. "How?"

Our first quiet time at camp turned out to be full of noise—booming thunder outside, pounding rain on the roof, and heated discussion inside. Fortunately, Rhonna Chen was occupied for the moment in a counselor's meeting somewhere. I'm not sure what she would have thought of the conversation we had.

"We could report Stan to the camp director and get him kicked out," Shauna said. But by the looks on everyone's face, no one was in favor of that.

"Or . . . we could form a society," I suggested, lowering my voice. "A secret society." I motioned for the girls to gather round. "We could make a pact—a no-guys pact. It's fabulous."

"Yeah," Paula said softly. "For girls only."

"Tell us more," Amy-Liz said, fooling with her tie-dyed tights.

I nodded. "Here's the deal: We create a pact with rules and stuff. And the first big rule will be to ignore boys."

Andie cheered. "Count me in!"

"You're amazing, Holly," Amy-Liz remarked. "What'll we call our secret society?"

"How about . . ." I thought for a second, then began laughing nearly uncontrollably.

"What?" Andie grabbed my arm.

I still couldn't stop.

"What's so funny?" Joy asked.

I coughed and sputtered, choking down the giggles. "It's perfect. Are you ready for this?"

My cabinmates leaned in even closer.

"Since the guys need a little help from their friends," I began, "we'll call it SOS, which stands for Sisters of Silence. Get it—SOS? Help for the guys—to teach them how to treat women."

The girls applauded.

"You and your wild abbreviations," Andie said.

"Remember that scrutiny test she put Jared through last fall?" Kayla asked. "What did you call it again?"

"STAN—Scrutiny Test to Analyze Nascence," Andie recited.

"Thanks," I said, tickled that they'd remembered. "So . . . what do you think about SOS?"

"I'd be delighted to join," said Kayla. "Show me where to sign."

"I'll show you, all right," I said, pulling my suitcase out from under Andie's bed. Thank goodness I'd packed my new spiral notebook.

I sat on the floor, using the top of Andie's suitcase as a desk. With pen in hand, on lined paper, I wrote the pact. The girls sat on the floor peering over my shoulder, some of them whispering to themselves as they read each sentence. Bottom line: We would ignore all boys to the best of our ability for the rest of camp week. Here's what I wrote:

The No-Guys Pact

We, the Sisters of Silence, on this twenty-third day of June, do promise and resolve to ignore the boys at Camp Ouray for the space of one week.

We may speak quickly to them, such as "Hey," or respond to a boy's greeting, but we will not be involved in any extended conversation.

We will not walk anywhere with a boy alone.

We will not sit with a boy in chapel.

We will not eat meals with a boy.

We will not sit around the campfire with a boy.

By following the above provisions, we hope to help the male population of this camp learn to respect us.

Everyone cheered when I wrote the final words. Andie was the first to sign her name. She handed the pen back to me, and I signed next. Then Paula, Kayla, Amy-Liz, Shauna, and Joy.

We sealed the pact with bright pink nail polish, the Miller twins' expensive stuff. When the polish dried a bit, I pressed my pen into the gooey substance and printed the letters SOS.

There. Now our pact was signed and sealed.

This was just the beginning.

Chapter 11

Paula broke the solemn silence. "When does the pact legally begin?" She flipped her hair for no obvious reason.

"Immediately," Amy-Liz replied.

"Hurray!" shouted the Sisters of Silence.

It was time for celebration all right. If I'd been at home, I would be reaching for my journal. So I went to the cabin window and stared out just as I did every day on my window seat at home. The rain had slowed up, and the sun had created a golden ribbon around the thunderclouds above.

Andie came up to me. "What's up?"

"Oh, just thinking about that rotten Jared person we used to fight over. Remember?" I turned to face her.

"The first crush of your life is a thief, Holly," she said softly. Sadly.

I nodded. "I want my hair tie back so bad I can taste it."

Andie stopped nibbling on her candy bar and offered it to me. "Here, try this."

I laughed. So did Amy-Liz, who'd overheard us talking. But the missing piano scores were no laughing matter. Andie had to find her music before choir. And I mean *had* to!

It was already one-thirty. Time for craft class for some of us. Archery class for the rest.

"We'd better get going," I suggested. "Rhonna probably won't be back here before we are. I've heard how long-winded those counselors meetings can be."

"How can we secure our cabin?" asked Andie.

"Yes, we have some very expensive make-up and clothes and things," Paula spoke up.

Kayla suggested pushing a chair under the doorknob so no one could just waltz in and rip off our stuff while we were gone. "But, then, how will we get out of here?" she asked.

Andie spied the back window and went to check out the situation. "Looks like this one's close enough to the ground," she said. "We can jump out over here."

Which is exactly what we did. We stuffed a chair under the doorknob and exited through the back window.

Just as I was swinging my left leg over the windowsill, I heard someone jiggle the doorknob. I froze—sat right there on the ledge like a stunned pigeon.

"C'mon, Holly," Paula said from outside, reaching up to assist me. "Are you scared to jump?"

"It's not that," I said, lowering my voice. "Someone's at our front door!"

I heard knocking. "Anyone home?" a voice called.

I whispered out the window to the girls, "It's Rhonna!"

The Sisters of Silence freaked out.

"Quick! Everyone back inside!" Then to Rhonna I called, "Uh, just a minute. I'll be right there."

It was the only logical solution. If we were caught leaving through the window and barring the door like this, well, I wasn't sure what might follow.

My heart pounded as Andie and Shauna pulled Joy back through the window and into the cabin.

"Not a word about anything," I whispered, thinking of the pact we'd made against the guys. Quickly, I removed the chair from under the doorknob.

Rhonna came inside, smiling big as you please. I'd expected a tongue-lashing for blocking the door like that. But she was as cool as you can get—still wearing her red cap. Only now it sat sideways on her jet black hair. "Having a private meeting, girls?"

We nodded, grinning like crazy.

She glanced at her watch. "So, who's doing crafts today?" she asked, looking around.

Andie, Paula, and I raised our hands.

"Anyone for archery?"

That took care of Kayla, Amy-Liz, Shauna, and Joy.

"Okay, let's go," Rhonna said, still smiling. It was like she actually remembered being a teen at camp. Without another word, we split up and headed in different directions.

♥ ♥ ♥

During basket-weaving class, my hair came loose three times. I had to keep winding it into a bun because it was too thick and heavy to stay put. Mrs. Campbell, an expert basket weaver and our instructor, finally gave me a long pencil to stick in it. The pencil worked much better. Probably looked better, too.

More important than my hair, though, was Andie's music. She was worried sick. And I *had* to do something. After all, Stan was my brousin. If I couldn't outsmart him, no one could.

Finally I excused myself, using the rest room as my reason to leave.

I left the great hall via the same exit as Stan had at lunch almost two hours ago. *Which way did he go?* I wondered, following the dirt path to the front of the building.

I needed something to go on. Just one minuscule shred of evidence . . .

Hiding behind the trunk of a dripping wet poplar tree, I spied out the land. Peering down, I scanned the path carefully and the wild grass on either side of it, hoping to find a clue.

To my far right were the guys' cabins; to my left, the girls'. In front of me, the commons area stretched across a flat, wide meadow bordered by tall pine trees that rose like pointed arrows straight to the sky. A flagpole stood in the center of the area. Behind that lay the sports area and pool.

I decided to scout things out in Stan's cabin. Surely, that's where he'd hidden the music folder. But I'd have to go around to the back of the great hall so I wouldn't be seen by the kids in the craft class. Mrs. Campbell would know I hadn't gone to the rest room if she spied me sneaking across the commons area to the boys' side of the camp. A definite no-no.

I backtracked, heading around to the rear of the dining hall. Down the steep slope behind it was the amphitheater, and even farther down, a rugged, wild area of rocks and cliffs leading to the valley floor. I sneaked down low so I wouldn't be seen by the cooks in the back windows.

Crouching, I noticed the blond cowboy carrying his raincoat and hurrying to the boys' cabin. Curious, I followed close behind.

He hurried inside the cabin. Probably to drop off his raincoat, I thought. One look at the sky and I knew the thundershower had passed. I stood outside the cabin, wondering what to do now that I was here. I certainly couldn't barge right in with him inside!

That's when he came out, looking mighty surprised to see me. Surprised . . . and, I must say, definitely pleased.

"Hey," I managed.

His eyes searched mine.

"Have you seen a music folder with 'Andie Martinez' written on the top?" I described the size and color.

"Oh, that." He disappeared into the cabin and emerged carrying the folder under his arm. "Stan Patterson found this somewhere," he said.

"No, he didn't find it," I insisted. "Stan stole it!"

He frowned. "Are you sure?"

"Positive. Danny Myers saw everything," I said. "Stan must be mad at Andie. That's why he'd do something like this."

His face lit up, bright with amusement. "Looks like you're mad, too." Suddenly I remembered the pact. *No extended conversation.*

"Uh, thanks for the music folder," I said, turning to leave. "You saved Andie's life."

But he called after me. "Wait!"

I turned around.

"I hope I'll see you again, Holly."

He knows my name!

The afternoon sun enhanced the blondness of his hair. And the blue in his T-shirt brought out the blue in his eyes. "My name's Todd Stillson." He paused. "What're you doin' later?" he asked. "Maybe we could take a walk . . . or something."

"We will not walk anywhere with a boy alone."

"Look, I'm sorry . . . I've gotta go." I forced my gaze away from his face and started down the path toward the dining hall, proud of myself for sticking by the rules of the SOS pact.

"Holly?" he called after me.

But I just kept walking.

Chapter 12

Andie leaped out of her chair when I returned with her music folder. She hugged me. And . . . *whoosh!* My hair came tumbling down. Again.

"Oops, sorry," she said, giggling.

"No problem." I redid my bun.

Andie held the music folder close. "Where'd you find this?" she whispered.

"It's a long story."

Mrs. Campbell glanced up, nodding. "Everything okay?" she asked, coming over to our table. I had been gone quite a while.

"I'm fine, thanks."

She scrutinized my half-woven basket, then looked at me a little too sympathetically. "If you hurry, hon, I think you might be able to finish your project today."

"I'll try," I said, smiling. The smile was really for Andie. I'd retrieved her music. A triumph!

When the teacher left to help someone else, Andie whispered in my ear, "Tell me everything." I should've known she wouldn't give up easily.

"Todd Stillson found it in his cabin," I said, enjoying the sound of Todd's name on my lips.

I couldn't help but notice Andie's bewildered frown.

♥ ♥ ♥

After crafts class, we waited for Mr. Keller to arrive for choir. Jared, Danny, Stan, and a bunch of kids from Buena Vista started showing up. Todd came, too.

All of us in Cabin B sat on one side of the stage area, which also doubled as the platform for chapel services. We women were sticking together, all right. Making a statement.

My hair kept coming loose, and it was really starting to bug me. And how awful that it had to happen in front of Todd.

Andie offered an idea. "As a favor from one friend to another, I'm gonna chop your hair off tonight . . . while you're asleep."

"You wouldn't!"

"Maybe, maybe not," she teased.

Recapturing something as ordinary as a music folder had completely rejuvenated my friend. As for my stolen hair tie, well, I didn't dare think about it, or I'd come uncorked.

The side door opened, and Mr. Keller burst into the room. He motioned for Andie to move to the piano. I watched her take her seat and arrange her music. I was certain that she'd never follow through with her threat. Besides, she was such a heavy sleeper.

Reaching up, I touched my hair. Maybe I could braid it later, do something to make the ends hard, to keep it from unraveling. *Elmer's glue might be a possibility,* I thought. *Glue washes out.*

Mr. Boyce showed up, and while he spoke with Mr. Keller about our Sunday chapel performance, I wondered if he might have some extra rubber bands floating around in his office. Surely he wouldn't mind offering assistance to a damsel in distress. The more I thought about it, the more I knew it was something worth pursuing. I would pay the camp director an impromptu visit right after choir.

Mr. Keller and Mr. Boyce stepped outside, and Jared took advantage of the moment.

"Psst, Holly!"

I turned around without thinking.

A pink flash!

Jared waved my hair tie in midair. Then, in a split second, it disappeared back into his pocket.

"How immature," Paula scolded.

"We really shouldn't have looked at him," I whispered to her.

"In keeping with the pact we made, you're right," Paula said. "*Ignore* is the key word."

By now Kayla and Amy-Liz were leaning forward in their seats, trying to hear what Paula and I were saying.

"We'll discuss this later," I assured them. The six of us—Andie was sitting prim and proper at the piano—leaned back in our chairs. Almost on cue. That synchronized motion surely had Jared and Danny wondering by now. In fact, the guys were beginning to lose it. Todd, however, looked more confused than amused.

Jared whispered that my hair looked like something out of *Little Women*.

I didn't flinch or move a muscle. A little respect would've been in order about now. After all, we were in the area where chapel services were held. Where worship and praise were given to God.

"Hey, Holly!" Jared called to me again.

I kept ignoring him.

"We've been talking about you. And we were wondering . . ." He paused dramatically to get everyone's attention. "Did you happen to notice that a flying saucer has landed on your head—complete with antenna?" He meant the bun and the pencil poked in it.

There was rousing group laughter now. And out of the jeering crowd I heard, quite distinctly, my stepbrother's voice.

That Stan, I thought sadly. *He's just as rotten as the rest of them.* Humiliated, I wanted to melt into the floor. But I kept my cool and refused to look at Jared. Or at any of the rest of them. I didn't even look at Todd, who hadn't joined in the laughter at all.

Paula reached over and touched my arm. "Don't pay attention to them, Holly-Heart," she said. "Your hair's beautiful no matter how you fix it."

I smiled. Leave it to Paula to comfort me. What a good friend she'd turned out to be. I felt more confident than ever about the pact. SOS was working! My sisters and I were in agreement—a unified front.

When Mr. Keller returned, he allowed us to stay seated for the first song. "It's good to see so many of you here," he said without cracking a smile. "Mr. Boyce tells me that we should have two choir numbers prepared for Sunday morning."

He went on to remind us not to chew gum, talk when he was talking, or sing like a soloist. "Blending is everything." He adjusted his wild purple tie. "I don't need thirty show-offs. If you want to make a statement, sign up for horseback riding, please." His face broke into a wide grin. "Any takers?"

No one.

The question was designed to weed out smart alecks on the first day of practice.

"Good! Now, sing as though your life depends on it," he shouted. "Because it might."

We laughed along with him. That was Mr. Keller. He spoke precisely what was on his mind. The nice thing about people like that is you always know exactly what's expected. Exactly where you stand.

As for standing, we lined up when we sight-read the second song. I stood proudly with my Sisters of Silence, ignoring Jared, Danny, and Stan. Billy Hill was missing. Evidently, he was out riding a horse . . . making a statement.

♥ ♥ ♥

After choir, we had fifteen minutes before afternoon devotions. My sisters were headed off to the rest rooms when I explained that I was going to hunt down some rubber bands.

Mr. Boyce's office was housed in a former boys' cabin. The

exterior was even more rustic than the other cabins, and I noticed several chairs lined up on the porch. Apparently the counselors had gathered there for their meeting.

I felt strange marching off in the direction of the camp director's cabin. Jared seemed uneasy, too, when I passed him standing near the flagpole. I made a point to walk with determination—straight for Mr. Boyce's office.

"Holly!" Jared called to me. "Let's talk!"

Oh, yeah, Wilkins. Not on your life.

Suddenly it dawned on me why Jared might be so concerned. Maybe he thought I was going to report him for taking my hair tie. This was perfect.

"Holly!" Jared said again. "Wait up!"

I chuckled to myself. Jared was playing right into my hands.

He caught up with me. "Where're you going?"

I spun around. "Where do you *think* I'm going?"

"Hey, relax," he said, taking a step backward. "This is camp, remember?"

"I remember, all right," I said. "Now, if you'll excuse me, I have to see Mr. Boyce."

He glanced anxiously at the camp director's office just ahead. "C'mon, Holly, lighten up."

"Later." I pushed past him.

"Wait, you're not gonna—"

"Not gonna what?"

"Listen, Holly, will you drop this if I give your hair thing back?"

Bingo!

I turned around, holding out my hand silently. Jared reached into his pocket and pulled out my pink hair tie.

Looking around, I hoped my sisters weren't watching. *Extended conversation.* The words pounded my brain.

Here I was less than two hours into the pact, and I had already broken the first rule.

Twice.

Chapter 13

"Happy now?" Jared asked me.

I ignored him, trying to make up for the pact rule I'd already fractured.

He cleared his throat. "Uh, Holly, could I ask you a favor?"

"Nope."

"C'mon. We're still friends, aren't we?"

"That depends."

"Look, I think you could be a little, uh . . ."

"What?" I snapped.

"A little friendlier" came the reply.

"Forget you."

"Why?" he asked. "What's going on?"

"None of your business." I turned, clutching my hair tie, and ran across the grassy area toward the path leading to the girls' rest room. At last I could get rid of this crazy hair bun!

I heard a group of kids laughing and talking as they came up the slope from horseback riding class. Several girls from Buena Vista were there, along with Billy Hill.

I darted inside the bathrooms, yanking the pencil out of my mound of hair. Like a waterfall, my hair cascaded around me. So much for bun head!

Luckily, my cabin sisters were still there. They'd finished washing up, and now they were primping in front of the mirrors.

"Look, everyone." I waved the hair tie at them. "I got it back!"

They crowded around me, buzzing. "How did you do it?" Andie asked.

I peered under a few stalls. "Anyone else here?" I asked. No way did I want outsiders overhearing what I was about to say.

"It's just us," Amy-Liz piped up.

"Good." And I told them what I had done.

Shauna and Joy listened intently as I told my tale. Kayla and Paula stopped combing their hair and stood spellbound, brushes in hand. Andie looked on with ever-widening eyes.

"But," I concluded, making a face, "I feel bad that I had to break the pact to get my hair tie back. I said I wouldn't have any extended conversation with a boy, and—"

"Well, you didn't talk to him *that* long!" Shauna interrupted.

"Besides," Amy-Liz chimed in, "you had to get your hair tie back."

"And in a decidedly clever manner!" Paula observed.

My Sisters of Silence were so sweet and forgiving that I began to calm down and feel better. Until Andie spoke up.

"Okay, enough sympathy," she said, clapping her hands briskly. Her dark eyes were fixed on me. "Holly broke the very first rule of our pact. It's not the end of the world, but it should never happen again."

I looked around, hoping to get some support, but they all looked down at their shoes, refusing to meet my gaze. The Sisters of Silence were *too* silent. Here I was, supposedly on friendly— *sisterly*—turf, having just suffered a tremendous blow to my self-esteem, and Andie sounded like she was threatening to kick me out of my own secret society.

"I know I'll do better next time," I said. Just then Todd's smiling face flashed into my mind. Would I be able to keep from talking to *him* next time?

The girls' solemn faces told me I'd better—or else.

Chapter 14

The bell rang for devotions at that precise moment, so my pact-breaking transgression was forgotten in the rush to the main hall. Danny was seated behind the pulpit with Mr. Boyce and Pastor Rob. I nudged Andie, rolling my eyes. "Look who's going to preach," I joked. "It's Pastor Danny."

Sure enough. After Mr. Boyce opened with prayer and Pastor Rob led us in a few songs, Danny stood up and gave a high-and-mighty exposition on a verse in Ephesians—about becoming mature in the faith. I sure hoped Jared was paying attention.

Todd was sitting two rows in front of me. His hair was charmingly messy. I could tell he wasn't a guy who was always checking himself out in a mirror. Not like Jared—Mr. Vanity himself.

Then I caught myself. *C'mon, Holly,* I scolded. *Ignore the boys— all boys. Cute and troublesome alike.*

The secret society must come first. *Besides, there's always next summer,* I thought, proud that I was sticking to my resolution.

After chapel, Todd came up to me. "Hey, Holly," he said, falling in step with me.

My face grew warm.

"Last one to Cabin B's a poached egg!" Andie announced as we approached the front entrance.

Amy-Liz, Shauna, and Joy dashed off, leaving the Miller twins and me behind. They gave me a searching glance. I could tell they'd noticed Todd with me.

"Let's go," I shouted, thankful for a graceful excuse to ignore Todd. Speeding up, I forced myself to match strides with Paula and Kayla. They had been on the track team during spring semester and were still in great shape.

The thing that slowed me down was the steep slope leading to our cabin. At last, exhausted from lack of sleep and too winded to go on, I slowed down. That's when I saw Rhonna.

She was coming out of the camp office, and her eyes were red. Had she been crying?

"Hey, Rhonna," I said.

She smiled a little. "How were devotions?" she asked. But I could tell she was making small talk.

"Are you okay?" I asked.

She nodded quickly, then shrugged her shoulders. "Well . . . no, I guess I'm not," she said. "Truth is, I was just talking to my mom. She and my dad are going through a pretty nasty divorce."

"Oh," I said. "I'm sorry."

"Your parents are divorced, right?" Rhonna asked. I had explained my weird family situation during the introduction time.

"Yeah. It was really hard for me," I said. "But that was a long time ago."

She had a faraway look in her dark eyes. "The only thing that seems to help these days is running. I get up early and jog till I drop. Every day."

I hardly knew what more to say, even though she seemed so open and friendly—not nearly as adult and distant as I'd expected.

"Maybe your parents will work things out," I offered—the fantasy I'd entertained in my own mind and heart for many years.

"No hope of that, Holly," she said softly. "Unfortunately."

"I'm sorry."

She nodded, adjusting her red cap. "So am I."

That seemed to end our conversation—at least that aspect of it. Now I knew what had drawn me to her earlier. Now I understood the pain in her eyes. I determined to keep the information private. Just between the two of us.

When we arrived at the cabin, Kayla was applying mascara to her already dark lashes. Joy and Shauna leaned into the wall mirror like Siamese twins attached at the shoulders.

Andie was obviously ready for supper; in fact, it appeared that she couldn't wait another minute. She reached under her bunk and pulled a blueberry muffin out of a shoe box.

Not surprised, I watched her hide her stash of leftovers under her bed. "You're not hoarding food, are you?" I teased.

She didn't seem to mind. "It's just in case I get hungry in the middle of the night."

Reaching for my brush, I unbraided my hair, brushed it out, then rebraided. Since the cabin was a bit crowded, I went outside and sat on the porch, waiting for the rest of the girls.

Rhonna sat on the porch, too, Bible in hand. I didn't know if she was preparing for our evening devotions—or finding some comfort in her situation. I let her read quietly.

I thought of the secret pact and wondered what Rhonna would think of the drastic measures my Sisters of Silence and I had taken.

The supper bell rang. Five-thirty.

Rhonna closed her Bible, then gave me a sweet "don't-worry-about-me" smile. It seemed that reading God's Word had helped.

"Girls!" she called, clapping her hands together.

When we'd all gathered on the porch, she announced, "We're going to have fun tonight. We have plans to get all of you interacting with one another."

Andie looked at me, frowning. "Like how?"

"You'll see," Rhonna said secretively.

"Tell us!" we girls shouted, swarming her.

Rhonna wrinkled her nose. "Among other things, you get to

pick someone you don't know and spend ten minutes talking to that person."

I groaned inwardly. This could be real tricky for the SOS! The rest of the girls stared wide-eyed.

"What?" Rhonna said, raising her hands. "Did I say something wrong?"

Andie rolled her eyes. "Oh no. Nothing at all."

Rhonna looked surprised. Probably at the lack of enthusiasm from us and the sarcastic way Andie had responded. "C'mon, girls, here's your chance to meet some new guys," she prodded, obviously thinking we'd be overjoyed at the thought.

Guys? Right.

The mere mention of the word made us sick.

Chapter 15

At supper, we filled up one whole table. We took our sweet time eating, chattering about the events of the first day at camp. But we avoided any mention of the pact since Rhonna was sharing the meal with us.

But we certainly did ignore the boys—in spite of their continuous attempts to get our attention. All through supper, Stan, Billy, Danny, and of course, Jared kept watching us.

Once, Danny strolled past our table, obviously going out of his way to get seconds. Not one of us spoke as he waved, smiled, and then . . . frowned. Andie nearly choked trying to keep a straight face.

To make the boys even more curious, we got into a string of joke telling.

Andie got us started. "What did the upper denture say to the lower denture?" she asked.

Kayla bit. "What?"

"We're going out tonight," Andie said.

"O-o-oh, Andie," the girls groaned. "Sick joke."

And we knew the guys wondered what on earth was so funny.

"Here's another one," Andie said, glancing over at the guys' table. "It's better."

"It *better* be," I said.

"What kind of boat does a dentist like best?"

None of us knew.

Andie grinned. "A tooth ferry!"

Then came a flood of camp riddles. Shauna started; then the Miller twins each had a turn. I kept waiting for Rhonna to share a good riddle. But she was silent, observing, not really joining in with the rest of us. "Hey, I know," Andie spoke up. "Here's a joke I just made up."

She glanced at me. "Did you know Jared spent all night trying to wake up his sleeping bag?"

We laughed, forgetting ourselves for the moment. Rhonna looked around at us, a small frown on her face. "Who's Jared?" she asked when we'd calmed down a bit.

We shot glances at each other. But no one said a word. The pact thing was top secret. Not even a cool counselor was allowed to be clued in.

♥ ♥ ♥

When it came time to clean up tables and get ready for the orientation, I caught Todd looking at me. He was sitting between Jared and Danny, and I wondered if they'd filled him in on what a sweet person I was. Seriously, I wondered what rotten things they'd said about me. I tried to avoid his gaze.

Ignoring Todd worked well enough until Mr. Boyce asked everyone to pair up and introduce themselves. I spotted a redheaded girl with braces two tables away and hightailed it over there. My sisters hurried to make contact with several new girls from Buena Vista, as well. We were meticulous in following the rules of our pact. I was doing well, that is, until Todd intercepted me.

"Hey, again," he said.

"Oh, uh . . . hey." I had no idea what to say next.

"How's your first day at camp?"

"Okay."

"You doing anything special for Talent Night?" he asked.

Everyone loved the big finale—the last fabulous night at camp. But I hadn't even begun to think about what I'd be doing.

"Well . . . I sing," I mentioned feebly.

"Great," he said. "I play guitar. Will you sing a duet with me?"

A duet? With Todd? I swallowed hard.

"Oh, that's very nice of you," I managed to say, "but—"

Andie was waving at me. Frowning too.

"Excuse me a second," I said to Todd and rushed over to see what Andie wanted.

She was caught up in animated conversation with one of the girls. Turning to me, she said, "Holly, you remember Alissa Morgan, don't you? You took her spot during the spring choir tour in seventh grade?"

Of course I remembered. If it hadn't been for Alissa leaving Dressel Hills, I might never have become good friends with Danny Myers.

Andie kept talking. "Well, this is Alissa's cousin, Emily. She likes to write stories, too."

"Hi, Emily," I said, wondering what to do about Todd, who was still standing off to the side, probably waiting for my return.

"I read one of your stories," Emily said. "In that magazine *Sealed With a Kiss.*"

"You're kidding. Really?"

Emily nodded. "Your story, wasn't it called something like 'Double Love' or . . ." She paused. "I don't remember the exact title, but it was great."

"Thanks," I said, deciding not to correct her. The actual title had been "Love Times Two."

I noticed the pin on the collar of Emily's camp shirt. It was a simple gold pen, and seeing it and meeting her made me miss writing in my journal more than ever.

Mr. Boyce asked us to take our seats, ending the ten-minute

encounter. The entire staff, including camp nurse, maintenance, and cooks, had assembled and were ready to be introduced formally.

My mind, however, was on Todd, the all-time cutest cowboy who wanted *me* to sing a duet with him.

I sighed. Was I breaking the pact rules to sneak a glance or two at him?

♥ ♥ ♥

Back in our cabin, it was nearly time for lights-out.

But I couldn't help myself; I opened my suitcase and located the spiral notebook containing the SOS pact rules. I wasn't referring to the rules or anything; I just needed a blank page. I had to write!

Way in the back of the notebook, where no one would ever see, I began my secret camp journal.

Thursday night, June 23: I can't believe how exhausted I am. We walk everywhere—to chapel, to classes, to the dining hall. Saturday, a big hike is planned. I'm worn out just thinking about it. And I'm peeling like crazy. But, oh well, getting sunburned was worth getting Amy-Liz to camp. I really think she's having a marvelous time.

This guy, no, this wonderful person, Todd Stillson, asked me to sing a duet with him for Talent Night. I'm torn apart— ripped, really. If I snub Todd, he'll think I'm rude. But how can I compromise the Sisters of Silence? (That's our secret society.)

I must be true to the pact—it's a no-guys pact, a list of things we absolutely refuse to do this week. Besides, the guys have it coming . . . our Dressel Hills guys, that is.

The first day of camp has been a nightmare!

There was so much whispering going on, nobody paid attention to my journal and me. Thank goodness. When I closed the spiral notebook, I slipped it safely into my suitcase and closed the lid.

There were three rounds of pillow fights before Rhonna signaled lights-out. That's when the giggling started. And the secrets . . .

It was a good thing the cabin was dark. And Rhonna was too tired to care. Or at least she was pretending to be asleep. Her parents' divorce must have been heavy on her mind.

Eventually all of us got tired and fell asleep, dreaming of boys and pacts and camp.

Chapter 16

Rhonna's alarm clock went off, shattering my early morning dreams.

Friday. Second day at camp.

I groaned and rolled over. *Let Rhonna do her predawn jogging thing,* I thought as I fell back to sleep.

Soon the rise-and-shine bell rang. I sat up—half of me still in my sleeping bag—and reached for my suitcase. Inside, I discovered some stationery and three self-addressed stamped envelopes.

Thanks to Mom. She knew me well.

I wrote her a quick letter, assuming that Uncle Jack would read it, too. I described our cool counselor, Rhonna Chen, and all the fun we were having. I left out the SOS and the no-guys pact, of course.

I could almost see Mom sipping iced peppermint tea on the front-porch swing of our home as she read my letter to Uncle Jack. When I licked the envelope, I sensed a twinge of homesickness. Only a twinge.

It was Joy who had a serious case, I discovered on our way to the showers. As we headed down the dirt path and over the log bridge, she confided her feelings to me. Not only was she homesick, she was worried about what the camp chef had cooked up for breakfast.

"Let's see if we can't get you some vegetarian meals," I suggested. "I'm sure a few other kids here are in the same boat."

Joy slipped her gym bag over her shoulder. "That's sweet of you, Holly. Thanks."

♥ ♥ ♥

I stuck close to Joy when we went swimming later that afternoon. Homesickness is untreatable and can easily turn into a debilitating disease. The rest of the Silent Sisters were ultraconsiderate of her, too.

We weren't being very nice to the guys, though. In fact, the pact and all its implications were beginning to take shape. Not only were we living up to our rule of no extended conversation, we weren't even returning *heys*. *Bye*s were out, too. So was everything else verbal.

We acted as though the guys weren't even sharing the same pool with us, steering clear of them so effectively that none of us noticed what was going on outside the pool. Outside . . . on the grassy area where we'd laid out our beach towels and sports bags.

Andie and I were getting out of the pool when Paula and Kayla let out matching shrieks. I turned to see what the noise was all about.

"Look! Our sports bags are gone," Paula wailed.

"With all our makeup!" Kayla cried.

"What?" I said. Andie and I dashed over to check on our belongings.

Shauna was already shouting, "Mine's gone, too!"

Sure enough, not a single one of us had our bags. Or our clothes.

Amy-Liz put her hands on her tiny hips. "You don't suppose—"

"Yes, I do!" I declared. "I think the guys know something about this."

Kayla looked like she was going to cry. "We *have* to get our stuff back."

"Wait, girls!" Andie called out. We stopped chattering and looked at her. "We're not going to let the boys get to us, right?"

We nodded.

"We're committed to ignoring them, right?"

We nodded again.

"It's really no big deal missing a few things, *right?*" She stared at each of us in turn. And like loyal sisters, we nodded again.

"And," she concluded, "we've got plenty of clothes back at the cabin. Right?"

"Right!" we cheered.

I could see what Andie was getting at. No makeup, who cared? If we acted like it didn't matter—which it didn't—we were actually defeating the guys' attempt to aggravate us. Perfect!

"Hey, you know something?" Amy-Liz said. "We don't have to mess with primping. And it's not because our makeup's gone."

I knew what she was getting at. "Because we don't wanna attract guys anyway, right?"

"Bingo," Andie said.

I couldn't help thinking that Jared, Billy, and Stan usually had more smarts than to risk being sent home for ripping off our sports bags. But then again, they were behaving like males, so maybe their smarts had gone ker-ploo-ey!

Kayla still looked frantic. "We can't wait too long to locate our things," she said. "I simply must have my makeup by supper."

"You'll be fine without it," I reassured her. "Just look at the rest of us."

Paula wasn't taking this business of zero makeup nearly as hard as Kayla. Not long ago, though, she would've been freaking out right along with her twin. Thanks to an afternoon at my house, Paula had seen the light. She'd abandoned her mascara-laden eyelashes. The heavy blush, too.

When it came right down to it, Paula's more natural look enhanced her true beauty. It did something else, too. Her fresh, clean look set her apart from Kayla. It gave her a new identity—her very own. Except now—at the moment—the two of them looked exactly alike.

"Couldn't I at least borrow from another girl somewhere?" Kayla asked sheepishly. This was a major concession from a girl who wore only designer clothes and used the most expensive makeup on the market.

"Listen, if it comes down to the wire, Kayla, you're welcome to beg makeup from the girls in Cabin A," Andie offered. "But"—and here she let her mischievous side surface—"if you do, you're out of the SOS."

Kayla's face drooped.

"Andie's kidding," I said, grinning. "But really, if none of us wears makeup, no one will stick out." I was hoping to soften the blow for Kayla.

"Besides, you don't wanna attract guys this week anyway, remember?" Andie teased.

Paula patted her twin's shoulder. "If you did, you'd just have to ignore them."

We laughed at that, heading to our cabin, wrapped in beach towels—feeling smug about not letting the loss of some petty things like makeup and a change of clothes spoil our afternoon.

SOS rules!

♥ ♥ ♥

That evening we had a cookout featuring barbecued chicken, corn on the cob, baked beans, and watermelon for dessert.

In line, Jared took one look at us and burst out laughing. "What's this . . . the natural look?"

"Right," Stan said. "So natural, you don't wanna look!"

The guys howled with laughter. Except Todd. He sat there in the middle of it all, surrounded by a pack of ignorant Dressel Hills males, behaving like a perfectly wonderful gentleman. Man, what our guys could learn from a Buena Vista cowboy!

None of us were moved in any way by the ridicule. We were as cool as cucumbers.

♥ ♥ ♥

After supper, all the campers hiked the half mile into Ouray. We ignored the boys the whole time, but they kept bugging us anyway. Stan untied Andie's shoelaces while she read a brochure, but she kept her nose up and completely ignored him. Jared bumped into Shauna "accidentally" when we stopped for ice cream, knocking the ice cream out of her cone. She simply picked it up, tossed it in the trash can, and went inside to order another. By the time we headed down the street to the San Juan Jeep Company, the guys were totally mystified.

Mr. Boyce and the counselors were collecting some brochures. And after they conferred together, Rhonna told us we were sched-uled to go on the wildest jeep trip of all—the Black Bear—next Wednesday, the last full day of camp!

Before heading back, we were allowed to split up for one hour. Several groups of guys headed for the Buckskin Trading Co., a store specializing in history books and mining. Danny and several other studious types made a beeline for a bookstore called Food for Thought. Jared and Stan followed us girls around, taunting us about being in public without our "faces" on. After a full thirty minutes of no response, they got bored and left. At last.

We wandered from one specialty shop to another. Then I saw it. Dozens of brightly colored shirts filled the window, and wild neon lights spelled out "The You-Name-It T-Shirt Shop."

"Come on, girls," I called, gesturing toward the store.

"What's up?" Shauna asked.

"I don't wear T-shirts," Kayla sniffed.

But I dragged them over to the shop anyway. A brainstorm was brewing.

"Here's my idea," I said once all the sisters were gathered around me. "How about if we get matching pink T-shirts with the letters SOS on the front!"

"And let's put a picture of a guy on the back, X'd out," Andie joked.

We all laughed. But—"Too obvious," I said. "This way, with only the letters on the front, the guys'll never know about our secret society. Besides, it will drive them crazy trying to figure it out."

"As if they aren't going crazy already," Shauna observed.

We laughed, rejoicing over our successful strategy.

"Which shade of pink?" Kayla asked. "Fuchsia goes best with my skin tone." Surprisingly, she seemed excited about the idea, even though the shirts were on the cheap side. At least, compared to the kind of money both Kayla and Paula usually spent on clothes.

"How about this one?" Shauna pulled a pink shirt from the stacks on the shelf and held it up.

"Fresh," Paula approved.

Then I noticed Amy-Liz hanging back from the rest of us. She caught my eye, then said bravely, "Sorry, girls, you go ahead, but I can't get a shirt."

"Why not?" Andie said without thinking. Then she remembered and blushed. We all looked at each other, embarrassed.

"I have some extra cash," Paula volunteered, opening her tiny shoulder purse.

Amy-Liz freaked out. "If I can't afford it, that's my problem."

"But you're in the society," Shauna argued. "You *have* to have a matching shirt."

"It's okay, really," Amy-Liz insisted. But it wasn't okay, and I could see this whole thing escalating. Whew, it was a good thing she didn't know how the church had gotten the money for her camp scholarship!

"We'll just forget the whole idea," I said.

"Look," Amy-Liz said, sitting down. "I'm not going to spoil everyone's fun. Go ahead, get the shirts. I insist."

Kayla's eyes sparkled. "Listen, Amy," she began. "What if I loan the money to you?"

Amy-Liz stared at the floor.

I held my breath.

"You can pay me back later," Kayla said. Wisely, she waited before digging into her wallet.

It was fabulous—Amy-Liz agreed.

Chattering excitedly, we headed to the counter to place our order. Fuchsia pink shirts with white letters. SOS.

"Hey, let's wear them now," Amy-Liz suggested. So we used the dressing room to change into our shirts, stuffing our old shirts into the plastic bags they'd given us.

The hike back to camp was a blast. Everyone, even the other girls from our church, asked us what SOS meant. But it was the guys who bugged us the most. When we didn't give them answers, Jared came up with his own solution. "SOS. Yeah, these girls need help, all right," he said loud enough for everyone to hear.

My sisters and I laughed right along with those foolish boys. If only they knew!

Chapter 17

Back at camp, we undressed for bed, recounting the T-shirt episode, careful not to divulge anything to Rhonna, who was definitely listening. She knew something was up, but she was being awfully cool about not prying.

Shauna volunteered to sleep on the floor. "If it's okay with you," she said, "I'll trade permanently."

I was surprised. "How come?"

She looked sheepish. "Well, if you want to know the truth, I'm not comfortable up there." She pointed to the bunk above Joy's bed. "I'm afraid I'll fall off the bunk and hit my head—get a concussion or something."

No one laughed. We could see she wasn't kidding.

"Sure, I'll trade," I said. "But what about Joy? You two are best friends." I glanced at Andie, who was already snuggling down for the night. "Maybe Andie and Joy could trade, too," I suggested—which they did after a quick change of sheets and blankets.

So, Joy slept in the lower bunk beside Shauna, who crawled into the sleeping bag on the floor, and that was that. Well, almost. None of us really settled down until Rhonna started devotions.

She began by reading the Golden Rule. " 'In everything,' "—she emphasized *everything*—" 'do to others what you would have them do to you, for this sums up the Law and the Prophets.' "

I felt strange. Guilty, I guess. We sure weren't treating the guys the way Jesus had commanded us to. *But they treated us pretty lousy in the first place,* I thought, justifying our actions in my mind.

Rhonna continued. "All of us are unique in God's eyes. We're made in His image. Just because certain people are different doesn't mean we should decide that they're inferior."

I wondered how much Rhonna had been listening to our conversations.

Andie blurted, "But what do you do when guys act like . . ." She stopped, looking at me. I could tell she was struggling with how much to share.

Rhonna finished Andie's sentence. "When *certain* guys act like jerks?" She smiled knowingly. "*All* guys aren't jerks, Andie, if that's what you mean."

It was exactly what Andie meant.

"Certain guys, is right." Andie groaned.

Rhonna grinned. "Let me tell you a story—a true story—about when I was your age."

You could almost hear a collective sigh. An interested sigh, that is. We leaned back on our pillows, our hands supporting our heads as we listened to Rhonna tell about her past.

"There was a boy," she began. "A very *fine* boy."

We giggled. Rhonna was so cool.

"His name was Mel, and he was far and away the best-looking guy in the youth group." She stopped, like she was thinking ahead to the good part. "Only thing, Mel was biased in a big way. Prejudiced against slanted-eyed girls like me. He even had a nickname for me. Honestly, I've forgotten it now. Maybe I blocked it out of my memory because it was so painful."

I was beginning to feel sorry for Rhonna.

She continued, "One night after church, I tried to introduce myself, to let him know I actually had a name. He turned away from me and started talking to some other girl . . . like I barely existed.

Well, later my older sister found out through the grapevine that he refused to have anything to do with Asians."

"Why?" Amy-Liz asked, wide-eyed.

Rhonna shrugged. "Some people can't accept others who look different from them. It's sad but true. But just because Mel was a jerk didn't mean that *all* the guys in my youth group were in the same category."

Andie smiled. "So you're saying that just because certain guys bug us doesn't mean we should shut 'em all out?"

Yeah, Andie, I thought. My mind was on Todd. Again.

Rhonna nodded. "Some boys take a longer time to grow up, I guess you could say. But by ignoring the obnoxious ones—which you all did very well"—she grinned knowingly—"you are showing them you can't be hurt by their antics."

"So," I piped up, "you think we did the right thing?"

There was a mischievous sparkle in her eyes. "Just don't turn it into some organized society or something. In other words, don't carry things too far."

I gasped. It sounded like she knew about SOS!

I glanced around at my sisters. For once, we were really earning our name. The sisters were solemn—and silent.

♥ ♥ ♥

The next morning at breakfast, I noticed several Buena Vista girls casting snooty glances from the next table. A short redhead was one of them.

I decided to ignore them—something I was getting better and better at all the time.

Most of the guys had cleared out when Miss Carrot Top strutted up to our table. It seemed she had planned her strategy well, since she waited for Rhonna to excuse herself before showing up.

"You don't know me." She smiled, a mixture of braces and lip gloss. "I'm Laina Springer, Cabin E."

I forced a smile, trying to be cordial.

Laina leaned down, whispering, "The guys from your church are scheming something lowdown and dirty."

"Like what?" I asked.

"I . . . uh, we heard it's something about getting someone's attention." Springer's braces twinkled momentarily.

"Who said?" I asked.

She fidgeted, looking around at her friends still sitting at the table behind ours. "Well, according to Billy Hill,"—and with the mention of his name her face burst into a wide grin—"your church guys are ticked off. So they've got some big surprise planned."

Andie shot up out of her seat. "What sorta surprise?"

"Beats me," Laina said, turning to leave. "Just thought you'd wanna know."

Yeah, right! I wasn't going to let *her* scare me.

"Listen, Laina." I reached out to touch her arm. "We really appreciate the tip. Thanks a lot." I forced the biggest, most sincere smile I could conjure up. "Oh, and if you happen to hear anything else, could you let us know?"

Her shiny lips twisted over her braces into a weird little pained expression. "Sure," she peeped out and returned to her table.

What was the guys' motive in giving us this advance warning? Maybe they planned to get us all freaked out, on the edge of our seats, anticipating something drastic. And then absolutely nothing would happen.

I pondered these thoughts for a moment. Then quickly, before Rhonna returned, I shared my theory with the rest of the SOS.

Andie frowned. "Surely the guys aren't *that* stupid. I mean, just look at the trouble they could get into just from taking our sports bags and stuff."

Paula eyeballed Laina Springer and the girls at the other table. "I can't believe Billy would tell her anything."

"Well, *I* can," Amy-Liz interrupted.

And so could I.

Kayla looked a little foggy, like she wasn't so sure about any of this.

Amy-Liz set down her lemonade glass. "You know, Holly might be on to something. Maybe we oughta keep watch."

"I'm still trying to figure out what makes guys tick," Andie said.

Paula flipped her hair. "If Holly's right, this would be one way for the guys to ruin our week without doing a single thing."

Kayla nodded, like the light had finally dawned. "Sounds feasible."

I grinned. "It's the coward's way to get us guarding our cabin door."

Shauna sat up. "To tell the truth, I think Jared's still mad because Holly told him she wouldn't be his girlfriend anymore."

"Well, we can't let it spoil our camp experience," Kayla commented.

"Kayla's right," I said, grateful to see Laina and friends get up and carry their trays off to the kitchen. Followed by her string of straight-faced girl friends, the spunky redhead looked like a contemporary Pied Piper. I couldn't imagine Billy spending time with the likes of her. But Billy Hill was the epitome of an unpredictable male, as were his cohorts.

♥ ♥ ♥

Another busy day sped by.

Swimming, craft classes, a noontime picnic, horseback riding, and finally the twilight hike. Not once did any of the makeup-less SOS speak to a guy. Not a single time.

After supper, we headed off on our hike with Rhonna.

Several other girls and their counselors joined us, but fortunately not Cabin E.

I was looking forward to this hike. I figured since I had given up guys, the least I could do was enjoy the rest of God's creation. Sunsets included.

Rhonna insisted that each of us carry a water bottle in our backpacks, as well as granola bars and flashlights, even though we were only going for a moderate hike. She was like that. "Be prepared for anything," she said.

Steadily, we worked our way up a gradual incline, stopping occasionally to catch our breath and view the sights, hearts pounding from exertion. Andie and I linked up as hiking partners, and even though lately Paula wasn't too eager to hang out with her twin, she teamed up with Kayla automatically.

Rhonna and Joy led the way, with Shauna and Amy-Liz close behind. The trail was wide enough for two to walk side by side.

"This trail will adjust us gradually to the altitude," Rhonna said when we paused for one of our huff-and-puff stops.

"How high up are we, anyway?" Joy asked.

"Almost eight thousand feet," Rhonna said.

"Whew!" Andie whistled.

I sat down on a log to tie my tennies and catch my breath. Suddenly out of the stillness came a high-pitched whistle. I leaped off the log. "What's that?"

Rhonna chuckled. "Sounds like a marmot saying hello."

Andie searched everywhere for the furry little guy, but the rodent must have scurried off to his burrow for the night.

I squinted as the Saturday sun sank behind the mountains beyond us to the west. "Look, Andie, it's almost sunset," I said, enjoying the peaceful moments of the evening. What a fabulous contrast to the conflict of the first three days at camp.

We hiked farther before stopping midway up one of the highest mountains overlooking Ouray. Andie and I found a place to sit on a massive rock at the edge of the trail. There, I stared in awe at the sunset. Red and gold streaked the western sky, and the sweet smell of pine filled the air. In the hushed stillness of twilight, the SOS, the pact, and the hassles with boys disappeared.

After a long silence, Rhonna whispered, "Girls, look!"

Far below in an open meadow, a deer meandered from the protection of the pine forest, searching for cool mountain waters. I held my breath as she located the stream and drank.

Rhonna said softly, " 'As the deer pants for streams of water, so my soul pants for you, O God.' "

I recognized the psalm she quoted. It was one of Mom's favorites. For a split second, I wished Jared and Billy and the other guys—Danny, too—could have been here to witness the inspiring scene. Ripping off our sports bags and making lowdown, dirty threats seemed almost insignificant at a time like this.

♥ ♥ ♥

After the hike, we headed back to our cabins, ready for a full night's sleep. I wondered if the guys had pulled a fast one while we were gone—that deed our weasel-like informant had warned us about at supper. But as we crossed the log bridge leading to Cabin B, things appeared to be perfectly normal.

"Nothing happened," Andie whispered as we rummaged around for our toothbrushes and towels.

"Right, and let's hope it stays that way," I replied.

Andie and I were the first to make the nightly trek to the bathroom. "Here, we'll need this," she said, pulling a flashlight out of her backpack.

When we arrived, Andie pointed her flashlight into the darkened log structure. "Anyone home?" she called out. I giggled as she groped for a light switch.

Nothing.

Again she tried the lights.

"Something's wrong," she said. "The electricity must be off."

A quick glance toward the dining hall/chapel building told us differently. "That's weird, lights are on everywhere but up here," I said.

"Well, whatever's wrong, I can't wait forever," she stated. "You guard the door, and I'll take the flashlight with me." Andie hummed a song of courage as she disappeared into the darkness.

Outhouses and outdoor rest rooms had never been my favorite places. Maybe because I had gotten locked inside a nasty-smelling outhouse on the top of Copper Mountain last summer.

Suddenly Andie's humming stopped. The night was too still. I inched forward. "Andie?"

"I can't believe this," she wailed. "There's no toilet paper!"

"I'll go find some," I said, bravely entering the darkness to aid my friend. When I made the turn into the stall area, my eyes became better adjusted, thanks to Andie's flashlight. I opened the door to the stall beside hers.

No paper there, either.

I went to the next one and the next. "How bizarre. Do you think the camp maintenance people just forgot to restock?"

"Oh, this is great," Andie said with a sigh. "Remember what that Laina Springer said about the guys?"

I gasped. "It *is* them. They did this. It's so despicable!"

"So, what am I gonna do?"

"Wait here," I said. "I'll get some tissues."

On my way back to the cabin, I met up with the other girls. Quickly, I filled them in on the situation. Hearing the news, the sisters grew more determined than ever to ignore the boys.

Amy-Liz summed it up for all of us. "One thing's for sure," she said, "if this is how the guys think they're gonna get our attention, they're still *absolutely* wrong!"

♥　♥　♥

Later, while lying in bed, I thought of the events of the day. If taking our light bulbs and toilet paper was the lowdown, dirty deed Laina had mentioned, then the rest of camp week was going to be a cinch.

Still, I wondered how the guys would respond to zero reaction from us girls. Would they become even more determined?

Joy and Shauna were still whispering as I gave in to the scratchy feeling behind my eyes. I dreamed a marmot was chasing me, but when I woke up, I realized the sound of the marmot's whistle was coming from Andie's stuffy nose.

Sometime later, in the misty, wee hours, I was sure I heard people tiptoeing around in the cabin. Cracking open my eyes, I saw something shiny gleam in the moonlight. But when I tried to sit up, my body went stiff as a board. Absolutely numb. The sleep stupor overtook me, and I sank into it.

♥ ♥ ♥

Rhonna's alarm rang too early the next morning. But I fell back to sleep. Much later, I awoke to the sound of Paula and Kayla whispering. I opened one eye and saw them gather up their towels and clean clothes for the day. The twins headed out the front door.

I squinted my other eye open, yawning. Looking around, I saw that Andie and I were the only ones left in the cabin. Joy, Amy-Liz, and Shauna must have wanted to be the first to hit the showers.

I peeled dead skin off my arm while relaxing on my upper bunk. Wide awake now, I leaned over the side, peeking down at Andie. She looked so little all curled up in a ball beneath me. I was proud of her stand against my brousin, even though I knew it was painful. After all, Stan had been Andie's longest-running guy friend.

I stretched in my bunk, eager for another busy day at camp.

The twins hadn't been gone more than five minutes when I heard Kayla yelling, "Those horrible boys!"

"Holly! Andie!" Paula called as she came back into the cabin.

I tossed off the covers. "Wha-at?"

"Come look," Kayla said, peeking her head into the cabin. "You'll never believe this!"

Andie appeared unconcerned. She rolled over, pulled the blankets over her head, and snoozed on.

I swung down off the top bunk, then grabbed my bathrobe and pulled it on as fast as I could. In my bare feet, I ran out the door and down the path behind Paula and Kayla.

When we came to the clearing at the bottom of the slope, I stopped cold in my tracks. Directly in front of the chapel stood three stately pine trees, uniquely decorated. Their branches displayed underwear—pink, blue, and white bras, matching panties, and two pairs of baby-doll pajamas.

An underwear raid!

And not just *any* underwear raid. I could see Andie's iron-on name tags adorning numerous items. Paula's and Kayla's bras were obvious by their size. My own intimates were recognizable, of course. At least by me.

"Lowdown and dirty, all right," I muttered, completely stunned. "How embarrassing."

Kayla and Paula stared in silence.

"We've got to get this stuff down before breakfast," I said. "Mr. Boyce will have a cow."

"Shouldn't the guys be worried about that?" Paula asked.

"You'd think so, but once again, we're not dealing with intelligence here," I reminded them.

We hurried back to the cabin. Thank goodness we'd discovered this state of affairs so bright and early.

"Andie!" I hollered, out of breath. "Get up!"

She moaned pitifully from her mound of covers. I pounced on her bed. "C'mon, Andie. This is war!"

"What's war?" she muttered in a sleepy, throaty voice.

Such a way to begin the Lord's Day.

Chapter 18

Andie got up immediately when I announced that her baby-doll pajamas were waving in the breeze in front of the chapel.

Just then Shauna, Joy, and Amy-Liz arrived back from the showers, their hair still damp. "What's going on?" Joy said when she saw our faces.

Paula explained the situation, and panic ensued.

"My brand-new bras!" Kayla moaned.

"You think you have it bad. My underwear is *labeled*," Andie complained.

"The guys are begging for battle," I said.

In no time, all of us were standing in front of those three pine trees. Paula reached up, trying to retrieve her dangling blue bra.

"Our Dressel Hills guys, all right. Has to be," Andie fumed. "But let's deal with who did it later. We need some long-handled brooms . . . or something."

Amy-Liz found a rake around the side of the girls' rest room and shower area. "Too convenient, don'tcha think?"

I wondered about that, too. Had the guys actually come into our cabin and used this rake to do their wretched deed?

"Wish we could dust for fingerprints," Andie said, eyeing the rake handle.

"No kidding." I watched as the Miller twins carefully located their personal items, getting them down with the long rake handle.

One after another, we stretched and strained, poking at pine branches with the rake, bobbing for underwear. Andie was last. She was too short to reach her baby-doll pajamas and panties and things. I volunteered to help while the rest of the girls headed off to the cabin.

"We won't let the guys get away with this," she hissed.

I agreed, shoving the Golden Rule out of my mind. "I have a plan."

"Good, because if you don't, I do," Andie said.

It turned out that the entire SOS—once we were gathered in the cabin—was in agreement. We would deliver a declaration of war describing why we were retaliating and what we wanted. It all boiled down to this: The guys wanted our attention. Well, they would get it. I scribbled furiously.

We, the girls in Cabin B, do declare war on the boys at Camp Ouray. You have taken our personal items and displayed them disrespectfully for the world to see. You have stolen our makeup and clothing. You have hurt our feelings and tampered with our self-esteem.

Therefore, we declare all-out war. Starting from the second this envelope is opened. In return, we want respect. From all of you!

> *Signed,*
> *Holly, Shauna, Andie, Joy,*
> *Amy-Liz, Paula, Kayla*

Andie was champing at the bit when she signed—no, scribbled—her name. Kayla could hardly write her name, she was so angry.

After we had all signed the document, I added a P. S. at the bottom: *The Bible says, "There is a time for everything. A time for war and a time for peace." Well, guess what time it is!*

I folded the paper and put it into one of my stationery envelopes. "I'll deliver this," I said grimly, waving it in the air.

On my way to the camp post office, I ran into Todd.

"Holly!" he called to me.

"Oh, hi," I said. *Perfect timing!* "Could you give something to someone for me?" I said sweetly, then realized how perfectly insensible that sounded.

"Sure," he said, glancing at the envelope in my hand. "Like who?"

"You know Jared Wilkins, right?"

He nodded.

I handed Todd the war letter. "Thanks a lot," I said, dying for Jared to read it and spread the word.

He frowned. "What's this about? You two are really fighting, aren't you?"

"Uh, not just him and me," I explained. "The girls in Cabin B have had it with the entire male camp population."

He looked stunned. "Why? What happened?"

I turned to go. "It's a *long* story."

"Wait, Holly, about the Talent Night . . ." He looked serious. "Have you decided on anything yet?"

No way was he going to fit into the scheme of things. Not *this* summer.

"Maybe you should ask someone else," I said. "Sorry, but thanks for delivering the letter. See ya." I waved and was off before he could pursue the matter. I wasn't too thrilled about conversing with the enemy, polite—and cute—or not. As far as my sisters and I were concerned, there was no neutral ground in our battle plan.

It was all-out war, beginning with water balloons to be administered during quiet time, right after the noon meal. Over lunch, we drew up our strategy.

Andie wanted to blow a trumpet or something and march around the boys' cabin, Jericho style.

"You've gotta be out of your mind," I said.

"Yeah," Amy-Liz agreed, fooling with her bandanna. "We'll attract too much attention."

"Okay, then, what?" Andie asked, looking too eager to embark on the first attack.

I made a quick sketch of the boys' cabin area, showing the route we could take—down the steep slope, through the pine forest, around the amphitheater, and up the hill.

"Masterful," Kayla said, tracing the imaginary path with her well-manicured finger.

Instead of Joshua's army, we were the SOS battalion.

♥ ♥ ♥

Our initial attack was so fabulous! We never even looked where we were throwing. Just opened the guys' cabin door and pelted those boys good!

At first they yelled. Then their shouts turned to enthusiastic hooting as some of the balloons came flying back in our direction.

Shaving cream, too.

The cabin was filled with white foam, spilling out through the doorway, hissing through the screened windows. What an unexpected counterattack!

Kayla screamed. Some of the shaving cream caught her in the eye, and Paula guided her away from the chaos, toward the girls' rest room.

"Retreat," Andie shouted, and all of us followed.

Our quiet time before devotions officially ended with our explaining to Rhonna why we were angry at the guys and that they deserved any prank we might play on them. Of course, we left out the part about a zillion water balloons and where we'd been. Fortunately we'd rinsed off the shaving cream before returning.

Paying attention to Rhonna's devotional and her prayer wasn't easy with my mind on our next strategy conference. Even so, I heard snatches of words like overlooking wrong deeds, forgiveness, getting along, etc.

❤ ❤ ❤

Later, Andie had the bright idea to ask permission for us to take a short hike. Without Rhonna. It was free time, anyway.

Rhonna agreed. She looked worn out, probably from all those early jogging sessions. Surely it had nothing to do with keeping track of seven conniving females.

When we were far enough away from the cabin, our meeting began under the covering of the pine forest.

"What happened back there?" Kayla asked, referring to the guys' ammunition.

"Yeah, where'd the shaving cream come from?" Shauna complained.

I shrugged. "They must've planned to launch an attack of their own."

"Well, we beat 'em to it!" Andie cheered.

Paula touched her damp hair. "What's next?"

"Tomorrow morning—early—we get 'em good," I said.

Andie grinned. "Yes!"

"We'll get up really early. When the guys take their showers, we'll be hiding outside, around the back, waiting to turn off the hot water."

Joy looked uneasy. "Do all of us have to?"

"We're in this together, right?" I said.

"SOS," said Andie, "SOS."

Eagerly, we picked up the chant, heading to inspect the pipe system outside the girls' rest room. Afterward, I sneaked through the trees behind the guys' rest room and studied the plumbing there.

Perfect! They were identical.

❤ ❤ ❤

Monday morning, Rhonna was long gone on her morning jog when my watch began to play its wake-up tune at six-thirty. Ten minutes later, Andie and Paula were on either side of me, ready for mischief! We stared at the network of pipes and spigots outside the boys' shower area.

"That's not it," I whispered, searching for the hot-water pipe.

"Where *is* it?" Andie hissed. "Remember where we found it behind our rest room? Think!"

I envisioned the identical setup behind our rest rooms.

"We've gotta find it," Paula said, glancing at Kayla.

My eyes scanned the pipes once again. "There, I think that's it," I pointed toward the hot-water spigot.

"We'll know soon enough," Amy-Liz said, crouching down.

"Who's going to stand post?" I asked.

Shauna volunteered. Silently, she headed to a clump of aspen trees around the side of the log cabin structure. It was the perfect hiding place, especially in the early morning light.

Jared and Danny headed inside the small building first, followed soon by Billy and Stan. We'd assigned numbers to the boys so that whoever stood post could flash the appropriate fingers to the rest of us behind the building. Jared was number one, Stan number two, and so on.

The gentle rumble of pressure pushing through the outside pipes told us the water was on. We could hear the guys talking their easy-going, boring nonsense. Probably soaping up . . .

We waited a few more seconds.

"Ready . . . set . . . now!" Andie said.

I turned the hot-water spigot all the way. Hard.

Off!

Howling followed. Loud, freaking howls.

"Let's go," I whispered.

Shauna dashed over to catch up with us.

"Outta here!" Andie said as we flew up the dirt path, across the log bridge, and into the safety of our cabin.

"Listen," Amy-Liz said, standing in the doorway.

"Can you hear them?" I strained, listening.

"It's most likely your imagination," Paula said.

We stood by the window, grinning.

"What a horrible thing to do," Joy said.

Yet we were still grinning long after the deed was done.

Chapter 19

The guys sent a delegation—Jared and Stan—to talk to Andie and me during lunch. The four of us moved to a vacant table with our trays. It seemed strange having an extended conversation with the guys like this.

Jared got things started. "If it's respect you girls want, let's talk."

"So, shoot," Andie said. She wasn't making it easy for the guys' first attempt at a peace conference.

"Okay," Jared said, winking at me. "For starters, how about Holly and me spend a little time together, for old times' sake?"

"Focus, Jared," Andie piped up. "This isn't about past friendships. Don't you guys pay attention at all?"

Stan looked puzzled. "We're here to talk peace," he reprimanded Jared. "The thing about Holly can wait till later."

"Just a minute!" I said. "Are you saying this peace thing hinges on certain people being your girlfriends?"

Jared ran his fingers through his dark waves. "You could say that."

Andie stood up. "Well, then, just forget it!" She motioned to me, and we picked up our trays.

"Hey, Andie, you want your makeup or not?" Stan taunted.

"Keep it!" Andie called over her shoulder.

But Jared and Stan didn't return to their table. They followed us to our table, focusing on Amy-Liz now.

"I need to talk to you, Amy," Jared said, shooting a sly glance at me.

Amy-Liz turned to look at me. "What's this about?"

"Why don't you just go away, Jared," Andie said. She was as nervous as I was about Jared wanting to talk to Amy-Liz.

Jared stood his ground. "We *have* to talk, Amy-Liz."

"Leave me alone," she said, turning her shoulder to him.

Jared's eyes narrowed. "It's about your camp scholarship."

No, not that!

The SOS gasped in unison.

Amy-Liz frowned. "What about it?"

Jared leaned closer to her. "Let me be the first to tell you where the money really came from. . . ."

All of us squirmed while Jared enjoyed himself to the hilt. Amy's face turned white. She looked first at Jared, then at Andie and me. "What's he saying?"

Before I could respond, Jared took her by the arm. "I think you'd better come with me," he said.

Horrified, we watched as Amy-Liz left us to go sit with the archenemy at a table near the dessert window. "The war rages on," I said, worried about the consequences of Jared's deed. This would surely be the demise of the Sisters of Silence. And Jared knew it.

"We might as well kiss Amy-Liz good-bye," Andie said mournfully.

"You can say that again," Paula said. "Remember how she freaked when we tried to give her money for her SOS T-shirt?"

Kayla sighed. "Do you think she'll leave camp?"

Joy looked wistful. "I hope not."

I shook my head. "Amy's probably so upset right this minute, who knows what she's thinking or saying." And I had no doubt Jared would worm the secret society information right out of her.

"Hey, wait a minute," Andie said, gawking at them. "Check it out."

I couldn't believe my eyes. Amy-Liz was marching back to our table, and her face literally shone with delight. Jared, on the other hand, sat alone with a dejected look on his usually cheerful face.

"Interesting," I said.

Amy-Liz started hugging us. First Andie, then me. "You two did that? You baked all those cookies so I could come to camp?" She was blubbering all over us about what we had done. Whew, what a relief.

Once again, the guys' attempt to destroy our unity had failed. We were stronger than ever!

♥ ♥ ♥

Hours after lights-out, the SOS found some bowls in the camp kitchen. After filling them with warm water, we tiptoed to the boys' cabin area.

Since Jared was my main target and Stan was Andie's, the two of us crept inside first. If all went well, Paula would dish out the hand-in-warm-water trick to Billy. Kayla's target was Danny, and the rest of the girls would stand guard outside.

We were so good, we never even made a sound. Silent sisters, all right.

Jared's limp right hand went willingly into the bowl. Quickly, I left the cabin and hid behind a tree with Paula, waiting for Andie.

Soon she emerged. Victory!

One by one, the girls administered the prank. Miraculously, we pulled it off.

I wrote in my notebook by flashlight when we returned. *Monday, June 27: We did it! We pulled off a major, I mean MAJOR, attack tonight. I still can't believe we didn't get caught.*

Wednesday morning's the jeep trip. We're going to experience hairpin turns and switchbacks. After that, we'll come back to camp for a wiener roast, and then . . . Talent Night.

I still don't know what I'm doing for my talent. Todd Stillson wants me to sing a duet with him, but that's impossible. Too bad things turned out this way.

How I wish I could be a little mouse hiding somewhere in Jared's cabin tomorrow morning. Man, I'll bet those boys will be ticked. When they see the bowls of water, they'll know the truth. The SOS doesn't mess around!

More later.

♥ ♥ ♥

Sleeping bags were hanging out of every single one of Jared's cabin's windows Tuesday morning! We honestly tried not to giggle about it on our way to breakfast. It was mean, what we had done, but a powerful message had been sent. Maybe as strong a message as we'd ever sent.

After lunch we swam in the pool, just the girls. The guys had gone into Ouray to the hot springs.

So . . . it was a complete mystery when a white truce flag found its way onto the ground beside my beach towel.

"Hey, look at this," I said to my dripping, shivering sisters. Reaching down, I read the note pinned to the makeshift flag.

Andie peered at the note as I read it. "Looks like the guys bit the dust," she cackled. "They want an end to the war."

"And check this out," I said, laughing. "They're calling for 'a time of peace'! They actually want to meet and have a talk."

"Cool, a powwow," Amy-Liz said, and we cracked up.

"So, when do we talk?" Joy asked.

"The note suggests we meet the guys after the campfire, in front of the three pine trees," I said. "Everyone agree?"

"Sounds fine to me," Shauna said.

"Let's wait for the guys to do the talking," I suggested. "We'll see how sorry they really are."

We hurried off to the showers, wondering what would happen after the campfire.

♥ ♥ ♥

After supper was a volleyball tournament—boys against the girls. We played Cabin D the first game. And then we had to play Jared's cabin.

Groan.

"C'mon, girls, let's show 'em," Andie said.

The game turned out great. Strong competition. The works. Almost like a real war. Except for one thing: The opponents— especially Jared, Stan, and Billy—were being super nice. Giving us the benefit of the doubt during the game. Concerned when one of us tripped and fell. Stuff like that. They weren't letting us win, though. I wondered why.

In the end, we got creamed—21 to 4. Jared and Billy came up afterward and shook hands, like in professional sports. Stan hung around Andie and me, behaving like a cool stepbrother . . . and friend. It didn't even bug me when he turned on the John Wayne charm.

When it was dusk, we built a campfire and sat around singing. Rhonna passed out marshmallows, and our guys offered sticks to roast them. I accepted the offer from Jared and watched as he used his pocketknife to sharpen the end. I marveled at his change of spirit. He even *looked* repentant. Whoa!

During devotions, Pastor Rob talked about unity within the family of God. I wondered, had someone spilled the beans? Did he know about the guy-girl war?

"What kind of important info can we learn from Romans 12:16 today?" Pastor Rob asked.

Danny raised his hand. "That we should 'live in harmony with one another.' "

Pastor Rob slowly made eye contact with each of us around the campfire. "What does that mean for you and me?"

Laina Springer raised her hand. "I guess we're supposed to try and get along." She glanced sheepishly at me.

Pastor Rob nodded. "That's right. Now jumping down to verses eighteen and nineteen"—he shone a flashlight on his New Testament—" 'If it is possible, as far as it depends on you, live at peace with everyone. Do not take revenge, my friends, but leave room for God's wrath, for it is written: "It is mine to avenge; I will repay, says the Lord." ' "

I could hardly swallow as I listened to Pastor Rob. What he was saying hit home. Hard. We had treated the guys—our own brothers in Christ—like enemies. The pact, and the war, too, were wrong. The boys had treated us poorly, that was true, but we'd carried things too far.

Long before the coals died out in the campfire, I was ready to talk peace. And talk we did. We met the guys at the pre-appointed spot. Silently, they piled the sports bags in front of us.

How desperately I wanted to erase the memory of my underwear rippling in the breeze. Could I forgive the boys for that?

"Okay, who wants to start?" Danny asked, looking around.

I took a deep breath, ready to speak, but Joy beat me to it. "I'm sorry for ignoring you guys all week." She coughed nervously. "It was wrong."

"I'm sorry, too," Billy confessed, "about setting up Laina and her friends to raid your cabin."

I couldn't help it; I had to gasp. "*Laina* did your dirty work?" I was totally confused. Then I remembered the shiny glint in the moonlight; I *had* seen her braces!

Paula stepped forward, looking at Danny. "I'm really sorry about making you wet your bed." She was sincere, but we girls burst out laughing.

Danny turned beet red. I could see it even in the fading light of dusk. "Don't ever do that again," he said softly.

"You're supposed to forgive her, Danny," I teased. "Practice what you preach."

Jared turned to me and apologized for taking my hair tie. "And I didn't mean it about your hair," he said, moving closer. "I love your hair, Holly-Heart. Honest."

"Uh-oh," Andie muttered while the rest of my sisters groaned audibly.

I couldn't contain myself. "SOS was my idea," I confessed. "So was the pact. I guess we got a little carried away."

Jared looked puzzled. "What was SOS supposed to mean, anyway?" he asked.

"Sisters of Silence," I said.

"Oh . . . yeah," he said, thinking it through. "You girls *were* way too quiet."

"Maybe talking things out would've been better," Andie offered.

"No kidding," Stan admitted.

Danny fidgeted.

"Well, what's it gonna be?" Andie asked. "Forgiven or not?"

The guys looked at each other. Jared shrugged. "Okay, fine."

Stan said, "Forgiven."

Billy agreed, "Completely wiped out of my mind."

Danny piped up: "Hey, there's a really cool verse about forgiveness I memorized just today."

"Whoa, Danny, you're avoiding the subject," Jared said. He shot a look at Stan and Billy. And—as if they'd planned it hours earlier—they promptly picked up "Preacher Danny" and hauled him down the slope to the cold mountain stream.

I could still hear Danny yelling for mercy as we picked up our sports bags and made our way back to good old Cabin B.

But it didn't take me very long to forget about our church boys, because I was already planning what I would say the next time I saw Todd Stillson.

Chapter 20

"I feel like a new person," I told Andie later that night. She was at the sink next to me applying makeup like crazy. "And it has nothing to do with this." I studied my lip gloss.

Andie glanced at me in the mirror. "You're right." She sighed. "Just think, we almost messed up our entire week with that stupid pact."

"Thank goodness we've still got some time left to enjoy the cease-fire," I said.

"And to spend with our brothers," Amy-Liz said.

"Call them brothers if you want." I smiled. "I, for one, prefer to think of *some* of them as *more* than brothers."

Andie and company turned simultaneously to stare. But I didn't give them a single clue as to what I was thinking.

♥ ♥ ♥

Jared and Todd both hung around during the end-of-camp late-night hike, walking on either side of me as we made our way up the trail. The rest of my sisters ended up with male counterparts, as well, something none of them seemed to mind.

At a rest stop, when Jared was busy talking to Billy, I invited Todd to sit with me on the jeep trip.

"I'd be honored," he said, adjusting his cowboy hat, or was that a gentlemanly tip of the hat?

"And about that duet," I said, "I have a great idea. That is, if you still want to sing with me."

"We can practice our harmony tomorrow," he said in a slow drawl. I took that as a yes.

"Perfect," I said.

Out of the corner of my eye, I noticed that Jared was watching. Apparently he'd overheard Todd's last words. I didn't dare look at him too closely, but I was sure he was pouting. I could tell from the way his hands were jammed in his pockets.

I hid a smile. Jared never gives up. . . .

💙 💙 💙

Wednesday. Last full day of camp!

The open-jeep ride was even scarier than the brochure advertised. To keep from being too freaked about the steep drop-offs on either side of the trail, Todd and I sang. One song after another.

The jeep stopped at an overlook and I gasped. "I'm too young to die!"

"I won't let you, Holly," Todd said, smiling that cowboy grin. "I'm just getting to know you."

It sounded a little hokey, I guess. But that was the part I liked about Todd. Sometimes along with hokey comes downright honesty.

I thought back to the times when Todd hadn't gone along with the crowd—the guys—and joined in with their jeering. He was his own person. Different from most of the boys I knew but special just the same. A true gentleman.

We backed up and headed down the same way. I held on to my seat for dear life, convinced my knuckles would stay white forever. Volcanic rock towered above us on switchbacks so narrow that the slightest wrong move by the driver meant a plunge to certain death.

The most comforting aspect of the trip was the way Jared and the rest of our church guys weren't embarrassed about turning ghost-white right along with us girls. No one was being macho about this excursion. The guys were equally as freaked. Even Danny, who was heard quoting Psalm 91 for the Miller twins' benefit.

During one of the rest stops, Laina Springer smiled at me. "I heard you found out who raided your cabin Saturday night," she began, blushing. "It was a dumb thing to do," she admitted. "Sorry."

"I think we're all sorry about a lot of things," I said, smiling at her. Billy strolled up just then.

"Well, see ya," I called, feeling good about how things had turned out with everyone here at camp.

💜 💜 💜

Todd and I ended up singing "Let There Be Peace on Earth" for the talent program—to the accompaniment of his cool guitar. My now not-so-silent sisters joined in on the *ah*s and *ooh*s, making a fabulous backup for the finale.

The song, the way we arranged it, had never sounded so good to me. The rest of the guys must've thought so, too, because they gave us a standing ovation. A far cry from the way they'd treated us before we introduced their sleepy hands to warm H_2O.

I was encouraged. If things kept going this well between all of us, there was hope that the Dressel Hills youth group might actually become super close. Like a family. And what a benefit that would be for all of us.

💜 💜 💜

On the last morning of camp, Rhonna and I were alone in the cabin, doing last-minute cleanup. As I swept the wood floor, I glanced over at her, wondering how she felt about going back home. She looked up just then and caught my gaze.

"Rhonna?" I said tentatively. "I just want you to know that I'll be praying for you and your parents."

She smiled. "Thanks. We'll need it."

"I'm no expert at this stuff," I offered. "But things *do* improve over time."

She nodded. "I don't know which hurts worse, watching your parents' marriage crumble at my age or going through it when *you* did." She looked at me. "You said you were only eight when your dad left?"

"It seems like a lifetime ago," I whispered, remembering.

"Well, maybe by the time I'm thirty, this'll seem like that for me." She sighed.

"I really hope so, Rhonna, " I said. Then added, "Prayer really helps, you know."

She smiled. "I know."

♥ ♥ ♥

As for Todd, he walked with me, just the two of us, for the last time. He insisted on carrying my luggage to the bus. Sighing, I wished I'd had more time to get to know him. More time, without pathetic pacts and wars.

"Will you answer my email?" he asked.

"Sure."

"I'm not so hot at writing, I guess. But I will if you write me first," he promised.

Isn't the boy supposed to write first? I thought. "Maybe *you* should," I suggested.

"How come?" he said as we passed the commons area and the dining hall.

"I don't know." I wondered why we were wasting our last precious minutes on silly things like the proper procedure for starting an email correspondence.

"I might be able to talk my dad into coming to ski next fall," Todd said, sounding hopeful.

"To Dressel Hills? That'd be fun," I replied. "Maybe your whole youth group could come, too. You could get to know *all* of us better." I said that only to let him know ours wasn't an exclusive sort of relationship.

Besides, what I longed for it now was peace. That and my window seat . . . my cat, Goofey . . . and my family. Only not in that order.

Actually, a good night's sleep wouldn't feel half bad right about now!

Holly's Super-Duper Snickerdoodle Recipe

These cinnamon-sugar cookies have been known by their silly name since they started showing up at Dutch tea tables in colonial times. "They're my favorite cookie in the world," says Holly.

Mix well:
  1/2 cup butter, softened
  3/4 cup sugar
  1 egg

Sift together:
  1 3/8 cups sifted flour
  (Note: For high altitudes add 1/4 cup additional flour.)
  1 tsp. cream of tartar·
  1/2 tsp. baking soda
  1/4 tsp. salt

Mix and set aside:
  2 tbsp. sugar
  2 tsp. cinnamon

1. Chill dough one hour in refrigerator.
2. Roll dough into balls the size of small walnuts.
3. Coat balls in sugar-and-cinnamon mixture.
4. Place balls about 3 inches apart on ungreased cookie sheets.
5. Bake at 400 degrees F until center is almost set and cookie appears lightly browned, 6 to 8 minutes.
6. Cookies will puff up at first, then flatten out with crinkled top.

Makes 3 dozen fabulous cookies.

Andie's Mexican Wedding Cookies (Polvorones)

A festive basket filled with polvorones makes a perfect home-made gift for friends and relatives. Andie dares you to eat just one!

Ingredients:
2 cups all-purpose flour, sifted
1/2 cup confectioners' sugar
1 cup finely chopped pecans
1 tsp. vanilla extract
1/2 cup butter or margarine, softened
1 tbsp. ice water (more or less as needed)

Set aside:
Confectioners' sugar for garnish

1. Preheat oven to 350 degrees F.
2. Mix flour, confectioners' sugar, and pecans in large mixing bowl.
3. Add vanilla and butter; using mixing spoon, blend until mixture forms a soft ball. Add about a tablespoon of ice water if mixture is too crumbly.
4. Pinch off pieces of dough and roll into balls the size of Ping-Pong balls.
5. Place balls about 1 inch apart on greased cookie sheet. Bake for about 12 minutes or until set and golden.
6. Remove cookies from oven and sprinkle them with confectioners' sugar.

Makes 2 dozen delicious cookies.

HOLLY'S HEART

Little White Lies

For two very loyal fans—

Joy Zartman,

who thinks Holly

should have a boyfriend.

And . . .

Elyse Hall,

who has more

pen pals than Holly

and Andie combined!

LITTLE WHITE LIES

Chapter 1

"Please say it's not true," Andrea Martinez said, pedaling hard to keep up with my bike. "You're going to California *again?*"

I nodded, amused. "It's not like you didn't sorta figure this, right?"

She didn't say a word.

Side by side, we rode our bikes down the tree-lined street in total silence. I stared straight ahead, letting the soothing summer breeze ripple the length of my hair.

I didn't have to glance at Andie to know she was fuming. Shoot, I could *feel* the frustration oozing out of her. When Andie didn't get her way, she often behaved like this, and I braced myself for the fierce argument that was sure to come.

Two weeks without her best friend wasn't exactly Andie's idea of summer fun. In fact, by the gray cloud on her face, it looked like she was going to have herself a full-blown pouting party. Just when I thought she might've grown up a little. After all, we *were* headed for our freshman year next fall. Besides that, we'd had the same ridiculous conversation last summer.

"Look, Andie," I said, trying to be kind, "just because I want to visit my dad doesn't mean I enjoy leaving you behind. You should know that by now."

There. Maybe that would calm her down.

Andie kept pedaling, standing up now as she worked her short legs. "All the coolest things happen in July around here, Holly," she insisted, slightly out of breath.

Whoa! Had she already forgotten our fabulous time at Camp Ouray? And what about that zany no-guys pact we'd concocted?

"So . . . church camp wasn't all that cool, then?" I asked sarcastically.

"That was *last* month," she shot back.

"Well, it's not like we haven't spent time together this summer," I pointed out. We coasted down a hill.

"Aw, c'mon," she argued. "Please stay in Dressel Hills. We'll have so-o much fun."

I could see this conversation was going nowhere fast. "Hey, I have an idea." I turned the corner and headed toward Andie's driveway. "Let's pretend we're having fun right now." I couldn't stop a mischievous smile from spreading across my face.

We parked our bikes on the front lawn. Andie cast a furtive glance my way. "Holly Meredith, you're completely hopeless." And with that she dashed into the house, calling to let her mom know she was home.

Completely hopeless?

I situated myself on Andie's front steps. Completely hopeless fell into an entirely different category than the simple teasing I'd just dished out. Completely hopeless had more to do with obnoxious little sisters like mine—Carrie, who was nine, and Stephanie, my stepsister, who was eight, going on infancy. Without the two of them forever sneaking around, my life might seem perfect right now.

Last week I'd squelched my excitement when Mom informed me that she didn't think Carrie would be going to California this time. "You know how close Carrie and Stephie have become," she explained.

"Sure, Mom," I said, absolutely delighted.

When Uncle Jack came home for lunch, Mom asked his opinion. It took only a split second of whining from Stephie—telling how *horribly* lonely she'd be without Carrie—to bring Uncle Jack to his decision.

So it was settled. Carrie could skip the summer visit if it was okay with Daddy. And Mom lost no time phoning him in California. She escaped with the cordless phone into the living room while Carrie and I cleaned up the kitchen. I tried to listen in on Mom's end of the conversation, but it was difficult with all the kitchen clatter. As it turned out, Daddy had no problem with Carrie staying put here.

I was secretly thrilled. Daddy and I would have more time to spend together. At least this way, Carrie wouldn't jabber away every single second of our visit.

I leaned back against the warm steps leading to Andie's front door and closed my eyes. Cheerful birds chirped around me everywhere. It was summer all right—one of the best times of year in Colorado. The heat from the porch steps radiated through my white shorts, so I stood up, letting the sun's rays warm my face instead.

"Thirsty?"

I twirled around. There stood Andie, holding out a tall glass of lemonade. "Mmm, looks good. Thanks." I reached for the icy glass.

Andie shot me a hesitant look. "Are you totally sure about going off to California in just four days?"

"I don't have second thoughts if that's what you mean."

Her big brown eyes did a little rolling number. "Hey, can't a girl ask a question?"

I was silent. She was pushing way too hard.

"If I could, I'd try and talk you out of it, you know." Andie took a long drink of lemonade, then looked up. "C'mon, let's go around to the backyard."

I followed her through the side yard toward the back of the house. Andie didn't wait for me to catch up. She kept twisting one of her dark curls around her finger, which *always* spells trouble. She was acting downright weird, like she had some big secret or something.

Around the back, positioned near several small aspen trees, a large jungle gym stretched out across one end of the yard. The play set had been purchased earlier this summer for Andie's three-year-old twin brothers, Jon and Chris. Numerous times, Andie and I had entertained the busy little boys while their parents were away. For pay, of course.

I went to the swings and sat down, swaying gently as I sipped my lemonade. Andie plopped down on the bottom of the slide.

"Look out—it might be hot!" I said, just as she scooted off and fell into the sand.

Getting up, she brushed off her shorts. "We oughta go swimming. You can get in on my Y membership." She sat on the swing next to me. "Want to?" she asked.

It *was* hot; a cool dip would feel fabulous. "Sure," I said. But Andie seemed suddenly distant—preoccupied—as she drank the rest of her lemonade. Was she still brooding about the California thing?

I chewed on the ice at the bottom of my glass. "Something bugging you?" I asked.

"Sorta," she said softly.

"So talk to me."

She shuffled her feet around in the sand a bit before she spoke. "It's just that . . . I, oh, I don't know."

It wasn't like Andie to stall. If something was on her mind, she never hesitated getting it out in the open. Especially with me. Andie and I had been close friends since preschool days.

"What *is* it?" I asked, my curiosity getting the best of me.

The sun glistened on Andie's hair, and she studied me with a clear, steady gaze. "What would you think if I went along with you?" She seemed almost shy. For the first time in her life.

"Let me get this straight," I said, smiling. "*You* want to go to California?"

"Yep. With you," she emphasized.

"Sounds like a good idea to me, but what about your parents? Do you think they'll agree?"

Her smile faded quickly. "I don't know. My parents are real protective."

"Well, why would you want to go in the first place?" I asked, eager to get to the bottom of this.

"It's just that I never get to go *anywhere,*" she exaggerated. "I was born here, and except for camping, we hardly ever leave Dressel Hills." She stood up just then and flung her arms wide. Something like the way Maria does in the opening scene to *The Sound of Music.* "There's a world out there just waiting for me. I don't want to stagnate and die here in Colorado."

I giggled. Now, *this* was the Andie I knew and loved. High drama at its best.

"Okay, okay, I get the picture. But don't forget our choir tour to California, and there was the Grand Canyon, and—"

She grabbed the chain on my swing. "So you'll take me along?" she begged, her face inches from mine. I could smell the lemon on her breath.

"It's not up to me to decide," I said more seriously. "Even if it's okay with your folks, I'll still have to clear it with my dad and stepmom." Then I remembered Jon and Chris. "Who's going to help with your brothers while you're gone?"

"Two weeks?" She waved her hand like she was swatting flies. "No problem."

"So you think your mom can manage?"

"I guess we'll just have to ask." She motioned for me to go with her into the house.

"Wait." I stopped at the back door. "Maybe we should talk this over with my dad first, uh, you know, since he hasn't seen you for a while."

Andie's countenance dimmed. "Oh yeah. Maybe he won't want his daughter bringing home her *Hispanic* friend."

I stared at her, shocked. "What's that supposed to mean?"

She put her hands on her hips. "He doesn't care that I'm Hispanic, does he?"

"Look, Andie, I don't know what you're getting at, but Daddy's not prejudiced. Not even close. Besides, he's a Christian now."

Her voice quivered. "I know. But I've heard how it is in some places for different ethnic groups—even worse than in a small town like Dressel Hills."

I reached for Andie and gave her a hug. "You're my friend. Nothing will ever change that."

Andie started to tremble.

"Andie?"

Quickly, she wiped her eyes, pulling away.

"What's wrong?" I whispered. "Are you all right?"

She shook her head, eyes filling with tears.

"Has someone said something?"

"I don't want to talk about it," she managed to say. "Maybe we should just forget the whole dumb idea." She turned away quickly so I couldn't see her cry. "I'll see you later, Holly."

"No, wait," I called to her. But it was too late. Andie had gone inside. She closed the door without even the slightest glance back.

Tears stung my eyes as I imagined someone, anyone, insulting my friend. How rotten!

It was obvious Andie wanted to be left alone. As much as I hated leaving her like this, I knew it would do absolutely no good to ring the doorbell, hoping she'd answer. Andie was too hurt to talk.

She and I were opposites in that way. If I was hurting, I wanted someone around. Someone who would talk to me and help me through my tunnel of pain. Andie and my mom were both good about pursuing me at times like that. Even when I might insist that I wanted to be alone, they knew deep down I really didn't.

Feelings of concern pricked at me as I got on my bike. Andie had actually become hostile, and all it took was a single comment about Daddy not having seen her lately. She'd mistaken my words completely—jumped to conclusions.

Something, or *someone,* was bugging her. Why, I didn't know. But I was determined to find out.

Chapter 2

When I arrived home, supper was almost ready to be served.

I sniffed the air as I came into the kitchen. *Oven-baked chicken, yum.* "Smells like the Fourth of July all over again," I said.

"Oh, there you are, Holly-Heart." Mom gave me a quick hug. "Hungry?"

"Starved."

"Well, good," she said, turning around to check on the oven. "I didn't make thirty pieces of chicken for nothing, did I?"

"Thirty?"

Some quick math told me that with six kids, plus Mom and Uncle Jack, there were eight of us. Divided into thirty, that's about four pieces each. "Why so many?" I asked, even more puzzled when I spied two huge steaming bowls of mashed potatoes.

"Well," she said, a twinkle in her eye, "we're having company."

"We are?"

"Stan has a new friend." She reached for two potholders and opened the oven door. Tantalizing smells escaped and wafted their way through the kitchen.

"A girl?" I asked, hoping not—for Andie's sake.

"No girl," Mom said. She carried a huge oven tray over to the island bar and began to place pieces of chicken on a large platter.

"Who, then?" I checked to see if the dining room table was set. It was.

"Oh, just a guy he met down at the Y," Mom said. "I'm sure you'll find him interesting."

"What's that supposed to mean? You're not setting me up with . . ."

"Oh, Holly, you know how I feel about girl-boy stuff at your age." She untied her apron and flung it over the drainboard near the sink. "Can't I say something nice about a boy without you getting defensive?"

"Sorry, Mom, I just—"

"Just what?" It was Carrie. My little sister had materialized out of thin air.

"Carrie," Mom reprimanded. "How many times have I told you not to do that?"

I sighed. "Oh, give or take two thousand."

"That's *not* true!" Carrie shouted, shooting daggers at me with her beady eyes.

"You mean you haven't been getting A-pluses in sneaking up on people? Tell me it isn't so," I sneered.

"Girls, girls," Mom said, wagging her finger in front of our faces. "Be sweet to each other. You only have a few more days together before Holly leaves for California."

"Yes," Carrie whispered, flicking her long ponytail.

I didn't say what *I* was thinking. It wouldn't have pleased the Lord. Mom either.

"So," Carrie inquired, "who's coming for dinner?"

"Never mind," I said, turning her around and giving her a gentle shove.

Mom smiled. "You'll both find out soon enough."

Carrie turned around and wrinkled her nose at me.

"Holly, will you pour the iced tea, please?" Mom asked.

Gladly. Anything to get away from my pesky sister.

When everything was in its place on the table, Mom rang her dainty white dinner bell. Mark, Phil, and Stephie came running up the family room steps. Stan and his friend came barreling up next. I wondered why Stan avoided my eyes as he walked through the kitchen.

Funny. Just when things were perking along on an even keel with my fairly snooty stepbrother, a thing like bringing a friend home for supper threw everything out of whack. How could that be?

I studied Stan's friend discreetly. Medium frame . . . not quite as tall as Stan. Average brown hair, sort of mousy, actually. And horror of horrors—a ripe pimple. Right next to his nose!

Uncle Jack waited for us to get situated at the table before he offered the blessing. Afterward, he turned to Stan, who sat across from me, and asked him to introduce his friend.

"Sure, Dad," Stan began. "Everyone," and here he made eye contact with each of us at the table, even me, "this is Ryan Davis, one of the guys on the swim team at the Y."

Stan introduced each of us individually, starting with Stephie, the youngest. When he came to me, he said, "Ryan's into creative writing . . . like you, Holly." He paused. "Maybe you could show him that story you got published last year." He smiled like he was actually proud of my accomplishment.

"Really?" Ryan said, his hazel eyes lighting up. "Published?" He said it like it was a sacred act or something. "What magazine?"

"I'll show you after supper," I said, not really caring about this little charade Stan was playing, using me to impress his pimple-faced friend.

"Okay," Ryan said, smiling too broadly for my taste.

Mom and Uncle Jack carried the conversation with Ryan and Stan clear through dessert. Now and then I caught snatches of Carrie and Stephie whispering next to me. Sounded like they were making plans for the two weeks I'd be gone. I grinned. What a fabulous break from these two—escaping to Daddy's wonderful beach house overlooking the ocean, relaxing in the sun, sipping iced tea. Ah, what a way to spend fourteen carefree days. No time pressure. No stress. I could scarcely wait.

I was daydreaming, blocking out Stan and Ryan's jibber-jabber, when suddenly I heard Andie's name mentioned. I spooned up some of Mom's apple crisp and a scoop of ice cream on the side, trying to act disinterested. Staring at my plate, I chewed in silence, but I was all ears.

Stan was saying he and Ryan had bumped into Andie at the Y yesterday. "We were going in and she was ready to leave," he said nonchalantly.

I waited for him to mention that Andie was his former girlfriend and that they still spent time together off and on. But he was silent about that.

Strange.

Mom wiped her mouth with a napkin, then reached over and touched my left hand. "I think Holly and Andie must have the longest-running friendship around Dressel Hills," she said. "Right, honey?"

I nodded.

Uncle Jack nodded, too. "I'd say they're nearly sisters."

A smirk swept across Ryan's face. "Well, they sure don't look it." He snickered.

"Very funny," I replied.

"Well . . . you know," Ryan muttered.

"No, I don't," I said. "And I think you'd better spell it out."

Stan frowned, casting at stern look at me. "Just drop it," he said.

"Look," I said, directing my comment to Stan, "Andie's fabulous and *you,* of all people, should know that."

He didn't comment, and it infuriated me. Why wasn't he sticking up for Andie? I didn't get it.

I slid my chair away from the table, remembering the way Andie had cried earlier. "Excuse me, please."

"Holly!" Mom said stiffly.

Ignoring her, I ran to the kitchen and grabbed the portable phone.

"What's your problem?" Stan said as I flew through the dining room.

Turning around, I stared him down. "Think about it," I said in my coldest voice. "Andie was perfectly fine for you"—I forced my gaze away from him and looked at Ryan—"until now."

The entire family was staring at me. I could almost hear the wheels in Mom's brain turning. *What's gotten into her?* she was probably thinking.

Sure as shootin', Uncle Jack was thinking something along the same lines, except his face was less revealing. He leaned back, scratched his chin, and winked in a fatherly fashion—to let me know he'd have a talk with Stan later, no doubt. It was just what I needed from my stepdad—the best around.

Ryan's voice rose out of the silence. "Very nice meeting you, Holly."

I wanted to say "Go pop your pimple," but I turned and fled to my room. I choked back the horrible thought, only to have it rise up like a flood: *Had Stan's friend ridiculed Andie to her face?*

I closed my bedroom door behind me. My hand shook as I gripped the portable phone. It was time to get to the bottom of things.

Chapter 3

The phone rang a zillion times. *C'mon, Andie, pick up,* I thought.

Two more rings.

Where is she? I wondered.

Frazzled, I let the phone continue to ring.

At long last, someone answered. It was Andie's father. "Martinez residence," he said.

"Is Andie there?" I asked hesitantly.

"Oh, hello, Holly." He paused. "Uh, I believe she is, but I think she's in her room. May I take a message?"

I switched the phone to my left ear. "Is . . . is Andie all right?"

"Well, I don't know that she's ill if that's what you mean." He cleared his throat.

I figured he didn't know what I was talking about.

"Okay, well, just tell her I called, and she can call me back whenever."

"I will certainly tell her."

We said good-bye and hung up.

This wasn't working. I *had* to talk to Andie!

I figured I'd better wait awhile before leaving to go visit her. The way I felt right now, it wouldn't be smart to go dashing downstairs. I didn't trust my feelings toward Stan or his disgusting friend.

Why did they talk that way about Andie, anyway?

My cat leaped up onto my window seat, as though he were inviting me to join him. So I did. There, on the padded pillows, I snuggled with Goofey, letting the rumble of his purring comfort me. More than anything, I wished I could talk to Andie. Maybe she didn't need me to help her through whatever was bugging her, but I needed her—to find out if what I suspected was true.

To keep from freaking out, I began to pray. "Dear Lord, I don't know what's going on between Stan and Andie, but you do." I paused, hesitating to pray about Ryan Davis. What a jerk!

I took a deep breath, then continued my prayer. "Uh . . . Stan's friend, you know him, his name's Ryan. Well, I don't think he's the best kind of friend for Stan, but then, you know all things, so I'll let it go with that, Lord. Amen."

It was the most pathetic prayer I'd ever prayed.

I glanced at my watch. Almost seven o'clock. I got up and gently laid Goofey down on my window seat. Then I opened my bedroom door and leaned my head out, listening. Stan and Mom were talking in the kitchen. Closing my eyes, I tried to visualize the kitchen cleanup schedule.

Fairly certain that it wasn't my turn, I breathed a sigh of relief. Maybe, just maybe, I could slip out of the house without encountering Stan. Or Ryan. It was worth a try. Besides, my curiosity was propelling me over to Andie's. I had to know what was going on. She would easily clear things up for me if I could just get her to talk. One thing was sure—with Ryan hanging around over here, it would be next to impossible to get a straight answer out of Stan.

Quietly, I closed my door and tiptoed down the hall to the stairs. I made my way cautiously to the landing.

Carrie came racing through, nearly slamming into me. "Holly," she said much too loudly, "I need your help."

"Not now," I whispered, looking around, hoping Stan and company weren't nearby.

Just then Stephie came in from the living room. "Ple-ease help Carrie and me," she begged. "It won't take long."

I glanced over my shoulder toward the kitchen. Too late. Stan had spotted me.

"Can't now." I pushed past the girls. "Maybe later." Heart pounding, I hurried toward the front door.

"Wait up!" Stan called after me.

I ignored him and kept going.

"Holly, would you wait?"

There was no looking back now. I hopped on my bike and sped away. When I was out of reach, I glanced back, surprised to see Stan sitting on the front steps, staring at the ground. Had he sensed where I was headed? And if so, what didn't he want me to find out?

Now I was *really* curious. If I could just get Andie to talk.

Three blocks away, still on Downhill Court—my street—I saw the Miller twins riding their bikes, heading west toward the main drag through our ski village resort.

"Hey, Holly," the girls called in unison. Funny how that worked with twins. Not only did they look alike, they thought alike, too.

"Hey," I said, riding up to them. "Where're you two headed?"

Kayla spoke up. "Footloose and Fancy Things is having a giant sale on their summer stock. Why don't you join us?"

"I'm almost broke," I said, which was true. I'd spent nearly all my summer baby-sitting money on a year's sponsorship for an overseas child.

"I'll be glad to loan you some money," Paula offered, smiling brightly.

"Thanks, anyway," I said. "I'm pretty well set with clothes for summer."

Paula moved her bike out of the street and onto the sidewalk. Kayla did, too. I stayed put, eager to get going. Unfortunately, it looked like the twins wanted to engage in small talk.

"I'm in a hurry," I said apologetically.

"Headed to Andie's?" Paula asked.

"Uh-huh." I said it casually, like it was no big deal.

Kayla flipped her shoulder-length brown hair. "How's she doing *today?*"

Before I could answer, Paula added, "We were really concerned about her emotional state yesterday at the Y."

The Y?

Quickly, I moved my bike out of the street and up onto the sidewalk beside Kayla's. "What happened at the Y?"

Kayla's eyes widened and her thick, mascara-laden lashes fluttered. "Andie didn't tell you?"

"Not exactly."

Paula put the kickstand down on her bike and came over to me. Kayla too. Something was up. We were actually huddled.

Paula started filling in some important details. "Kayla and I had just arrived at the Y yesterday afternoon when we ran into Andie. She was crying as she came out."

I swallowed hard. "Crying?"

Kayla sighed. "It looked like she and Stan had gotten into it, or worse."

"Stan?" I echoed.

"He and some guy were standing inside the lobby," Kayla explained. "And Stan looked upset."

"Who was the other guy?" I asked.

Paula glanced at Kayla. "We'd never seen him around here before," she said.

"Not at church or school," Kayla added.

"It's possible that he's a high school student," Paula suggested. "He seemed a little older than Stan."

"What did he look like?" I asked.

Paula glanced up, like she was trying to pull a description out of the air. "I don't remember."

"I remember something," Kayla said with a giggle. "He had a very large pimple near his nose."

Paula nodded, laughing, too.

My pulse raced. "You're saying the guy with Stan had a pimple?"

Paula and Kayla stared at me. "Why?" Paula asked. "Do you know him?"

I exhaled. "Maybe."

"Well, whoever it was," Kayla said, "he sure was a master intimidator."

"Yeah," Paula piped up. "He was downright sarcastic."

Whew! Things were beginning to take shape.

Kayla draped her arm around her twin's shoulders. "The jerk made a comment about Paula's eyes—that they didn't match mine. And if we were really twins, one of us ought to wear a little more mascara."

I gasped. "He said *that*?"

Paula nodded. I could tell by her grin that she was rather proud that someone had noticed she'd opted for the more natural look.

"I tell you, the guy's outspoken," Kayla said.

"No kidding," I whispered. Man, it was anybody's guess what the guy had said to Andie!

♥ ♥ ♥

By the time I got to Andie's house it was almost eight o'clock. I could see the light in her bedroom upstairs as I rode my bike into the driveway. Walking around the side of the house, I stood under her open window and called up to her. "Andie, come to the window."

In a flash, her perky curls appeared at the window.

"What are you doing down there?" she asked, her brown eyes questioning my return.

"We have to talk," I said matter-of-factly.

"Now?"

"Can you come out?" I stepped back away from the house, trying to see her better. "Or should I come up?"

She frowned slightly. "Well, I guess I could. Meet me out front."

I hurried to the front of the two-story house, to the same steps I'd sat on earlier. Now they felt cool to the touch as I eased myself down onto the cement, waiting for my friend. It seemed strange that I'd be sitting here again, especially since I knew Andie needed some space from whatever had happened. But I needed to hear the story from her lips.

Crickets chirped noisily as Andie finally emerged from the front door, barefoot. "What's the occasion?" she said as she sat down, a bottle of red nail polish in her hand.

How should I start? I wondered. I sure didn't want to put her through the same kind of pain she'd seemed to be feeling earlier today.

"Hey, can't your best friend just show up for no reason?" I said. "I was worried about you." I put my arm around her shoulders.

"I'll survive."

"Of course you will. And I'm going to make sure you do." I removed my arm as she leaned over to paint her toenails.

I sat there, fidgeting with my fingers, studying my cuticles and pushing them back till I could see the round white moon shapes underneath. I wished for some sort of breakthrough. Some way to open up the subject of Stan and Ryan without causing Andie additional pain.

"Have you thought any more about taking me to California with you?" she asked, still bending over, talking to her toes.

I hadn't had time to think about that. I'd been too busy worrying about her encounter with Stan to contemplate my trip to California. "It'd be fabulous" was all I said.

"What about your dad and stepmom?" She straightened up and dipped the brush into the polish. "Did you ask them?"

"They do have a huge house," I said. "Plenty of room for you. But what about your parents? Think they'd let you go with me?"

"Here's the deal," she said. "If you get the okay from your dad, I'll take it from there with my parents, okay?"

"Sure, that'll work."

She started polishing her toenails again. "You're flying out this Monday, right?"

"At 12:15," I said. "Think you can get up before noon?"

She laughed. "Yeah, right. Isn't summer terrific?"

I nodded. Summer made the whole rest of the year worth living. "Guess we'd better start planning things, or you might not get a seat on my flight. I'll call my dad tonight."

This conversation was going in a totally different direction than I'd intended. I wondered how to address the subject of what had happened yesterday at the Y. Then an idea popped into my head.

"So . . . does Stan know you want to go with me?" I asked.

She stared at me incredulously. "Stan who?"

I realized I'd opened up a fresh wound.

"He couldn't care less where I go or what I do," she announced to the approaching sunset. "I'm sorry to inform you, Holly, but your stepbrother is a despicable bigot."

I frowned. "Excuse me?" I needed more to go on than this impromptu indictment.

"And that friend of his . . ." She blew air out through her lips.

"What friend?" I quizzed her, almost sure she was talking about Ryan Davis.

"Oh, Ryan somebody." She waved her hand in front of her face. "You should've heard what he said to me."

Bingo. Just what I'd been waiting to hear!

Chapter 4

"What did Ryan say?" I asked.

"Stan was in on it, too," Andie insisted. "He acted like he hardly knew me. Especially after his friend carried on about how nice it must be to have such a good tan." She tightened the lid on her nail polish and held out her feet, swinging them in the air. "It was like he was trying to flirt with me in a backhanded sort of way."

"So . . . what did you do?"

"I went over and stood beside Stan, expecting him to be his normal, cool self . . . you know, clue this guy in on the two of us."

"Yeah?"

"But Stan clammed up. Didn't say a word in my defense. And even worse, his friend didn't seem to know when to quit."

"What else did he say?"

"Stuff like where was I during Cinco de Mayo this year and was English my second language." She sighed. "It was the cocky, sarcastic way he said it that bugged me the most. Like he thought he was better than me just because he's white."

This was so bad! I couldn't believe Stan would tolerate something like this, especially since Andie was the victim.

"I don't blame you for being hurt," I said. "Stan knows better."

"Well, I'm not crying the blues anymore," she said, getting up. "I'm plain mad. And if I don't split this town soon, I'm gonna burst."

I could see that a change of scenery might do her good. "I'll go home and call my dad," I said, heading for my bike.

Andie hugged me before I left. "Holly, you're the best."

"I'll call you the minute I know something." I hopped onto my bike. "Don't go anywhere, okay?"

"I'll wait by the phone," she said, waving. And I knew she would.

♥ ♥ ♥

Mom was talking on the phone in the kitchen when I arrived home. She sounded pretty involved, so I didn't bother her. When twenty more minutes had passed, I went back downstairs and waved my hands in front of her face.

"Excuse me," she said to the caller, then covered the receiver with her hand. "Holly, what is it?"

"I need to use the phone. It's important."

Mom's eyes got squinty. "Well, Andie will just have to wait," she insisted.

"It's not Andie. I have to call Daddy."

"Tonight?"

"Just some last-minute stuff about the trip."

"Okay, well, I'll be done in a few minutes." She uncovered the receiver, and I could tell by the sound of things it'd be more than a few minutes before the phone was actually free.

Heading upstairs to my room, I located my journal and began to write.

Thursday, July 7: Today's been a real eye-opener in lots of ways. I've discovered that Stan isn't half the man I thought he was, given the circumstances. He's got some weird friend

445

*named Ryan Davis, and the guy's a total loser. I can't believe
what Ryan said to Andie. I mean, this is prejudice at its
worst!*

*I just hope Andie can work through things. I don't know
what this rotten world's coming to!*

I continued to write, pouring out my woes. Then I glanced at
my watch. If I didn't get Mom off the phone, it would be too late
to call Andie. Her dad had a rule that she wasn't allowed to use
the phone after ten o'clock at night.

I signed off in my journal and stashed it safely away in the
bottom dresser drawer. Then I hurried down the hall to the stairs.
Time to claim the portable phone.

Mom was yawning as I tiptoed into the kitchen, motioning to
her for all I was worth. I made some hand signals to her. She nodded, smiling, catching my unspoken message.

Sitting down at the bar, I munched on a couple of snickerdoodle
cookies. Mom had made a batch this morning in the cool of the
day while we kids slept in. I glanced around for Carrie and Stephie.
They were nowhere in sight, thank goodness.

Mom was still engaged in animated conversation with someone—I hadn't figured out whom—so I slid off the barstool and
headed downstairs to the family room. There they were, my five
siblings, stretched out in various degrees of vegging out all over
the carpet. Carrie and Stephie sat cross-legged in front of the coffee
table, eyes glued to the TV. Mark and Phil, my younger stepbrothers—I called them brousins since they were really cousins-turned-
brothers—were gobbling popcorn. Stan took up the entire sofa
part of the sectional, reclining with his legs sprawled out across
the length of the furniture.

"What's on TV?" I asked.

"Shh!" they answered in chorus.

Inching into the room, I saw the reason for their interest. It
looked like some sci-fi show, complete with weird music. Why
Stephie and Carrie were fascinated I had no idea.

"What a waste," I muttered, heading for the stairs.

That's when Stan called to me. "Hey, Holly."

I turned around to see him getting up. "What?" I said as he came over.

"How's Andie doing?" His face looked serious. No . . . he was actually worried.

"Who wants to know?"

"C'mon, Holly, don't do this."

"Don't do what? You're the one who got all this garbage with Andie started." I turned to leave.

Stan reached out and touched my arm. "Just tell me, is she okay?"

I pulled away. "If you're so worried, why don't you ask her yourself?"

"She won't talk to me," he said.

"Well"—I eyed him sarcastically—"I wonder why."

"Okay, I'll admit it, Ryan said some stupid things, but I—"

"You?" I wanted to scream. "You just stood by and let him go off like that?"

He frowned, concerned. "Is that what Andie told you?"

I nodded. "I heard it straight from her, and that's not all. Paula and Kayla thought Ryan was bad news, too."

He ran his fingers through his hair. "I didn't mean to hurt Andie."

"Okay, but what about *me*? What was all that at supper?" I turned around and ran up the stairs.

Stan didn't follow me, and it was a good thing because Mom was just hanging up the phone. "Phone's all yours, Holly-Heart," she said. "You might want to use the hall phone upstairs. This one needs recharging, I think."

For a long-distance call, I didn't want to chance it, so I hurried upstairs, hoping the rest of the kids would stay put in front of their ridiculous intergalactic flick.

Quickly, I punched the numbers for Daddy's luxury oceanfront house. The phone rang only twice. Saundra, my stepmom, answered. "Meredith residence."

"Hey . . . uh, this is Holly. Is my dad there?"

"He's on his way home from work," she replied.

"Work . . . this late?"

"Well, you have to remember it's only eight-fifteen here, dear," she crooned into my left ear.

"Oh, I forgot." Time zones aside, I wondered why Daddy was working so late.

"Is there a message I may give him?" Saundra asked, pouring on her not-so-subtle charm.

"I guess not." I hesitated, thinking about the time crunch involved in getting Andie's plane ticket. Hmm. Maybe I'd better go ahead and chance it and get Saundra's opinion on the matter. "Well, actually, it's about my trip out there," I continued. "I was wondering if you and Daddy would mind if I brought a friend along."

"A friend?" she said. There was a delicate pause. "Sure, since Carrie's not coming, there'll be plenty of room."

"Are you sure it'll be okay with Daddy?" I asked politely. It didn't hurt to make points with the woman who pretty much ran my father's social life.

"I think your dad will be delighted to entertain you and your friend."

"Her name's Andie—short for Andrea," I said. "She's going to try and work things out on this end with her parents. I'll let you know as soon as it's definite, okay?"

"That's fine," Saundra said. I could almost see her perfectly manicured nails wrapped around one of their expensive telephones.

"Tell Tyler I can't wait to see him and that Carrie says hi," I said, referring to Saundra's son.

"He'll certainly miss seeing her this time," she added.

"Well, I guess I'd better get going. But tell Daddy I called."

"He should be home any minute. I will."

"Okay, thanks. Good-bye."

"Good-bye, dear," she said.

I hung up, hoping Daddy wasn't becoming a workaholic or something.

Quickly, I surveyed the stairs behind me. I didn't want Stan or anyone else listening in on my next conversation—with Andie. Our plans were going to be kept private, at least for now.

"Hello?" she answered on the first ring.

"Guess what? It's all right with California," I said, excitement rising in my voice.

"Really?" She sounded ecstatic. "Your dad said it's okay?"

"My stepmom will fill him in, but she's all for it." I heard the steps creak behind me. I spun around. "Just a minute, Andie." I left the phone dangling on its cord. I crept toward the stairs and peered down. Stan was there, all right. "What're you doing?" I said.

"I need to talk to you, Holly," he said sheepishly.

"Not now. I'm busy."

Stan turned away, leaving me alone with Andie, who was waiting impatiently. "What's going on there?" she asked. "I thought I heard Stan's voice. Does he know anything about this?"

"He knows squat," I said, laughing.

"I'll talk to my parents and call you back tonight . . . before ten," she said. "Thanks, Holly, you're terrific!"

We hung up, and I danced a jig through the hallway and into my bedroom. What a fabulous trip we were going to have!

Mom and Uncle Jack came upstairs just as I finished another set of twirls and spins. "Everything okay?" Mom asked, peeking into my room.

"Everything's perfect." I grinned at Uncle Jack, who had a long piece of celery hanging out of his mouth—complete with leafy green ends.

"We're tired," Mom said, eyeing my stepdad. "Jack's been working long hours."

"Sweet dreams," I said. "I'll make sure the crew doesn't stay up all night."

"And don't you, either," Mom said with a grin. "You might want to think about packing pretty soon."

"I'll start tomorrow."

"Good night, kiddo," Uncle Jack called, still munching on his celery stick.

"Love you," Mom said and closed their door.

Inside my room, I undressed and found my favorite pair of pj's in my drawer. The rosy pink tank top had a matching pair of pink-and-white heart shorts. I curled up in my canopy bed with a brand-new Marty Leigh mystery, wondering how long before Andie would call.

Nearly a half hour passed. I couldn't believe it was almost ten when I looked at my watch. That's how it was with this incredible author. She could keep you spellbound, make you forget real life even existed.

I put the book down and went into the hallway, listening for sounds from the troops below. Surely the sci-fi movie was over.

I reached for the hall phone and was surprised to hear Stan's voice on the other line. No wonder I hadn't received Andie's call. *He* was hogging the phone.

"Excuse me, Stan," I interrupted. "I'm waiting for an important call."

"Uh, is that Holly?" another voice came on the line. It sounded familiar.

"Who's this?"

"Ryan Davis," he said. "Remember, we had supper together?"

Was this guy pushing it or what!

"Hey, I really wanted to see that magazine of yours," he went on, sounding way too eager for my liking. "You know, the one with your story in it?"

I wanted to say "forget it" but bit my tongue. "Look, I'm leaving for California in a couple days," I told him. "I'm real busy. Sorry."

"Maybe we could talk about it over a Coke before you go."

I nearly choked. Who did he think he was—insulting my best friend, putting her down in front of me at supper, and now asking me out? This was outrageous!

"I'm not allowed to date," I answered. Hopefully that would change his attitude about me.

"Oh, it wouldn't be a date," he went on. "Stan could come, too, if that would make you feel better."

Nothing would make me feel better about you, I thought. *Not now, not ever!*

"I'm waiting for a call," I said, dying to hear from Andie.

"Hey, cool," Ryan said. "Anything the pretty blonde says."

I tried not to gag. Andie was right. This guy was a total nightmare!

I hung up, waiting a few seconds for Stan to do the same. Unfortunately, I could still hear him downstairs yakking with Ryan, and it really bugged me.

Finally I could stand it no longer. I grabbed my bathrobe off the back of my door and dashed downstairs.

"Get off the phone," I told Stan.

"Deal with it," he shot back, waving me out of the room.

Wanting to cut the phone cord, I stood just outside the kitchen, waiting in the dining room where Stan couldn't see me. As I expected, he took his sweet time and eventually hung up a meager three minutes before ten o'clock. He sauntered out of the kitchen, heading toward his bedroom without even speaking to me. Just as well.

Within seconds, the phone rang, and I flew to get it. "Hello?"

"Very bad news," Andie moaned. "I'm stuck in Dressel Hills forever."

"You mean you can't go?"

"Mom says no."

"What about your dad?"

"He's not home yet," she said tearfully. "Besides, he won't agree to something Mom's already vetoed." Sounded familiar.

"Well, maybe another time?"

"Probably not," she said, exhaling into the phone. "I was really living for this."

"I know," I said, trying to soothe her disappointment. "Maybe they'll change their minds."

"Dream on."

"See you tomorrow?" I said.

"Yeah, see ya."

I hung up, feeling lousy. Andie was stuck here in town. And in three days she'd be without me to protect her from that rotten Ryan Davis. Not to mention my own stepbrother.

Chapter 5

The next morning I woke up earlier than usual. I heard Mom and Uncle Jack talking quietly in their bedroom, down the hall from my room.

Yesterday's events came flooding back. The ethnic slurs Ryan had made to Andie . . . the way Stan hadn't spoken up to defend her . . . and the latest blow: Andie's mom had put her foot down about California.

I crept out of bed, found my journal, then crawled back into bed. Time to tell all.

Friday, July 8: Here I am, wanting something so badly, and BAM, the wish bubble pops right in my face! Translation: I was hoping Andie could go with me to visit my dad, but things got changed around way too fast. Her mom said no. It's no good to tell Andie to talk to her dad about it. That would just make things worse in the long run.

I laid down my pen, thinking. What if *I* were to talk to Andie's mom? Just sorta wander over there today and test the waters . . . find out why she'd decided against letting Andie go. Maybe it would open the door for some discussion. Maybe I could put her mother's fears to rest. No doubt she had some.

With a renewed sense of urgency, I bounded out of bed and headed for the bathroom. When I was dried off from my shower and wrapped in a towel, I hurried to my room again, anxious to get over to Andie's.

When I made my kitchen appearance, Mom was already scrambling eggs and frying bacon. "How'd you sleep?" Mom asked. It was her standard line.

"Morning, sweet toast," Uncle Jack said, shuffling through the newspaper. He had such weird nicknames for all six of us kids. And I mean *all* of us. Uncle Jack was cool that way. (The uncle part came from the fact that he'd been married to Daddy's sister before she died.) So even though he wasn't really related to Carrie and me, it felt good knowing that he loved us enough to dream up individual nicknames.

"What do you have planned for today?" Uncle Jack asked, studying me as I settled down onto the barstool next to him.

"Not much."

"Well, I hope whatever it is, you won't forget your mother here. I think she could use some help around the house." He winked at me and reached for a glass of orange juice. "What do you think? Can you squeeze a chore or two into your social schedule?"

It wasn't *what* he said that made me want to do exactly what Uncle Jack asked, it was *how* he said it. "Sure, I'll help," I said as Mom placed a large plate of eggs and toast in front of me. "What's up?"

"Only about twenty-five loads of laundry, give or take," Mom joked. "You probably want to freshen up your summer things for your trip, too, right?"

I nodded, scooping up a forkful of eggs. "Can I run over to Andie's first?" I asked before taking a bite.

Uncle Jack turned to me. "I've got an idea. Why don't you put in a load of wash right after breakfast, and I'll drive you to Andie's on my way to work." He glanced at Mom. "Okay with you, Susan?"

"Sounds good." Mom sat down with her usual peppermint tea. "Just don't be gone too long."

"I'll catch the bus home," I said. It was perfect. Dressel Hills had public transportation via city buses—free to the public. That made getting around our little town a cinch.

Mom stirred honey from the plastic bear into her tea, humming softly. She seemed a little distant, though, like she was contemplating something important. Uncle Jack reached across and covered her hand with his big one. "What's on your mind, Cupcake?"

She smiled a whimsical smile at me. "Guess I'm just going to miss my number-one girl, that's all."

"Aw, Mom, I'll be fine. You know that," I said.

"Of course you will." She brightened. "It's just such a different world out there on the West Coast." She was thinking about big cities. Mom hated them. Too many people packed into one area gave her stress. Lots of it.

Uncle Jack squeezed Mom's hand. "Holly's going to be okay," he said. "True, she's not a big-city girl, but she knows how to handle herself." He nodded at me. "Right, kiddo?"

"Uncle Jack's right," I said, smiling. He sure knew how to lighten up a conversation.

He got up and carried his plate over to the sink. "Holly won't fall for some big, bad beach bum," he said more for my benefit than Mom's. "I guarantee it. Right, angel face?" His eyes twinkled, but I caught the serious glint behind them.

He must have heard from Mom that I'd pretty much written off the boys around here. After the way things turned out at camp, I figured it was a good idea to cool it with the boy-girl thing. Far as I was concerned, being just friends with the opposite sex was perfect at my age—almost fourteen and a half.

"That's one of the reasons why I thought it would be fun to take Andie along to California," I said glumly.

Mom's eyebrows shot up. "Andie?"

Oops! The California thing was supposed to have been kept

a secret. Except now that things were at a standstill with Andie's parents, maybe it wasn't such a big deal anymore.

I tried to laugh it off. "Well, it was a fabulous idea while it lasted," I said. "Andie asked if she could go along, so I talked to Saundra about it. She said it was fine with her, but now Andie's mom says no."

Uncle Jack came over and leaned his hands against the bar. "That's really too bad, isn't it, hon? I think Andie's going is a really terrific idea."

A minute later, Mom was agreeing with Uncle Jack. Yes! With both of them on our side, maybe, just maybe, Andie and I could talk her mom into letting her go. What a fabulous turn of events!

♥ ♥ ♥

It started to rain while I was at Andie's. A dismal outlook for the day. Trying to be cheerful, I helped Mrs. Martinez by dressing Chris and Jon. The twins seemed happy to see me. Andie too. But there was an underlying sense of disappointment in the air.

"It's going to be so boring around here without you, Holly," Andie blurted out when her mom left the room.

I wanted to find the bright side of things. "Maybe it'll still work out for you to come."

"Huh?" She looked at me like I was crazy. "You don't know my parents. Once they decide something, that's it."

"Well, listen to this." And I began to fill her in on Uncle Jack's reaction.

Andie beamed with anticipation. "So your stepdad liked the idea?"

"Would I kid you?" I laughed. "Let me hang around your mom for a while, you know, help her out a little. Maybe the subject will come up gracefully."

Andie sighed. "Yeah, don't you wish."

I did my thing with Andie's mom, following the twins around, picking up after them and assisting with anything that would bring me in close proximity to Mrs. Martinez.

Several times the conversation touched on my California trip, but mostly in reference to my dad and the fact that he'd become a Christian recently.

"Are you looking forward to going to California?" Mrs. Martinez asked politely.

I nodded. "It's always perfect on the beach, you know. I always feel close to God out there."

"What's your stepmother like?" she asked rather pointedly.

I wanted to be careful about the way I described Saundra. After all, she wasn't exactly the best role model around. If I told the truth and launched into a description of my stepmom's materialism, it might limit Andie's chances of going for sure.

"Saundra and I are getting to know each other better every time we're together." What a pathetic statement. I wasn't really saying much of anything.

Andie's mom sat down at the kitchen table with Jon on her knee. "Is she starting to go to church with your dad?"

"I don't know exactly." It remained to be seen how Saundra was responding to Daddy's conversion. "The best I can do is pray for her."

"Good for you, Holly" was all Mrs. Martinez said, and since I didn't feel the timing was right, I dismissed the idea of pushing for Andie to go.

When the phone rang, I suspected it was my own mother, reminding me of my duties at home. My assumptions were correct, and reluctantly I said good-bye to Andie and to her mom before scampering out into the drizzle to catch the bus.

On the ride home, I thought of the logistics involved in getting Andie's ticket in time for the Monday flight. Even if her parents agreed, it was unlikely that there would be a seat available at this late date, especially at such a hectic vacation time of year. Yet something in me held out hope.

♥ ♥ ♥

When I arrived home, Carrie and Stephie greeted me at the back door. "You're late," Carrie bossed.

"Yeah," Stephie echoed her. "We've been sorting your dirty clothes."

I pushed past them and ran down the steps to the laundry room. The place was crammed with piles of whites, colors, and darks. "You weren't kidding," I said to Mom about the dirty clothes. "This is a mess."

Mom ignored my comment. "What took so long?" she asked, her hands on her hips now. "I thought you were coming right back."

I couldn't tell her that my plan to approach Mrs. Martinez had bombed. That I'd tried to worm my way into the conversation over there, only to end up discussing Daddy's new wife. So I muttered, "Sorry, things took longer than I thought."

"Well, I hope we have *all* your dirty laundry." She glanced around. "Carrie and Stephie brought everything down from your hamper."

I wondered if my sisters had taken advantage of the moment and snooped elsewhere in my room. I could see Mom was feeling frantic about getting me ready for the trip. After all, I was going to be gone two full weeks.

"Have you made a list of things to take?" she asked.

"That's a switch," I said, laughing. "I'm usually the one asking you."

She nodded. "Well, I think a list would be a good idea."

"Sure, I'll make one." I started sorting through the underwear. Then I loaded the washer, sprinkling detergent around before I closed the lid.

I gathered up the next load, but Mom kept hanging around. It seemed she had something on her mind. I knew I was right when she said, "Any chance that Andie's folks might change their minds?"

I shook my head. "Probably not."

She leaned against the dryer, pushing a strand of blond hair away from her face. "I don't know why we didn't think of this earlier. Andie would be marvelous company for you." What Mom was trying to say wasn't coming out too clearly. She really meant to say that if Andie went to California with me, maybe she wouldn't be as worried about me.

Just then a fabulous plan hit me. "Do you think Andie's mom would be more open to the idea if you gave her a call?"

"Oh, I don't know about that," Mom said, backing out of the laundry room.

"Aw, come on," I said, laughing. Maybe by keeping an upbeat, cheerful attitude about this, I could get her to see the light. "Let's discuss this." Playfully, I reached for her arm.

"It's not my place to interfere with Andie's family." She let me pull her back into the room.

"But you're such good friends with her mom, and—"

"I don't think it's fair to use our friendship like that," she said. "Rosita can be a very stubborn woman at times, and I think this may be one of those times."

"But, Mom, can't you at least call her and find out why she said no? Ple-e-ase? I'll do anything, any chore you ask."

Mom folded her hands in front of her and stepped toward me, grinning. "Does this mean *that* much to you?"

I hugged her nearly off balance. "Thanks, Mom. You're so fabulous."

She cocked her head. "Oh, so now I'm your favorite word."

I tried to maintain my composure as she headed upstairs to get the portable phone. Minutes later, she came down with the phone in her hand. "I want you to hear what I say, Holly."

Strange. Mom *never* wanted us to listen in on her phone conversations. What could possibly be on her mind?

Chapter 6

"Hello, Rosita? Yes, this is Susan."

I held my breath.

"How are your little ones?"

Another medium-sized pause. I could just imagine Andie's mom telling something humorous about one of the twins. Except Mom wasn't laughing.

"Oh, that's good," Mom said, nodding. "Yes, we're just fine. Thanks." A short pause. "Well, yes, Holly mentioned something about it."

About what? What did I say? I wanted to know where this conversation was headed.

"Jack and I thought it was a very good idea," Mom said, much to my surprise. Could she be referring to Andie going with me to California?

I studied Mom's face. Her eyes grew serious; her eyebrows knit into a hard frown. "I know. Sometimes things don't make a bit of sense, but if you feel that way, I understand completely." Mom glanced at me. "Well, it was no picnic the first time I let Holly go out there, but I guess letting go is a rather slow process."

There was an exceedingly long silence on this end. Mom shook her head from time to time but nothing more.

"What?" I whispered, but Mom waved at me to be still. This was *so* agonizing, standing here in the middle of the laundry room, listening to Mom discuss my summer plans with my best friend's mother.

The rinse cycle came on with a whooshing sound as water sprayed against spinning clothes. The noise triggered the end of Mom's conversation with Mrs. Martinez. She said she'd talk with her again. I couldn't wait for Mom to hang up. Maybe then I'd get some straight answers at last.

Finally she beeped the phone off. "What?" I demanded. "What did Andie's mom say?"

"Holly-Heart," Mom said, smiling, "I think you can relax about the whole thing."

"What are you saying?"

She sighed. "Rosita's just a little fearful, that's all." She placed the phone on top of the dryer. "There's really no logical reason for her to have said no, but who knows, maybe next year. Things like this take time."

"Time?" I was beside myself. Here we were, approaching the goal, and Mom was talking about our biggest enemy. "We don't *have* time!"

She smiled. "We do if you want this thing to work itself out."

Mom was probably right. Again. "So . . . how long do we have to wait?"

Her eyes twinkled. "Only until Rosita calls a travel agent. How's that?"

"Oh, Mom!" I ran to her open arms.

"Happy?" she whispered.

I showed her just how very happy with the biggest bear hug I could muster.

Hours later, Andie's mom called back. She'd gotten the information she needed. It was celebration time. Which, unfortunately, only lasted five seconds.

Turned out the Monday flight was booked—not a single coach ticket available. Which meant Andie would have to fly standby or not go at all—her mom said she really didn't want Andie traveling alone for her first flight. Don't ask me why; after all, I've seen lots of much younger kids flying alone. But Mom had said Rosita was stubborn, and boy, was she right.

♥ ♥ ♥

Saturday, Mom and I met Andie and her mom at the Soda Straw for lunch. Mom said it was just going to be a little get-together before Andie and I left town. No big deal. Well, what was supposed to be no big deal turned out to be a mini-lecture, more for Andie's benefit than for mine. And at one point during the conversation—even before the waitress had a chance to bring us our burgers and fries—Mrs. Martinez asked me point-blank if I would watch over Andie.

Who did she think I was? Andie's worst enemy? Of course I'd be looking out for my friend, and I said so.

Andie's mom eyed me quite seriously. "Now, you know that Andrea has never been away from home like this before. She's very naïve."

And I'd like her to stay that way, Mrs. Martinez was probably thinking.

I nodded, trying to avoid looking at Andie. We both knew her mother's image of California had come from the media. White sand, tanned bodies, wild beach parties . . . the whole sun and surf thing. I didn't want my laughter spilling out while she was speaking so directly and seriously to me. I respected Mrs. Martinez and her feelings; still, there was just a little too much hovering going on at the moment.

"Andrea has led a sheltered life," she continued. "You know what I'm saying?"

Of course I knew. Andie and I were in the same boat when it came to being a bit overly protected. Personally, I didn't mind. It beat having more freedom than you can handle, like most teens I knew.

Andie's mom gave her daughter a sweet-as-molasses look before switching her gaze to me. "Except for your stepbrother Stan, Andrea's never really spent much time with a guy friend. And since she's only fourteen—"

"Almost fifteen," Andie interrupted.

"Well, almost, yes, but nevertheless, you're much too young for boy-girl nonsense." Mrs. Martinez leaned back against the red vinyl booth. Her eyebrows had been waxed to a narrow line, framing her large deep-set eyes. When she frowned, as she was now, the too-thin eyebrows made her eyes look almost mournful.

I could tell she was desperate. She wanted a firm commitment from me—something she could count on to make her feel more comfortable.

"I'll take good care of Andie," I volunteered, meaning it.

"I can take care of myself," Andie spouted.

Mrs. Martinez rolled her eyes exactly the way Andie always did. "Now, Andrea," she whispered.

Mom leaned forward at that moment. "Holly's made some nice friends at her father's house. I don't think we have to worry. The main thing is for the two of you to stick together. Don't go pairing off with boys"—and here she looked directly at me. "Holly can't car-date yet, either. You girls are on your honor."

"We'll be just fine," I assured both mothers. And I had no doubt that we would.

When the door jingled, I looked up. Jared Wilkins and Billy Hill strolled inside. They waved when they spotted us in the corner booth—the same one Jared and I had shared over a year ago when I'd first had a crush on him.

Jared was the last person I wanted to see today. He and I were still decent friends, sort of, but I didn't want to be tied down to hanging out with one boy anymore. The boy-girl thing had gotten too complicated last school year, and I just wanted to cool it. Not only with Jared—with all guys.

"Hey," he said, coming over. Billy waved, looking a little shy when he realized we were with our moms. Jared wasn't bashful, though. "Looks like you've got a cozy mother-daughter event going here. Nice to see you again, Mrs. Meredith . . . er, Patterson."

"Same to you, Jared," Mom said politely, ignoring the mistake with her new married name.

"How are your little boys?" he asked Andie's mom. "Chris and Jon, right?"

Mrs. Martinez nodded. "Lively as ever."

I smiled. Andie didn't. She was still ticked, I think, at what had happened at youth camp last month. It was a very long story, but as far as I was concerned, all was forgiven.

"So, what's the occasion?" Jared asked.

"It's our farewell lunch," I said. "Andie's going with me to California on Monday."

Billy piped up. "Really?"

"That's the plan," Andie said, grinning.

Jared flashed his dimples at me. "Well, have fun."

"We sure will." I wanted to reinforce my stand, in case he thought I'd softened on my decision.

"See ya," Jared said, and he and Billy headed to the counter to order.

♥ ♥ ♥

Later that evening, Andie and I sat on my front-porch swing talking between slurps of root beer floats.

Ryan had come by to pick up Stan about thirty minutes before. They were going to see some show downtown.

Andie looked like she was going to pop. But I knew there was no way she'd hold her breath for an apology from either Ryan or Stan. If Stan had any smarts, he'd certainly have offered a humble one. And Ryan? He was as rude as they come.

After the guys left, Andie spewed out her feelings.

"I guess my mom was right. I *have* been sheltered." She sat cross-legged on the porch swing next to me. "At least I've never had to deal with any sort of prejudice before. Never." She continued to rant about Ryan's slurs, rehashing the scene at the Y a few days ago. "Just where do you think Stan was during all that?" She huffed. "It was like he was totally out to lunch instead of standing right there beside me."

"I know," I said, touching her shoulder. "I know."

"Just when you think you've found a guy you can really be friends with, something like this has to happen."

"Mom says there's lots of good fish in the sea," I said, trying to comfort her.

"Yeah, right. The problem is *finding* the fish."

"Don't worry about that. We'll pray 'em in."

She turned to look at me. "You honestly pray about everything, don't you?"

"Close." It was true. For some reason I talked to God about most everything.

Andie played with the chain on the porch swing, deep in thought. "Sometimes God answers with 'no,' sometimes a 'maybe' . . . not always a 'yes.' At least, that's what Pastor Rob says."

I nodded. "Bottom line, though, He knows what's best for us. I guess, for some people, trusting is the hardest part."

Silently, we contemplated the fact. Andie seemed restless about something, though, and when I mentioned it, she asked, "What are my chances of actually making that flight, really?"

"Don't worry," I said casually. "I've seen zillions of passengers get on with standby status."

"Honest?" Her eyes lit up.

I nodded. But deep down, where my greatest fears always simmered before surfacing, I knew this standby thing was very tricky.

Andie *had* to get on my flight. Or else we were right back where we started.

Chapter 7

Denver International Airport was wildly congested. Vacation season was in full swing, and crowds of people flocked to the enormous airport east of the big city. Andie and I waited near one of the many automatic doors, juggling luggage, while Uncle Jack drove the van to the short-term parking area. At the last minute, he'd decided to drive us instead of Mom because he had some business to tend to at his Denver office. The car trip from Dressel Hills to Denver zoomed by surprisingly fast, and all because of Uncle Jack's continuous flow of airplane jokes.

"Bet you're going to miss your stepdad, huh?" Andie said as we waited.

"There's no one quite like Uncle Jack, that's for sure."

She squeezed her gym bag. "I can't wait to see your dad again . . . your real dad. It'll be so great to see what *he's* like now."

I spied Uncle Jack outside, hurrying across the street. "Oh, you'll like Daddy. He's very articulate—handsome, too—but he doesn't joke around a lot." *He doesn't have time to; he works too much,* I thought.

My uncle helped us lug our bags into the long line where I'd be checking mine. The plan was that Andie would carry her single bag onto the plane—that is, if she even got on.

At last we were past security, where Uncle Jack was given a pass, allowing him to escort us to the gate. Then we headed for the underground tram and on toward the correct concourse, keeping our eyes peeled for gate eleven. Uncle Jack helped navigate while Andie chattered like a chipmunk. This was her first flight anywhere. She was acting like a kid about to eat her first ice-cream cone.

"Oh, Holly, this is going to be so amazing." She grabbed my arm as we walked.

I agreed. "Maybe you'll get hooked on flying and want to fly all over the place."

When we located gate eleven, the waiting area was crammed with people. Andie and I searched for three seats together, with no luck. Uncle Jack saved the day and discovered two vacant seats close to the window. "Here you go," he said. "Window seats for the ladies." He waited till we got situated before excusing himself to make a phone call.

Andie and I whispered and giggled nonstop—a preview of what was surely ahead for us in California. "Just think, we've got two whole weeks away from our mundane, boring Dressel Hills lives," she said. "When we're old and crotchety, we'll be telling our grandkids about this trip."

"Oh, did I tell you? My dad has passes to Universal Studios," I said, suddenly remembering.

Andie's eyebrows leaped up. "Really? When did this happen?" Before I could answer, she said, "What else haven't you told me?"

"Absolutely nothing." I scratched my head and put on a frown. "Oh yeah, I forgot to tell you about my wicked stepmother. I figured you wouldn't want to come along if I said anything. But now that you're committed to going—"

"Holly, you never call her that," she interrupted, glancing around to see if anyone was listening.

I lowered my voice and leaned closer to Andie. "You'll be calling her wicked, too, when you find out what she makes you do."

She giggled. "Don't be silly."

"Okay." I folded my arms across my chest. "But don't say I didn't warn you."

She cocked her head at me, trying to decide if what I'd said was to be taken sincerely.

I shook my head, keeping a straight face. "Yep, Saundra will have you cleaning out cupboards and closets all week long. Oh, and she likes the pantry alphabetized according to brand names."

"You're kidding," she said, a tiny smirk waiting in the wings.

"You just better hope you make this flight so you can see for yourself."

"I don't believe you." She was about to toss her gym bag at me when the announcement came for first-class passengers to board the airplane. I felt my stomach lurch. This was it. We'd know in a few minutes whether Andie was coming or not.

I grabbed her hand. "Have you prayed about this?"

"Me? I thought you were the one doing all the praying."

"But this was *your* idea, right?" I stared at her. "Well, don't you think you ought to?"

"Okay, I'll pray," she said, bowing her head right there in front of everyone. Her lips started moving, and I could see that she was squeezing her folded hands like crazy. Andie wanted this trip bad. I remembered lots of times when I couldn't get her to pray over her food in public, but this . . .

She was really going at it. I sent a powerful silent prayer heavenward as I got up and headed over to the check-in counter. "Excuse me," I said to the man dressed in a navy blue uniform. "Could you please tell me if there are any no-shows for the coach section?" I explained that Andie was flying standby and wondered what her chances were.

"Just one moment, miss." He pulled up the information on the computer. His eyes darted back and forth, scanning the screen.

"Looks like there are three no-shows so far." He smiled a comforting smile. "But your friend will have to wait until all passengers have boarded before we can give her the go-ahead."

"Thank you very much." I was more hopeful than ever and hurried over to Andie, who was still squeezing her eyes shut in earnest prayer. I touched her hand. "I think God heard and answered already."

"Oh, Holly, this is so cool." She hugged the living daylights out of me.

I pulled back, filling her in on the details. "Let's wait to celebrate until you're on the plane, okay?"

She turned around and stared out the window overlooking the runways. The plane—our plane—was a DC-10. We watched as the luggage carriers glided along the ground loading the luggage.

"Hey, look." I pointed. "There's my suitcase."

Andie leaned forward. "You're right."

The large piece of pink yarn tied to the suitcase handle would make it easy to spot in L.A. I'd gotten the idea from one of Marty Leigh's mystery books. One of her characters obsessed over identifying her own luggage. She decorated it with brightly colored ribbons and yarn. Every piece, every time.

That's when I heard the announcement for standby passengers. I felt tense, jittery—tried to picture Andie walking down the long, narrow Jetway to board the plane with me.

I glanced around, checking on the short line of standby passengers filing down the enclosed walkway connecting the terminal to the plane. "Shouldn't be long now," I whispered, half to myself, half to Andie.

The names of a Rudy and Jayne Kish were called over the intercom. I watched the young couple hurry to the podium and show their IDs. Promptly, they were given a boarding pass and returned to their seats.

Andie's eyes filled with worry. "How much longer . . . before my name is called?"

"And it *will* be, you know," I assured her.

Uncle Jack strolled to the window, his hands in his pants pockets. I wondered if he was as concerned as I was. Actually, I'd never seen my uncle freak out over anything. He was calm and cool, the way I wished I could be. Especially now.

Soon, another standby passenger was called to the podium.

My pulse raced. I could scarcely breathe. And just when I thought I'd burst, another name was announced. A tall, good-looking man hurried to the check-in counter.

Andie grabbed my arm and clung to it. "Oh, Holly," she moaned. "I can't stand the suspense."

"We're *both* getting on this flight. I can feel it." I let Andie hang on to me as the beady-eyed man in uniform offered a boarding pass to the tall man.

About that time, Uncle Jack wandered over to us, checking his watch. "The flight's scheduled for departure at 12:15. That's twenty-five minutes from now."

"So . . . I'll know soon if I'm going or not," Andie said softly.

First-class passengers were invited to board. Then coach passengers, beginning with rows twenty-five to thirty-three. A bunch of people lined up in response to the announcement. Parents with small children, older folk, men in business suits.

Still, I wanted to hold out for a miracle.

"I can't believe this," Andie was saying, tears in her eyes. "I guess this is good-bye."

We were both in tears, and Uncle Jack came over and put his arm around Andie as he leaned over to kiss my cheek. "Don't let this ruin your time, sweetie," he said. Then, turning to Andie, he winked at her. "Hey, kiddo, you and me—let's paint the town, okay?"

Uncle Jack was so cool. He would see to it that Andie had a fabulous day. She'd probably end up having more fun than I'd have the whole two weeks.

"Better get in line now, Holly," Uncle Jack said. "They won't hold your plane forever."

"Bye. Love you." I hugged my stepdad and then Andie again. "You too!"

"Send me lots of emails, okay?" Andie said.

"I'll write at least twice a day."

After showing my boarding pass and ID, I hurried down the walkway. I wiped my cheeks, too upset to look back.

Andie wasn't coming with me to California. God had said no this time. But why?

Down the long ramp, I headed toward the plane. Maybe God had something else planned for Andie. I could only hope it was something wonderful.

Just as I was about to enter the plane, the tall, handsome man— the last standby passenger called—was being escorted out of the plane by a male flight attendant. Evidently there was a problem. The name on his boarding pass didn't match the name on his checked lugguge, so he had to get off the plane. His luggage would have to be removed, as well.

"Excuse me," I said to the flight attendant. "Does this mean there's room for one more standby passenger on this flight?"

The uniformed attendant nodded. "Only one." He headed up the ramp with the ousted passenger.

Wow. This was so fabulous. I didn't know what to do first. But I knew I had to run back up the Jetway and let Andie know this good news.

"Miss," the flight attendant said as I passed him, "if you haven't boarded by the time the door is closed on the plane, you will miss your flight."

So I hurried to the waiting area and looked around. Andie and Uncle Jack were nowhere in sight!

Rushing to the podium, I was out of breath. "Can you please page someone for me?" Quickly, I filled him in about Andie and how she'd already left with my stepdad to head for the terminal. "She thinks the plane is full, but it's not."

"One moment, please." He checked the monitor, then nodded with a smile.

I heard Andie's name over the entire airport intercom. Darting out into the wide concourse, I searched frantically. People crowded my vision, making it impossible to spot Andie. Or Uncle Jack.

My heart pounded uncontrollably. This was worse than any nightmare I'd *ever* had!

Chapter 8

The attendant frowned. "Now, young lady, if you don't go this instant, you will miss your plane."

I had no choice. Daddy and Saundra would be waiting for me at the L.A. airport. If I didn't show up they'd be very worried. So, with great reluctance, I obeyed.

The flight attendant brightened when he saw me coming. "Oh, good, you're back."

"Uh, they're paging my friend right now. Is there any way you can hold the plane for her?"

"Is your friend the Queen of England?"

I caught the joke, but it wasn't funny. I tried to explain my problem, but he couldn't give me any reason to hope that Andie would catch this plane.

He asked to see my ticket. "You're in row seventeen, seat C."

My heart sank as I made my way through first class—all those comfortable, spacious seats were filled. In fact, the entire plane was filled to capacity. Except for one aisle seat five rows into the coach section. I nearly cried as I passed it. It could've been Andie's seat. If only . . .

I couldn't stop thinking about her. Even if she and Uncle Jack *had* heard the page, it was unlikely that she could make it in time. Not with the crowded concourses or the way the flight attendant glowered when I asked if they could please hold the plane.

I found my seat. It was also on the aisle, and every few seconds I leaned around the seat in front of me, hoping to spot Andie.

A flight attendant came down the aisle, offering magazines. Who could read at a time like this? Instead, I prayed under my breath, begging God to please change His mind about things.

I remembered how Andie had bowed her head in prayer inside the concourse. It was one of the few times she'd ever done such a thing—closing her eyes like that in public—and I asked God to reward Andie for her courage. For her faith. To give her this trip she longed for.

I said "amen" audibly, not caring what the lady beside me thought. When I opened my eyes, I couldn't believe it. There was Andie Martinez in the flesh. Trooping down the aisle as though she owned the place.

"Yes," I said, leaping up. "Andie!"

Her face burst into an enormous grin. She waved triumphantly and sat down just as the second officer's voice came over the intercom. "Flight attendants, prepare for cross-check."

I fastened my seat belt, making sure it was tight. What an incredible day.

♥ ♥ ♥

When the plane leveled off at peak altitude, the seat belt sign was turned off and passengers were allowed to move around. Andie didn't waste any time getting out of her seat. She stood in the aisle beside my seat, beaming. "Is this incredible or what?"

"I know. I mean, here I was coming to get on the plane, and I find out that tall guy isn't getting on, after all. So, I make a mad dash back up to find you, and you're gone!"

Her eyes danced with excitement. "You must've been totally freaked."

"Worse," I said, remembering the panic.

"Well"—she handed me a note—"read this while I use the rest room."

"Thanks." I felt like at least a zillion bucks as I opened her note.

Hey, Holly,

This is just too cool. I'm really going to California with you! Can you believe it?

You were right about trusting God and all. It really looked like He'd said no loud and clear—but this . . . this is so-o-o totally cool. I think between the two of us, our prayers got answered. Pronto!

You should've seen your uncle Jack's face when we heard my name being paged. Actually, he was the one who made it possible for me to catch this plane. He grabbed a luggage cart, I hopped in, and he pushed me faster than lightning back to gate 11. It was so weird. I'm glad you have such a great stepdad. And, in case you didn't know it . . . you're not so bad yourself!

Love ya, kid,

Andie

I refolded her note, smiling. What a sight they must have been, flying down the concourse like that with Andie in a luggage cart.

When she finally came back down the aisle, I stopped her. "I have a fabulous idea. Let's write notes."

"You're on," she said, trotting back to her seat.

I pulled a fresh piece of lined paper out of my backpack. I always carried a small six-by-nine-inch tablet with me. Essential equipment for a writer.

Dearest Andie,

You won't believe this, but while you were racing to catch this plane, I was praying. I asked God to reward you

for praying in public. Remember back there when you prayed
while we were waiting to find out about this flight?

    I know it was probably tough for you, but I was really
proud. I'm sure God was, too!

    Hey, this is weird. I almost feel like we're in Mr. Ross's sci-
ence class passing notes. Now you owe me one.

                Friends forever,

                Holly

We passed notes back and forth while the flight attendants served us pretzels and a beverage. But afterward, I started feeling wiped out. Andie, however, was wired up and ready for anything. I had to talk her into letting me catch some *z*s during the remainder of the trip. It wasn't easy.

"How can you sleep when we're in the middle of a miracle?" she said when she passed my seat on her way back from returning a magazine.

I yawned. "Ever hear of adrenaline depletion?"

"Oh that."

"Yeah, that," I said. "Traveling with you is exhausting."

She actually gave up and let me rest.

♥ ♥ ♥

Much later I had the privilege of introducing Andie to Daddy, Saundra, and Tyler at the L.A. airport. They seemed pleased that she had come. Daddy was especially interested in hearing about God's answer to our prayers. Saundra didn't seem to care.

Once we arrived at the luxurious beach house, Andie and I began settling in. I showed her down the spiral staircase—I called it the Cinderella stairs—to the guest bedrooms. We had two spacious rooms, each opening to a large, cozy sitting room where bookshelves were filled with classics and poetry. And a complete set of the Marty Leigh mystery series. Along with a desk and chair where quiet thoughts could be recorded, there was a huge flat-screen TV and an entertainment system to boot.

After I gave Andie the tour of the lower level, we made quick work of unpacking. She was anxious to swim in the Pacific Ocean. "Do you realize, Holly Meredith, that I'm nearly fifteen years old and I've never been in the ocean?" She was already changing into her bathing suit.

I sat in a leather recliner near the windows, drinking in the spectacular view of the blue Pacific. "The water's salty," I told her. "You shouldn't swallow if you get any in your mouth."

"Yes, mother." She came over to have another look.

I glanced at her. She was spunky, all right.

"Whew, it feels good putting a couple of states between me and that lousy Ryan whatever-his-face-is."

"Yeah," I said, watching the sea gulls swoop and sway in the distance. "I wonder what Stan sees in him as a friend."

"Beats me," Andie said, investigating the room. There was an oil painting of the tall red-topped lighthouse at St. George's Reef on the wall opposite the window. "Wow," she whispered. "This picture looks expensive."

"It's an original."

She moved close to the painting. "How can you tell?"

"See the artist's brushstrokes?"

"Yeah, I see what you mean." Then she stepped back, surveying the whole room. "Man, your dad must be rich."

I nodded, content to sit in the comfortable chair. "I suppose so."

She looked at me with surprise in her eyes. "You mean you don't know for sure?"

"It doesn't matter, really. Besides, I don't want to get into this right now." The whole thing with Daddy coming out here when Mom didn't want to move, back before their divorce, sometimes still hurt. Like now.

Thank goodness Andie understood. She took my lead and dropped the subject. "Well, I'm ready to hit the beach. You coming?"

"Give me five." I pulled myself out of the chair and hurried through the sitting room to my own room. Inside the room, which was decorated in creams and greens, I closed the door. Andie and I would probably end up discussing my feelings about Daddy's remarriage sometime while we were here. But . . . maybe not. I just wished it hadn't come up right off the bat like this.

Locating my swimsuit, I put it on, taking my time. I could almost feel the vibrations coming from Andie's room, she was so hyper.

I sighed. Hopefully she'd slow down a bit. Maybe a good swim in the ocean was what she needed.

With towels and a beach ball in hand, we dashed to the sandy path. It sloped down a bit, leveled off, then dipped a little, leading us to the beach.

It was a fine, hot day, complete with a balmy ocean breeze. Eagerly we marked our territory with giant towels given to us by Saundra. They were thick ones that felt new. My stepmom wanted only the best for us.

We used our sandals to anchor our towels; then, with total abandon, we raced to the ocean. The waves called to me, and I swam out past the breakers. Andie followed.

"I'm never going home!" she shouted as we floated free and easy under the California sun.

"I know. This place is total heaven."

She grinned at me, riding a low swell. "Do you think there's an ocean in heaven?"

"Well," I said, thinking, "there's the sea of forgetfulness where God dumps our sins. How's that?"

"But I want waves." She giggled blissfully.

We let the tide pull us closer to the beach, where giant waves picked us up like tiny corks bobbing in the water. What a fabulous way to spend the afternoon.

After a while, we decided to get some sun. Andie was already tan, thanks to her natural skin color, but even though it was summery back home, I was whiter than white. Since the sun was still fairly high, I knew I'd better get some sunscreen. "I'll be right back," I said. "Need anything?"

"Some music would be nice," she said, turning over on her stomach.

"I'll see if Daddy has a radio we can borrow." I hurried up the worn path to the house and climbed the steps to the deck. I wiped the sand off my feet before I entered through the sliding glass doors.

Inside, Saundra was stirring something on the stove. I wondered if Daddy had gone back to work. Probably. I crept into the open, distinctly modern kitchen. "I'm sorry to bother you, but could I borrow some sunscreen?"

"Certainly, dear. I have some in my bathroom just above the sink. You're welcome to it." Saundra pointed me in the direction of her and Daddy's bedroom.

The room had dazzling décor, with an elegant king-sized bed positioned so that it made the most of the sweeping ocean views. The nature-inspired hues of the room's palate reminded me again of my stepmother's exquisite—and expensive—tastes. The room made me almost forget what I was looking for.

Sunscreen. Yes, that's why I was in this magical place. I moved quickly to the large bathroom, trying to ignore its uncommon beauty. Opening the medicine cabinet, I located the sunblock easily. As I reached for it, my hand bumped a container of pills. The plastic bottle clattered into the sink below.

I picked it up. *Robert Meredith* was printed on it. What was *this?*

Quickly, I slipped the pills back into the cabinet and left the room. Back in the kitchen, Saundra was still stirring noodles. I stood there, wondering if I should inquire about Daddy's pills.

Tyler came up behind me in the hallway. "How's the water?" he asked, glancing toward the ocean.

"Oh, Andie's having a fabulous time," I said. "It's her first visit to the ocean, you know."

"Really? Way cool."

Saundra looked up just then. Her reddish hair was drawn back in a fancy hair clip at her neck. "Is there anything else I can get you for your swim?"

"Well, Andie just wondered if you have a portable radio, that's all."

Tyler seemed eager to help. "You can borrow mine." He disappeared down the hall to his room.

Saundra's silver earrings danced as she stirred the pasta. "I hope you and Andie like spaghetti and meatballs."

"Sounds delicious, thanks." I wondered about the lack of excitement in her voice. "Everything all right?" I ventured.

She smiled, her lips bright with red lipstick, one of her trademarks. But she avoided my question. "How soon do you think you girls will be ready for supper?"

"Whenever you want to eat will be fine," I replied. But I had something else on my mind. I inched farther into the kitchen, wondering how to approach Saundra with my concern. "Where's Daddy?"

"He had to finish up some work at the office. He'll be back later, dear." She reached up and turned on the fan above the stove. It seemed to signify the end of our conversation.

Tyler returned with his box radio. "Here you go." He gave me his radio, which had a dock for an MP3 player. "Thought you might wanna listen to some of my music, too."

"Whatcha got?"

"Oh, a little country . . . a little R and B."

"Thanks," I said and headed back outdoors. Saundra's son, now ten, never ceased to amaze me. He was perceptive, thoughtful, and much more grown-up than most kids his age.

I wondered if Daddy had taken Tyler to church with him yet. Tyler had shown some interest in God, openly discussing things like prayer and the creation of the world when I'd visited last. When Saundra wasn't around, of course. Daddy had said once that she didn't believe in a personal God. I assumed Tyler didn't, either.

I tucked the sunscreen under my arm, leaving my hands free

to carry the radio. Like everything else in Daddy's house, this, too, was probably expensive.

Partway down the sandy slope leading to the beach, I noticed a guy in purple-and-blue surfer pants talking to Andie. He was tall, Hispanic, and bare-chested . . . and he was sitting on *my* beach towel.

Andie's eyes danced with excitement when she saw me. "You're back!" She seemed elated.

What was she so happy about? I glanced down at Tyler's radio. Maybe it was the possibility of music on the beach. Then I saw a familiar glint in the guy's eyes as he grinned at Andie. Oh, so *that's* what it was. . . .

Andie waved me over. "Holly, you're just in time to meet Rico Hernandez."

"Hey," I said, wishing she wouldn't do this. Introductions to perfect strangers were always awkward for me. Besides, I wanted to get on with our afternoon. Andie's and mine.

She turned and smiled up at him like she'd known him all her life. "Rico, this is my friend Holly Meredith."

"Hey." He glanced up at me, still perched on my beach towel.

I got a better look. And cringed. This guy—this *stranger*—was at least eighteen!

Chapter 9

Honestly, I didn't know what to say or think.

I tried to figure out how long I'd been gone. Ten minutes, max. By the looks of things, Andie had gone and flipped over a complete stranger in the time it took me to go for sunblock.

"Time for music." I set the radio down on the sand because there was no room on my towel. Rico only had eyes for Andie, so it still hadn't hit him that he was trespassing on my spot.

"Thanks," Andie said, as though I'd hauled it out here for their exclusive use.

Rico found the tuner and scanned the airwaves. His wet hair glistened in the sun. "What's your style?" He was facing Andie.

"You pick," she said, grinning at me. I gave her my cutthroat gesture, which meant cool-it-with-this-guy-and-let's-get-on-with-our-plans, but it didn't seem to register.

I was about to leave to get another towel when Rico suddenly snapped to it and remembered his manners. Leaping up, he sputtered, "Here, have a seat."

"Thanks." But I didn't feel comfortable shooting the breeze with a guy neither of us knew. Why wasn't Andie being more cautious?

It wasn't like Rico looked suspicious or anything. And I couldn't imagine him turning out to be a serial killer, but what was he doing hanging out with fourteen-year-olds?

Rico turned to Andie, then me. "You wanna see something cool?"

"Sure," Andie exclaimed.

"Like what?" I said.

"Up there," he pointed, "at the high tide, there are lots of shells packed in the sand. Wanna see?"

"That's okay," I said, "you go ahead." And surprise, surprise, Andie got up and off they went, leaving me to deal with what sounded like a rumba blaring over Tyler's radio.

"Don't be long," I called to Andie, lying on my stomach facing the water. "Supper's almost ready."

I sounded just like Mom. Which reminded me of my promise to Andie's mother. I'd told her I would watch out for Andie while we were here. And watch her I did. Pretending to sunbathe, I spied on my best friend—watched her walk barefooted in the foamy surf. The wind made a point of tossing her curls against her face now and then. I heard her laughter, too. Rico was much taller than she, but her height didn't seem to matter. I watched him kneel in the sand, showing Andie how to skip stones into the receding tide. It was a scene for a painting. And my friend looked happier than I'd seen her in ages.

I remembered her tears after the Ryan Davis incident. And Stan doing zilch about it had made things even worse.

Pushing my pointer finger into the sand, I dug a tiny hole, feeling a little lonely . . . and wondering about Rico Hernandez.

♥ ♥ ♥

At supper, Andie was quiet, subdued. I wondered what she was thinking. But, really, I knew. Rico was already part of her thought processes. I could see it in her eyes. Recalling the way he'd looked at her all afternoon, though, made me even more nervous.

Daddy's chair remained vacant until the tail end of supper.

Finally he arrived, rushing into the kitchen just as Saundra was dishing up dessert—warm apple pie with ice cream on the side.

"Hello, dear," he said with a quick kiss. He looked at Andie and me. "Well, how was your first day in sunny California, girls?"

I wished he hadn't asked. Surely Andie wouldn't launch off on meeting Rico. I decided not to give her the opportunity. "Well, we're completely unpacked and settled." I sent Andie an eyeful. She caught it this time and kept her mouth shut. "I took Andie out for a long swim."

"So you got a taste of our ocean," he remarked.

"You could say that," I said.

Tyler talked about his summer school class for a while before Daddy began to talk about his work. Saundra listened attentively, but she couldn't hide the concern in her eyes. What did she know about Daddy that I didn't?

Andie and I sat politely long after our dessert was finished. It was Tyler who brought up the question of going to Universal Studios.

Daddy leaned back in his chair. "Well, we can go any day you'd like. What do you think, hon?"

Saundra tapped her long manicured nails on the tabletop. They matched the red on her lips. "I think it would probably work best on Friday."

"Friday's out," he said. "I have to be at the office all day."

One glance at Saundra's face told me she was disappointed. "Weren't you going to take some time off this week?" I could almost imagine the last part of her sentence. The part she'd left out: *while your daughter's here?*

He looked uncomfortable. "I'll have to make up for the time on Saturday." He didn't look at me. "Friday it is, then."

Tyler clapped his hands. "Yes!" he shouted.

That little problem settled, Andie and I began clearing the table. Saundra actually let us help, which was highly unusual. In fact, I was convinced by the unspoken words at the table just now that maybe Daddy and Saundra needed some time alone. So

I volunteered to finish up the kitchen. "We'll put everything away for you," I said.

Saundra smiled and put her arm around Daddy. "Thanks, Holly, you're a dear."

"Yes, Holly, you're such a dear," Andie said impishly when they'd gone. Tyler snickered, but I didn't say anything.

I waited till he'd cleared the table and left the room before I spoke. "I think we have to talk," I began. "And I think you know what about."

She tossed her head from side to side comically. "If it's about alphabetizing the canned goods, forget it."

"Very cute."

"No, really, I don't think your stepmom's all that wicked."

"Shh!"

"You mean she doesn't *know* she's a wicked stepmother?" Andie was really sneaky. Trying to get me off the subject.

"Andie," I tried again. "Just listen to me."

She was leaning over the dishwasher but remained motionless like a statue.

Exasperated, I turned around, my hands all soapy. "Stand up and listen."

She cranked herself up slowly like a windup doll. "There, how's that?"

I turned around and finished wringing out the dishcloth. "You're hopeless."

"I am?"

"Yeah, just forget it." I wasn't in the mood to approach her about Rico Hernandez. Not anymore. Mostly because I could see she was euphoric. And he was the reason.

We worked in silence, finishing off the kitchen in nothing flat. Andie was smarter than to push the issue. After all, she and I had been best friends for as long as I could remember, so she probably already figured out what I was thinking.

Both of us phoned home to our families to let them know we'd arrived safely. When Andie talked to her mom, I noticed she purposely left Rico out of the conversation. She kept asking her mom to repeat things. Probably because her twin brothers were crying in the background.

After she hung up, Andie cornered me near the refrigerator. "Holly, I want you to promise not to tell my mom about Rico."

"Sure, fine, whatever," I said glibly. "What's to tell?"

"I really like him, Holly. We're so much alike." Her eyes, normally quite round, grew narrow now. Almost slits. "I know you're my best friend, but I need to hear you say, 'I promise.' "

Not only was she glaring at me, she was squeezing my arm!

"Why? What's going on?"

"Nothing, but you know how my mom is . . . she jumps to all sorts of ridiculous conclusions. So, will you promise?"

"What's the big deal?" I said.

"It's important to me, that's what."

I could see she wasn't going to let this go till I gave in. "Okay," I reluctantly agreed. "I promise."

"Good." She looked perfectly relieved.

Tyler called to us from the living room, wanting us to play Monopoly. "C'mon, girls, I'll take you on."

"You're no match for me," Andie said.

I laughed. "Just you wait." We settled down for an evening of popcorn and Park Avenue.

Daddy came in later, wearing his robe and slippers. Saundra seemed awfully attentive to him, plumping the cushions behind his overstuffed chair and helping him find just the right position for his footrest. Then she put on some soft music in the background, lit all the candles in the room, and dimmed the lights.

"Mom!" Tyler wailed. "We can't see our game."

She tilted her head as if to say she was sorry and turned the lights up just a bit. "There, dear, how's that?"

"Still too dark," he said, sounding less spoiled than before. "But we'll live with it."

I grinned at Andie. This kid had his mom wrapped around

both his little fingers. Not only that, he wiped Andie off the board within the first hour of play.

I hung in there, with some cheering from Andie. Daddy too.

Shaking the dice, I held my breath for a nine. A six, seven, eight, or ten meant certain bankruptcy. Any other number meant I was headed to the poorhouse. Tyler owned so many hotels he couldn't fit all of them on the board. I wondered if living with a tycoon stepfather had made any difference.

"Throw!" Tyler rubbed his hands together, anticipating his triumph. One die rolled off the board, and Tyler cupped his hands over it. "A six!"

The other die was a two. Game over.

"Once again, I win," Tyler said, beginning to count his wad of money.

I pushed my remaining dollars together without tallying them. "Here, you can have mine, too."

He looked surprised. "Don't you want to know how much you ended up with?"

"Not really," I said. "Money isn't everything."

He snorted humorously. "If you wanna win, it is!"

Saundra shook her head, smiling. "Okay, Tyler, I think a little humility would do well here."

He looked sheepish, like he'd been caught doing something dreadful. "Thanks for playing my game, girls."

"Any time," Andie replied, laughing.

"It was very enlightening," I said, helping to fold up the board and put away the little green houses and red hotels. It was obvious Saundra hadn't taught her son about the dangers of greed.

When the game lid was secure, I turned around to ask Daddy something, but he was sound asleep. His head had dropped down against his chest, and his hands were folded across his lap. "Looks like someone's had a rough day," I whispered to Saundra.

"Your father's a tired man." The gentle, motherly way she said it made me wonder even more.

Chapter 10

Much later in the evening, Andie and I finally had a chance to have our little talk. Actually, it turned out to be a big deal. Much bigger than I ever dreamed. Andie had totally lost it over a chance encounter on the beach. And on the first day, no less!

I propped myself up with one elbow on the queen-sized bed in Andie's room, studying her as I lay on my side. I couldn't believe what I'd just heard. "Let me get this straight," I said. "Did you say you think this guy could be your future husband?"

Her eyes sparkled as she rolled over, staring goo-goo-eyed at the ceiling. "In my entire life, I've never met a guy like this. And to think he's Hispanic, just like me."

I could see that Stan and Ryan had done a number on her back home. "Okay, so he and you have the same ethnic background. So what?"

"Don't you see?" she said. "This could be the reason God let me catch the plane this morning."

She's turning irrational on me!

"You're kidding, right?" I looked at her. Then I sat up and peered down into her eyes. "Who are you, and what have you done with my best friend?"

She sat up, nearly knocking me over. "You're not funny, Holly. I'm serious. I want to get to know Rico while I'm here." She sighed, her eyes getting that dreamy, faraway look in them again. "Please don't say I shouldn't."

"Remember what our moms discussed about not pairing off?" She shook her head. "This isn't like that. Rico's different."

Now I was really confused. "He's a *boy*, right?"

"Double duh . . ."

"But you hardly know him," I pointed out. "Besides, do you even know if he's a Christian?"

"We didn't talk about that." Her face looked glum for a moment, then it brightened. "I could witness to him and lead him to the Lord."

"That's risky," I said. "And while you're spending time talking to him about Christ, you're getting in over your head. It doesn't work that way."

I waited for a comeback, but she was silent. Finally I dealt with the real issue—the thing that was really bugging me. "I thought you were coming here to spend time with *me*," I said softly.

"Oh, Holly, we'll be spending lots of time together. Rico won't be able to come around every day. You'll see." She hugged me playfully. "You don't have to be jealous. No one could ever take your place."

After several more minutes of guy talk, I excused myself and headed to my own room. Andie had more than flipped; she'd completely lost her ability to reason.

I pulled out my journal and wrote my feelings about this first day at Daddy's.

Monday, July 11: I'm confused. Andie met a guy on the beach today. His name is Rico Hernandez. She thinks he's Mr. Wonderful, but I think her objectivity is totally out of whack.

One minute she says maybe he's her future husband. Why? Just because he's Hispanic. Then she says maybe she's supposed to lead him to Christ—that's why she met him. And last, she thinks maybe this was the reason she got on the plane today. Like meeting Rico is somehow providential.

Whew! She's got her mission mixed up big-time. And short of locking her in her room, I have no idea what to do with her.

Andie's trying to convince me that he won't be hanging around all the time. But the way he looks at her . . . Well, I'll guess we'll find out soon enough.

I closed my journal, feeling dejected. Andie's mom had put her good faith in me. I couldn't let her—or Andie—down.

♥ ♥ ♥

The next day, after Tyler's summer math class, he convinced us to build a giant sand castle with him. Saundra had several errands to run after lunch, so I agreed to baby-sit. Since she was expecting a call from Daddy, I brought the portable phone out on the beach with us.

Tyler, Andie, and I were well into the blueprint planning when Rico showed up. At least he wasn't walking around here half naked, like yesterday. Today, he wore a sleeveless blue T-shirt over his bulging chest muscles and a pair of gray nylon surfer shorts. High on his left shoulder, he balanced two Boogie boards, steadying them with his super-tan hand.

"Cool castle," he said, acknowledging me with a nod of his head. But his gaze quickly found Andie's, and before I knew it, they were headed for the ocean.

"Who's he?" Tyler asked.

"Some guy," I said. "Ever see him around before? His name's Rico Hernandez."

Tyler packed the sand hard with his cupped hands. "I think Sean might know about him."

What was that supposed to mean?

I dropped the subject of Rico but asked Tyler about Sean

Hamilton, the boy I'd met last Christmas when Carrie and I came to visit. "Does Sean still come over and hang out with you sometimes?"

"Sure," Tyler said, standing up and surveying his so-called moat. "He's over here a lot. Dad likes him."

"Really?"

"Yeah, we go to his church sometimes."

Fabulous news!

"You do?" I was dying to know if Saundra ever went along. "What about your mom; does she go, too?"

"Nah, Mom's not into church much. I'm not exactly sure why."

I wished he had said she went at least occasionally, but then, I guess I could understand why Saundra wouldn't want to. Church, after all, was worship, freely giving love and praise to God. Since she didn't believe in a personal God, she would probably find worship rather tedious. I determined in my heart to pray more often for the new Mrs. Meredith.

The castle was nearing completion when Andie and her possible future husband came racing out of the water and onto the beach. He'd taken his shirt off and was chasing her. He looked intent upon *catching* her, too. They ran down the beach and out of sight.

I sighed, frustrated. Andie was making it hard for me to watch over her. Besides, her mom would be very upset if she knew what was going on.

I tried to focus my attention on my young charge, who seemed eager to finish his castle before suppertime. Since I didn't want to abandon Tyler and possibly spoil things between Saundra and me—I wanted to show as much responsibility as I could—I tried to forget about Andie and Rico.

More shouts drifted to my ears. Then there was a long silence, followed by giggling, Andie's giggles!

I raced to the grassy mound a few yards from Tyler's castle, peering into the distance. The heat of the midday sun beat against my shoulders, and I shielded my eyes from the glare.

My father's beachfront property was rather small compared to his sprawling house. I could see Andie and Rico sitting on a boulder overlooking the ocean, and judging by the distance, they were probably trespassing on someone's property.

Just then the phone rang. I hurried back to the beach blanket and grabbed it. Pressing the On button, I said, "Hello, Meredith residence."

"Is this Holly?"

"Yes, it is."

"This is Rosita Martinez. How's everything there?"

Oh, great, she probably wants to talk to Andie.

My heart was pounding. "We're having a great time," I said, trying to remain calm.

"Is Andrea nearby? I'd like to talk with her."

I gulped. There was no way Andie would ever hear me calling this far away. "I'm sorry, Andie can't come to the phone right now," I managed to squeak out.

"Oh, she's tired? Bless her heart."

I didn't want to lie. Mrs. Martinez thought Andie was taking a nap.

"May I have her call you later?" Smart move. This would buy me some time.

"No, no," she insisted. "I'll call her back in about an hour."

"Okay, I'll tell her. Good-bye." I zapped the Off button and flung the phone back on the beach blanket.

Tyler noticed my anger. "What's wrong?"

"Stay here; I'll be right back." I stormed down the beach, avoiding the tide foam as it crept close to my bare toes. "How dare Andie put me in this situation," I whispered, feeling the anger rise in my face.

I could see the cozy twosome half snuggling on the giant boulder. Well, they weren't really touching, but their shoulders seemed somewhat connected. When I reached yelling distance, I held my hands up to my mouth and shouted her name.

Andie turned to look.

Good. I'd gotten her attention. Now I was too stubborn to holler out the message. Instead, I motioned to her with my hand, making large round motions over and over until I was sure she would catch on. But she didn't respond instantly, as I'd hoped. And I was too angry to stand there and wait for her. Turning back, I headed into the salty wind.

Tyler wanted to do an inspection of his castle creation with me. We began our ritual. He stood guard on one side while I recited the names of the towers and gables and things. He'd written everything down for me. Then we traded, and I was the guard and he did the same on the back of the masterpiece.

Minutes had passed since I'd called to Andie. I was beside myself because she hadn't come. No way I was going back down and calling for her again. I refused to cater to her obvious game playing.

I wanted to run inside and check the clock. Andie's mom had said she'd call back in an hour. This was treacherous. I hated being caught in the middle like this.

"You want a snack or something?" I asked Tyler.

"Sure." We headed toward the house.

While Tyler poured lemonade for both of us, I stood out on the deck overlooking the beach to the south. Two specks of humanity sat suspended in space and time on the same large rock as before. What was so important that Andie hadn't responded and come as I'd requested? Was she talking to Rico about God? Was *that* it?

I wished I had some binoculars. Then I remembered Tyler's telescope. He'd set it up on a tripod in one of the guest rooms last Christmas when Carrie and I were here. "Do you still have your telescope?" I asked when I went back inside.

Tyler handed me a glass of lemonade. "Sure, wanna have a look?"

As it turned out, the "spy tube" was set up in Tyler's bedroom, just down the hallway on the main level. He helped me get it focused, and I purposely aimed it toward the ocean so he wouldn't know what I was doing and spill the beans to Andie later.

"I'll be right back," he said, running out of the room. Just the break I needed.

Quickly, I moved the long black tube in the southernmost direction. There they were—Andie and Rico. I focused again, pulling them in closer.

Yikes! Rico was holding Andie's hand. And by the look on his face, their conversation had nothing to do with God. Nothing at all.

I thought about the promise I'd made to Andie last night. How loyal should I be if it meant lying to cover for her?

"Dear Lord," I whispered, still looking through the telescope. "Please help me do the right thing."

Chapter 11

I headed back to the kitchen, remembering to check the clock. Nearly four-thirty! It was an hour later in Dressel Hills. Andie's dad was probably home with the twins, giving her mom a chance to chat in peace. Now, if I could just get Andie to be here when her mother called back.

An idea struck me just then. I waited for Tyler to finish washing his hands, then the two of us went back down to the beach. I knelt on the beach blanket in front of the radio and scanned the tuner, hunting for a Christian station. When I found a contemporary one, I told Tyler to cover his ears. "Let's crank up the music." He nodded, smiling, and I turned up the volume all the way.

Marching down the beach a short distance, I checked to see if Andie had heard. Yep! She was getting up and heading this way. And not surprisingly, Rico was tagging along beside her, holding her hand.

"It worked," I muttered to myself, heading back to turn the music down—just a tad. I wanted the Christian music to be playing when they arrived.

Tyler and I fitted a drawbridge for his castle while I waited for

Andie's return. Without turning to look, I knew they were back by the sound of Andie's laughter.

Rico came over to check out Tyler's creation. "Incredible," he said.

Andie followed close behind. "Wow, Tyler, you're good."

Tyler grinned, obviously proud. "Thanks, but Holly did a lot of it, too."

I wondered how long before Andie would notice the choice of music or if she'd even comment about it. She avoided my eyes as she sat down on the beach blanket, brushing the sand off and smoothing the wrinkles. Rico sat beside her and reached for the radio. "Anybody listening to this?" he asked me.

"Tyler and I are," I said.

"Okay, then. No problem." He set the radio back down on the blanket, the music still going strong. "Sorry."

I don't know why I was surprised that he was polite about it. Sitting on the edge of the blanket, I held up the portable phone. "Your mom called while you were gone," I told Andie.

Her eyes bugged out. "She did?"

"Uh-huh. And she'll be calling back any minute."

Andie glanced at Rico. Her face turned a little pale. "What did you tell her?"

"Nothing. She thought you were napping."

Andie burst out laughing. "You said that?"

"No. It didn't happen like that." I turned away, hoping she'd drop the subject.

Then the phone rang. I held my breath, hoping it was Daddy, which it was.

"Hi, Holly. Having fun?"

"Sure am," I said. "But it would be lots more fun if you were here."

He didn't comment on that. Instead he asked to speak to Saundra.

"She's out running errands. I'm in charge of the house."

"Holding down the fort, eh?" His chuckle disguised the tiredness in his voice, but only for a second. "Well, when Saundra returns, tell her I'll be a little late tonight. She'll know what that means."

I drew in a deep breath. "Everything okay at work?"

"Oh, work's not a problem," he said.

Something else is?

"Tell her not to wait for supper," he continued. I heard the heaviness in his voice. "I'll pick up something on my way home."

"Okay, Daddy," I said, wondering what was so important to keep him late. Again. I was starting to feel like he was an absentee person around here. Just like Andie.

Discouraged, I turned the phone off. Something seemed wrong. I couldn't overlook the obvious sigh in Daddy's voice.

When the phone rang again several minutes later, Andie and Rico were still flirting.

I reached for the phone. "Meredith residence, Holly speaking."

"Hello, Holly, it's Rosita again." Andie's mom!

"Uh, just a minute." I pointed to the phone, motioning for Andie.

She shook her head, waving her hands as though to say she wasn't there and had no intention of talking.

I frowned, covering the mouthpiece. "It's your mom."

She stood up and said, "I just talked to her last night," and walked away.

Andie was taking this way too far. I wanted to shout at her, make it obvious to her mom that Andie was right here—let Mrs. Martinez know she was pulling her spoiled brat routine. But I didn't dare. After all, I'd been the one who'd begged to have Andie come along.

Giving up, I uncovered the mouthpiece. "Uh, hello?"

"Yes?"

"I'm sorry, Mrs. Martinez, Andie still can't come to the phone." I swallowed hard, wishing Andie would get over here and take her call. It was her mother on the line, for pete's sake.

"She isn't ill, is she?"

Depending how you looked at it, sick was definitely a possibility. I watched Andie run into the ocean with Rico and the Boogie boards.

"Holly, are you there?" Mrs. Martinez sounded concerned.

"Uh . . . yes, I'm sorry."

"Did Andrea get airsick on the plane?"

"Oh no, she didn't have any trouble flying," I said, grasping at straws. "But . . . she hasn't been herself lately."

"Well, I hope Andrea's getting plenty of rest and watching the junk food." She paused. "You girls aren't staying up all hours, are you?"

I laughed. "My stepmom would never allow that."

"That's good." She seemed satisfied to hear that. "Well, I want Andrea to call me when she feels better. Have her use her phone card."

"Okay. Good-bye." It was all I could do to control my actions this time as I turned the phone off.

Andie saw that it was safe to come back, but I was too furious to look at her. I called to Tyler, "Come on, kiddo. Let's get cleaned up for supper."

Between the two of us, Tyler and I gathered up the beach blanket, his castle-making equipment and radio, and the phone. Without a glance back, we headed to the house, leaving Andie with her precious Rico.

💜 💜 💜

I was in the shower when Tyler started pounding on the bathroom door. "Holly! Someone's on the phone for you."

I turned the water off for a second. "Who is it?"

"Sean Hamilton," he said. "Should I tell him to call you back later?"

"That'll be fine. Thanks." I finished soaping up, then rinsed off, wondering about Sean. If he wanted to see me, I'd have to make it perfectly clear that I wasn't interested in anything but friendship.

After dressing, I towel-dried my hair and fluffed it with my fingers. I stood in front of the mirror, holding the long strands out. Andie was forever teasing me about getting my hair cut, but the way I figured, if I ever *did* decide to cut it, and then if I hated it, I'd be stuck with it for a very long time. Whew, I couldn't begin to imagine how many years it would take to grow my hair this long again.

Still, the washing and drying thing was a pain sometimes. Especially in humid weather like this. In order to hurry up the drying process so I could braid it before supper, I pushed the sliding glass door open and stepped out onto my private balcony overlooking the ocean.

That's when I spotted Andie with Rico, standing side by side in the shallow ocean tide, facing into the sun. He had his arm draped around her shoulder, and she leaned her head against his arm. If I hadn't been so upset with her, I might've thought they looked sweet together out there.

But anger welled up inside me, and I clenched my teeth. Nope, I wouldn't even begin to acknowledge her tender moment. I turned on my heels and flew into the house.

♥ ♥ ♥

Sean did call back later. The phone rang as Andie and I helped Saundra clean up the kitchen. Tyler got the phone, and a big smile stretched across his face when he announced that it was Sean.

I excused myself. "Hey," I said.

"Welcome to Southern California" came the deep voice.

"Thanks, it's nice to be here."

"How long this time?"

"Two weeks," I replied. "Long enough to get a decent tan. Maybe."

"Tans are way overrated," he teased.

I chuckled. "Don't I know."

"Well, I was wondering if I could see you sometime while you're here." He paused for a moment, sounding a little unsure of himself. "Maybe we could take that walk on the beach after all."

I wanted to set some ground rules right away, but when you're standing in the kitchen with several pairs of ears listening in, it's not so easy.

"That'd be fun," I said, thinking that I would explain my decision about guys when we walked together.

"How does tomorrow after lunch sound?" Sean asked, sounding more confident.

"That'll work." I bit my lip, hoping I was doing the right thing.

"Okay, I'll see you then." And he hung up.

Walking in broad daylight on the beach with Sean Hamilton couldn't be classified as a real date. Besides, I knew my mother would approve of him because of his Christian faith. She'd even met Sean last April when he and Daddy came to Dressel Hills to ski. She had wanted to be introduced to him formally right there at the ski lodge. At the time it seemed sort of awkward, but now it made good sense. Caring parents were like that—wanting only the best for their kids.

So why was *Andie* fighting against her parents' wishes?

Chapter 12

I went outside and sat on the deck, waiting for Daddy to show up while Saundra was in the living room entertaining a neighbor lady. Tyler had run back to the beach to check on his sand castle.

I was beginning to wonder where Andie was, when she showed up in a T-shirt and long, white skirt, ready for a relaxing evening.

"Look, Holly, I know you're mad, but could you at least tell me what my mom called about?" Andie stood there, hands on hips, waiting for my answer.

I set my soda down deliberately on the table next to me. "Well, it's about time. I thought you'd never ask."

"So?"

"Your mom wants you to call her back." There. Now let's see what Andie did with that tidbit of information.

"Did you tell her about Rico?" she asked almost sheepishly.

"Of course I didn't." I leaped off the chaise. "Does this look like the face of a friend you can't trust? Does it?"

Her eyes suddenly seemed sad. "What *did* you say to my mom?"

"That you're breaking every one of her rules. That you're going crazy out here; you're totally out of control. And if you don't get your act together, I'm shipping you home on the very next plane." I studied her as I eased myself back down into the lounge chair. "Is that what you wanted me to say?"

Andie sat down. "Is that how you feel? That you want me to go home?"

I inhaled and held my breath for a moment. "Well, I think it might be a good idea, especially if you're going to lose your head over a guy who can't get a date with girls his own age."

"Holly!"

"C'mon, Andie, face it. You're only fourteen. What could he possibly want with a girl your age?"

"You don't even know Rico." She folded her arms. "Listen, I don't want to hurt your feelings. Is that what this is about? Are you mad because we're not doing very much together?"

Sure, that was part of it, but I was tired of taking the rap for the rift between us. Jealousy was becoming less and less of an issue. I'd seen the lusty look in Rico's eyes. "Don't you remember the lunch we had at the Soda Straw, all of us together? What was the point of telling your mom you were going to follow her rules when the minute you get out of her sight, you go nuts?"

"Okay," she agreed. "I need a break. What am I doing that's so bad? I mean, we've all been together . . . most of the time. And nobody's going out on dates or anything, not really." Her face was red and angry. She was fighting too hard for Rico.

I looked away, letting my eyes roam over the beach to the boulder where she had sat with Rico. "You're in way over your head, Andie," I said without looking at her. "If you have any sense, you'll cool it."

"You're getting preachy."

I sighed. "I'm sure you've heard this stuff many times from your mom, at church, from our youth pastor."

She looked at me like I was from some other planet. "Holly, save your voice," she said. "We're not doing anything wrong."

"Maybe not yet, but things lead to, you know, other things."

I was having a hard time getting this out. "You can't fool around physically without getting hurt . . . eventually."

"I can't believe you're saying this," she said, standing up. "Everything's under control with Rico, if that's what you mean." She walked to the sliding door. "I have to make a phone call." Picking up her long skirt, she stepped inside and slid the glass door shut.

Reaching for my soda, I thought of the stress I'd endured back home with Carrie and Stephie constantly in my face—how I couldn't wait to get away from them. Away from their snooping. Away from Stan and his constant stupidity.

Peace and quiet—what a joke. So far, the past two days had been nothing short of total chaos. How ignorant of me to think I was finally going to have a real vacation.

♥ ♥ ♥

The word *stress* hung in my mind as I tiptoed inside and hurried downstairs to my room. I found my journal and began to pour some of the tension onto the lines of the notebook paper.

Tuesday, July 12: I think Andie and her friend Rico are not only freaking me out, they're turning me into a watchdog. Tonight when I talked to Andie about her spending time with him, I honestly sounded like somebody's mother! I hate this role, yet I agreed to take it. In a way, it's Andie's mom's fault for asking me to "watch over" her daughter. I'm turning into someone I don't like.

If Andie would take more responsibility for herself, I could relax. Relax. Hmm, that's something I think my dad oughta do, too. He sounded so exhausted when he called from the office this afternoon. Here it is already 8:30, and he's still not home.

I'm beginning to worry. And I don't think I'm the only one. Saundra isn't herself. I can see it in her eyes. She's worried, too.

After I finished writing, I knelt down and began to pray for Saundra. And for Daddy. Then I felt compelled to pray for Saundra's salvation. "Make her want to know you," I told the Lord. "And let me be more open to her during this visit. In Jesus' name, amen."

I was surprised how quickly the time had passed. It was nearly dark outside when I stood up. I reached for the green lamp on the table next to the bed. Turning it on, I sat there on the floor in the stillness of my empty room, reveling in God's peace.

The quiet moments spent there were the calm before the hurricane. When I went back upstairs, I didn't really mean to eavesdrop, but as I was turning into the kitchen, I heard Saundra talking to her neighbor lady. It sounded as if they were standing at the door, saying good-bye to each other. "Do take care of that husband of yours," her friend said.

"Doing my best," Saundra answered. "But he's not slowing down enough, I'm sorry to say." I heard her sniffle. "I'll know more when Robert gets home later."

I strained to hear. Saundra was saying that Daddy had to stop and get some lab results. I held my breath, afraid to breathe. So *that's* why he'd called this afternoon.

I didn't like the sound of this. When Saundra came into the kitchen, I stuck my head in the fridge, pretending to look for something to eat.

"Hungry already?" she asked.

Slowly, I withdrew from the refrigerator. "Not really," I whispered.

"What is it, dear?" She put her hand under my chin and lifted my face to meet her gaze. "What's wrong?"

"I heard what you were saying just now," I muttered, tears coming fast. "What's wrong with Daddy?"

"Oh that." She waved her hand as though there was nothing in the world to worry about. "Your father's a workaholic, that's all. His doctor wants him to slow down, but—" she sighed—"you know how your father is."

"So he's not sick, then?"

She pondered the thought. "I think he's a little stressed, that's all."

I honestly didn't believe her. The answers she'd given sounded like white lies to me. Which made me even more concerned. What was she hiding?

♥ ♥ ♥

The next day was Wednesday. Daddy stayed home from work, which was fabulous. He lounged around in his silk pajamas and robe most of the morning. Maybe he and I would have a chance to talk. Maybe not an intimate heart-to-heart talk, but a good, solid one would do.

We sat outside on the deck, where Saundra served Andie, Tyler, and me a breakfast of bacon and eggs. Dad got granola and an orange without his usual coffee. My stepmom played the energetic hostess, rushing in and out of the house, bringing more platters of jelly toast and bacon.

Tyler seemed to enjoy himself, chattering on and on about the sand creations he was planning to make.

"What are *your* plans today?" Daddy asked me, including both Andie and me in his gaze.

"Sean and I are going for a walk after lunch."

Andie jumped on that statement. "Sean Hamilton's coming over? You mean I finally get to meet him?" She was too eager. Or maybe she didn't really care at all about meeting Sean. In her mind, maybe my having a guy around would get her off the hook with me about Rico.

Before I could answer her, Daddy spoke up. "That Sean . . . he's really terrific." He smiled, leaning back in the sun, like he was remembering a fond moment. "I can't think of a nicer fellow for my daughter to be seeing."

"Daddy!" I blushed. "I'm not *seeing* anyone. I'm too young to date, remember?"

"Oh, sure," he said. "But if you ever decide to do such a thing, well, Sean's my first choice."

Andie's eyes danced with glee. She was obviously delighted that the subject of boys had come up.

Then I did something I'd probably live to regret. I asked Daddy about Rico Hernandez. "Do you know him?"

Andie's eyes shot warning signals.

"Rico, you say?" He shielded his eyes from the sun. "Now, there's an interesting kid." He didn't say Rico was a *good* kid.

Andie must have read more into his statement, though, because she sat up straight in her chair, sporting a huge grin.

"So you *do* know Rico?" I asked.

"I certainly do," Daddy responded, holding his glass up for more ice water. Saundra hopped to it and got him some fresh water. "Rico lives up the beach. I've known his family for a number of years; in fact, his dad's a brilliant doctor—one of mine."

Andie's eyes did a complete flip.

"What kind of doctor?" I asked, but Saundra didn't give Daddy time to answer. Instantly, she changed the subject.

Exactly what was she hiding?

Chapter 13

My walk with Sean that afternoon took us several miles down the beach. Tropical palm trees dotted the bluffs jutting high above the coastline, making the setting seem all the more exotic.

"I was going to send you an email before you came," he said cautiously, "but the timing didn't seem quite right." His light blond hair rippled in the breeze. "I've been thinking about you, Holly."

I swallowed. This wasn't supposed to happen. "Look, Sean," I said, realizing now was as good a time as any to lay down my ground rules, "I wanted to tell you on the phone about something, but it was—" I paused—"shall we say, inconvenient at the time."

Sean looked puzzled.

I continued. "Last month, after church camp, I came to the conclusion that I'm not happy with the way things have been going for me with boys. I mean, I don't have a problem with being friends or anything."

Sean nodded enthusiastically, like he could see my point one hundred percent.

"I won't be fifteen for another seven months, but it's not really the age thing so much as the pressure most boy-girl relationships involve. Know what I mean?"

He said he did.

"So, for that reason, I'm going to level with you. I don't want to hurt your feelings, but I'm not interested in dating while I'm here. Besides, my mom wouldn't approve anyway."

"That's cool. I respect that."

We found seashells at the high-tide line, packed close together in the sand, as we walked leisurely toward Daddy's house. Sean was nice enough to fill his pants pockets with my beach souvenirs. He told me about the secondhand car his folks were helping him buy and his summer job at a Christian radio station.

"Sounds like fun," I said. "Do you want to become a disc jockey after high school?"

"Nah, it's just one of my hobbies." He ran his fingers through his short, thick hair. "I'm actually thinking about going to med school."

This was news to me. "What kind of medicine?"

He turned to look at me, smiling. "For as long as I can remember, I've been interested in hearts." His smile broadened. "I'm not talking Holly-Heart here, so relax, okay? But ever since sixth grade, when Dr. Hernandez came to school for Professional Day, I've thought about being a cardiologist."

Dr. Hernandez . . . a heart doctor?

"Rico's dad's a cardiologist?" I blurted.

He nodded. "So . . . you've met Rico?"

"Well, actually, he's Andie's friend," I said quickly.

"Rico's a little old for her, don't you think?"

I could hardly make sense of things—my brain was clouded with the fact that Daddy's heart needed help. That's why Saundra had been covering for him. She didn't want to worry me. Daddy's heart . . . what could be wrong?

I wasn't doing very well carrying my end of the conversation. "I'm sorry, what?"

Sean repeated himself. "Rico's been out of high school for a year. He ought to be dating girls his age."

"No kidding!"

"Does Andie know he's not a Christian?" he asked.

"Well, she says she wants to witness to him," I explained, letting Sean know in no uncertain terms that I was opposed to their friendship. "It's kinda touchy, though, because Andie had problems with a couple of guys back home. They, well . . . *one* of them made fun of her for being Hispanic, and because of that I think she's more vulnerable to Rico right now."

Sean nodded. "Prejudice is widespread around here, too. It's everywhere, really." He seemed to understand my concern for Andie, and I felt instantly better for having confided in him.

♥ ♥ ♥

Daddy seemed more relaxed when I arrived home. He was sitting in his study, reading a poem to Andie. She sat across from him in a comfortably cool leather chair. Rich, gleaming cherrywood bookshelves shone against the sunlight streaming in from the skylight above.

I tiptoed in, standing silently as he read. When the poem was finished, Andie applauded. "You never told me your father writes poetry," she said, observing me.

"He does?" I came around, leaning over his chair. "You do?"

He held up the printed pages. The title, "A Year to Celebrate," made my heart glad. It must have been inspired by his newfound joy. Daddy had become a Christian last April.

"You wrote this?" I walked slowly around his chair, scanning the lines on the page. It was free verse, beautifully flowing with a loose rhyming pattern.

"Well, what do you think?" His eyes searched mine.

"It's fabulous!"

Andie agreed. "You get your writing talent from your dad, Holly."

Daddy's eyes shone. He reached for a pencil and began scribbling on the back of his paper.

I walked around his large study, stopping to inspect the goldframed family pictures on his enormous desk. Baby pictures. One of me wearing a red Valentine dress with white lace edging, one of Carrie cuddling a white bunny with pink ears.

Andie wandered over, looking at the pictures. "Aw, how sweet. Holly, you were such a doll."

"Look how light my hair was then," I said. It looked the color of real butter—almost white.

"And it was so short and wispy," she said. We looked at Carrie's picture together. The resemblance between us was uncanny, even as babies. "You could pass as identical twins," Andie said.

"Yeah, born four years apart."

Saundra poked her head in the door. "Anybody ready for tea?"

Andie looked at me, surprised. "Tea?"

Daddy chuckled. "Yes, we have afternoon tea around here every so often. Saundra's quite a hostess." He smiled proudly, and Saundra came over and laid a big smacker right on his lips.

I chose peppermint tea with honey, because that's probably what Mom was drinking back home right about now. I honestly missed her and wished I could confide in her about Andie's shenanigans. Unfortunately I'd promised to keep my friend's private life a secret.

After we pigged out on finger pastries and a variety of other sweet cakes, I thanked Saundra and asked Daddy if we could talk alone.

"Not now," Saundra said, standing up suddenly as though she'd forgotten something important.

"Time for my pills," Daddy said, apologizing for her. "We'll talk later, okay?"

I went over and kissed his cheek. "I'll be waiting."

Daddy smiled faintly, leaning his head back against the padded leather. "I don't think I can stand having two doting women in the same house."

I blew a kiss, wishing Saundra hadn't cut me off like that. Something must have shown up on those lab tests for Daddy to be staying home all day. Worried, I headed down the stairs with Andie trailing behind.

"Your mom called while you were out with Sean," Andie said, following me into my room.

"She did? When?"

"Right after you left."

"Why didn't Daddy say something?" I asked.

"Because he was asleep and Saundra was next door."

"So *you* answered the phone?" I couldn't believe this. Andie was certainly making herself at home here.

"Well, I kinda thought it might be Rico," she admitted softly. "That's why."

"What would *he* want?"

"Oh, nothing much," she said, but I wondered if they weren't making plans for later.

"Well, what did Mom say?"

Andie grinned. "She wanted to talk to you, what else?"

"What did you say?"

"That you were out with some boy, sneaking off with him into the night."

"You did not."

"Bet me." Her face looked serious, and she wasn't twisting her hair like she usually did at a time like this. Was she fibbing me? Or . . . was she trying to get back at me for my reaction to Rico?

"Your mom said you'd have to come home immediately." Andie's face was severely serious now.

"Andie, come on!" I wailed.

Her face broke into a spiteful grin. "How's it feel?"

I lashed out. "That's not fair. You lied."

"And you didn't?" She looked absolutely haughty. "Well, now we're even."

Even or not, I didn't like it one bit. I flew out of the room and upstairs to call my mom.

Chapter 14

The next morning, bright and early, I slipped out of bed and found my journal.

Thursday, July 14: Andie and I aren't getting along so well. I wish she'd drop Rico flat, but even after we talked late last night, she seemed more determined than ever to ignore me and do things her way. Shoot, she's not just being stubborn, she's outright defiant! Andie's acting really different here. I can't remember her being so rebellious back home.

    That bizarre comment she said she made to my mom about me sneaking off into the night with Sean . . . Where did that come from? If I didn't know and trust Andie the way I do, I'd think she was planning something like that herself.

    Whew—Mom sounded depressed when I called last night. She said Stan was giving Uncle Jack fits over his new curfew—guess he's been staying out too late, breaking house rules. I told her I thought Ryan Davis was a bad influence on him. She agrees.

    Mom thinks my coming out here might be just the thing

my little sister needed to make her appreciate me more. She said Carrie actually misses me. Stephie too.

Well . . . Daddy and I didn't get to have our talk, at least not yesterday. It seems like every time there's the slightest window of opportunity, Saundra shows up and slams it shut. I don't know what her problem is, but she's starting to drive me crazy. I have a right to know what's wrong with my father. And if she's going to keep being so secretive, well, I guess I'll just have to confront her.

I showered, dressed, and wandered onto my balcony. In the distance I could see a tall blond jogger on the beach with a black dog. I was sure it was Sean Hamilton and his Labrador, Sunshine.

I thought about our talk yesterday. Sean's face had shown his approval for what I'd said . . . and his words seemed to agree. But I had a funny feeling he was going along with my decision to appease me. Sometimes it was hard to read Sean. I wished I had a better handle on things—on how he really felt.

Tyler was more hyper than usual at breakfast. We ate at the breakfast nook, and Andie came dragging in late. She looked exhausted, like she hadn't slept all night. I played with the tan linen napkin under my fork. Still observing Andie, I listened half-heartedly as Tyler chattered about tomorrow's trip to Universal Studios in Hollywood.

"I can't wait to ride through the earthquake on the back lot," he said as Saundra finally came around and sat at the head of the table. "Power cables snapping and sparking with electricity, train wrecks, lethal fumes, and a sixty-thousand-gallon tidal wave coming right at us!"

"Cool," Andie said sleepily, her curls drooping as she tugged on her bathrobe.

I wondered why Saundra was sitting in Daddy's place. "Did Daddy go to work today?" I asked, watching for signs of him.

Saundra began passing a platter of pancakes around. "Since

your father is taking off tomorrow, he had to go in to the office early today." She volunteered nothing else. Zero info . . . zilch!

I breathed deeply, surveying the situation. Her eyes refused to meet mine. But I watched her anyway. I *had* to know. "Is he okay?"

Saundra nodded, still avoiding my persistent gaze. Then Tyler launched into his excited chatter about Animal Planet Live and the Rugrats Magic Adventure, along with everything else we were going to see and do tomorrow, and Saundra actually seemed relieved.

So . . . was that how she wanted to play this game? Just ignore me? Say whatever she pleased to get me off her back?

I was freaked out, and even more so when it came time to eat and no one said grace. "Excuse me?" I eyed Tyler. "Didn't we forget something?"

"Oh, sorry." He passed the pancake syrup to me.

"That's *not* what I meant."

Andie came to my rescue. "Somebody pray," she muttered, leaning her mop of curls into her hands.

"I will." And I did.

When I was finished, I noticed that Saundra had bowed her head right along with the rest of us. A first.

I spread butter and syrup on my warm pancakes and began to chow down.

After breakfast, Andie went back to bed. She said she hadn't slept well last night. I really wasn't interested in her sleep patterns, so I headed to my room to straighten things up and have my devotions.

Later, I went upstairs to see if I could help Saundra with anything. "That's very thoughtful of you, dear," she said, "but the cleaning lady will be coming tomorrow morning. The best thing for you to do is to have your room picked up a bit before she comes."

"It's nice and neat," I said, dying to broach the subject of Daddy's health. But she looked rather busy as she sat at her desk in the kitchen alcove, scanning her daily planner.

Glancing up, she said, "Since Tyler's going to be busy at summer school, how would you and Andie like to go to lunch with me?"

"Okay."

"We could go to Marcie's first and have our nails done. Would you like that?"

"Marcie's?"

"Oh, you'll adore the place," she said, all bubbly. "Marcie's is the most exclusive beauty salon in Beverly Hills. We'll get all dressed up and go, okay, dear?"

"Sure," I said, but getting all prissy wasn't my thing. Having a manicure was okay, but fake nails? Ick!

In a flash, Saundra picked up the phone and made lunch reservations at some exotic place in Beverly Hills.

I hurried downstairs to inform Andie.

Tiptoeing into her room, I whispered, "Andie."

She was sound asleep.

"Hey, wake up, we're going somewhere really fabulous for lunch."

No response. She was out cold.

I shrugged and turned to go back upstairs. Saundra was talking on the phone when I showed up in the kitchen again. I waited till she was finished, then explained that Andie hadn't slept much last night. "Maybe we should wait awhile and let her rest."

Saundra's eyebrows shot up. "How long do you think she should sleep?"

I glanced at the clock on the wall. "It's already nine-thirty. When's our nail appointment?"

"Eleven on the dot." Saundra went back to her daily planner. I noticed several mini-lists inside. She and I had *something* in common. Maybe it was a starting place.

"I make lists, too," I began, a little cautious at first. "I have a whole notebook full of them."

"That's nice, dear," she said, not really paying attention.

I took a deep breath now. "One of my favorite lists is my prayer list."

She looked up quickly.

"It helps me keep track of the people I'm praying for."

"You certainly sound organized." Her comment was a bit patronizing.

"Well, it sure helps . . . especially when the Lord answers my prayers. Then I check off my list with the date of the answer."

Saundra had a quizzical expression on her face. "Your father started doing something similar to that recently."

"Daddy? Really?"

"Yes, he's quite taken with the Bible and church and such things."

"That's really great, don't you think?"

"Well, I try to steer clear of his current obsession," she said, making it sound like Daddy's interest in spiritual things was merely a passing fancy.

"You'd be surprised how the Lord can help you, especially when things go bad. Like Daddy's health, for instance."

She frowned. "What makes you think your father's health is bad?"

"Well, if Rico's father is a cardiologist, and he's one of Daddy's doctors—"

"Well," she snapped, "your father has seen Dr. Hernandez only one time. So I don't think you can jump to any conclusions."

"That's just it," I said softly. "I don't want to jump to conclusions. I want the straight truth."

She tapped her nails on the desk, studying me. For a split second I wondered why she needed to have her nails redone. They were perfect. "Holly," she began, looking at me with sincere eyes. The tension between us felt white-hot. "Do you think I've been lying to you about your father?"

I sighed. "Well, I hope you're not trying to keep me in the dark. Maybe you're just protecting me, not really lying to me." Whew, I'd said it. Now it was her turn. Would she keep fibbing or was the truth about to emerge at last?

"You're a perceptive young lady," she said, throwing me for a loop. I honestly thought she'd continue her charade. "What would you like to know?"

Bracing myself against the possibility of bad news, I said, "I want to know what's wrong with Daddy."

"Let me see if I can explain this to you." She crossed her legs, smoothing her voile skirt. "Your father's heart, along with suffering severe stress from a minor heart attack about a year and a half ago—"

I interrupted her. "That long ago? Why didn't anyone tell me?"

She looked at the ceiling, like she was trying to get a grasp of things. "It was around the time of his sister's cancer diagnosis."

"Aunt Marla? She found out about her cancer in January—a year and a half ago."

"Yes, that's when your father had some trouble." She shook her head. "He started slowing down a bit. Remember when we drove over to that pretty little chapel to hear you sing with your youth choir?"

I nodded. "So, was Daddy's heart damaged back then? He seemed just fine to me."

"The heart attack was so slight, but it was enough to make him want to improve his diet and include more daily exercise. But as time went on, he got caught up in his hectic routine again."

"Does he follow a strict diet now?"

She ran her fingers through the length of her hair. "I'm doing my best to keep him on a low-fat diet. But he gets very little exercise, which isn't good, and he's so driven it's hard to get him to take time off. That's one of the reasons I was thrilled you were coming."

"Does he really have to work such long hours?" I asked.

She shook her head. "He's entirely his own boss, but that doesn't change his tendency to overwork."

"Can't you make him slow down?"

She smiled wistfully. "That would be nice."

"Well, maybe if I talk to—"

"No," she interrupted. "I don't want you to say anything about this to your father. He doesn't need the additional stress. And maybe if he thought you knew, he might be concerned that you'd be worried." She smiled a sweet, comforting smile. "You know how that goes."

It was obvious she knew Daddy well. But I wondered how his recent conversion to Christianity had affected their relationship. From listening to her, I could see there wasn't any change for the worse. That was good, because it sounded like Daddy needed someone very supportive now.

My next question was about his lab results. But I wasn't able to ask because the phone rang. Saundra caught it on the second ring.

"Meredith residence." A short pause. Then, "Yes, Andie's here, but she's resting." Saundra turned to me, covering the mouthpiece. "It's Rico Hernandez; he asked to speak to you."

"Me?"

What did Andie's guy friend want with me?

Chapter 15

"Hello?"

"Yeah, Holly, this is Rico. I thought you and Andie might wanna know about my beach party tomorrow night."

"Oh? What's the occasion?"

"Just some people getting together for a good time."

"What people?" I sounded like an interrogator, but I didn't care. I wanted to make things tough for him.

"Some of my college friends will be hangin' out. You know, just a bunch of kids."

Yeah, right. Sounds like a party I can't wait to miss!

"Andie and I have other plans," I said quickly. "Sorry. Bye." I was getting ready to hang up.

"Uh, wait, Holly. Is Andie doing okay?"

"Why wouldn't she be?"

"Well, uh, oh, nothing. Just tell her I said hi, and I'll see you two later."

See us later? Hadn't he listened? And why was he asking about Andie as though she were sick or something?

I dashed downstairs. "Andie, wake up!" She moaned and

groaned when I shook her awake. "C'mon, sleeping beauty. My stepmom's got some great plans for us."

"I'm sleeping," she said, her throat raspy.

"You'd better shake a leg if you wanna go with us to Marcie's." I told her it was some expensive salon in Beverly Hills.

She carried on like she was too tired. "Do I have to go?"

"You'll be fine once you wake up," I assured her, now playfully pulling on the covers.

"Holly, I'm tired," she snapped at me. "Leave me alone."

I stood back, surveying the rumpled pile of covers billowing around her. "Are you kidding, you actually want to miss this?"

"I'm telling you to just go without me. I'll stay home and sleep. Have fun with your wicked stepmother." With that, she rolled over.

"Okay, have it your way." I left the room, purposely keeping the beach party invitation a secret. Closing the door behind me, I wondered how fast Andie would have snapped to it if I had mentioned Rico's party.

❤ ❤ ❤

Saundra and I did the town, all right. I managed to get by with just getting my cuticles soaked, pushed back, and trimmed. After my nails were filed and shaped properly, I chose a pale pink polish that matched my shirt.

Several hair stylists went a little over the edge about my hair—especially the color and the length. No matter where I went, my hair seemed to attract people.

Afterward, Saundra and I headed for lunch in another posh area of Beverly Hills. During the drive there, and later after ordering our entree, I unsuccessfully tried several times to return to our former conversation about Daddy. I was still curious about the lab results, but Saundra was talkative about other things. Mostly the travel plans she was secretly making for their wedding anniversary in August.

"I tell you, Holly, your father is going to be so surprised." She looked happier than I'd ever seen her. "He's been talking off and on about Tahiti for years. What a wonderfully beautiful place for him to rest."

"When will you tell him?"

Her face glowed with anticipation. "I must plan a very special way to present the tickets to him." She gushed about the luxurious anniversary gifts he'd presented to her other years. Everything from cashmere sweaters to diamond bracelets. You would have thought, listening to her talk, that material things ranked highest on her list of important things in life. I wondered where simple words or deeds of kindness and affection came in.

By the time the dessert tray came around, I had decided I never wanted to be rich, and I was anxious to leave. The black-coated waiter held the gleaming silver tray with a variety of delicacies for us to choose from. His accent was French or Italian—I wasn't sure which. For Saundra, it was chocolate mousse, slightly chilled; for me, the most familiar dessert I could find: strawberry cheesecake.

We arrived home long before Tyler, and I rushed downstairs to Andie's room, expecting to find her up and reading in bed. The big surprise was that her bed was made and her room picked up.

"Andie," I called, even searching outside on her private balcony. "We're back!"

I checked her bathroom and found that she'd taken a shower. A pile of dirty clothes was left lying on the floor in the corner near the sink. Her makeup bag was unzipped, with mascara and blush shoved into it sloppily.

And then I spotted a clue to her whereabouts. Above the sink, on the flat piece of glass running across and below the mirror, I noticed a business card with the words *BEACH BUZZ, The Band*. Under the words were Rico's name and phone number.

"Oh, so she stayed home to see Rico," I muttered angrily, remembering the tired, worn-out-and-desperate-to-sleep charade she'd put on for me earlier. Talk about lies. Andie was the master of deceit!

Not sure what to do, I ran upstairs to the deck and scanned the beach area. She was nowhere in sight.

I headed to Tyler's room and focused his telescope, aiming north toward Rico's parents' estate. No sign of Andie.

Then I looked toward the ocean, turning the black knob, bringing a rectangular white speck into view.

Bingo! There she was. Way, way out—past the breakers—and floating on an air mattress built for two with her cohort. Quickly, I cranked the view in even closer. I could almost reach out and touch them, which is exactly what Rico was doing to Andie. Touching her hair, her face. Why was she letting him get so close?

Not only had Andie decided the first day we'd come here that Rico was husband material, but here she was acting like they were married already! Well . . . not exactly married like on a honeymoon or anything, but getting terribly close. I almost felt guilty watching the two of them carry on this way. I held my breath, scared he was going to kiss her.

Tyler came bursting into the room. "Having fun?" He came over to me. "Who're you spying on today?"

I backed up, moving away from the telescope. "I, uh, hope you don't mind."

"Go for it."

"You sure?" I inched forward, almost afraid to look again.

"Go ahead and watch them," he said, grinning. "They don't know it, but last night I caught them outside together."

Andie was with Rico in the middle of the night?

Tyler kept talking. "Man, would my mom have a cow if I did that!"

"Of course she would," I said, trying not to overreact to the shocking news. "You have no business sneaking out of the house with a girl."

"I didn't mean *that*," he said. "I meant leaving the house in the middle of the night. You never know what's lurking around out there on the beach." He sounded for real, but I didn't know what he was talking about.

"Are there prowlers or something?"

"Drug dealers, prowlers, you name it—we've got it going on up and down the beach. And the parties. Sometimes I have to put earplugs in my ears."

Now my heart was pounding out of control. Was Rico's party going to be one of those wild ones? And if so, was Rico involved with drugs or alcohol?

I got brave right then. I asked Tyler if he'd ever seen Rico drinking. "Oh sure. Some of his college friends come up from San Diego almost every weekend. They have some rock band; I forget what it's called. All I know is there're tons of beer bottles scattered around the next morning."

I shuddered to think about Andie and her dreams of Rico becoming her future husband. If she only knew!

Chapter 16

I shouldn't have been surprised.

Andie refused to believe me when I told her what I knew about Rico, his band, and his wild parties. I cornered her as she came into her room to shower and dress for supper.

"Holly, get a life!" she yelled. "I wouldn't think of butting into your time with Sean."

"Nothing's happening between Sean and me."

"Right." She threw her wet towel at me. "I'm sick of your holy-schmoly routine, Holly Meredith."

"You didn't have to lie to me today," I accused her.

"I didn't lie, just changed my mind."

"What? About sleeping in? Come on! You pretended to be tired so you could stay home."

She shook her head defiantly. "That's not how it happened, but it's really none of your business, anyway."

"Okay, fine," I said, throwing her towel down on the carpet. "But the next time your mother calls, I'm telling her the truth."

"See if I care!" She slammed her bathroom door, punctuating her words.

Jittery and upset, I went to the sitting room. Things were so far out of control. Andie couldn't even begin to see the truth about Rico. And worse, there seemed to be no way to get through to her. What could I do to make her see who Rico really was *before* she did something she might regret forever?

♥ ♥ ♥

At supper, Daddy announced that everything was set for our trip to Universal Studios.

"Cool," Tyler shouted.

"Tyler, please," Saundra reprimanded him. "We're having supper."

"Sorry," he said, but I could see his enthusiasm was oozing right out of his pores.

"What about the rest of you?" Daddy asked.

"Fine with me," Saundra said. I agreed, too.

Andie, however, looked a little nervous. "How long will we be gone?" she asked.

"Why? Got a date?" Tyler piped up.

Andie shrugged. "Just wondered."

"I thought we could have dinner somewhere special and then drive up the coast and see the sunset." Daddy pursed his lips, waiting for her response.

"Sure, sounds fine," Andie said eventually, even though I was sure Rico had told her about his beach party.

As it turned out, Andie refused to discuss anything about Rico later that night. We'd reached a standstill, Andie and I, and to push things with her would only bring more hostility between us. So I made the decision to back off, let her do her thing, and pray for her. Mom had always said that prayer was more powerful than anything you could ever do or say.

So I prayed before going to bed, and later while trying to fall asleep—every single time I thought about Andie or began to worry over the situation.

One thing for sure, the trip to Universal Studios would keep her from Rico most of the day. That was something to be thankful for.

♥ ♥ ♥

Andie chose to hang out with Tyler on both Jurassic Park, The Ride and the E.T. Adventure. It had to be obvious to the rest of the family that Andie and I weren't speaking. I hoped it wasn't spoiling things for them, and I tried to keep a positive, upbeat attitude.

Later, Saundra freaked out over the two-thousand-pound eating machine otherwise known as Jaws. When we least expected it, it leaped out of the water just inches away from her side of the tour bus.

"Oh," she squealed. What really got her, of course, was the water it sprayed at her while thrashing around in a frenzy to "devour" her. Then it was on to the earthquake, where we experienced an 8.3 heart-pounding tremor.

Out of the entire day, Daddy seemed to enjoy the WaterWorld show most—probably because his heart prevented him from being able to go on some of the rides. And I noticed him laughing at the tribute to *I Love Lucy.*

Of course, we scurried here and there, standing in long lines and snacking on junk food and pop while we moved from one attraction to another. One time, when Daddy and I were alone getting caramel corn, I almost told him about Andie's crush on Rico. Then, just as I was about to open my mouth and confide in him, I decided not to. I didn't want to worry him about it—and maybe cause more stress on his heart.

While waiting in line for sodas, Saundra spotted a girl with waist-length hair the color of mine. Her hair hung in gentle, vertical waves down her back. "Holly, look," she said. "Your hair would look wonderful that way."

"You think so?"

"Definitely," Andie said, the first she'd spoken to me all day.

"Really?" Now I was excited.

"If you think your mother wouldn't mind, we could have it permed while you're here," Saundra suggested.

"Daddy, what do you think?" I asked.

He cocked his head, looking at me with his eyebrows raised. "It won't kink up or anything, will it?"

"It better not." I touched my single braid, not sure now how I felt about Saundra's idea.

"Then I'm all for it." He paid for the sodas and passed them down the line to Tyler, Andie, Saundra, and me.

"So, are you gonna do it?" Andie asked.

"I'm probably too chicken," I said, filing the idea away for future reference. Who knows, maybe I'd get brave and have it done right before school started. A new look would be perfect, especially to start my freshman year.

♥ ♥ ♥

"Did everyone have a good time today?" Daddy asked as we drove back down the coast at dusk after supper.

"Universal Studios was way cool." Tyler answered from his perch in the rear seat, where he sat between Andie and me.

"Maybe we'll go again next summer," Daddy said, grinning. He turned around to glance at me. "What do you say, Holly?"

I glanced at Andie to my left, wondering if he was including her in the invitation. "Sure, let's do it," I said.

Daddy kept talking about the events of the day while Saundra nodded off every so often. We all seemed a bit frazzled from our hectic day. All but Andie. She seemed jazzed. Probably the beach party . . . and the prospect of seeing Rico again.

That thought made me cringe, but I kept my feelings hidden, praying silently instead.

After we were home only a few minutes, Daddy got the bright idea to invite Sean over. "We'll play that Bible board game I just bought," he said, opening the built-in shelving unit opposite the fireplace. "Okay with you, Holly?"

What a matchmaker!

"I guess," I said, trying to hide my smile.

Saundra looked completely baffled about the new game. But she was quiet and didn't raise a protest.

💜 💜 💜

We tried our best to get Andie involved, but she wasn't interested. Daddy literally begged her to play, but she declined. "Thanks anyway," she said without an explanation. And she scurried off, down the steps, while I shot another silent prayer heavenward.

It didn't take long for Sean to show up, and after a few instructions from the manual, we began to play. I couldn't stop thinking about my beach speech to him about just being friends. And here was Daddy throwing the two of us together.

In fact, Daddy was close to winning when he got up rather abruptly and excused himself. "Sorry, kids," he said, winking at Sean. "I think I'll call it a night."

That rascal! I couldn't believe he was going to simply abandon the game like this. And Saundra was no help whatsoever. She took Daddy's arm and accompanied him down the hallway, leaving Sean and me to finish the game amidst the light of candles and soft music.

Sean seemed amused. "Look what they've done." He chuckled a little, his eyes reflecting the twinkling light of Saundra's best-smelling French vanilla candles.

"What's so funny?"

He forced the smile away. "Oh, nothing." He said it with a silly straight face now.

"Uh-huh," I said under my breath.

"What's *that* supposed to mean?" he asked, not able to hold back his grin.

His gaze was downright attentive. And, I didn't understand it, but I felt giddy. Inside and out. Shoot, my hands were damp, and I wasn't sure, but it seemed like my heart was racing out of control. Why was this happening? Sean was just a friend, wasn't he?

"Holly," he started to say.

"No, please, let's just finish the game, okay?" My eyes stared down at the board between us.

He reached over and covered my hand with his. "I can't lie to you anymore, Holly." His voice was unbearably sweet.

I felt his gaze on me and couldn't resist. My eyes found his. "About what?" I whispered.

"About your friendship notion." He took a deep breath, like this wasn't the easiest thing in the world to be saying. "I guess I just can't go along with it. I do like you as a friend, but . . ." He was searching for words. "But I want you to think about something."

He was positively adorable, sitting here across from me in my father's living room. Yet what was he thinking, spoiling our evening like this?

I withdrew my hand. "So you're saying you didn't really agree with me before? That you were just going along with me that day on the beach? That you—"

"Holly, I think you're special. I want you to be my girlfriend." He spoke with purpose. "Those were little white lies I told you on Wednesday. I'm sorry."

This wonderful person had just asked me to change my mind. To break my promise to myself. And yet the gentle, kind way he approached the subject told me he was sincere. A true friend.

"I . . . I don't know, Sean. I really can't date yet. And what I said is really important to me," I replied, referring to my earlier decision.

"*You're* important to me," he said.

Silence settled in around us as the candles flickered and the distant sounds of a rock band found their way to my ears. Thoughts of Andie clouded my thinking, and I searched for the perfect words.

Sean smiled thoughtfully. "Will you please think about it?"

Thank goodness. At least I wouldn't have to decide anything tonight.

Chapter 17

I did myself a favor and didn't check on Andie before I went to bed, even though I was very curious. I figured what I didn't know wouldn't hurt as much. Besides, if she'd gone to meet Rico, there was only one thing I could do, down on my knees!

In my prayer, I didn't want to include a P. S. to God about Sean Hamilton, though. I was torn between feeling betrayed and knowing inside that Sean was probably the best thing that had ever happened to me.

He certainly wasn't an immature, obnoxious flirt like Jared Wilkins. And I couldn't imagine him ever acting spoiled or using Scripture to get his own way like Danny Myers.

There was one problem, though. A thousand miles separated Sean's home from mine. Long-distance romances were for the birds, and once I got back to Dressel Hills this fact would hit me for sure. I didn't have to pray about something so foolish. Sean Hamilton, like it or not, would just have to stick with my original decision.

I was starting to doze off when I thought of Andie again. What if she *hadn't* gone out to the beach with Rico? What if she was actually sound asleep in her room?

Tired but inquisitive, I hurried to check. The moonlight played on the floor near her bed and for a minute, I thought she was curled up there. Maybe praying?

A closer look told the truth. Andie was not in her room as I'd hoped. Now I wished I'd stayed in bed. Troubled, I pulled back her covers and lay down, resting my head on her pillow. I stared at the lighthouse painting on the wall across the room.

"Dear Lord," I whispered into the darkness, "I can't handle this thing with Andie. It's just too heavy."

My tears rolled onto her pillow. "Please watch over my friend, wherever she is right now. If she's in trouble, will you help her? I'm glad you always stay awake and never have to sleep, because I'm too exhausted to wait up all night, even though I wish I could. Good night, Lord, and thanks. Amen."

A peace settled over me, and I fell asleep in Andie's bed.

♥ ♥ ♥

The next morning when I awakened, I looked around. No sign of Andie. Then, going to my room, I found her snuggled down in my bed, mouth hanging open in a perfectly relaxed state. *Okay*, I thought, relieved. *She's back, safe and sound.*

After a quick shower, I had breakfast with Daddy and Saundra while Andie and Tyler slept in. Daddy seemed to be in a big hurry to leave for the office.

"It's Saturday, Daddy. Can't you stay home?" I pleaded.

"Someone's got to work," he said, reminding me that he'd taken off yesterday.

"What's wrong with two days off in a row?" I asked.

"All play and no work makes for a lousy retirement," he teased. When he finished his granola and grapefruit, Daddy made a beeline down the hall.

Saundra shook her head. "What will it take to slow that man down?"

"Well, it looks like you can't make him, and *I* sure can't. . . ." I buttered my toast, wondering what those lab tests had shown.

Surely they weren't anything to worry about, or else Daddy's doctor would have ordered bed rest or something else drastic.

Saundra began to clear the table while I was still eating, but suddenly she sat down. "Have you given that perm any more thought?" she asked.

"A little." I reached for the strawberry jam.

"Well, I have plenty of time today. If you'd like, I could drive you over to Marcie's. Afterward, we could pick up some sandwiches and have a picnic on the beach."

I twirled the perm thing around in my brain. If it turned out fabulous like the girl at Universal Studios, I'd be going home looking like a zillion bucks. "Let me think about it some more, okay?"

"Oh, sure," Saundra said. "We've got all next week."

Daddy hustled through the kitchen carrying his black leather briefcase. I hurried to catch up with him. "Wait a minute," I called. He turned around and let me kiss him good-bye. "I love you," I said. "Hurry home."

"You're a darling girl, Holly. I'll see you tonight."

A few minutes later, Tyler clumped into the kitchen looking like something the cat dragged in. "What's for breakfast?" he asked, his auburn hair sticking out all over.

"You're a little late, dear," Saundra said. "But . . . what would you like?"

He pulled out a chair and fell into it with a thud. "I could go for some waffles," he said, yawning.

Saundra had just cleaned up her now-spotless kitchen and put everything away, and here was Tyler requesting a full-blown breakfast. I wondered how his mom would react to the request.

"Waffles or French toast?" she asked.

His reply was, "Waffles, with a side of scrambled eggs."

This was so unbelievable. Saundra instantly set to work creating a made-to-order breakfast. She glanced at me from the counter where she was measuring the waffle mix. "What about Andie? Do you think she'd like something to eat?"

"I'll check." I dashed to the stairs to see if Andie was still in her former zombie state.

When I got downstairs, I looked for Andie in my room. She'd already made my bed and picked up her clothes. I figured she was back in her own room, so I hurried to the door and knocked. "Andie, you up?"

"Come in," she said. Her voice sounded muddled, like she'd been crying.

I went in and closed the door behind me. "Are you okay?"

She sat on her unmade bed, her arms crisscrossed in front of her. "Not really." She sighed. "It's just . . ." Her voice trailed off.

"What's wrong?" I sat at the foot of the huge bed, facing her. That's when I noticed she was trembling.

She pulled the covers around her. "Oh, Holly."

I rushed to her side.

She could hardly talk for the tears. "It's . . . it's Rico. And . . . you were right."

"Shh," I said, stroking her back. "Just relax." But deep inside I was starting to suspect what I might be right about.

"Rico . . . uh, we . . ." She coughed, still crying. "I went to his beach party last night. After his band played awhile, he said he wanted to talk to me. Somewhere private."

Yikes, such bad news.

I tried to listen, eager to help her through whatever seemed to be upsetting her. "What happened?"

She sniffled and reached for a tissue. "We were walking down the beach, holding hands, when he started kissing me."

"You actually let him?"

She nodded slowly, watching me, testing to see if I was going to totally freak out or keep listening. I opted to listen because it was obvious Andie needed a friend.

She started talking again. "His breath smelled like beer. I pulled away, but he wanted me to sit on the beach with him."

"What did you do?"

"His speech was slurred. I should've known better than to be alone with him."

"You're saying he was drunk? Oh, Andie."

She nodded. "I was so scared. I pushed him away and said that you were expecting me here. Then I ran home as fast as I could."

"Let me get you more tissues," I said, worried sick about her.

Andie blew her nose, taking deep breaths. "You knew all along, Holly. Rico was no good." She shivered.

I put my arm around her, and she leaned her head on my shoulder. "You okay?"

"Uh-huh," she whispered. "Nothing worse happened."

"Thank goodness," I said, realizing how risky the whole situation had been. "I was praying for you late last night."

"In my bed?" She blinked her big brown eyes, smiling. "You're a wonderful friend, Holly, and I promise I won't make you cover for me ever again."

"That's good, because I was running out of lies. Actually, I hated the deceit," I confessed. "And I wish I had confided in your mom about all this."

She nodded. "I know how you must've felt, Holly. It was *my* fault you didn't. . . . I made you promise, remember?" She flung her arms around me.

After a quiet moment, I began to pray. "Dear Lord, thanks so much for protecting Andie. Forgive us both for our faithless words, and help us remember this very hard lesson. Amen."

After the prayer, I tried not to think what might've happened to her out there—if God hadn't answered my prayers.

"I'm just glad you're okay."

"You're not the only one," she said, smiling through her tears.

I heard Saundra calling, announcing brunch.

"Oh, I almost forgot. Do you want some waffles?"

"Sounds good." She hopped off the bed. Together we went upstairs, my friend and I, both equally thankful for the end to the Rico nightmare.

Chapter 18

Andie was pouring syrup over her second waffle when the phone rang. Tyler leaped out of his chair, fully awake now, and grabbed the phone. When he'd said "Hello," he listened for a moment, then said, "For you, Mom."

"I wonder who that could be," Saundra said, making her way across the spacious kitchen.

I sat at the table, watching Tyler and Andie chow down, tuning out Saundra's conversation. But suddenly I realized her voice sounded strained. Really tense. And when I looked at her, I noticed that her face had turned chalk white.

She was clutching the phone with both hands. "Yes, yes . . . oh dear, this can't be. I'll come right away. Yes, I'll meet you there."

Hands trembling, Saundra hung up the phone. "Your father collapsed at work," she told me. "He's being rushed to the hospital."

I gasped. "Is it his heart?"

Tyler held his fork in midair, staring up at his mother.

She said no more but headed down the hallway. I followed at her heels, right into her luxurious bedroom. "I want to go with you, Saundra," I stated.

"I need you to stay with Tyler, dear."

"What about Andie? Let *her* stay with him."

She shook her head. "No, no, it'll work out much better if you're here." And she literally shooed me out of her way.

"Please don't do this," I cried outside her door. "Please, Saundra, he's my father."

My emotions went crazy—anger and terror mixed together. Anger at Saundra for shutting me out, and absolute, total fright for Daddy and his condition.

How could she do this? How could she make me stay home while Daddy was probably having a heart attack . . . possibly dying. What a wicked stepmother!

I sobbed, replaying his words to me this morning. *You're a darling girl, Holly . . . I'll see you tonight.* What if those were his last words to me? What if I never saw Daddy alive again?

I choked back the tears. Back in the kitchen, Tyler was staring at his half-empty plate. "Somebody better pray," he said, sniffling.

"Let's go into the living room," I said, leading the way. Tyler and Andie followed. It was Andie who offered to pray for Daddy, and I knew she did it out of love for me. Her prayer was a powerful one, and it took some of the sting away.

Just as she said "Amen," Saundra flew through the house, grabbing up a sweater from the closet in the entryway. "I'll call you as soon as I know something."

"The second you know?" I pleaded.

"Yes, dear," she said.

So, I had Saundra's word on it. Not nearly as good as being there myself, but it would have to do. Saundra was stubborn sometimes, and since I was a guest in her house, I couldn't actually throw a fit about it, could I?

The three of us stood in front of the window watching Saundra's white sports car back out of the driveway. I glanced down at Tyler. Big tears rolled down his cheeks. "I hope Daddy doesn't die," he sobbed. "He's the only real father I ever had."

Kneeling down, I threw my arms around him and drew him

near. "I know," I said, trying to swallow the huge lump in my throat. "I know."

It seemed important for me to be strong for him, letting his fears, and his tears, pour onto my shoulder.

Conscious of the passage of time, I felt the air going in and out of my nose, the pounding of my pulse—I was aware of Tyler's little body heaving against mine. And of something else.

Andie. She wrapped her arms around both Tyler and me. It was the dearest thing she could've done.

When the phone rang, I was the first to break up our huddle. I dashed to the kitchen. "Hello?"

"Holly, I just heard the news." It was Sean. "My older brother works with your dad. He just called. Are you all right?"

I couldn't speak. Hearing Sean talk about Daddy and what had just happened made me want to cry.

"Holly?"

"It's just . . . so . . ."

"I'm praying," he said in a whisper. "We all are."

I didn't know who "we" meant, but I figured his family was. "Thanks," I squeaked out.

"Anything I can do?" he asked gently.

"Yes . . . there is. Can you hold on a second?"

I covered the phone and called to Tyler, "Will your mom freak out if I show up at the hospital after all?"

"She'll get over it," he said. "She wasn't thinking clearly, that's all."

"You're sure?"

Andie piped up. "You go, Holly. I'll stay here with Tyler." Her eyes were serious, almost sad.

I turned back toward the phone. "Sean? I was wondering, would you mind driving me to see my dad? At the hospital?"

"Unfortunately I'm not old enough to drive passengers yet, but I'll get a cab and ride with you. I'll be there in fifteen minutes, max."

"Thanks." He said good-bye, and I hung up.

I leaned against the kitchen wall, hoping and praying Daddy was going to be all right. Then, remembering what Saundra had said about Daddy's prayer list, I felt compelled to locate his Bible. Hurrying to their room, I found it lying on the lamp table beside the bed.

Reverently, I turned to the back pages. There, I found his prayer list. Tears clouded my vision and I struggled to see through the blur. Saundra's name was number one!

I thought of the many years I'd prayed for Daddy's salvation. And God had answered. Now, Daddy's desire was to see his wife come to know Jesus, too.

I decided to leave his Bible here at home where it belonged . . . where *he* belonged.

♥ ♥ ♥

When Sean arrived, he came to the front door and rang the bell. He was wearing beige khakis and a light blue shirt. His warm smile comforted me.

Sean waited for me to say good-bye to Tyler and Andie. "I'll call the minute I know something," I promised.

Tyler stood on tiptoes and kissed my cheek. "Tell Dad I'm praying for him."

Thrilled to hear these words, I hugged my stepbrother. "You better believe I will."

Outside, Sean opened the taxi's back door for me before hurrying around to get in on the other side.

We rode in silence for a while. Then, looking concerned, Sean asked if Saundra had told me about Daddy's condition.

"Apparently he had a small attack about a year and a half ago. She didn't say much more."

He nodded. "How did Saundra take the news about your dad . . . today?"

"Frazzled, like she didn't know what to do first," I said, remembering how she'd hurried to her bedroom and then out to the closet to get her sweater and purse. "She's probably in denial."

"We need to pray for her," he said quietly.

"Sometimes things like this pull people toward Christ," I said, remembering how Daddy had reacted to his sister's death.

"And your dad has several prayer partners who are remembering Saundra right now."

I looked over at him. "Are you one of them?"

His face lit up. "As a matter of fact, I am."

"I have to be honest with you," I said hesitantly. "When I first met Saundra, I couldn't stand her. She really bugged me. Everything at the house—her clothes, the way she talked—had to be perfect. But since then, I've discovered another side to her. She's so caring, she'd give you the shoes off her feet, I think. Not that she doesn't have a zillion pairs."

He laughed at that.

"You know what I mean," I said.

We went for several miles without talking. But the closer we got to the hospital, the more I realized the seriousness of Daddy's situation.

Childhood memories began to flood back. Especially the times when Carrie and I were little. Daddy would read to us on Sunday afternoons. We'd snuggle into a big comfortable chair together in his upstairs study while he read the old classics aloud. Books like *Peter Pan* and *The Secret Garden*. To our delight, he would change his voice to match each character.

And there were those still, magical nights in deep summer when Daddy and I sang in harmony on the porch swing late into the night. Dear memories, never to be forgotten. How I loved my father. I loved him in spite of his leaving us. In spite of the divorce.

Quickly, I reached for my purse and pulled out a tissue, staring out my window. But Sean had seen the tears, and against my will my eyes filled to the brim.

"Hey, are you okay?" he asked tenderly.

I tried to reassure him, forcing a weak smile. "It's so scary to think that Daddy might . . ."

Sean reached over and took my hand, not saying more. His

hand enveloped mine, and despite the fact that he'd asked me to be his girlfriend last night, I knew this gesture was meant to be purely comforting, nothing more.

We rode in silence as I composed myself, and a short time later the hospital came into view. The driver let us out at the main entrance. Inside, Sean asked for directions to the cardiac unit, and after a quick elevator ride, we arrived on the fourth floor. The smell of antiseptic was strong as the elevator door opened. I hated the thought of Daddy being here.

I told the nurse behind the counter who I was. "My father is Robert Meredith."

Without blinking an eye, she said, "Come right this way." We followed her to a private waiting area around the corner and down the hall.

Saundra looked up with a tearstained face. "Oh, Holly . . ." She stood up and rushed over. "I'm so glad you're here." Spying Sean, she thanked him for getting a taxi for me. "I'm sorry I left you at home that way," she said, still holding my hands. "It was just such a frightening time, I—"

"I understand."

Sean slipped out to the hall, giving us privacy. I let Saundra hug me, and I cried in her arms. "How's Daddy?" I finally blurted out.

She held on to my hands as we sat down. "The doctors are with him now." She glanced up at a TV monitor high on the wall. "That's your father's room."

The heart monitor continued its monotonous beeping—a good sign. "Daddy's heart?"

She nodded. "I doubt that he'd be overjoyed about being televised like this."

I cracked a smile briefly. "Are they going to do bypass surgery?"

She seemed hesitant to respond. "Two of his arteries are ninety percent blocked. From what the cardiologist says, they're trying a clot-busting drug on him first." She sighed audibly. "If that doesn't work, they may consider angioplasty."

I was afraid to ask. All of it sounded hideous.

Saundra seemed to understand my reluctance to inquire. She let go of my hands and used her own to demonstrate the surgical procedure. "Angioplasty is used to open a coronary artery. A small balloon is inserted into the blood vessel, compressing the plaque against the wall of the artery."

I tried not to visualize what she was describing, maybe because she kept using the word *blood* as in blood vessel and blood work.

Frightened and worried, I went back into the hall to find Sean. "It's okay for you to come in," I told him.

He frowned. "Are you sure?"

"You don't have to leave, do you?" I asked. The truth was I didn't want him to go just yet.

"Not really," he replied. "If Saundra stays the night, I'll be happy to help you get home." He was so eager to do something.

The three of us flipped through magazines and talked occasionally, waiting for the doctors' decision. After another hour passed, I was beginning to wonder if something had gone wrong. Why was it taking so long?

Finally several doctors came into the private waiting area. I held my breath, wishing with all my heart this day might have a happy ending.

Chapter 19

All the doctor talk of blood and balloons—and that horrible hospital smell—had made me queasy. Quickly, I left for the rest room while the doctors informed Saundra of the results of Daddy's EKG and lab work.

Inside the ladies' room, I splashed cold water on my face. Leaning over the sink, I closed my eyes. "Dear Lord," I prayed, "I've learned not to hold on when it's much better to let go and completely trust you for things like this. I really can't do this hospital scene . . . I'm so scared for Daddy. And for me. Please help the doctors and Saundra know what to do to help. Amen."

When I finally got it together and returned to the waiting room, Saundra and Sean were nowhere to be seen. One of the nurses came in and said Sean had headed back to the beach house to get Tyler and Andie. "Your stepmother is in the prayer chapel just down the hall." She touched my arm, guiding me in the right direction.

I hurried to the chapel door. Holding my breath, I inched the door open and saw Saundra kneeling at the altar. A large crucifix hung on the wall above her. I tiptoed into the peaceful place, making my way soundlessly toward the altar to Saundra.

She turned slightly as I knelt close beside her.

"This is all so strange to me," she whispered, glancing up at the form of Christ on the cross.

I listened intently.

"I guess I've been wondering about God all my life," she explained, "but I was never truly able to bring myself to believe in a personal Being. But just now, as I was praying, I found myself talking to Him as though He were someone real, someone who cares about what happens to your father."

I wiped the tears from my eyes and found it curious that she simply let hers drip off her face. Searching in the chapel, I found a box of tissues on a chair beside the wall. I offered her one.

"Thanks, Holly," she said, without the dear. It was comforting to hear my name without her automatic tag.

She spoke of their first meeting—hers and Daddy's—with fondness, and even though I always thought I'd resist hearing this story, I found myself eager to listen. "Your father was floundering emotionally when I first met him. We happened to be attending the same support group. He was almost shy, definitely reserved. Desperately lonely."

Lonely for us? For the family he'd left behind?

She continued. "After several sessions, your father found enough confidence to share his story with the group. Such a sad, despairing tale. He told how he'd abandoned his family, how he'd been selfish and self-centered, how he'd hurt his wife and children. My heart went out to him." She paused, taking a deep breath. "You see, Holly, I'd been hurt desperately, as well, only not in a similar way. . . ." She didn't reveal the reason for her divorce, but I knew that her former husband had done the leaving—two weeks before Christmas, no less!

I touched her arm. "You helped Daddy through his pain, didn't you?"

She nodded. "We helped each other. Now we must do the same," she said, her head down. "If Christ can make himself real to your father, stubborn and strong-willed as he is, maybe there's something to all this God business."

I wanted to help. "Sometimes it's hard to trust," I said. "But if you ask the Lord to become real to you, I know He will." I put my arm around her. "I believe something else, too."

She began to cry again.

"I believe Daddy is in very good hands." By the tentative smile on her glistening face, I knew she understood.

♥ ♥ ♥

Much later, the surgeon, still wearing his green scrubs, met all of us in the waiting room. "Robert is stabilized and in very good condition. He held up well during the angioplasty, and we'll know better tomorrow how things stand after we do a follow-up EKG and some lab work." His serious expression transformed into a wide smile. "Things look very good at the present time."

Tyler stood up. "Will my dad be able to go Boogie boarding with me again?"

"That's certainly a good possibility," the surgeon said, chuckling.

"So you're saying he's going to be fine?" I asked while Andie draped her arm around my shoulders.

The surgeon nodded.

I heard Saundra whisper, "Thanks, God."

♥ ♥ ♥

After a while Sean returned again, this time bearing sacks filled with hamburgers and fries—definitely not appropriate food for the cardiac patients in the units surrounding our little waiting room. But the emotional day had depleted all of us, so we were thankful for Sean's gracious gesture.

"Here, let me reimburse you," Saundra said, opening her purse and pulling out a wad of bills.

Sean put up his hands. "The treat's on me."

Just then the head nurse came in and told us we could see Daddy. Each of us would have three minutes with him. Saundra first, then me, then Tyler. Only one family member could be in the room at any given time.

We were all so anxious to see him, crossing our fingers about the procedure. If his arteries stayed open, they'd have him up walking soon, and later doing the treadmill thing. Maybe, just maybe, Daddy would get to come home on Wednesday. If so, we'd have him all to ourselves for five whole days before Andie and I were scheduled to leave for home.

While I waited my turn, Sean and I went for a short walk down the hall to the sunroom. It was still light out, and the ferns and plants scattered around made the room pleasant and airy.

"I guess we need to talk," I said as we sat near one of the windows.

Sean smiled, which made his eyes twinkle. "Good news, I hope."

"Well, yes . . . and no."

He looked puzzled.

I continued, "Well, yes, we should continue being good friends, and no, I can't go out with you . . . at least, not yet." I explained that my mom had always said I should be at least fifteen before I actually dated anyone.

"I'll wait," he said calmly. "You're worth waiting for, Holly."

I swallowed. "Are you for real? You mean you're not going to try and change my mind?"

"Why should I?" His eyes studied mine. "Friendship is one of the highest forms of love."

Who said anything about love?

"Okay, it's settled, then," I said, feeling fabulously comfortable with this guy. "When I get back home, I'll send you some letters."

"Probably not as often as *I* will."

"We'll see," I said, grinning.

Quickly, he glanced at his watch. "I think it's your turn to see your dad." We hurried down the hall, and when our hands bumped slightly, Sean didn't reach for mine. There would be plenty of time for that—with or without Sean. For now, it was great to have someone who cared but wasn't pushy. A true friend.

Standing outside Daddy's room, I leaned against the wall, feeling hopeful. Saundra and I had shared a very special moment in the chapel. I was beginning to see who she was on the inside. And Andie? Well, there was no telling how far she and I were destined to go as friends. Hey, we'd been through a living nightmare together and survived.

Saundra came out just then, her eyes bright with joy. "He's doing wonderfully."

"Are you sure?" I whispered, glancing around the corner at Daddy, all wired up with monitors and IVs and things.

"Don't worry," she reassured me. "He's fine. Go give him a kiss."

"Okay." I tiptoed into Daddy's room and stood beside his bed. Touching his hand, I whispered, "Daddy?"

His eyes fluttered open. "Holly-Heart," he said. "You're here."

I leaned over and kissed his forehead.

"Guess your old man better slow down a little, eh?"

"For starters," I said. "We want you around for a very long time."

He squeezed my hand. "Oh, I'm not going anywhere."

"Promise?"

Solemnly, he nodded. "I promise."

I couldn't help it—a tiny giggle escaped my lips. What a fabulous day this had turned out to be.

♥ ♥ ♥

Sean showed up on Sunday. We sang a few hymns softly for Daddy, and when we came to "Amazing Grace," Saundra joined in. Later, she and I took turns reading to him from his Bible.

Daddy, being a highly motivated fellow, couldn't be kept in bed for long. By Monday morning he was up walking the halls and phoning Carrie long distance. On Tuesday, he passed his first treadmill test and was moved to a regular floor. Wednesday, after lunch, we brought Daddy home. He was discharged to a cardiac rehab clinic nearby, where he'd have to check in for therapy.

Andie and I took turns helping Saundra cook his fat-free diet. Tyler played waiter, serving him breakfast on the deck, picnics on the beach, and supper by candlelight in the dining room. Andie and I played Daddy's Bible board game and beat him three times in a row.

Sunday evening, Saundra pulled a trick on him and hid her newly written prayer list in his napkin. "What's this?" he remarked, holding it up as he sat at the head of the elegant table.

I giggled. "What's it look like?"

Saundra beamed, coming around and hugging him. "Read it, darling."

"It's a list," he said, frowning at first. "A *prayer* list?" He read it silently first, then out loud.

"Number one, Robert's complete recovery. Number two, many more anniversaries together. Number three, a surprise trip to Tahiti with my husband. Happy anniversary!"

Tyler, Andie, and I applauded the success of her secret mission and Daddy's steady recovery.

♥ ♥ ♥

When I called home to Dressel Hills later that night, Mom asked if Andie was around.

"She's right here, why?"

"Stan has something to say to her."

"Okay," I said cautiously as I handed her the phone.

"Hello?" Andie said hesitantly.

A short pause followed.

Then she said, "You're not friends with Ryan anymore? Why, what happened?"

I held my breath.

"Yeah, I know what you mean," Andie said.

Another pause. I wondered what was going on between the two of them.

Soon, Andie's grin gave her away. "Sure, I forgive you. Just don't let it happen again."

Perfect! My best friend and my brousin (cousin-turned-step-brother) had made up. As for the Ryan Davises and the Rico Hernandezes of the world—well, prayer changes things. And people, too.

I must never forget.

The Absolute Truth: How Honest Are You? A Quiz

Holly grabbed her beach towel and sun block. "Little white lies aren't really white, you know," she said to Andie.

"And not so little, either," Andie said, carrying a Thermos of lemonade and her beach bag. The two girls headed across the park to the Dressel Hills Portal Pool.

"Some kids lie all the time and think nothing of it," Holly remarked. "But the problem with lying is remembering what you said."

"Yeah, so you have to tell another one to cover up the *first* lie," Andie agreed.

Holly sighed. "When it comes right down to it, the best thing is to tell the truth, even if you're in trouble, and just deal with the consequences."

Andie giggled.

"What's so funny?" Holly asked.

"I was just thinking of Danny Myers. He'd be quoting Scriptures by now."

Holly nodded. "Like the one in Proverbs. 'Truthful lips endure forever, but a lying tongue lasts only a moment.' "

"Actually I was thinking about the verse in Revelation where it talks about liars being cast into the lake of fire," Andie said.

Both girls shivered.

"After what happened this summer," Holly said, "I think I'd rather go with 'truthful lips.' "

Andie agreed wholeheartedly.

♥ ♥ ♥

So, what about you? Does the temptation to lie give you the creeps, or is it no big deal? Let's see how honest you really are. Take the honesty quiz and find out.

1. You and your friends drop in on the nearest fast-food place. Instead of change for a five, the clerk gives you change for a ten. What's your response?
    a. Keep the extra money. (Who knows how many times you've been shortchanged before. This'll balance things out, right?)
    b. Give the extra money back.
    c. Donate the extra money to your favorite charity.

2. A new family moves into your apartment complex. They need an experienced baby-sitter, at least fifteen years old. You're experienced but only fourteen. You really need the bucks. What do you do?
    a. Wear your hair up during the interview and fib if they ask your age. (After all, you look sixteen.)
    b. Volunteer your actual age in hopes of impressing them with your responsibility and honesty.
    c. Tell the truth, but only if they ask.
    d. Don't bother to interview.

3. You're grounded for the weekend—no phone calls allowed. On Saturday, Mom and Dad go out for the evening. You're

bored and dying to call your best friend. What do you do?

    a. Call her. After all, you have homework questions.

    b. Surprise your mom and clean up the kitchen.

    c. Leave the house. Use the pay phone at the 7-Eleven.

4. Your friend loves her new hairstyle. But you liked it better the old way. When she asks your opinion, you say:

    a. "Looks cool."

    b. "It's okay, but I prefer the old way."

    c. "What are you doing for spring break?" (Change the subject—fast!)

    d. "Are you serious? Please, change it back!"

5. During a test, you can see the smartest kid's answers one desk away. The teacher leaves the room. You need a good grade to stay on the girls' volleyball team. So you:

    a. Sneak a peek. (The team needs you!)

    b. Rely on last night's cramming efforts.

    c. Finish the test quickly, in time to double-check the smart kid's answers. (It's not really cheating, is it?)

6. Your best friend asks you to keep a major secret. She emphasizes that you're the only one who knows. Another friend wants to hear the full scoop, too, and promises to keep it quiet. What will you do?

    a. Tell her, but make her promise not to tell.

    b. Keep the secret. You're loyal, aren't you?

    c. Tell her and five others. Your friend will understand.

7. At the amusement park, the Big Bad Wolf roller coaster entices you, but the lines are incredibly long. (A sign says there's a sixty-minute wait.) Your impatient friends begin cutting through to the front, telling people, "Mom and Dad are waiting just ahead." What do you do?

a. Save some precious ride time and go along with the story.

b. Wait at the end of the line . . . despite what your friends do.

c. Let your friends cut through the line, then tell people, "My pals are waiting for me just ahead."

8. Five of your friends are headed for the mall. You want to go, but your mom's not crazy about the idea. What do you tell her?

a. "All my friends have permission." (Well, maybe three.)

b. "You can trust me, Mom. You won't be sorry you let me go. You'll see."

c. "They'll kick me out of the group forever if I don't go."

d. "Please, Mom? I'll do all the dishes for a year."

9. After school, while your teacher is out of the room, you accidentally break her glass paperweight. No one sees it happen. You:

a. Say nothing unless she asks about it.

b. Apologize and offer to pay for the paperweight.

c. Deny breaking it if asked.

10. Walking along the beach, you find a wallet containing $500. There's no ID, only a name inside. What do you do?

a. Hit the nearest mega-mall and shop till you drop.

b. Exhaust every possible lead until you find the owner.

c. Attempt to find the owner. Keep the money if you fail.

Scoring:

Give yourself two points for each "b" answer, one point for each "d" answer, and zip for each "a" or "c" answer. Subtract one point for each time you answered "b" only because you knew it was the correct response, not because that's what you'd actually do. Be honest.

20 points:	Hey, you're "perfectly fabulous stuff." It appears that you take God's Word seriously and are growing stronger in your faith. Great job.
16–19 points:	For the most part, you're tops on truthfulness, not to mention a girl who can be trusted. Work on the rough edges and keep trying.
10–15 points:	Oops! You're in desperate need of some truth training. Crack open your Bible and take a hard look at Ephesians 4 and 5.
0–9 points:	Talk to Jesus about your untruthful tendencies. Ask Him to help you be a girl of honesty and integrity. Once you get on the right track, retake the test. You ought to see a major improvement.

Acknowledgments

Thanks to all who have helped to make the HOLLY'S HEART series a successful reality. I'm forever grateful to Charette Barta and Sharon Madison, who believed in Holly-Heart from her earliest beginnings, as well as to my superb editor, Rochelle Glöege, whose suggestions and encouragement are so valuable to me.

Big hugs to my terrific teen consultants— Mindie, Amy, Kirsten, Anastasia, Jonathan, Kristin, Aleya, Shanna, Andrea, Mindie, Janie, and Julie. With their fantastic ideas and input, they made the Holly's Heart series even more fun to create!

Hurrah for my SCBWI critique group, as well as reviewer Barbara Birch, my witty sis, who dreamed up the idea of Holly and friends being snowbound at school.

Three cheers for my husband, Dave, whose thoughtful comments, loving support, and super sandwiches made this series possible.

Thanks also to Kristie Frutchey, who shared information on the American Field Service, an international exchange student program; to Lynn Sanders and Linda Marsh, of Aaron Animal Clinic in Colorado Springs, Colorado, for answering my questions about sick cats; to Bob Billingsley for his knowledge of the classic Thunderbird sports car; to Kathy Torley, who answered my medical questions about angioplasty; and to Janet Turner, my travel agent, who helped answer airport security questions. Your expert advice was a huge help!

And finally, my deep appreciation to my many fans who think Holly really *does* live somewhere in Colorado. I've enjoyed every minute spent writing HOLLY'S HEART just for you!

From Bev . . . to You

I'm thrilled that you've chosen to read Holly's Heart. As my first young-adult protagonist, Holly Meredith remains dear to my heart, and I laughed and cried with her as I wrote every one of these books.

Holly-Heart and I have quite a lot in common. While growing up in Lancaster County, Pennsylvania, I wrote zillions of secret lists and journal entries (and still do!). I also enjoy my many e-pals, and sending snail mail letters and notes to encourage family and friends has always been one of my favorite things to do. And I know all about the importance of having a true-blue best friend. Mine was Sandi Kline, and while we didn't have Loyalty Papers, we did write secret-coded messages to each other. Once, we even hid a few under the carpet of the seventh step leading to the sanctuary of my dad's church!

Thanks to my books, I've had the opportunity to develop friendships with people of all ages, from the grade-schoolers who love my picture books to the teens and senior adults who enjoy my novels. Through the years, some of you have even written to confide in me or share some of the difficulties you've faced. Growing up can definitely be tough sometimes. I've always found hope in the words of Psalm 139, which describes the amazing love of our Creator-God. It's comforting to know that the same God who formed us in our mother's womb, who knows the number of individual hairs we're washing and blow-drying each day, also sees the fears and concerns of our lives. Our heavenly Father sees and understands. What an enormous blessing that is!

To learn more about my writing, sign up for my e-newsletter, or contact me, visit my Web site, *www.beverlylewis.com.*

Only Girls Allowed: More Fun Reads From Beverly Lewis

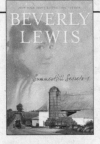

Meet Merry Hanson, a fifteen-year-old girl who happens to live in Amish country—only she isn't Amish. When strange things seem to be happening there, it's up to Merry to get to the bottom of it. Like when her friend's mom mysteriously disappears.

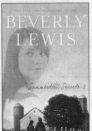

Whether she's solving mysteries, learning the ways of the Amish, helping friends, or just trying to stay out of trouble, you won't want to miss a single adventure with Merry.

SUMMERHILL SECRETS: Volume 1
Whispers Down the Lane, Secret in the Willows, Catch a Falling Star, Night of the Fireflies, A Cry in the Dark

SUMMERHILL SECRETS: Volume 2
House of Secrets, Echoes in the Wind, Hide Behind the Moon, Windows on the Hill, Shadows Beyond the Gate

Join Olivia Hudson, Jenna Song, Heather Bock, and Miranda Garcia as they follow their dreams of competing in the Olympics. From figure skating to gymnastics to skiing, cheer on your new friends as they go through life's challenges and triumphs.

GIRLS ONLY
Dreams on Ice, Only the Best, A Perfect Match, Reach for the Stars, Follow the Dream, Better Than Best, Star Status

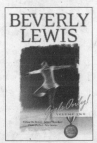